TEARDROPS OF THE INNOCENT:

The White Diamond Story

Allie Marie

Allie Marie

Teardrops of the Innocent

Published by Nazzaro & Price Publishing

Published in the United States of America

DEDICATION

In loving memory of my uncle and aunt,
Charles and Joan Carroll.

THE PROPERTIES

CONTENTS

ACKNOWLEDGMENTS

Thanks to the many people who helped make this book possible:

To my editor Helen Nazzaro, for taking a chance on an unknown. Thank you for the advice, guidance, and laughs. Here's to a long partnership.

To James Price, for taking my primitive sketch and turning it into the beautiful cover that resulted.

To my sons, Jack and Mike, for their geek team fixes every time I broke something on the computer, and to my nieces Brittney and Stefani for their social media advice. To the rest of my family, who listened to my endless chattering about fictional people, places, and things. Even if you were secretly rolling your eyes, you listened...sometimes. Love you all.

To the following friends for their help during the many phases of editing, revising, researching, and worrying: Laura Somers, Janice Philbin, Janelle Williams, and Yvonne Gray. Thank you, thank you.

To Jenny Hamilton and Frances Blake for cheering me on.

To fellow writers Lyn Brittan and Jennifer Keller, whose support and advice helped me tremendously. And to Màiri Norris, a sincere thank you for your faith in my story, and for the introduction that made this book possible.

To the new cousins I found through my own ancestry search. Karen Fontaine, your ancestry trees led me to discover our common 3rd great-grandfather Dosithe. Kitty Cooper Wilson, your ancestry trees led me to the extensive lineage of Dosithe's wife, Emily. Thank you both, cousins. To our 3rd great-Grandmother Emily, who conducted research in the days before Internet, email, and even telephones were invented—merci beaucoup, Grandmamma, for leading me to our family's own Revolutionary War hero, Antoine Paulint. Antoine and his wife Theotiste became the inspiration for my fictional characters Etienne and Clothiste.

To firefighters everywhere, for all you do every day. Thank you to retired Portsmouth firefighter Ed Ewing, for his answers to my research questions. Any discrepancies between the real PFD and the book are the result of my creative writing. And a special thank you to PFD Firefighter Brandon Upton for assistance with my cover. We've got your back!

To Ms. Patty Phillips at the Portsmouth Visitors Center for her quick help in a last minute query.

A very special thanks to my good friend and cohort Sandi Baum, for being there from the time the first chapter was put to paper to the final tap on the keyboard. I wouldn't have done as well without all those hours we spent on the phone, dissecting every line, word, and hyphen. I sincerely appreciate the support, encouragement, laughs—and Tom's patience.

And most of all, to my husband Jack, my hero always and forever. You are the wind beneath my wings.

Throughout this story, I tried to keep details of Olde Towne historically accurate and any errors are all mine. While researching the architecture of old buildings, I discovered that homes from the colonial time period of the story no longer exist, necessitating the introduction of the Civil War Wyatt family (whose own story may be told in the future.) Sadly, Pâtisseries a la Carte does not really exist in Olde Towne.

A chance visit to the Friendship Firehouse Museum in Alexandria, Virginia inspired the setting for Stephanie and Gage's first kiss. Thank you, Cathy, for answering my questions on the day we visited.

And to anyone who travels Virginia's I-95 when it turns into a rush-hour parking lot, I'm sure you will commiserate with the traffic issues the characters experience. There was nothing fictional about that scenario

PROLOGUE

Nicole and the White Diamond

It was in Portsmouth, Virginia, in the year 1781.

Even though I was only a little girl, just your age, I remember that day vividly. Fingers of ice-blue lightning raked the darkening sky like a cat's claws across flesh. The patter of rain on the metal roof rose to a crescendo, while a wooden shutter drummed a steady rhythm against the outside wall.

When the ensuing thunderclap rattled the window glass, none of us flinched. After living with the constant barrage of cannon fire for five years, the sudden rumble of thunder rarely bothered my family anymore. And for me, at four years old, I had spent my entire life living in the army camp, so thunder no more scared me than the big guns. I didn't remember my father or my brother, because they were always away somewhere, fighting in the war.

Then we had to go to that house when Mama became ill. People are making changes to it now. I've heard them say it's going to be a Bed and Breakfast, which I think we used to call an inn in my day. Now back to my story.

Even though we only stayed there a short time, I hated living in the step-grandmother's house. It was beautiful, warm, and comfortable, but young as I was, I always sensed an evil presence there. I did not understand what. I wanted to go back to the soldiers' camp where we used to live. But Mama was so sick, and my sisters sometimes cried. They would never tell me why.

Then that horrible day came. Mama asked us to gather our things and we waited in the small room. She was nervous, and walked back and forth in front of the window. My sister Marie Josephé paced near the door, and my oldest sister Theresé sewed a rip in her skirt.

I sat at the window seat, playing with my baby doll. She was old, and the paint flaked from her face. The step-grandmother said it was ugly, and once tried to throw it away. But my sisters painted her face, and made a new dress.

Then Mama called us to her, and told us she had gifts for us. She had a pretty brocade pouch, and from it she withdrew three smaller ones. One each of red, white, and blue velvet. I remember calling them the continental colors because Mama often talked about the new flag.

Mama showed me the white bag, and said it was mine. She emptied the bag in her hand, and held up a necklace with a small white diamond on the end. I remember the sparkle as she held it near the candle light.

She said, "This is for you, my innocent one. This little diamond shines like the tears of happiness I shed when you were born." She draped a pendant with a teardrop-shaped stone over my head.

I was so in awe of the beautiful gift, I scarcely paid attention when she gave my sisters their pendants. They were so happy, and talked and laughed. But Mama said we could only keep them for a few moments, and we had to give them back before we went on our journey.

I did not want to give mine back. I begged Mama to allow me to put the necklace on my baby. She smiled so sadly, but she said yes.

While Mama and my sisters admired their pretty blue and red stones, I ran to the window seat. I pretended to put the necklace over my baby's head, but when I saw that Mama and my sisters were occupied, I put the necklace in that secret lining of the hem, the place where I knew my sisters sometimes put papers with funny markings on them. They thought I was unaware of that hiding place, but I saw the soldier take the paper one time.

I checked along the hem with my fingers, and found no papers this time. I dropped the necklace inside the lining. I took the white pouch back to my mother. She did not look inside, just put the bag inside the bigger one. I rested my head on her arm. The storm increased its rage, and I looked toward the window. I wanted to go back and get my baby, but suddenly I was afraid.

Silver lightning streaked across the sky and lit the room. The doll's dark eyes glared at me from her pale white face. The thunder that followed boomed louder than any cannon I ever heard, rattling the house. I buried my face in my mother's arm, and she held me close.

I knew the storm was punishing me for taking the necklace.

And I can never forget, until I find it and give it back to Mama.

Below us, a door banged and voices shouted. My mother and sisters stood, staring at the door. I could sense their fear.

I heard the clomping of heavy boots, and like the others, I knew—the time had come.

"And then what happened, Grandma Nickel?"

"Tanner, where are you?" At the sound of his mother's voice, the little boy called, "Coming. Mommy." He turned back to the elderly woman.

"I have to go now, Grandma Nickel. When will little Nickel come back to play wif me? She can tell me the rest of the story."

The old woman sighed sadly. "She'll be here. She's always here with me, my dear."

As the child grabbed his toys and ran to the kitchen, the figure of the old woman evaporated into the air.

CHAPTER ONE

STEPHANIE
Alexandria, Virginia, present day January

Stephanie Kincaid pushed the heavy ornate door open as a salty tear trickled down her cheek. Melancholy silence greeted her. Not even a hinge squeaked.

She had often entered her parents' quiet home in the past. When they were on one of their frequent excursions, she stopped by to water her mother's plants, stack mail, and check doors and windows. Although she sensed their absence, she'd always known they'd be coming home.

The house's aura settled on her differently this time. As she crossed the threshold the reality struck her that they would never do so again. Fresh tears stung her eyes, and her breath caught in her throat as she leaned back on the wooden door.

The click of the latch closing behind her resonated like the turning cylinder of an empty gun.

She moved into the foyer. Had her footsteps ever sounded so loud in the past? Each time she took a step, the thud of her footfall dissipated into ghostly silence.

She kept her gaze fixed on the spiral staircase to avoid looking at objects that would only stir her memories, and bolted to the second floor. Taking the steps two at a time, she headed directly to the small upstairs bedroom her father had converted into an office. She planned to be there only long enough to find legal documents in the wall safe and escape the gloom as fast as she could.

Yet the moment she entered the room that personified her parents' lives in recent years, the essence of their beings lingered. The subtle fragrance of the Chanel No. 5 that her mother had favored mixed with the tobacco scent that still wafted from her father's collection of antique pipes displayed on the wall.

In this room, her father, long retired from the Department of Defense, had reluctantly learned how to surf the Internet and check the stock market using an ancient desktop computer. His first attempts resulted in hilarious predicaments, prompting him to call her often to ask how to navigate a web site or use a program. Within two months, however, he had become a self-taught computer enthusiast.

Her father's designated office area lined one wall; on the opposite side, her mother's dainty Queen Anne writing desk held her more modern laptop and office supplies, in complete but complementary contrast to the sturdy executive-style desk and old Dell computer.

The two desks were as different as their owners were, but like those owners, they belonged together.

She pictured the two of them at their respective spaces, talking over their shoulders about websites they found on the Internet or new vacation spots they discovered. They enjoyed frequent short trips, and Stephanie always suspected they took pleasure in the planning as much as— if not more than—their actual treks.

Stephanie walked softly to the wall safe tucked inside the closet. With a few flicks of her wrist, she sent the tumbler spinning and the door clicked open. She withdrew neatly stacked brown envelopes and slid them into a canvas bag imprinted with an Adirondack chair overlooking a sunny beach.

She debated for a moment whether to take the blue velvet cases holding her mother's valuable jewels. Aware they were more secure in the safe than at her home, she slid them toward the back and closed the door, twisting the lock until the tumbler clicked.

Once she sorted through all of the information for wills, bank accounts, property deeds, vital papers and certificates, and even car titles, she would schedule an appointment with the family attorney, Winston McGraw.

With the quiet weighing on her, she emptied the contents of their individual desks, filling a plastic file box for each parent. She smiled or sighed as she spotted little scrawled notes posted around their workspaces. Her mother usually scribbled notes on brightly colored paper, cut into shapes, while her dad preferred plain old yellow sticky notes.

Despite her intentions to move swiftly and leave, she lingered. Her gaze fell on one of her father's scrawled reminders to have the tires rotated on his car. Taped to the bottom, one of her mother's famous heart cutouts swayed in the breeze as Stephanie walked by. She leaned closer to read the flowing script. "I'll never grow 'tired' of you...here's an early Valentine...Love you!"

The sigh that escaped turned into a small gasp of grief and she clamped her hand over her mouth to stifle the cry. Her parents had always sent little notes back and forth, finding fun ways to hide them where the other wouldn't expect to discover them. During her youth, she often found similar notes from one or the other of them stuck in her coat pockets, tucked in the cover of a schoolbook, or nestled in her lunch bag, all places where she would eventually run across them. As she grew up, she invented her own unique ways to leave her own notes to her parents, such as over the visor of her dad's car or folded inside her mother's compact mirror.

She brushed her fingers over the calendar book on the Queen Anne desk, imagining her mother might sit down at any moment and write another date in it. Notations in red or blue marked reminders for doctor appointments, upcoming weddings, or lunch and dinner dates. She smiled at the neat script documenting the car appointment in the calendar. Since retirement, her dad no longer kept a formal calendar, so her mother's datebook backed up his sticky-note system.

Stuck on the corner of one page a yellow sticky beamed at her, bearing a smiley face with a winking eye, under which her dad had scrawled, "I've still got eyes just for you."

"Aw, daddy, you sweetie," Stephanie said out loud, biting back more tears and hugging the calendar to her chest.

Not allowing herself to wallow in misery any longer, she straightened her shoulders and moved to her parents' bedroom, just to glance inside. She had been in it several times since they died, but only to retrieve something she needed for the funeral. To actually go through their personal items would be the hardest task ahead of her, and one she was not yet ready to tackle.

She leaned against the doorframe, her gaze sweeping the room for a final glance at the French provincial furniture, the crisp white comforter and curtains against the blue walls.

Her eye caught a tiny sparkling light glowing from the standing jewelry armoire, where her mother kept inexpensive but elegant costume jewelry.

How strange. She hadn't planned to look through the antique chest during this visit, but the light drew her to it.

Made of cherry, the chest stood tall and slim, with a narrow door on each side where necklaces could be draped. Eight small drawers lined the front. Not seeing anything that could be the source of the beam that had now disappeared, she rested her cheek on the top to see from a different angle.

Normal daylight slanted through the partially-closed venetian blinds. "Trick of my eyes," she muttered crossly as she straightened. "Or is it my imagination?"

The top of the cabinet radiated odd warmth to the side of her face as she pressed it to the wood again. She raised her head, gently rubbing her hand over the satiny cherry finish that smelled lightly of lemon oil. A trace of Chanel No. 5 lingered in the air. Her fingertips tingled as if a light jolt of electricity passed through them, and then returned to normal.

Should I take the contents of the jewelry armoire to look through at home? Stephanie ran her fingers down the two long thin doors on either side. She pushed the doors open to reveal delicate chains hanging on individual brass hooks. She ran her fingers gently across the necklaces as a harpist might strum the strings of her harp. Next she pulled out the slim top drawer and peered through the rings nestled in felt-lined slots. Her mother always preferred simple but elegant jewelry, a trait Stephanie shared.

She searched the walk-in closet for a shoebox to hold the pretty trinkets, and as she walked back into the bedroom, her eyes again caught the sparkle of light and her mother's perfume seemed to drift by as if her mother had just walked by.

Where was that glow coming from? Somewhat annoyed, she marched over to look, tilting her head from side to side to see where the light came from. She could see no source for the light.

Oh, yeah, I'm imagining things.

Yet, as she touched her cheek to the wooden surface a second time, another electrical sensation tickled her face. She raised her head and as she had done earlier, touched the polished wood with her hand. Once again, a warm tingle coursed through her fingertips.

"Okay, Mom, are you there?" she called out to the empty room, looking around. "Are you trying to tell me something?"

She wasn't afraid, and she didn't feel silly talking out loud—*well, not too much anyway*—but something drew her attention back to the armoire.

She remembered the stand contained a vanity mirror hidden under the top. When lifted, the mirror raised and revealed a secret compartment below. Her nervous fingers located the tiny latch on the side. With a nearly inaudible click, the lid raised a half-inch.

The silence of the empty room reminded Stephanie of the somber atmosphere of the funeral home. She shivered, wishing now she had taken up her friend Jackie's offer to accompany her. But this was her parents' home, the place of comfort where she had grown up. Unsure why she felt such apprehension roiling in her chest, she bit her lip and lifted the lid.

Only her own face reflected in the mirror. No strange light or ghostly figure appeared in it behind her. Without thinking, she glanced behind her as if to ensure she was alone and laughed at her giddiness.

"Stop it, Stephanie," she commanded out loud, laughing again. "You're driving yourself crazy."

Drawing her gaze back to the concealed drawer, she fully expected to find a few special pieces of her mother's costume jewelry nestled on the soft felt lining.

Inside, however, rested a single item—a long white envelope with her name written in her mother's flowing script. She reached inside, her movement as tentative as one reaching into a viper pit.

Grasping the envelope and withdrawing quickly, she sat on the bed and stared. She gingerly pressed her thumbs against the paper and felt the outline of a key.

An ominous feeling washed over her as she slid her finger along the flap. Despite the room's comfortable temperature, she shivered. She peered inside the packet and then dumped the contents into her hand. The mixed fragrances of Channel No. 5 and her father's pipe smoke seemed to fill her senses.

An index card with a single key taped at the bottom displayed the address to a bank, with instructions on how she was to access a safe deposit box.

Why isn't this with Mom's other valuable papers? What could be in the bank that she didn't want to keep in the house safe?

Clutching the letter in one hand, Stephanie grabbed the sack containing the other legal documents in the other and raced to her car.

Something was definitely amiss. She fumbled with her keys as a vague memory formed. On her eighteenth birthday, she had accompanied her mother to the bank to sign some forms. Her mother told her that she had reached legal age and the bank required her identification and signature to access her parents' bank accounts. It never occurred to Stephanie to ask why it was necessary.

Hands still shaking, she backed out of the driveway, cutting the turn too sharply. Metal wheel hubs screeched against concrete curbing. She stopped to gather her senses. *You just lost your parents in a car crash. You don't need to go out in one too.*

After taking a few gulps of air, she continued her journey without further mishap. Along the way she conjured up images of the contents of the box. Was she about to learn her parents had engaged in illegal activities and they hid the evidence in this bank box? Would the contents reveal a stash of unexplained cash tucked inside the box, or other ill-gotten goods?

Despite her concern, she laughed out loud. Her mental pictures were as ridiculous as saying her parents were Bonnie and Clyde. They were more like Mr. Rogers and Mary Poppins—kind and loving.

Relieved to find the bank devoid of customers, Stephanie strode to a teller, clutching the card and key so hard they left creases in her palm. She inquired about access, and the teller directed her to the bank president. After she again explained her reason for being there, the grandfatherly-looking financial officer expressed his sympathies.

"I've known your parents since they started banking here when I was a teller almost thirty years ago. They were good people."

"Thank you so much, Mr. Kiner. Do you need my

identification?" She pulled out her wallet.

"Driver's license is fine."

He took her driver's license and tapped a few keys on his computer. Once satisfied she had the authority to examine the safe deposit box, he produced the admission slip for her signature and led her to the vault. He located the box, used the bank key with Stephanie's to remove it, and then led her to a private viewing area.

The hushed surroundings of the vault gave Stephanie the impression she had just stepped into a tomb. The safe deposit box turned out to be much larger and heavier than she expected. Her mind's eye had visualized a tin container about the size of a shoebox but in reality, the heavy metal box measured about twenty inches square and six inches deep.

Churning nerves created an acidic tempest in her stomach as she stared at the unopened container, as if she could sense in advance what it held. She bit into her bottom lip, suddenly unwilling to find out what secret had been locked away.

With shaking hands and a deep breath, she flipped the lid open.

Staged on top was another envelope, addressed to her in her mother's handwriting. She slid a cold finger down the flap and opened the folded note.

Stephanie darling,

If you're reading this, it must mean that your father and I are both gone and you are settling our affairs. Darling, we are so sorry, because we know this means you are alone. Please don't grieve too much. Celebrate the wonderful memories we shared. You have been the joy of our lives and we have treasured every moment of your life with us.

You are, without a doubt, our beloved daughter. No parents could have been any prouder to watch you grow into the lovely woman you have become.

This is the hardest thing to tell you now. Please forgive us for not having the courage to tell you this in person. We just never had the strength. You have been our whole world and we do not know if we could bear it if you couldn't accept what we have to say. But say it we must.

I nearly told you this on your eighteenth birthday. We had such fun that day, going to lunch and shopping, so I decided to wait. Then we went to the bank to sign papers, and I just couldn't.

You see, you are our daughter, but not our biological daughter. Your father and I have been your parents since you were three weeks old.

Adopted! Stephanie's heart rocked so hard in her chest she thought it would thunder out of her body and crash to the floor. She reread the beginning sentences again, her hand clamped to her mouth as she shook her head in disbelief. Finally, she continued to read.

The contents floored her. The long, heartbreaking letter revealed her adoption and why her parents—the ones she thought were her parents—were afraid to tell her. They'd kept it a secret from everyone her entire life.

The box overflowed to the brim with legal documents, photos, and memorabilia that she saw for the first time, of people she never knew existed. Overwhelmed, she dumped the entire contents in a canvas bag borrowed from a teller, and took it straight to Winston McGraw, the family attorney, remembering to drive with caution in spite of her jangled nerves.

Winston was in his office. His secretary, recognizing the near-hysteria rising in Stephanie's voice as she explained her need to see the lawyer right away, directed her to a small conference room. Stephanie sat with clenched fists gripping the canvas bag.

When Winston joined her five minutes later, the dam of tears broke as she blurted out her discovery, shoving papers across the table. He set the papers to the side and walked to her chair, dropping into the one beside her and offering a handkerchief. In spite of her misery, Stephanie could not help but smile at the design on the hankie. Black pirate skulls lined the edge.

"Father's Day gift from my grandson." The lawyer's eyes crinkled into a smile as he patted her hand.

Immediately, Stephanie relaxed. Winston had been one of her father's best friends and she adored him. To her, who never knew her own, he personified a grandfatherly figure. He had a shock of white hair and a matching mustache. Navy-blue suspenders over a crisp white shirt held up the portly gentlemen's khaki trousers.

"I'm better now. Tell Andy his pirates cheered me up."

"I will. Now let's see what you have brought me."

Stephanie gave him the letter first, then pushed the rest of the papers in front of him. He looked in silence at each document, sometimes returning to one he had already set aside when he found something in a new one.

For Stephanie, biting her fingernails as he pored over the papers and jotted notes on a legal pad, the knot of worry intensified with his every turn of page or scribbled note. She studied his face for any signs of reaction, but he remained stoic.

Finally, he leaned back in his chair and pushed his reading glasses on top of his head.

"First things first, Stephanie." He leaned forward, elbows on the table as he patted his hands in the air in a motion to keep calm. "You were legally adopted, so there is nothing to worry about in that regard. Even I had no knowledge of your adoption, which took place years before your parents became my clients. You are the sole heir to your parents' estate. The probate will still be a straightforward process, and it will be concluded in a timely manner."

Page by page, he explained his notes. He surprised her with the news that her parents had left two considerable trust funds. Financially, she was set for a long time.

"I'm sure this is another terrible shock to you, Stephanie," Winston said. "It's only been a week since the funeral, and you haven't even had time to grieve."

"But, Winston, the safe deposit key wasn't even in the safe with their valuables. Why would it be separate?"

Winston sighed. "I don't know, Stephanie. You always handled things for your folks when they traveled. I suspect your mother didn't want you to find it in the day-to-day activities. I noticed she mentions several times in her letter that she always wanted to tell you, but never could."

"Did she think I wouldn't love them when I found out?"

"Probably. You would not believe how many adoptive parents fear just that, Stephanie. We handle a couple of adoption cases every year. When to tell their child they are adopted is one of the parents' biggest fears."

By the time she left the attorney's office, she had answers to most of her legal questions. However, she remained perplexed by questions he could not answer about her real family.

It shocked her to learn in her mother's letter that the Kincaids had also adopted her birth mother, Jessica, who had died right after giving birth to Stephanie. Jessica had reacted negatively to the news of her own adoption. The Kincaids wanted to avoid a similar reaction from Stephanie.

It took Stephanie nearly six months to sort through the paperwork hidden in the safe deposit box. Besides legal documents, the box was filled to the brink with journals, school memorabilia and other treasures from her mother's short life.

The small spare bedroom in Stephanie's small house became her work zone. She perused every document, scattering memorabilia across the crisp white comforter of the old-fashioned poster bed. Papers covered the desk while neat piles of photos obscured the floor.

A pink leather-bound journal, edges darkened by the touch of hands, detailed Jessica's years after she learned of her adoption. Harboring deep anger and bitterness, she wrote of her estrangement from her parents that lasted through her first two years in college, and early into her marriage.

Through the picture painted in the diary, Stephanie could clearly see the young couple who fell madly in love at first sight. She savored every detail until she could imagine her parents in a way she never had the chance to do in real life. Her thoughts became a movie, in which her parents laughed, danced, and played with their baby girl.

Stephanie found one photo of her birth parents that included her...sort of. Her father stood straight and proud in sharp Marine Dress Blues. Her mother wore a sparkling red maternity dress and leaned on his shoulder, smiling into the camera. Their hands entwined over the bump of their soon-to-be-born baby girl. Stephanie had definitely inherited her father's dimple and her mother's sable brown hair.

On the back of the photo, the neatly-printed caption "Marine Corps Ball, Nov. 10, 1986" recorded the event and date. She slipped this photo into her wallet.

Jessica had also started to research her biological family tree, which Marla had carefully preserved in the box. While slowly recovering from the shock of her own adoption, curiosity about her real heritage and where she came from consumed her. Jessica painstakingly recorded notes by hand, long before the Internet brought records to a computer screen at the click of a mouse.

All alone now, Stephanie devoted her attention to her mother's carefully constructed genealogy, hoping the old records would guide her to other living relatives.

The most detailed and fascinating information Jessica obtained had come during a telephone conversation with an elderly distant cousin named Sadie. Through her, Jessica managed to identify relatives back to the Civil War era. In the process, she also uncovered family legends of a mysterious French ancestress with a melodic first name, but with the passage of time no one in Sadie's family could recall whether it was possibly Celeste or Chlotilde.

Although Stephanie yearned to know more about this unidentified ancestress, the lack of information stymied her. The small clues she could discern seemed to link the French family to her third great-grandfather Thomas Wyatt, a Civil War era soldier. Jessica's documentation indicated he had spent time in Portsmouth, Virginia during the war.

If Stephanie learned more about him, it could lead to discovering information about the puzzling French woman. On the spur of the moment, she decided to take a week's vacation and conduct a bit of research in Portsmouth, just three hours south of her home.

Decision made, she closed the journal and left the spare room to call her office.

She imagined the scent of Chanel and sighed deeply at the lingering reminder of her mother. She didn't notice how the small book's pages fluttered silently, then just as soundlessly settled back into position.

CHAPTER TWO

STEPHANIE
Portsmouth, Virginia, six months later

Stephanie's wiggling fingers hovered over the keyboard. With firm resolve, she tapped the "send" button, the blinking icon confirming the email delivery.

"That's that," she muttered, dusting her hands in an exaggerated movement of dismissive finality. She shut down her laptop, leaned back in the chair, and strummed her fingers nervously on the closed top. Then she bounced to her feet and leaned over the dressing table in the small hotel room. The grim face staring back from the mirror wore furrows on her forehead and a downturn to her mouth.

Glaring at her reflection, she said, "You've done it now, so no use worrying."

She paced the room, the sigh escaping before she could stop it. She'd just sent the second of two life-changing emails.

In the first email, sent an hour earlier, she had accepted an offer for the sale of her house.

In the second one—well—she had just provided her employer with her two-week notice.

Her mind drifted to the events of the last six months. Just after the Christmas holidays, rumors predicting major layoffs had run rampant at work. The uncertainty created office tensions that could be cut with the proverbial knife.

Then, she and her long-time boyfriend decided to call it quits, mutually agreeing to take separate paths. Although saddened, she was not heartbroken at all—more accurately, the breakup relieved her. She'd taken comfort in knowing Ethan had the same reaction.

Shortly after the break-up, a police officer and chaplain appeared at her office, bearing news that her parents had died in a car accident. With Jackie and Ethan at her side, she made it through the double funeral.

Nothing, however, had destroyed her more than the moment when she found out she was actually the adopted daughter of Jeff and Marla Kincaid.

Adopted! The word still stunned her as much as the first time she read it. As she stared out at the river from her window, she fingered the revealing letter she'd removed from her files but did not read it. The letter's contents were forever etched in her memory, and she shook her head to erase them.

She returned the document to the file and reflected on the life-changing emails she had just sent. Selling her house was fine news.

But quitting her job? The decision had been easy—but was it wise?

She was on the third day of her vacation—if you counted the weekend. Her first *full* day away from work, however, and by nine a.m. she had already received three text messages to check her email inbox. There she found seven queries anyone else in the office could have answered. Other emails contained inquiries on the status of two different reports, both of which the team had already completed and turned in days before.

As she dutifully but grudgingly replied to each message, she reached a decision she'd been heading toward for a long time. After the realization struck her like a bolt of lightning, her resignation took two steps to complete.

Write brief two week notice, check.

Hit send button, check.

Yes, it had been easy. And wise.

So, now she would begin her new mission. Lovingly she caressed the leather-bound journal containing her biological mother's notes. Her purpose for visiting the historic district of Olde Towne Portsmouth was to research her family tree, and that was damn well what she would do! She might consider a new career as a full-time researcher if this proved fruitful.

She didn't move, but continued to sit in her hotel room overlooking the Elizabeth River. Although she thought she had cried all of her tears, fresh ones slid down her cheeks unexpectedly. She missed her parents terribly—okay, her adoptive parents—but she realized she grieved now because they had never told her about the adoption while they were alive. She could have assured them it did not matter to her; they were the only parents she had ever known, and she loved them unconditionally.

However, she would not have the chance now. She wiped her eyes and blew her nose. Her raw emotions and the stress from the crying jag left her unexpectedly depleted. She would rest just for a moment and stretched out on the bed, closing her eyes—*just for a moment*, she reminded herself.

Silent and still, she drifted into a dreamless sleep— except for one instance when she imagined someone touched her cheek and brushed a trailing tear away.

If she'd opened her eyes just then—she would have thought she imagined the ruffling of pages in the journal.

***

For two days, Stephanie tracked through Olde Towne's old cemeteries, studying well-cared-for headstones surrounded by flowers interspersed with lonely weathered markers, the lettering on some nearly obliterated by moss, weeds, and time. She took photos of every Wyatt headstone she found. In the end, none of the information matched with any of the names in her tree, and in disappointment she returned to her room to search the

Internet for other clues.

While she waited for her laptop to boot up, she pushed the drapes aside to gaze at the river scene below and gasped. Tears of pride tickled her eyes at the sight of a mighty Navy ship passing in the harbor, dwarfing the red tugboats that guided it. The slow silent movement of the passing gray craft commanded her full attention. Small naval signal flags she didn't recognize flapped from the bridge.

Sailors lining the deck formed a majestic crown from bow to stern. Intermittently, one of the white-clad figures waved to observers on shore.

She had never seen a navy ship so close. Sometimes her local news in Alexandria covered a large Navy homecoming in Hampton Roads and she remembered the "Welcome Home" signs and balloons bopping in anticipation as the crowds cheered wildly. Watching coverage of the joyful families' reactions' as the ship docked always gave her goose bumps, and she imagined the family members currently waiting on the pier would have similar outbursts when this ship arrived.

Reluctantly, she tore her attention from the imposing ship and returned to her computer. She prepared a list of records to search for in the city courthouse on Thursday, something she realized she should have already completed. Then she would head home Friday.

She fingered her mother's worn journal. From the neatly-scripted pages, she had garnered most of her clues from her birth mother's interviews with the elderly cousin Sadie, a spry ninety-four years at the time Jessica spoke with her.

Through Sadie, Jessica found the trail of ancestry clues leading to a man named Thomas Wyatt who had been in the Civil War. Sadie also relayed colorful memories of a time in her childhood when her own grandmother told stories of a French woman in the family whose husband had fought for the Americans during the Revolution. Sadie could remember this woman had lived in the eighteenth-century, had an unusual name similar to Celeste or Chlotilde, and her husband fought with the French Army. Jessica had reached a dead end on further details.

Stephanie closed the journal and typed names in the computer. Since the notes indicated Thomas's birth occurred in 1847 and he spent time in Portsmouth during the Civil War, Stephanie checked census records for possible matches. Census records were a goldmine of information but she had to thoroughly examine each one to be sure she had found the right person, and not simply someone with the same name. It wasn't so easy—in the 1920 census alone, she found dozens of Tom or Thomas Wyatts listed.

Stephanie typed Sadie's name into her genealogy program. Still confused by extended relationships, she estimated Sadie to be her second cousin once removed. A quick record search revealed Sadie had never married, and died in 1991 at age ninety-nine. Stephanie saved the information to her files to scrutinize further.

By Thursday, she had not developed much new information. Tired of dead ends, disappointments, and sad forgotten headstones sloping in weeds, she took a break to forget the past and enjoy the present. Time now to explore the historic seaport town, visit some of the churches, and maybe visit the courthouse. Instead of writing notes, she could simply take close-up digital photos to review afterward. It would clear her brain, and she could tackle the tedious record searches again later.

She gathered maps and brochures and headed down to the lobby and outside to a beautiful sunny day. She paused at the intriguing "Lightship *Portsmouth*" near the hotel. She'd never heard of a lightship before. The brochure explained that such vessels were a portable navigational aid, similar to a lighthouse but moved as needed. Anchored at strategic locations, the versatile ships guided mariners away from dangerous shoals or into harbors. The lightship had been given to the city and turned into a museum. As she snapped photos, she made a mental note to come back another time and visit the quaint ship as well as the Railroad Museum a few blocks away.

Turning onto High Street, she studied the statue of Colonel William Crawford before she continued past shops, restaurants, the Children's Museum, and the Virginia Sports Hall of Fame. With its long history, Portsmouth had more to offer than she realized.

She next strolled along quiet side streets boasting restored homes. Examples of Colonial, Federal, Greek Revival, Georgian, or Victorian construction nestled among modern structures, a mix she found charming. Frequently she referred to the brochure as she tried to determine the architecture of an interesting building.

Her heart thumped wildly when she spotted a historic marker heralding the "Wyatt House." She took pictures of the house and of the street signs identifying the intersection. Then she turned to the historical marker to photograph the description written on its face.

It wasn't until she read the information the second time that she realized she had misread the family name. Her shoulders slumped in disappointment. The actual name was "Watt."

Still, she mused as she stood on the corner and consulted the map. Names were often misspelled in old records. Maybe she could still find a clue. Returning her camera to its case, she headed toward the riverfront.

Mother Nature, however, had different plans for her. Or perhaps an unseen force dictated her route.

Deeply engrossed in walking the quaint old streets, she failed to notice the roiling clouds overhead until a clap of thunder startled her. Caught off guard, she tilted her head and looked toward the darkened sky. Large wet raindrops smacked her face.

She looked around. The nearest public building was a small bakery, so new she wasn't sure it was even open.

At the moment, she didn't care if the restored building represented Colonial, Victorian or modern architecture; it was her only option to avoid the rain.

As she dashed up the few steps to the wrap-around porch, the rain drilled into the top of her head. The name *"Pâtisseries a la Carte"* stood out in raised letters on a brass plaque beside the doorframe.

Please be open. The antique brass doorknob turned easily in her hand and she sighed in relief. Delightful bakery scents reached her nose even as she opened the door. She stepped inside, a tinkling bell over her head merrily announcing her entry.

The surroundings exuded the aura of a French sidewalk café, reminding her of one she visited with her parents while on a summer vacation in France.

Before she could absorb the atmosphere, a drop-dead gorgeous woman dashed around a glass counter toward a table near the door. Arms laden with white cardboard boxes, she called "Sit anywhere, I'll be with you in a minute," as she plopped the cartons on a table and dashed away.

Stephanie stood in place, taking in the retreating figure in a navy blue power suit, no shoes, running on perfectly-pedicured bare feet sporting fire-engine red toenails, hair piled haphazardly on her head. Stephanie experienced a rare twinge of jealousy. On the other woman the chestnut-colored hair formed a glamorous crown, a stylish look Stephanie could never achieve with her own locks.

When the well-dressed woman returned with more boxes, Stephanie asked, "Is this a bad time? I can come back later."

"Yep, it's a bad time and no, you don't need to leave. Anyway, it's still raining." She smiled and handed Stephanie a menu printed with French on one side and English on the reverse. "I want you as a customer, so please sit where you like and I'll be right with you. We just opened a few days ago and still have some kinks to work out."

She retraced her steps, calling over her shoulder, "The cook and server decided they didn't like each other this morning and both left. My cook will eventually be back, not so the server. Fortunately, they'd prepared this large order before they had their spat. I'm just bagging it now— hoping I don't have to deliver as well. Sorry if I'm babbling. My nerves are jangled. Oh, man, it's pouring down now." The woman disappeared behind the counter.

Stephanie shook her head in bewilderment and dropped into a chair near a bay window. Hanging baskets of colorful flowers were a stark contrast to the gray moisture building on the glass from the change in temperature. Outside, rain fell in slanted sheets, with a light wind waving branches on the trees lining the street. A dark blue SUV pulled in front of the building, but no one got out. She assumed they waited to catch a break in the rain.

"Wow," Stephanie exclaimed as she used a napkin to wipe vapor from the glass. "I made it inside just in time." She didn't realize she had spoken out loud.

"You did indeed," the other woman answered as she came back into the dining area, stacking more boxes beside the others. "One more load and I will be done. Today's special is broccoli cheese soup and chicken salad on a croissant. Be right back." She vanished again.

Stephanie wondered if the woman moved like a whirlwind all the time. She glanced at the simple menu, the description of the chicken salad catching her eye. Prepared with grapes, walnuts and celery, it sounded different but delicious.

She glanced around, enjoying the subtle French accents in the bright, airy dining area. Three small sets of two-seater ice cream parlor tables shared the space in front of a huge bay window. Five larger square tables on the main floor could each seat four. An empty pastry display case separated the dining area from the kitchen and bore a large sign taped to the glass declaring "COMING SOON!" On top of the case, three chrome cake pedestals with glass covers held a small array of luscious-looking éclairs, cupcakes and cookies.

Above the pastry case, a cheery red-and-white striped awning unfurled as if to shade patrons from the imaginary sun. The ceiling, painted a light blue with puffy white clouds airbrushed in clusters, combined with the awning to create a sidewalk café effect for diners.

Stephanie studied the décor. A whimsical copper plaque depicted a Frenchman furiously pedaling a bicycle with long bony legs, typical beret on his head and baguette under his arm. The black beret and bright red cravat at the cyclist's neck gave color to the otherwise all-copper cutout.

Small paintings featuring quaint outdoor Parisian cafés decorated the walls. In one corner, a wide screen television hung silent and dark.

Immersed in the atmosphere of the bistro, she racked her brain to translate the name of the café, *Pâtisseries a la Carte*. Her high school language class kicked in as she recognized other long-forgotten French words on the menu and she settled on "Pastries by the Menu" as the translation. She confirmed when she flipped to the English side.

The woman returned, this time carrying shopping bags while she wedged a phone between her chin and shoulder, loading boxes as she talked.

"I just found the shopping bags to hold everything. Can't someone make a pick-up, please, Gage? I'm in a real dilemma here and I have a customer patiently waiting. Please, please, pretty please?" She flashed a charming smile Stephanie's way and winked. Stephanie suspected the unseen caller would be hard-pressed to resist the charm. The jubilant fist-pump confirmed poor Gage had indeed given in.

"I love you, Gage, kiss, kiss."

"Oh, thank you, God!" the woman disconnected and directed her gaze skyward as she dropped into a chair opposite Stephanie. "I am so sorry. We just opened shop a couple of days ago, and today all hell is breaking loose. We had our first major catering order ready for delivery, rain's pouring, and I'm due in afternoon court in one hour. Did you decide what you wanted? My treat, since you had to wait."

Stephanie could not switch brain gears fast enough to keep pace with the energy radiating from this female powerhouse. She managed to mumble that the special sounded fine, and the woman jumped up and dashed behind the bakery counter.

"Oh, miss?" Stephanie went to the counter and leaned to call into the kitchen area where the woman clanked dishes and rattled pans. "Can you add an unsweetened tea, please?"

"Just call me Terry. Tea is coming up." Terry brought out two glasses of tea, placing one on Stephanie's table and one on the next. A few minutes later she carried platters with soup cups and sandwiches to both tables. She sat at her table facing Stephanie and said, "I might as well grab a bite while I can. The way this day is going, it might be my only meal."

"Do you always move around so fast?" Stephanie asked. She half-expected Terry would scarf down her sandwich in one bite, as energetic as she appeared, but surprisingly she nibbled her food daintily.

"Most days, yes, warp is my normal speed. I own this bakery with my best friend. I'm actually the silent—okay, not so silent—partner. In real life, I'm a lawyer. My office is just two doors down, so I take care of our legal and investment issues." She pointed to her left. "Next door, we are converting an old house into a B and B. Right now, the owner is in the Army serving in Afghanistan but believe me, she's been running the show long-distance. We've been working hard in her absence. We just finished and opened this week, but my sister-in-law, the manager, had to go out of town on a family emergency today. Voila! Here I am."

Relaxing considerably, Terry paused to sip tea. "My friend designed the café with an obvious Parisian flair. In addition to offering pastries and light meals, she wants to hold cooking classes for kids twice a week, and sell pint-sized kitchen gadgets as well. 'Boutique de le Petit Chef' will be her shop for the little cooks in a room off the kitchen." She nodded toward the kitchen and Stephanie's gaze followed.

"Kid's cooking classes—and a shop for the little chef. What a clever idea," Stephanie replied, wondering if she should sign up for one. Her own culinary skills probably equaled a child's capability. Her own specialty consisted of buying take-out food.

She wanted to ask more questions but the slamming of a car door and the sound of laughter distracted her. Through the bay window she noticed the rain had eased, and the three occupants of the blue SUV dashed through the remnants. A little boy about four stepped in every puddle as he ran with the boundless energy of a child. An older couple followed behind, using newspapers as a shield from the scattered raindrops falling on their heads.

The child burst through the entrance first, slamming the door against the wall. The bell sounded in overdrive. He exuberantly shouted "Aunt Terry! Aunt Terry! I'm here!" as he flung himself into her arms.

"You sure are. I heard you laughing all the way to the door." Terry laughed and gave him a noisy smooch on the cheek. "How are you, Tanner Bear?"

Her cell phone rang just then and she set the child down to answer

"Hi, Gage, what's up?" Terry listened for a moment and said, "*What? How* many more?" She grimaced as she glanced toward the glass display. "No, no problem, we should have enough." However, it's going to take me about twenty more minutes to get the sandwiches ready...yes, I can add them to the original order, but I still need someone to come pick it up; I have to be in court and this will cut it close...okay, will do...yes, I love you too but you are so going to owe me, Mr. Gage Dunbar."

"Can I speak to Uncle Gage, please, Aunt Terry?" Tanner begged before she could hang up.

"Yes, but hurry, baby boy, I have to do some work and you have to leave soon with grandma and grandpa if you want to catch your airplane."

Tanner grabbed the phone and yelled, "Hi, Mr. Uncle Gage Dunbar!"

Stephanie smiled at the endearing way the child repeated the name, mimicking the tone his aunt used.

That has such a nice ring to it. Gage Dunbar, Gage Dunbar, I wonder who you are? As the name danced over and over in her head, a brush of warm air skittered across her cheek in spite of the cold air-conditioner blasting nearby, as if gentle fingertips had stroked her skin. She touched her face.

"Are you at a fire right now?" Tanner listened to the answer and his excitement dimmed. He frowned and his shoulder slumped. "Skew-el?" stretching the word "school" into two syllables. "But it's summer, why are you in skew-el? We're leaving for Disney World now. Cause if you weren't in ske-wel you could go wif us too." He remained quiet for a moment and then laughed. "Yeah, I can't wait to see Mickey Mouse. Love you, Uncle Gage. I have to go now. Bye!"

He unceremoniously tapped the phone to hang up, and turned to the older couple. "Can we go now, Grampie?"

"Yes, partner, we need to scram. Give Aunt Terry a hug and let's get the goodies she made for us."

"They're right here, Pops." Terry handed her father a bag and a box, and pecked his cheek. "Chicken salad for you and Mom, PBJ for the little prince here, and loads of chocolate chip cookies for everyone. Hate to give you the bum's rush now, but Gage just called in an additional order for the fire training class. I'm all alone here—not to mention I have court shortly."

Terry's mother spoke. "I wish we could help you,

honey. Hannah called and told me what happened, but we're a bit late as it is, and thanks to the little man here, I need a roll of paper towels to clean the mess he dragged in."

"It's all right, Mom, I've got it. You guys need to get on your way before the next cloudburst hits."

"Thanks for the goodies, sweetie. It's a no-frills flight. We'll enjoy them on the plane." She hugged Terry and turned around to playfully admonish her husband and grandson, "Now come on, fellas, it's time to scoot! We have a mouse to see."

Tanner leapt into Terry's arms and this time, he gave her the loud smooch on the cheek, adding "Bye!" as he shimmied out of her arms and charged for the door. "Love you, Aunt Terry." He turned, faced the back of the room and with a wave shouted, "Bye, Nickel." Next, he looked at Stephanie and called, "Bye, lady!" His exuberance left her taken aback but she raised a hand in reply.

Terry kissed her dad on the cheek and ushered them out the door, standing on the porch calling "Love you guys. Have fun. Bye." She waved until the car drove out of sight and then stepped back inside.

"Geez, now my feet are wet!" she complained good-naturedly as she wiped her bare feet on a mat and shut the door. "And I have size two muddy shoe prints all over my skirt, which could have been avoided if I had taken a minute to put on an apron." Showing no sign of annoyance, she brushed at the telltale marks Tanner left when she'd lifted him into her arms.

Stephanie reached for her tea, impressed by the other woman's calm demeanor. While a three-ring circus had played around her, Terry had taken it all in stride.

That suit undoubtedly cost five hundred dollars and yet she's not upset at all. Anyone else would probably have berated the child to tears. The interaction of the obviously close family had also elicited a brief twinge of envy.

"Sorry for all of the commotion," Terry called over her

shoulder. "My family is like a three-ring circus at times."

Stephanie nearly choked on a sip of tea, wondering if she had revealed her thoughts on her face.

"Are you okay? Did something go down wrong?" Terry asked in concern.

"Fine, I'm fine. I've never had chicken salad like this before. It's delicious—and the soup as well."

"Glad you liked it."

"I have a question, though. Your nephew called out and waved to someone, but there's no one else here."

Terry laughed. "My sister-in-law brings him with her to work sometimes, and he becomes so bored that he has conjured up an imaginary friend named 'Nickel.' Sometimes he says she is a grandmotherly lady telling him stories, but most times he says she is a child that plays with him. He has an overactive imagination, but it keeps him out of trouble."

At the word "Nickel," unseen fingertips brushed against Stephanie's cheek and a warm shiver surged through her body. The bell on the entry jingled once but the door never opened, the eerie tinkle causing the hair on the back of her neckline to stand. She rubbed her neck as she glanced from the door to the kitchen.

Terry seemed oblivious to the bell as she walked to the glass display case. She removed a tray of pastries with one hand while making phone calls with her other, punching speed-dial numbers with her thumb.

"Hi, Pam, it's Terry. I'm at the café and wanted to see if you could help me for an hour or so. Can you call me back?" She frantically punched more numbers, leaving similar messages three more times.

By the fourth call her voice shook as she organized pastries into boxes. She then placed the containers in shiny gray shopping bags emblazoned with the dainty *Pâtisseries a la Carte* crest in black.

"Geez, now I've got to get a dozen more meals ready and I can't find a single person who can help on such short notice. Oh, my God, what am I going to do?" Terry spoke aloud as she shoved her phone in her pocket and brought more bags to the table where the earlier order waited.

Stephanie chimed in, "Can I help you do it?" Then she panicked. Had she actually just vocalized those words? She'd simply thought them and not spoken out loud. *Right? Please, please, that's what happened, right?*

But she knew she had spoken loudly and clearly by the way Terry's head shot up, pouncing on the idea much like a tiger on unsuspecting prey.

"Oh, God bless you, would you? Would you really?"

CHAPTER THREE

CLOTHISTE
Portsmouth, Virginia, 7 July 1781

Clothiste struggled to raise her head from her bed. Barely two months had passed since her illness had forced her to leave her beloved Etienne. Life following the army was harsh on good days and grim on most days. She needed recovery.

This house where she had come to heal should have been a safe haven for her and her daughters.

But in this terrible house, she became weaker and felt as if death edged near to her door.

There may not be much time left for her now.

Would she ever see her beloved husband again before her life ended? She feared she would leave her beautiful little girls in the hands of that wicked woman.

She opened her journal but her body slumped, the minimal movement sapping her remaining energy. Will I even be able to write in it much longer? *She had no other gift to leave her daughters, save for those three precious pendants safely tucked away.*

The lovely bedroom with its lace curtains at the windows and the exquisitely canopied four-poster bed should have afforded comfort following five years of living in battlefield tents and sleeping on meager pallets. Ornate candlesticks and pretty vases of white and blue scattered across the mantle, reminded her of the luxuries she had once known in her own home.

Drawing the small leather-bound book to her chest for comfort, a tear slid down her cheek. Through her stories her children would know of their courageous father, and all their family had suffered— and lost—helping America in the war against the British.

The clink of glass and a rattle of the door handle warned Clothiste that the servant Lizzie was bringing a tray. Wishing one of her daughters was nearby so she could feel protected, she tucked her journal under her coverlet. She pretended to sleep, praying she would not cough and reveal she was awake. The maid-servant's dress brushed her hand as the girl reached the bedside table and rattled dishes.

"Is her breakfast still sitting there?" The sharp voice of the wicked one shrilled from the doorway and sent shivers down Clothiste's spine.

Lizzie answered meekly, "Yes, ma'am, she left most of it unfinished."

"Well, take it away. Take both trays back. If she is not going to eat, there is no need to leave food around all morning and all afternoon."

"Yes, ma'am. Should I leave some small bread…?"

"Do as you are told! Take it all away at once!"

"Yes, ma'am, I will." She bobbed a quick curtsy and fled. The soles of her slippers squeaked as she scurried across the room and out the door; with her every step dishes clattered on the tray.

Clothiste sensed the presence of evil as the wicked one—her stepmother-in-law Abigail—stepped further into the room. She forced herself to remain motionless as the wicked one rattled glass near the head of the bed. For a brief moment, Clothiste feared a blow to the head.

The room fell into eerie silence. The wicked one bent closer, her voice a low feral snarl. "May you rot in hell, French whore." Her heels clicked in a rapid staccato as she retreated toward the door.

The frail figure in the bed remained still, silent relief washing over her. What would Abigail think if she knew the step-family referred to her as the "wicked one"?

Clothiste shuddered as she turned to one side, unable to find warmth under the coverlet. She rolled to the other side and curled into a ball. Indeed, that cruel woman would relish the title.

Clothiste could not stop the tears that burned her eyes.

She let her memory drift back to the day when she and her three daughters, wet and disheveled, arrived unannounced on the dark

41

doorstep of the grand home during a raging storm. The maid who answered the door appeared taken aback by their appearance and demanded they leave. When Clothiste explained that they were the daughter-in-law and grandchildren of Phillip Roker, the maid asked them to wait at the door, and went upstairs to report the arrival to her employer.

Abigail had descended the staircase, jaw clenched and eyes narrowed. Clothiste told the carefully-cultivated story: Phillip's son Etienne had brought them to America intending to start a business in the north but had to leave unexpectedly and return to France. The Americans commandeered their home and the women had no place to go. With nowhere else to turn and fearful of the soldiers, they fled to Virginia to evade the American army.

In reality Etienne had never returned to France at all, but fought in the Army right here in Virginia, with the Americans. His family traveled with him, as hundreds of other "camp-followers" did, but when Clothiste had become deathly ill, he had insisted she go to his father's house to recover.

They kept the story simple, and as intended, Abigail assumed Clothiste came from France but was loyal to British ties because of her father-in-law.

It did nothing to diminish Abigail's growing resentment toward her husband's French family.

STEPHANIE
Portsmouth, Virginia, present day July

Once the words had escaped, Stephanie had no opportunity for retreat as Terry plowed through a variety of bribes. "I'll buy your lunch. I'll pay you cash. I'll pay you both my baker and server's wages. Hell, I will pay you the retainer on my case today."

Stephanie gulped but rose to the challenge. "Well, that's not necessary. I can't promise any exceptional skills, but you seem to be in a bind, and I can handle slapping some sandwiches together. Just tell me what to do. And where is the bathroom?"

Terry gestured toward the back.

Wanting to kick herself in the butt the entire way, Stephanie walked toward the door marked "Femmes." She pressed her hands to her temples and shook her head disgustedly.

She glared at her reflection in the mirror. "What were you thinking, you dummy? You can't even boil an egg without a disaster. You do take-out four nights a week."

But she washed her hands, put on her game face and joined Terry, who had spread slices of rye bread across a chrome countertop.

"Grab a pair of plastic gloves from the gray box right there. If you can move along with me like an assembly line and daub the mixture from the glass bowl on all of these, I'll add the lettuce and tomato, and then we can add the deli meats. You don't know how much I appreciate this."

"Glad I can help but I won't be as fast as you," Stephanie warned.

"It's okay. Someone should be here any minute to pick these up, and with your help, we'll be ready. Put a sandwich, a container of potato salad, and a dill pickle in each lunch box." She pulled off one plastic glove, punched a number on the cell phone resting on the counter, and put it on speaker so she could use her left hand to place lettuce on the bread.

"Dunbar and Cross," an amplified female voice filled the room.

"Becky, it's me." Terry leaned toward the phone. "No time to talk, but I almost have the crisis under control here. I will be heading out in a minute. Can you have someone put my briefcase in my car so I can go straight to court? My files are already in it."

"Okay, Ms. Dunbar, will do."

"Thanks," Terry hung up without waiting for a response and replaced her plastic glove. "It's a good thing I'm just a five-minute drive from the courthouse," she grumbled. "By the way, what did you say your name was?"

"I'm not sure I did." Stephanie laughed. "Things were already hectic when I came in. I'm Stephanie." She extended her hand and Terry automatically reached to take it, when they both realized they were wearing the plastic gloves. They laughed but even though they withdrew without touching, a small spark snapped between their fingers.

"Ouch!" Terry yelped, shaking her wrist. "You would think these gloves would be a shock absorber for static electricity."

"I agree." Stephanie rubbed her encased fingers. "That was weird."

The bell over the door jangled as new customers entered. Terry sighed, saying, "Well, Stephanie, don't look now, but it's about to get hectic again." She raised her head and called out over the counter to the elderly couple, "Be right there!"

"Could you possibly take their order?" she whispered to Stephanie. "If it's the special, we can knock it out, but if it's anything else, it will take longer."

"Uh—okay," Stephanie said. She still reeled from the earlier commotion, but took menus to the newcomers and scooped up her plate and Terry's half-eaten lunch on the rebound.

Terry nodded toward Stephanie. "Thanks for cleaning those tables."

After working for a few minutes in silence, Terry spoke next. "Grab that bucket of potato salad right there." She motioned with her chin. "If you can start scooping into those little plastic cups, I can finish these sandwiches. Use the ice cream scoop beside it to measure it out."

Stephanie scooped a dozen servings of potato salad before returning to the dining area to take the new arrivals' orders. Their selection of the soup and chicken croissant combo elicited another jubilant fist pump from Terry, in the kitchen out of their sight. As Terry prepared the order for the new customers, Stephanie continued to scoop potato salad into cups.

When the platters were ready, she served the meals to the customer as Terry bagged the take-out boxes.

"Mary Jo won't use foam boxes, but after this fiasco I think I'll try to talk her into at least using those sectional ones for takeout orders. It would have saved us having to scoop individual cups," Terry said. "This became one major pain in the ass, and you certainly saved mine."

"It just seemed like the right thing to do and I'm glad...oh, my gosh, those shoes are gorgeous! Are they Italian?" Stephanie's gaze focused on white pumps with a gray geometric design, abandoned in one corner where Terry must have kicked them off.

"Yes they are. They're Manolo Blahniks. I just love them but they weren't made for the kitchen, that's for sure." Terry braced herself against the butcher-block table to slide her feet into the snakeskin high heels.

The bell over the door jingled as two more customers entered. Terry leaned close to Stephanie and whispered, "A pair of these shoes will be yours if you will stay until I get back. I shouldn't be gone more than an hour, but I have to leave right now or I will be spending the night in the hoosegow. I arrived late last week and already got one warning from the judge."

"Are you kidding? I can't help you. I don't know anything..."

"Sure you can." Terry grabbed a paper encased in plastic and grinned mischievously. "Here's a cheat sheet I made up for the sandwich ingredients. All the meats and cheeses are in marked containers, as well as the chicken salad. We have a very limited menu, so you won't have to worry about too many variables. We close at two, so it won't be too much longer anyway. I'll attach the final bill for the fire department order to one of the bags and all you have to do is collect from the person who picks it up. Cash drawer is over there for transactions." She pointed her chin to a small drawer under the counter as she grabbed her purse. "I'll get out of court as soon as I can. I just need you to stay until then."

"You're pretty trusting. How do you know I won't clean out this cash drawer while you're gone?"

For a moment, Terry stared as if assessing her, then said, "Because I have very good judgment about people and I trust you—besides, on my way out I'll be snagging your quite expensive camera, which you left on the window sill, as ransom."

"Wait, wait." Stephanie held her hands up in protest. "This is too much for me. I can't do this."

"I need you. Please." Terry gave her a pleading look, and added "Pretty please?"

Stephanie now understood why the unseen Gage had given in; the woman had an absolutely irresistible charm.

"All right, but I want it written in blood, preferably not mine, that I'm not responsible if this place catches on fire or something."

"Consider it done," Terry called as she and her great shoes danced across the room. She snatched Stephanie's camera from the window and waved airily as she headed to the door, just as it opened and the bell jangled.

Two of the most prime specimens of firefighting manliness Stephanie had ever seen rushed through the door, Terry nearly colliding with them on her way out.

"Hi, fellas! Sorry you had to pick this up, guys, but thanks a bunch," she said as she sailed past them, planting a big kiss on the cheek of one and patting the cheek of the second. "We've had some major glitches today, but your order's ready. I have to run. If I'm late for court again Jabba the Judge will throw the book at me."

And in much the same hasty way as little Tanner had ended his earlier phone conversation with his Uncle Gage she called out "Bye" over her shoulder and disappeared.

"I see she is a whirlwind as usual." The shorter firefighter said admiringly, as his gaze lingered on her departing figure. "Is she still tearing them up in court?"

"Yep, she sure is." The first firefighter stared at Stephanie with interest. "Hi. You aren't the same girl who was here this morning."

"No, I am just an innocent bystander who got drafted."

As he kept his gaze locked on her face, she became flustered and fumbled with the menu before asking, "Who is 'Jabba the Judge'?"

He seemed to choose his words carefully. "Well, it's the local attorneys' name for one of our judges, who is rather—shall we say rotund. Complete with three chins and sagging jowls."

"Oh, I see," said Stephanie, although she didn't see. After a second, she realized the description matched the *Star Wars* character "Jabba the Hutt" and laughed at the image of Jabba in a judge's black robe. Her eyes met the electrifying blue pair that perfectly complemented the firefighter's dark navy uniform shirt. A little flutter tickled her tummy.

"Good one, Gage." The second fireman also laughed and leaned slightly to study the pastries in the glass display.

Stephanie's gaze fell on the nametag of the man in front of her and she read the name "Dunbar." *So, this must be the "Mr. Uncle Gage Dunbar" that the little boy had talked to earlier.*

Then, she remembered Terry's call over the speakerphone and the faceless voice answering with "Dunbar and Cross."

Darn! He was her husband. A wave of disappointment drowned the fluttering.

Stephanie averted her eyes and said the first thing that came to mind. "I met your nephew earlier. He's so cute."

"Ah, our little man Tanner. He's a pistol. Should be taking off for Orlando just about now, I should think." He glanced at his watch. "Disney will never be the same. He's a whirlwind like his Aunt Terry and keeps us all on our toes." He looked around. "Where's Hannah?"

"Hannah? Is she the cook?" Stephanie spoke uncertainly, trying to remember if Terry had mentioned names earlier. Every time she looked at Gage, a teen-age giddiness washed over her, which she tried to immediately tamp down.

"Yeah. She's not back yet? Her tantrums are legendary, but she always comes back."

"Well, I'm not sure. Apparently, she and the waitress had some sort of clash this morning and they left. Terry seemed to be doing everything and had to leave for court, so I just kind of pitched in."

"Just like that?" Gage snapped his fingers, then shook his head and withdrew several bills from his wallet.

"Yes, just like that." Stephanie mimicked his movement with a crisp snap of her own, her tone annoyed. "And she didn't even run a police check on me. So it must be my honest face." She emphasized the words with sarcasm and sneered along with it. "Oh yeah," she added ruefully. "She's holding my two-thousand dollar Nikon as collateral until she comes back."

"Aha, now that sounds more like her. No offense meant. Will you tell her we appreciate the last minute order?" He paused and cocked his head at an angle as he studied her. "You know, you have a cute little dimple which appears whether you smile or grimace." He tapped the side of his face.

"I do not grimace." Stephanie straightened her posture, indignantly pursing her lips as Gage pressed bills into her hand, holding for what Stephanie considered to be just a moment too long as their eyes made contact. She took the money, and tried to withdraw, not quickly enough to avoid the small electric jolt that coursed through her fingers before she drew free. She narrowed her eyes at him.

"Yes, you do. You just grimaced again." He tapped the side of his mouth once more. "And the dimple showed up again. Keep the change. And thank you for helping her. Maybe we'll see each other again." Gage stared directly into her eyes, frowning slightly as he then turned to his partner.

"Grab some stuff, Mark. We need to get this back

48

ASAP." The firefighters grabbed the bags as Stephanie studied their sinewy backs. Gage began to whistle "The First Time Ever I Saw Your Face." He paused at the door, glanced back at her and winked as he pulled it shut with his free hand.

The overhead bell tinkled, reminding Stephanie of a child's giggle.

She fisted her hands to her hips in total annoyance and glared at the door, irked at several things. The man named Mark certainly cast adoring eyes at Terry as she nearly collided with him on her way out, while not directing so much as a flutter Stephanie's way after he entered. That didn't bother her; she was used to being in the shadow of more striking women. But he might have at least looked her way once!

She fluctuated between disappointment and annoyance. The handsome Gage was married to Terry, yet he'd just made a pass at her. Her immediate attraction to him, as well as the fact that she wouldn't mind experiencing it again, perturbed her more.

And like it or not, what really pissed her off was Roberta Flack's tune now playing over and over in her head.

CHAPTER FOUR

CLOTHISTE AND NICOLE
Portsmouth, Virginia, 7 July 1781

Clothiste resented the way her stepmother-in-law forced the older girls to do housework as if they were household servants, but she could not prevent it.

Her daughters did more than clean and serve. They were both quick of wit with clever minds that worked fast, always listening for useful information in the conversations around them.

From her observations in the army camp, she had surmised that men, especially soldiers, tended to drink too much, and ale or wine loosened their lips. If things went well tonight during the dinner, the girls might overhear valuable information which could help the Americans and possibly bring her beloved Etienne to her soon. She had received news his unit marched toward Yorktown.

Her four-year-old Nicole wiggled beside her on the bed. "Mama, do you know what? This morning the step-grandmamma took my baby and threw it in the trash bin." She glared and pouted for a moment. "The step-grandmamma—she called it ugly and dirty. She is so mean! She grabbed my baby right out of my hands and threw it in the bin. When she turned her back on us, Marie Josephé wanted to hit her. Like this." The little girl held her hand up as if to deliver a slap. "So did I! But Theresé wouldn't let us. She waited until the step-grandmother left the room, and went right out and found my doll, and brought it back to me. I love my sisters, Mama!" She kissed the doll as she settled under the coverlet and sighed. "They said I have to hide it from the step-grandmamma. I shall never let her see it again!"

Nicole played with the rag doll, humming innocently. Clothiste smiled to herself as she hugged her youngest child tighter. How fortunate her inquisitive little daughter did not know the secrets of *that old doll.*

Stephanie
Portsmouth, Virginia, present day July

In Terry's absence, Stephanie had managed to serve, without incident, two more couples: a raucous family of five who left no tip, and a grumpy older man in a business suit who placed an order to go and left a large tip. She was ready to close up shop.

When the bell over the door jangled again and two women entered, Stephanie glanced at the clock. One forty-five. Inclined to tell the new customers the café was closed, she pushed the idea aside with a pang of guilt. She'd made a promise and she'd keep it. She pasted on a bright smile and rounded the glass case, deftly snatching two menus to offer to the two women standing at the door. Heads together, they mumbled back and forth, pointing at the walls.

One woman, short and stocky, red hair cut in a rigid line at chin length, pursed her lips. The other woman stood slightly taller, with brown hair and similar facial features. "Good afternoon, ladies." Stephanie surmised they were sisters. "Have a seat anywhere you like, and I'll be right with you."

The red-haired woman glanced at Stephanie from head to toe with a slight smirk. "Not on your life. This place can't be any good if there aren't even any customers in it."

Stephanie bristled at the snide remark. Feeling she needed to defend the café, she retorted, "You just missed the lunch crowd. It's quiet in here now."

"Is Mary Jo here?"

"Mary Jo, the owner? I'm sorry, but she's not here. I understand she is on deployment."

The red-haired woman nodded slowly. Still pursing her

lips, she strolled further into the room, a speculative look in her eyes as they darted from side to side and rested on the display case.

The woman's furtive movements were disconcerting and Stephanie frowned as she stepped protectively in front of the glass case as the woman inched closer. "How can I help you?"

"When will she return?" The woman ran her finger down the base of a pedestal cake stand as she stretched her neck to peer over Stephanie's shoulder.

Stephanie drew to her full five-feet four inches and angled her body to block the view of the kitchen area. "Ma'am, I'm just filling in here for the afternoon. I can relay a message to her partner if you like."

"You tell her Mary Jo isn't going to get by with just returning my son's property. I gave him the money for this glass case and I want it back. I want it all."

"Ma'am, I'm sorry, but I don't know anything…"

Before Stephanie could finish, the woman turned on her heel and headed for the exit.

"Come on, Georgette. Let's get out of here before a roach crawls on us or something." She tore open the door with a flourish, letting it bang against the wall as she stomped out. The bell jangled furiously, sounding more like a hammer on metal than the usual tinkling sound. Georgette followed, glancing back with a shrug as she pulled the door shut behind her.

Stephanie clenched the menu in her fist, the laminated plastic cutting ridges in her palms as she ran to the window. Her heart thumped wildly against her chest. She kept her gaze on the two women standing on the sidewalk, gesturing back and forth between the café and the other building as the shorter one snapped pictures with her cell phone.

Turning from the window, Stephanie sank into the closest chair, her emotions dancing between anger and confusion.

What have I gotten myself into?

***

At precisely two o'clock, Stephanie locked the door and turned the sign around to the "Closed" side. She leaned her forehead against the doorframe and sighed, still shaken by the encounter with the two women.

She cleared tables and washed dishes, finding the right storage spots for the various plates and glasses. Then she scrubbed the surfaces of the dining tables, wiped down chairs, and cleaned the butcher-block table and the countertops in the food preparation area.

"This has to be the craziest day of my life," she mumbled out loud. "I'm out for a walk and a sudden storm directs me into a loony bin. Then a lawyer with great shoes railroads me into waitressing and her husband makes a pass at me. Then an angry woman comes in saying crazy things."

She'd managed to calm down after the encounter and put the angry women out of her mind.

But the mental image she couldn't clear sported the sizzling hot firefighter with those blue eyes. Despite her best efforts to clear his face away, it burned in her memory. She scrubbed a non-existent spot on the counter, which did nothing to erase the image.

Under other circumstances, she might even have tried to flirt a little more, or joked about him holding onto her hand. However, a poacher she was not, and as she contemplated the seemingly hard-working Terry juggling her personal career to help a friend in crisis while her husband…

Disgusted, she threw the towel into the trash and dug it out after she realized what she had done.

She refused to admit she'd felt a spark, something she had never experienced before, and could not explain.

"You were just caught off guard," she muttered to herself, tapping her fingers rapidly on the glass display case. "Maybe he wanted to make sure you had hold of the money. Oh, yeah, right. Do I say anything to Terry? No, no need to. After today, I'll never see them again anyway. I'll just mind my own business, get my camera back and be on my way. That louse!"

Stephanie rolled her eyes skyward at the lengthy and disjointed conversation she'd just had with herself, then went to the kitchen to give it a last survey. Stainless steel counters shared one entire wall with a matching commercial-grade refrigerator. Two huge stoves covered most of another wall. An enormous stainless steel island and a much smaller butcher-block table stood side by side in the middle of the kitchen; overhead, pots and pans hung from various racks suspended from the ceiling.

Stephanie glanced around, satisfied at the pristine condition. Chrome and glass literally sparkled, although she admitted it was because of the obvious care already put into maintaining it.

Then she frowned and stared at the center of the stainless steel table. All of the glass pedestals that originally stood atop the display case were stacked in the middle of the metal island, contents undisturbed.

"Now wait a minute." She alternated her gaze between the display and the island "That dish was sitting on the case when that woman came in. And I didn't move it." She shook her head. Whatever was going on was none of her concern. As soon as she got her camera back, she was finished with this place.

She counted the money in the cash box, pocketing the sixteen dollars she earned in her own tips and left the fifty-dollar tip from the fire department order for Terry. She had just sorted the currency and stacked all the bills facing the same direction—something she did habitually—when the bell over the café door tinkled lightly, followed by a little girl's laugh.

Puzzled, she set the cash box to the side, sure she had locked the door. She peered around the display case. No one stood near the closed door. She walked over and checked the handle. Locked. She turned the knob and opened the wooden door to peer outside, sending the bell overhead into jingles.

No one walked outside or even on the sidewalk near the building.

With a frown, Stephanie stepped back inside and turned the lock, looking above her head at the jangling bell. She checked the small rooms beside the kitchen and found nothing amiss. *It must have been children passing by outside.* She shrugged and went back around the counter, rummaging through the food receipts, separating the additional orders she'd handled so Terry could match them with the till.

A raspy voice screamed in her ear, "Don't move!"

Stephanie jumped, dropping the receipts and knocking over the cash drawer as she whirled around to face a tiny gnome of a woman wielding a mop by the handle, water dripping from the scraggly strings.

"Don't move," the woman croaked again. "Who the hell are you?

Stephanie raised her hands palms out, although she doubted the mop was loaded with anything more lethal than dirty water. "I'm not moving," she said, as her heart thumped wildly. She figured she could easily yank the mop out of the gnome's hands and turn the tables.

As if the shriveled little woman could read her mind, she narrowed her eyes at Stephanie and snarled, "You just stand still, dearie, while I call the cops," as she reached for the phone on the wall.

"There's no need for police. I helped Terry through an emergency. I just closed and was cleaning after lunch."

The wizened woman narrowed her eyes again as she assessed the situation and slammed the phone back into the receiver. "Damn phone still isn't working anyway. They were supposed to send someone to fix it today." She clenched her jaw, her mouth a stern line as she said, "Now tell me again exactly why I shouldn't consider you a burglar and just knock you over the head with this mop," her voice like sandpaper. "And don't think I can't do it either."

"Look, can I put my hands down? Call Terry's office, maybe someone can verify I'm supposed to be here. Call her husband. He just picked up the order for the fire department."

"Call who...?" the tiny woman started to speak.

"Hannah! What are you doing?" Terry screamed as she rushed in the back door, high heels clacking on the tile floor. "Give me that mop and tell me what is going on." She yanked the mop out of Hannah's hands and Stephanie gratefully dropped her own to her sides.

Hannah glared toward Stephanie. "I saw the 'closed' sign on the front door so I came around back to start my baking for tomorrow, and I found this one in here, going through the cash drawer. Looked like a thief to me." She sniffed and shot another glare at Stephanie.

"I just finished cleaning and she scared the bejeezus out of me, Terry. My heart is still pounding." Stephanie dropped onto a bar stool behind the counter and held her hand over her heart. "Is this place always so full of drama?"

Terry laughed and kicked her elegant shoes off. "Well, no, not usually. Or maybe it is. My drama is usually in the courtroom." She shrugged indifferently.

"First thing is putting this weapon back in the arsenal." Terry marched in her bare feet to a closet door and placed the mop beside several brooms. "And, by the way, Miz Hannah, if you hadn't gotten into a fight with Kim, she would still be here this afternoon and all of this would have been avoided."

"Bah! I am not going to have some snot-nosed brat tell me how to run my kitchen," Hannah snarled, then sniffed knowingly. "Besides, she wouldn't have lasted past today anyway."

Stephanie had never heard such a gravelly voice emanate from a woman before and scrutinized Hannah's features. Spindly thin, she stood about five feet tall, with tanned skin as wrinkled as a prune. She wore a flowered shirt and Capri pants, her feet encased in poison green Crocs. Her snow-white hair, cut short, stuck out in small spikes on top, reminding Stephanie of a rooster.

Terry massaged her temples. "Okay, okay, let's just forget this morning. I have a splitting headache. Jabba the Judge held my case for last and then made me sit through his lecture on the virtues of timeliness. While I was in court, I got a parking ticket and then got pulled for speeding on my way back here. Luckily, the officer let me off with a warning.

"Then, I wasn't sure whether or not I'd find the shop burned to the ground. No offense, but those were your words." She grinned at Stephanie.

"None taken. My waitressing days from college paid off, and I took care of five more customers after you left. I did shut the door right at two, since no one else came in."

"It's this darn weather, it causes mass confusion. Rain one minute, hot and humid the next."

Hannah interrupted abruptly. "Well, if you two are gonna stand there and play weather girls, go do it somewhere else. I need my kitchen."

"Yes, ma'am," Terry said, "It's all yours, ma'am." She kissed Hannah on the top of the head, then took Stephanie by the elbow and led her around the counter to one of the tables. Motioning for Stephanie to sit in one chair, she dropped into another.

She leaned forward conspiratorially and whispered loudly, "Hannah isn't always such a shrew."

The raspy voice of Hannah croaked out, "I can hear you," as she banged pots and pans.

"She does have good ears," Terry commented dryly, and leaned forward, continuing in a stage whisper, "Ears like an elephant, I might add." This prompted an "I heard

57

that too" retort from Hannah.

Terry leaned back in her chair. "I can't say enough how much I appreciate what you did today, Stephanie. My sister-in-law Beth—she's the mother of Tanner, the little guy who came by on his way to the airport—will be back tomorrow. She can have all of this dining drama and I can go back to my chosen profession."

She yawned wearily. "This day has been a disaster!"

"Obviously. You also mentioned a Bed and Breakfast next door. When will it open? I'd love to be able to stay and have a cute place like this next door."

"Unfortunately, our progress there is tied up in a legal issue." Terry grimaced. "My friend Mary Jo's fiancé died unexpectedly, without a will. His parents, as next of kin, are entitled to his property, but his mother thinks she should get a share in these projects. However, Jay was never involved and put no money into them. We have to go to court when Mary Jo comes home. It's a mess but we'll get through it soon."

"Oh, gosh, that reminds me. Two women came in here just before closing and said some ugly things." She repeated the brief exchange and described the women.

"The short one is Della, Jay's mom. The other sounds like her sister Georgette. They must have gotten wind of the bistro's opening and came by to check it out."

"What a sad situation."

"Yep, but that's life and we'll deal with it. There's nothing in this place she can get her hands on, but it'll have to be resolved in court."

"She seemed quite interested in the big glass case." Stephanie pointed to the pastry display.

"Oh, yeah, she wants that case. We have the receipt for it. She has no stake in it. She tried to file a claim after Mary Jo deployed, not knowing the court would continue the case until she returned. In reality she thought the court would just award her everything she claimed." Terry waved her hand dismissively. "Enough shop talk. You saved us today and I owe you."

"No, you don't, honestly. I am glad I could help, and I had a bit of fun," Stephanie remarked. *Except when Gage flirted with me.* Fun until she realized he was a married man.

Feeling somewhat guilty because she still felt a little pull toward Gage, she briefly told Terry about the genealogy research which led her to Portsmouth.

"You make it sound so interesting." Terry padded back to the counter and gathered the money Stephanie had scattered. "It makes me ashamed of myself, however; my family has records back to the seventeen hundreds and I just take it all for granted."

She sat back down and snapped her fingers with a loud click. "What are your plans for tonight? We are going to a great little pub with colonial charm, which you will love in spite of the big-screen televisions all around. I'd like to hear more about your research and maybe I can offer some help with getting old records or something. I'll get Gage to meet us."

"You'll love him. He's really into history."

No way! "Thanks for the offer, but I can't." Stephanie hoped her guilt didn't show through. "I haven't even tried to search actual records in person yet. I'm still investigating a lot of clues and data online, but I need to look at physical records at the courthouse. I leave tomorrow."

"The records offices close shortly. In fact…" Terry glanced at her watch, "It's too late. They're closing right now, and it's my fault you missed the chance. So come to the pub. We can square away what I owe you and I will take your shoe size for those shoes I promised."

Stephanie laughed. "I made sixteen dollars in tips, so you don't owe me. But I really should go now."

"Maybe, but I still have your camera, so you will just have to retrieve it at the pub. Come on. Meet me there at six. They have décor and architectural aspects from the original building dating back to the eighteenth century. It'll whet your appetite for your revolutionary war research."

With a sigh, Stephanie agreed to go, and wrote down the address. She had already learned it was futile to resist a request from Terry Dunbar.

***

Terry was right. Stephanie surveyed the room as she sipped on her third mojito. Despite the big screen TVs and the modern equipment, she could imagine she sat in a colonial tavern. The after-work crowd bustled through the bar while the restaurant hostess escorted a steady stream of patrons to tables and booths.

Unsure if the atmosphere or the two previous drinks prompted her, she told Terry everything, even the story of her adoption. She told her about Jessica's diary and genealogy charts and the family information that led to her visit Olde Towne.

"It must have been quite a shock to have your life turned upside down." Terry sipped a Cosmopolitan. "I can't imagine the pain you've been through. Did you uncover any helpful information here?"

"I hate to admit this, but it turns out I didn't prepare at all and didn't accomplish nearly as much as planned," Stephanie responded with a sigh. "I fielded so many inquiries from my office this week I didn't get much done the first day. It even prompted me to send in my resignation right then and there."

After another sip of mojito—now her new favorite drink—she continued. "Then I stretched on the bed for a moment and literally zonked out. For the next two days, I followed the trail of historical markers and poked around the old cemeteries. Reportedly, a family member served here with the Union during the Civil War. I decided to take a break from researching and just stroll around the historic area today. Something seemed to draw me to the side streets, and then that rain drove me into the café."

She sipped again, enjoying the tart lime and mint combination. "And so I became an impromptu waitress. And now I am here, chugging back mojitos like they are going out of style. I make it a rule to never drink more than one alcoholic beverage, and here I am on my third." She giggled, and to her ears, it sounded like the bells tinkling over the bakery door.

"And I think I may have a buzz," she admitted as she sipped again.

"Well, enjoy yourself. We're not very far from the hotel. If need be, I can roll you there when we get done."

"Like the colonial kids who rolled their hoops down the street with a small stick? But you'd have to prop me inside it and roll me back." She laughed at the mental picture of the well-dressed lawyer running down the street with a stick rolling a drunken Stephanie tucked in a fetal position inside a skinny hoop. She hiccupped and blushed.

"Sorry," she said and giggled again. She never knew her laugh sounded like bells. Terry's laughter also jingled in little bell sounds. *Bells are pleasant,* she decided as she bent her head over the glass and sipped through the skinny straw, savoring the tart, minty flavor. "This is so good."

"But seriously," Terry continued talking, "I hope you do find some information before you leave. It's too bad Mary Jo isn't here. She didn't have a good childhood and at one time got curious about her roots but abandoned the idea. Now, in *my* family, someone started researching years ago. I know we have some connections to Civil War ancestors; I just haven't paid much attention." She leaned forward and grinned. "Did you notice how hectic it was today? I love my family dearly, but sometimes I could pack them all off to Siberia."

Terry clapped her hand to her mouth. "Oh my God, I am so sorry. That sounds so callous after what you just told me. I am so sorry."

"Oh, no biggie." Somehow Stephanie recognized her words sounded slurred and waved her hand airily. She liked

Terry and could not explain the instant bond. She continued to sip her mojito, catching a mint leaf in her mouth and chewing on it. She would pay with her head tomorrow, but tonight she would enjoy herself.

Terry's phone rang and she plugged a finger in one ear to reduce the background noises as she answered and listened. "Hi, Gage...Yes, I am still here, are you coming...No, I haven't ordered anything, we'll wait for you...Okay, bye."

She clicked her phone off and said, "Gage is on his way. But now, please excuse me—I have to pee. Be right back." Terry scooted from her chair before Stephanie could respond.

All of a sudden, the pleasant atmosphere faded and she had a guilty flashback of those blue eyes.

Stephanie watched Terry wend her way through the crowd, stopping here or there to speak to someone. When she passed a tall man in a gray suit standing at the bar, he grabbed her arm and drew her to him, whispering in her ear. Terry tossed her head back and roared in laughter, her mane of hair spilling down her back. She took the man's chin in her hands and planted a big kiss on his lips before she continued on her path to the bathroom.

"What's with these people?" Stephanie muttered under her breath. Were Terry and Gage a couple of swingers? She did not approve of this at all, and rummaged in her wallet for her credit card, when Gage himself walked in. He glanced around, catching the eye of a passing waitress, who gave him a kiss as she pointed towards Stephanie's table.

Gage glanced over and nodded to Stephanie, spoke a few more words to the waitress and headed over just as Terry reappeared. They hugged and sat down.

"You met Gage already after we had our hectic sandwich rodeo," Terry said by way of introduction, as she waved her hand toward him. "We can't thank you enough for your help, Stephanie. Our shop's first major catering order threatened to become a total disaster until you saved the day."

"I didn't do anything special." Stephanie shook her head, feeling uncomfortable.

"Nonsense. We are buying you dinner, plus I still owe you those Manolo Blahniks. Gage, Stephanie's been telling me of her fascinating genealogy research, and how a family member may have been buried here during the Civil War. You're such a fan of that period. You might be able to help her with anything local."

"Oh, no, honestly, that's not necessary," Stephanie protested in panic. Being in Gage's company was the last thing she needed. "Tomorrow is my last chance to search for records, and then I'm heading home."

"Well, that's too bad," Gage replied, fixing his blue eyes on Stephanie. "There's a lot I could show you."

"Yeah, I'll just bet." Stephanie imagined those sarcastic words bounced around in her mind. Shock tore through her when she realized she had actually muttered them out loud. Three drinks, being well over her normal intake, certainly caused a strange effect on her. She slapped her hand on the table and glared at them.

Gage and Terry both looked at her quizzically.

"What is it with you two?" she snapped. "You flirt and carry on, kiss and hug every other person you see. I don't mean to pass judgment, but I am not comfortable being around this at all." She gulped the last of her mojito, a small piece of mint clinging to her lip.

"And your point is?" Terry seemed genuinely puzzled as she tapped the corner of her mouth and Stephanie impatiently wiped her own, the mint still clinging.

"You're married. Act like it!" Stephanie slapped the table again for emphasis, eyes narrowed.

"Who's married to whom?" Puzzled, Gage and Terry glanced at each other for a minute, then their eyes widened and they burst into raucous laughter.

"Stephanie, you goose." Tears rolled down Terry's cheek as she tried to dab a napkin to remove the stubborn mint and Stephanie backed away impatiently "Are you thinking Gage is my husband? Eeewwww!"

"But—when you called your office they answered with 'Dunbar'—and his nametag had the same last name. And Tanner called you Aunt Terry and Uncle Gage. I just assumed …" Stephanie's voice trailed off and she blinked in confusion.

"You goose," Terry repeated. "Gage is my brother. And we're both single."

Mortified, Stephanie wished the floor would swallow her. How could she have made such a mistake? She clamped her hand over her mouth, staring at the siblings who regarded her with amused faces.

"I am so sorry, oh my God, what was I thinking?" she mumbled and shook her head.

Gage leaned across the table and with a wink, said, completely deadpan, "Since we've established that I'm single, does this mean you will marry me now?" and took a napkin to brush the stubborn mint that had now migrated to Stephanie's cheek. In spite of her embarrassment, she laughed.

"I've never felt so awkward in my entire life." She pushed her empty glass toward the center of the table. "No more for me."

"You know, now that I think of it," Terry mused. "I probably would have assumed the same thing if our roles had been reversed. We never had a real opportunity or even a need for proper introductions when I rushed out of the cafe."

"Well, I remembered someone from your office answered on speakerphone with 'Dunbar and Cross.' Then I read your brother's nametag, and your nephew called you aunt and uncle, and in your phone calls you said 'I love you kiss-kiss' so I just assumed. Even if you were married, it would still be none of my business. I spoke in a brusque way and I am embarrassed. Plus I'm babbling now."

She wanted to leave. The siblings convinced her to stay.

Jokingly they agreed, for her sake, that they wouldn't kiss or hug anyone for the rest of the night.

She finally agreed to forget the incident for the moment. *Tomorrow would be a different story.*

In spite of her embarrassment, she relaxed. Terry and Gage made it easy. Once she had eaten, the effects of the alcohol eased somewhat and she laughed a bit during conversation. She decided they were enjoyable people to be with, laughing easily and naturally, and seemed to know every other person who came into the restaurant.

As the din of the crowd evolved from the cozy dining murmur to a noisy bar scene, it became more difficult to talk and Stephanie sat back to observe her surroundings, her gaze frequently drifting toward Gage. *This Dunbar family certainly has an abundance of good looks!* He wore his dark brown hair close-cut on the sides but a little longer on top. He stood probably close to six feet tall, with a strong sinewy build.

When she accidently brushed knees with him he didn't move away, so she didn't move either, enjoying the contact. She liked the feeling. When they were both resting arms on the table, their elbows nearly touched. The light tickle of the hair on his arm and the warmth radiating from his skin sent thrills through her body.

I'm so glad he's not her husband. Her fingers itched to touch his amazing biceps but she kept them to herself. *I don't understand this at all. I've never experienced such an instant connection to a man before.*

She found him incredibly attractive, and hoped he had a similar opinion of her—aside from her embarrassing outburst. She couldn't imagine how she could catch the eye of a man like Gage Dunbar. While some considered her cute, in her opinion she was average. Small and slim, she wore her brown hair in a layered cut. Her most distinguishing feature was the little dimple that appeared at times. She certainly felt inadequate beside the dazzling Terry.

Terry leaned over to Stephanie and tapped her arm. "Will you excuse me for a moment? A couple of my colleagues just came in and I want to talk shop for a few minutes. I'll be right back." She wandered over to a table of men in suits and after exchanging noisy greetings, they scrambled chairs to make room for her to join them.

Stephanie drummed her fingers nervously as she looked around. Several times she locked eyes with Gage, and found him regarding her with a look she could not quite decipher.

Finally, he reached over and put his hand over her dancing fingers. She stopped the movement but did not draw her hand away.

"Do I make you that nervous?" he asked, his eyes serious.

"What? Oh, no—well, yes, you do—but this is just a bad habit of mine. I find you incredibly attractive." *OMG, those damn mojitos.* One hand still trapped under his gentle hold, she slapped her forehead in disgust with her free hand." I can't believe I just said that." *I will never drink another one!*

Gage leaned closer, his flirty blue eyes twinkling with amusement. "Well, Stephanie Kincaid, now that we have that straight, I plan to get to know you better. Are there any other bad habits I should learn about in advance? Do you rob banks? Do you kick dogs? Do you kiss strangers?"

Stephanie burst into laughter, slowly drawing her hand free from his and straightening in her chair. "Of course not!"

"Then there you have it. Neither do I, therefore we are perfect for each other." He leaned closer, and in a husky whisper added, "Except for that 'not kissing strangers' part. We may have to reconsider that."

Butterflies danced a tango in her tummy as Gage's warm breath brushed her cheek. Her fingers started their nervous drumming.

He winked, and skimmed his fingertips over hers to still

the tapping. This time, she let her hand remain under his.

They talked for the next hour. He had known he wanted to be a firefighter since the age of six. The earliest age he could apply was eighteen, and on his eighteenth birthday, he took the entrance test. Fourteen years later, he was a fire captain and assigned to the fire training academy. He had just recently been promoted to battalion chief.

He caught the eye of the waitress and raised his empty beer mug. When he pointed to Stephanie's glass, she shook her head. She knew her limit.

Gage continued. "My dad is retired from the Navy and Mom taught mathematics at the community college. I grew up in Portsmouth but after my graduation, the family moved to an old farmhouse in Driver on the Nansemond River. The whole family joined in the project to renovate the house, which is nearly complete. Plans are in the works for a major celebration at Christmas to introduce the old house back to the world—or at least to family and friends."

"Driver?" Stephanie asked. "Where is that?"

"It's a small community in Suffolk. Fifteen miles from here."

While Stephanie and Gage chatted, Terry's "few minutes" with her colleagues turned into an hour. Stephanie saw her glance at her watch and turn toward her, eyes wide as she mouthed the word "Sorry." Terry bade a hasty good-bye to her friends and dashed back to the table.

"Stephanie, I am so sorry. We got carried away with shop talk."

"It's fine." Stephanie brushed it aside and stood up "I've had a lovely evening, but I really do have to get back to my hotel."

Apologizing again, Terry settled the bill. Then she and Gage accompanied Stephanie to the hotel lobby.

"I'm grateful I can walk on my own two feet." Stephanie giggled. "And not tucked in a hoop with Terry rolling me down the street."

Terry laughed as Gage stared quizzically.

"Never mind, little brother." Terry pinched his cheek. "You had to be there."

They reached the lobby door. Terry asked, "Are you sure you can't stay another day, Stephanie? Tomorrow evening they have a concert on the Water Stage near the hotel. You'd have a great time."

"I'd love to," Stephanie replied. "But I really have to be home tomorrow evening."

Although both siblings tried to convince her to stay, she resisted. At their urging, however, she did promise to stop by the *Pâtisseries* café at noon before she left.

Terry hugged her and Gage brushed a kiss across her cheek.

Stephanie's gaze followed the brother and sister until they disappeared from view before she danced into the lobby.

A burst of happiness she had not known for months filled her heart like fireworks in the sky.

CHAPTER FIVE

Stephanie awakened the next morning, realizing quickly that the pleasant tinkling bell sounds from the night before were now replaced by the combined tolling of bells from Notre Dame, St. Peter's Basilica, and any number of small churches around the world. Surely every one of them clanged in unison inside her head at the moment.

Last night was the closest Stephanie had ever come to getting drunk, and never, ever in her life had she felt this awful. She had no idea of the time, and made the mistake of trying to look out the window. As she parted the room-darkening drapes, she winced as the glare of daylight assaulted her eyes. *If this is what a hangover feels like, I'll never have another drink.* Groaning, she snapped the curtains shut, stumbled to the bathroom and rummaged for a bottle of aspirin in her toiletry kit, downing four with a gulp of water.

She flopped back in the bed when a knock on the door exploded like cannons in her suffering head.

"Coming!" she cried out, gripping her temples as she stumbled to the door and tried to glance out the peep-hole, seeing a spray of flowers on the other side.

"Delivery," a young male voice replied, and Stephanie opened the door as far as the chain block allowed. After all, she had heard about fake deliveries to fool tourists into opening the door to a robbery.

"I have a flower delivery for you, Ms. Kincaid." A delivery boy sporting a floral shop logo on his shirt lifted a vase to eye level and lowered again.

"From whom?" she asked, frowning at the flowers.

"I don't know who, ma'am. The front desk just told me to bring them up."

"Are you sure they're for me?"

"Yes, ma'am, these are for Ms. Kincaid, room four-fifteen."

"Oh, okay, hold on a moment." Cautiously Stephanie opened the door and took the flowers. She patted the pockets of her robe and started to reach for her purse for a tip when the young man said politely, "Ma'am, I was told not to accept a tip; it's been taken care of."

"Oh, okay," Stephanie repeated. She shut the door and locked it behind her, studying the slender vase with an array of daisies and tiny white roses. "Besides, why would I tip on something I didn't order anyway?" she muttered in annoyance, staring suspiciously at the card, which she finally took out of the envelope and read out loud:

"Hope you are well this morning. I am still single. Will you marry me?"

After a moment, she burst into laughter, which amazingly enough, did not shatter her head. She debated which best cured her headache—the four aspirin or the note with the flowers.

She reached for her phone and called the number Gage had left on the card, disappointed when his voicemail answered. He was probably still involved in the fire training class. She spoke her words carefully, "Hi, it's Stephanie. I am fine this morning, thanks to an abundance of aspirin and your nice surprise. The flowers are perfect, and I suspect they did more to relieve my threatening hangover than the aspirin. How nice to meet you, Gage—and I'm glad you're not married! Maybe we could discuss that subject again sometime in the future. If you're ever in Alexandria, give me a call."

She disconnected and was gathering her shower supplies when the phone rang.

"Hello?"

"It's Gage." Her heart squeezed in a funny little flutter when she recognized his voice. "I just got your voicemail. I know you said to call if I was ever in Alexandria, but I didn't want to wait until then."

She laughed. "Okay."

"Sorry, I missed your call. I slipped out of my class to phone you back. I'd really like to see you again. Do you have to leave today?"

"I have to, Gage, there's too much to do at home. I gave my notice at work and have to get back to finish my last two weeks. Then finish packing for two houses and prepare to move to whichever house deal closes second. I've still got to look for somewhere permanent to live. And I'm not as ready to be a genealogist as I assumed. I have to research more fully before I continue."

"Will you be coming back soon?"

"Yes, I plan to. I could use Terry's expertise with court records—and I could take you up on your offer to show me around Portsmouth's historical areas for my research."

"It's a deal. Look, I have to get back to class. If I don't see you at the bistro today, I'll be calling you soon. Very soon."

"I'd like that, Gage."

"Great. We'll talk again. Ciao." And in the "said and done" manner, she now recognized as a Dunbar trademark, the conversation was over.

"Whew!" she breathed. Whatever her immediate future held for her, she really hoped it included a phone call—make it many phone calls—from Gage Dunbar.

***

True to her word, Stephanie stopped by *Pâtisseries a la Carte* bistro at noon. Finding an unoccupied table, she sat and waited for Terry, who breezed in a few minutes later. Dressed in a gorgeous powder blue suit with matching shoes, she walked, fast-paced as usual, while clutching a phone to one ear.

She ended her conversation with, "I'm with a client,

Edgar, and I can't talk now. I will try to call you later." She wrinkled her nose as she tapped her phone to end the call and said, "Sorry for the fib. Edgar is a nice man but can't seem to take no for an answer and always calls at the most inopportune time." She waved to a woman at the counter. Stephanie turned and observed a petite blond woman walk toward them, a pencil tucked behind her right ear.

"Hi, Beth," Terry called. "Stephanie, I want to introduce you to my sister-in-law. And Beth, this is Stephanie, who pitched in yesterday and helped me get the fire department order out on time." Terry and Beth hugged, and then to Stephanie's surprise, Beth gave her a hug too.

"Oh, we're so grateful for your help yesterday," Beth exclaimed. "Things have been quite weird around here lately while we have been trying to iron out our kinks, then I had to go out of town unexpectedly."

"Beth is married to my brother Connor, who is a firefighter in Suffolk," Terry interjected. "And I already told her about your research, Stephanie."

"What you are doing must be fascinating. Now that I have Tanner, I think about preserving his family tree. His dad's side is in good shape, but mine is almost non-existent. I just don't know when I will find the time."

"I'm just starting on this myself." Stephanie sighed. "Unfortunately, I didn't accomplish as much as I had hoped. I just sense I'm on the verge of discovering a simple clue here which will break open the floodgates on my mother's family. I'll probably need to come back again soon but I have to be much better prepared next time."

"Well, I hope you let us know when you are back and we can get together. We might be able to help. Here's the menu. I hear Hannah terrorizing the new girl, let me get back there before I lose another waitress. Order what you want, Stephanie, it's on me."

"Oh, no need, Terry already repaid me with dinner last night.'

"I still owe you a pair of Manolo Blahniks, that's how much we value your help. I need a special to go, Beth," Terry called to the disappearing figure.

Stephanie declared ruefully, "I just can't keep up with the pace of your family." She shook her head. "My parents—my adopted parents—had no other relatives, and I was an only child, so I've never had the experience of a big family. I don't think we ever hurried anywhere. By the way, I'm curious. What's Hannah's story?"

"You mean when she is not catching burglars in the act or terrorizing the help?" Terry laughed. "Hannah is a distant relative of my mother. Her husband was killed in Vietnam, and she drifted around for a while, kind of the hippie life, I guess. She got sick and nearly died, and Mom asked her to stay with our family to recover."

Terry set a small basket holding napkins and salt and pepper shakers in front of Stephanie and continued. "My parents were so busy back then and when Hannah got better, she just stayed and started to cook dinner for them as a way of thanks. Then she kind of became a housekeeper slash sitter for my family when we were growing up and has been with us ever since. As cranky as she is, we all love her to death. She specializes in baking scrumptious pastries, and does all of the baking for the shop right now."

Terry stopped talking and it took a moment for Stephanie to realize it.

"What's the matter?" she asked.

"I notice you keep glancing around, Stephanie. Expecting someone?"

"No."

"Yeah, sure."

"No—well, to be truthful, I did hope to see Gage and say goodbye, but he wasn't sure he could make it when I talked to him this morning."

"Oh, you talked today, huh?"

"Oh, stop. I just called him to thank him for the

flowers …"

"*Awww, fwowers too?*" Terry mocked playfully. She plopped her hand on her chin and leaned forward conspiratorially. "Oh, do tell. And make it quick, I have to be out of here in five minutes."

"There's nothing to tell, Terry. He just sent flowers. It was kind of nice. He left his number so I called and thanked him. The end."

"That's interesting. I've *never* known my brother to send a woman flowers."

"Come on now; let's not make a big deal out of it, please. It was just a sweet gesture."

"Okay, sure. Here comes my order. I have to go, Stephanie, but I truly do hope you can come back and see us. I'd love to show you around Olde Towne, and Gage has a wealth of knowledge about local Civil War history. For that matter, he's well-versed in the Revolutionary War history of our area as well." She dug a business card out of her pocket. "Here's my contact info, please call me when you come back."

"I will, Terry." They hugged, as natural to Stephanie now as if she had known Terry her whole life instead of just a day.

Her phone rang, and when she answered, Gage's voice brought a smile to her face.

"Hi, Stephanie, I wanted to see you to say good-bye, but our classes are running late. I'm on break, and have to teach in five minutes. Can I call you tonight when you are home?"

"I-I'd like that, Gage."

"Great. I want to see you again too. I'm tied up with this course through next week, but I will be in touch to arrange something."

"Okay. Call me anytime. It was nice to meet you, and thanks again for the flowers."

"Great," he repeated. "I've got to go. Bye—for now."

The phone clicked in her ear. Did anyone say no to a

Dunbar?

***

Halfway through the now-gridlocked drive back to Alexandria, Stephanie nibbled from the fruit and cheese plate she'd picked up in the bistro. In order to keep her mind off Gage, she concentrated on her shortcomings as a researcher and the valuable genealogy lessons she had learned. She'd embarked on this trip woefully unprepared and would have to do a much better job of organizing in order to conduct a proper physical search. It was not enough to have a family tree drawn on a chart, or names and dates of birth or death. She needed to do her homework in advance and prepare a profile for each person she wanted to investigate.

She should create a list of the addresses and phone numbers of courthouses, churches, cemeteries and any other sites she might want to visit in person. Ideas rushed into her head so rapidly she grabbed her cell and recorded them.

About the time she hit the usual traffic bottleneck on I-95 north of Richmond, thoughts of Gage crowded research planning out of her head. She liked being around him, a fact that had increased exponentially when she happily found out he was not married to Terry. Their conversation had been casual in the noisy pub, but something seemed to simmer under the surface, something she wouldn't mind exploring further.

If he didn't call by Saturday evening, she would just call him!

***

Gage Dunbar, one of the best instructors at the Fire Academy, simply could not concentrate on his lecture materials. For the past twenty-four hours, a certain Stephanie Kincaid seemed to occupy his every waking moment, and he didn't even know why. They had just met yesterday, and she'd even mistaken him for a married guy—a misconception he was glad they'd cleared up.

He had enjoyed their flirting; then this morning he'd sent her flowers. He smacked his forehead, questioning the wisdom of the innocent gesture. The only flowers he'd ever given a woman before were the ones he sent his mom on Mother's Day. And obligatory corsages for his prom dates back in high school, but those didn't count either, from his point of view. Sending those flowers the day after meeting her could have freaked her out, perhaps make her think he was a stalker or something.

Geez—what were you thinking, man? A bit of worry unsettled his stomach. And how had this woman gotten such a grip on him? He shook his head to clear his mind, swiftly realizing he still stood at the blackboard, hand poised to write something for his students. He didn't have a clue what it could be. As a sea of curious faces stared at him expectantly, he did the first thing that came to mind. He grabbed his phone out of his pocket, and answered, "Dunbar...yes, sir, I'll get on it right away."

He noticed the missed call from Stephanie, shoved the phone back in his pocket and opened a notebook. "Sorry, class, emergency call from the chief. Take five and I'll be right back." He flipped through the book as the students filtered out. As soon as they cleared the room, he withdrew the phone and punched buttons. Disappointed when Stephanie's voice mail kicked in, he left a quick message. "Sorry I didn't catch you. The rest of this class is a hands-on practical scheduled to run late and I won't have another chance to call. I will try again tomorrow. Bye for now."

Gage replaced the phone and turned around, staring at the blackboard. What he had been trying to say finally dawned on him, and he cleared his head to devote attention to his class.

"All right, you guys," he stuck his head out the door and called out, "Break is over, let's get back to business. We have a long night ahead of us."

CHAPTER SIX

ABIGAIL
Portsmouth, Virginia, 7 July 1781

She should attend to her dinner plans, but bitter pangs continued to eat at her peace. Having the French woman in her house stirred memories she'd suppressed for forty years, back to the day she lost her fiancé to a different French woman. James had gone to France on holiday but upon his return, he exuded an air of fatigue, and he was gaunt. His greeting lacked warmth; it was kind, but devoid of enthusiasm.

"Come sit by the fire and have some tea," Abigail had invited. "You must be tired from your journey."

But he refused. She reached for his hand, but stopped at the look in his eyes. When he looked at her she could see the vacancy in his gaze, and she knew. She knew—he had found another love.

Oh, he had been such a gentleman about it. The bitter memory slid into her mind as she picked up a wine glass and set it down with a sharp tap. James could never be anything less than a gentleman. He said all the proper things. I never meant for it to happen. It was completely unintended. We met at a picnic and had several polite encounters. We sat together at a dinner party, and danced through the night.

In the end, he simply said, "I love her, Abby. I truly love her. I'm so sorry, I must go back to her." He left without a backward glance.

The memory as vivid as yesterday, Abigail's face distorted with pure venom, her jaw clenching as she remembered those words.

Oh, she did not make it easy for him. She carried on the high drama for days and weeks, calling on him at his home, even resorting to falling to her knees and begging him to stay—an action she deeply regretted afterward—demanding to know what was so special about this woman. He never explained, but left England and returned to

France, where he married and became a shoemaker. Shoemaker? A man of his stature? When she had learned this last piece of news, her singular wish was that he would be dirt-poor and unhappy for the rest of his life.

From that moment forward, she allowed no one to call her Abby, the pet name James had given her and her family had adopted. She flew into a rage whenever someone forgot.

She directed her anger toward gaining material things and possessions. But where to find someone who would give her what she wanted?

Before long, she set her cap on the dashing Frenchman who had come to England to open a new office in London for his shipping company. In her tortured mind, marrying Phillipe de la Rocher would exact revenge on those harlots from France.

A sly smile spread across her face at the memory.

Phillipe, a widower with a young son, had created a fortune building a small shipping empire in France. He had moved to England to increase his holdings and planned to expand in America.

It was not difficult to initiate contact. She and Phillipe traveled in the same social circles; her parents entertained lavishly. He was a frequent guest, as was her family at his estate.

But soon she caught the rumors that he might propose to the pretty French governess recently hired to care for his four-year old son Etienne.

Abigail remembered how she had discreetly observed the woman with her young charge and his father. The face of the governess blurred into the features of the woman who had stolen James from her. Abigail's body nearly convulsed from the rage churning within as she began to make plans.

As a governess, Monique fell into that peculiar undefined state such women endured when employed in a grand home; they were neither a family member nor a servant. She was foreign-born at that, but her fluency in French and English were the key assets that Phillip wanted in the governess of his child.

Abigail learned the habits of the household; how and when the young teacher would be out with her small charge. She found it easy to orchestrate ways to encounter them in the park or in the shops.

So Abigail easily befriended—and all the while hated—Monique, who spoke excellent English with a pretty little accent. Four years younger than Abigail, without friends in England and isolated from all her familiar home life, the young guardian reacted gratefully to the interest and concern the older woman displayed. With complete trust, she openly confided her love for her employer and his son, and how she hoped he would soon propose to her.

Abigail was not about to lose another love to a French woman. During one of those "chance" encounters Abigail planted the seeds of doubt in the younger woman's mind: how Phillipe described Monique as a delightful diversion but he would soon look for a more suitable woman to marry and care for his son. Abigail smoothly fabricated stories of vicious gossip and finger-pointing behind Monique's back, making it clear she would be scorned by society if she remained in the home. Abigail had consoled her, encouraged her, and convinced her if she slipped away and returned home quietly, she could escape the scandal that was soon to break. And so, on a cold rainy night, a broken-hearted and ashamed Monique slipped from the house and found her way back to France.

Abigail Weston had a true knack for convincing people to do as she wished without seeming obvious. She threw away the brown bottle of poison she did not have to use.

When the aroma of baked ham wafted through the windows and reminded her of the dinner party, Abigail broke from her daydream and returned her thoughts to 1781.

She patted the small bottle in her pocket and walked downstairs.

STEPHANIE
Portsmouth, Virginia present day July

If Stephanie expected things would be calmer at home, leaving time to gather more information for her family tree, she was certainly wrong.

When she arrived, she found several messages on her answering machine. As she punched the play button, she wondered why no one called her cell phone.

Her best friend Jackie, an FBI agent who recently

returned to town, left two messages. Her rich melodic voice on the recording pointedly ordered, "Buy a decent cell phone and chuck that useless piece of crap you carry. All I got was voice mail. Call me as soon as you can. I want a Girls' Night Out."

Additional messages related to the contract on her house. Two subsequent calls referred to the impending sale of her parents' home. Stephanie did a little happy dance. Yes!

After talking with her agent about the two contracts, reality suddenly struck her. She would soon be without a home. She had placed both houses on the market at the same time, speculating one might sell quicker than the other in the unpredictable market. She would simply live in whichever house did not sell first. Neither she nor her agent had expected *both* houses to sell so quickly.

A good dilemma to be in, but a dilemma all the same. Now she had to pack and find a place to stay. She still had a two-week commitment at work and a lot of sorting, packing, and storing to do.

Stephanie broke out of her reverie and started a list of the most pressing tasks to tackle first. When she reached for her ancient cell phone she noticed the symbols for missed calls as well as a voice message. Realizing she had accidentally turned the ringer off, she turned it on and tapped the message callback displaying Gage's number. At the sound of the recorded message that he would call her tomorrow, she smiled, in spite of the disappointment they would not talk again until the next day.

In the meantime, she had plenty of projects to get out of the way—but where to begin?

She snapped her fingers and made a command decision to call Jackie and suggest a girls' night out for Monday evening, when they would catch up on all the news. *Important things should never be neglected.*

Stephanie suspected she would be the one doing most of the talking.

Motivated now, she tackled her to-do list and worked though tasks until she fell into an exhausted heap on her bed.

For the first time in months, she slept soundly.

***

Rejuvenated, Stephanie rose early Saturday morning and tackled more of the "million" things she had on her list. She started with phone calls.

In the first of several lengthy phone discussions, her real estate agent jubilantly explained the sales of both homes would close in about a month. Stephanie plastered her memo book with sticky notes to remind herself to make phone calls to the attorney for the closings, and to a construction firm to handle minor repairs on both houses.

Every time she completed five chores on her to-do list, she allowed a half-hour for conducting family tree research. Determined to find the connection in her family line with the mysterious French woman who might have been named Christelle or Celeste, she studied Jessica's records of her old cousin Sadie's memories. Stephanie imagined a short, plump woman sitting in a rocking chair, dressed in a dark silk dress with white lace at the neck, her white hair pulled into a bun at the collar.

While waiting for the computer to boot up, Stephanie unrolled her charts and tacked them back to the wall where she could see them and make updates. She had accomplished pathetically little on her first "field trip" to search her roots. It had been a learning curve. She must focus more on one particular target, person or location before she set out on another trek.

In the end, she hadn't been as prepared to research as she'd anticipated and considered the entire experience as an eye-opener. The main reason she traveled to Portsmouth in the first place was the easy drive from

Alexandria, and her birth mother's notes had indicated a Thomas Wyatt had been in the town sometime during the Civil War.

With a few key strokes, she pulled up her file on Thomas Wyatt. He'd been sick or died in Portsmouth, had maybe even been buried there, but for some reason, Jessica never had further contact with Sadie to add details. Stephanie calculated Thomas to be her third-great grandfather but had precious little information to go on.

She perused census records, certain if she found the right clue the floodgates would open. She decided to track Thomas in a different way, and typed in the name Rosalee Wyatt with an estimated lifespan between 1840 and 1930. She found an 1870 census record for Rosalee Wyatt, wife of Arthur, with a ten-year-old son named Jeremy. Also living in the same household were Arthur's brother Frank and his wife Celestine.

Stephanie's heart skipped a beat. Could this Celestine be the mysterious French woman she sought? She could hardly contain her excitement as she circled the name, until she remembered the French ancestress she sought would have lived during the Colonial days, not the Civil War period.

"Darn it!" she yelled out loud. In aggravation, she scratched through the name, poking a hole in the paper with the last jab. "Wrong again."

Still, she mused, this was the first possible connection she had for someone with an unusual first name *and* the family name Wyatt. Could Celestine be a derivative of the name Celeste or Christelle? She made a note to study the possibilities further.

So far, Stephanie had identified every grandparent in Jessica's maternal line leading back to Thomas Wyatt. If he had brothers named Arthur and Frank, maybe she could find them all together in an earlier census. She added those names into her online tree as Thomas's siblings. She placed three question marks by their names, a tactic she had developed as a reminder that the actual relationship to a family member still needed to be determined.

Stephanie took out Jessica's notes. The leather covering on the journal, already frayed with constant handling, radiated warmth at her touch. She frowned at the small book in her hands. *Did I leave this too close to the computer tower?* She had to be more careful with her originals, and immediately created copies to handle on a daily basis.

Turning her concentration back to Thomas Wyatt, she circled his birth year, 1847. She tried to balance the leather-bound book, holding it in her left hand with her elbow propped on the desk while she typed with her right hand, but it slipped through her fingers and fell open on the desk. As she picked it back up, her eyes glanced at Jessica's neat writing and the name Arthur seemed to jump out of the page at her. She straightened and read her birth mother's notes:

Sadie says her grandfather Arthur and her great-uncle Thomas both fought for the Union during the civil war. They were members of two different companies from New Hampshire but they often talked about how they crossed paths during the war in Portsmouth, Virginia sometime during the early 1860's. They may have met a cousin there as well. According to Sadie, one of the Wyatts is buried there, but I didn't record the name and now I don't know. Next time we talk, I will have to ask if she knows.

Stephanie sat bolt upright. "Arthur Wyatt!" she said out loud, clapping her hand to her head. "How could I have missed that name the first time I read this?"

Concentrating so hard for information on her direct ancestor, she had not yet mastered the art of identifying siblings as a possible source of information. She read through the journal to see if there were any other references to Thomas's siblings or other relatives, but found no further mention. Jessica probably concentrated on finding clues for her direct lineage and therefore missed the possible connections through siblings.

Stephanie leaned back. With the confirmation of Arthur and Rosalee as relatives to her ancestor, she had a new avenue to follow for clues.

Jumping up and nearly knocking her chair over, she rushed to the chart on the wall to document the connection to the family tree. Placing sticky notes to the right of Thomas's name, she wrote "Arthur and Rosalee Wyatt" on one and "Frank and Celestine Wyatt" on the other to keep them in the proper generational bracket.

Without that chart, she would not be able to manage the who's who of her growing ancestry line. Counting through the generations she calculated Arthur would be her fourth great-uncle.

Going back to her computer, she typed furiously. Once she entered the names Arthur and Frank Wyatt into the online tree, a number of tiny icons appeared by each name. There were eventually a dozen possible clues she could follow to other family trees for men named Thomas Wyatt, as well as to census and military record databases.

It was easy to lose track of data with so many possibilities. She had learned to save any potential leads as she uncovered them; she might not be able to locate them afterward.

Engrossed in following the hints in the genealogy database, she nearly jumped out of her seat when her cell phone rang. The LED displayed 10:45 p.m. *Who could be calling so late?* The phone showed "out of area" where the caller's number normally appeared.

"Hello?" she answered tentatively.

"Stephanie? I hope I didn't wake you."

"Gage!" Her heart turned a somersault as she said his name. "No, no you didn't. I was involved in my research, and the phone startled me. It showed 'out of area.' How are you?"

"I'm good. I'm calling from the office. We just finished the training a little early. We're practicing night fires, and everyone did pretty well, so we wrapped up and sent them to bed. They'll be called out again for another practice soon." He cleared his throat. "Um—I keep thinking about you. I know we just met, but—I like you a lot. Um—before I go any further, are you seeing anyone? If not, I want to see you again. That is, if you're interested."

Stephanie danced a happy little jig but replied demurely, "No, I'm not seeing anyone just now. As we have established beyond a doubt that you are single, I would like to see you too. It might be difficult with the distance though, and I have a busy week ahead."

"I know. I'm committed for the next week with the fire training, but maybe we can exchange emails in the meantime? Then perhaps we can see what might work out after next weekend."

"It could work out very well." She would make it work.

"Do you have time to talk for a minute? Um—I don't want you to think I'm a stalker or some nutcase, or anything, and I don't want to scare you off. And why am I stumbling over my words?"

"Well, stumbling makes you human, and I don't think you're a nutcase—at least not yet anyway." They both chuckled. "I have plenty of time to talk now if you do. There does seem to be a definite spark between us," she added cautiously.

"Well, there you have it. Who better to deal with a spark than a firefighter?"

Stephanie burst into laughter. *So let's just see where this spark leads.* She clicked her computer into sleep mode and turned off the desk lamp. She headed to her room to stretch out on her bed like a giddy teenager, flat on her tummy with feet in the air while she talked on the phone.

As she left her small study, there was no reason for her to look back into the room—but if she had, she might have seen a tiny little light dancing a merry jig on Jessica's journal.

***

Gage leaned back in his chair, feet propped on his desk in the training office while he talked to Stephanie. He'd planned to make a quick phone call to hear her voice, then leave his office and head for bed. The recruits were undergoing a special twenty-four hour session to replicate a typical fire shift. Although they slept now, they would have a practical exercise in the early hours of the morning, responding to a simulated night fire call. He needed to be in his place well before it started.

As he pondered, the same thought crossed his mind over and over. *Why was Stephanie so special?* She wasn't glamorous like his sister Terry, or athletic like Mary Jo, or even sisterly like Beth, but when he looked at her—well, he just couldn't explain the magnetism. What he was doing was so out of character for him. He didn't rush in when it came to women. Sure, he'd had women in his life before but he usually took a little time to get to know them first. Certainly no one had ever caught his eye the way Stephanie Kincaid had.

And now he sat here, like a teenager chatting into the phone as he envisioned Stephanie's pretty face. He liked how tiny she was; the tip of her head barely came to his shoulder. He could readily imagine how it would feel to put his arms around her and hold her close. She had a cute tilt to her nose, and dark brown eyes that sparkled yet held such intense sadness. Her short hair reminded him of dark brown silk. Her mannerisms were quiet and unpretentious, but her laugh! He found her laugh infectious, so engaging with its musical lilt. It often brought out her dimple, and he wanted to be the one to make her laugh often.

He didn't know why, but whenever she laughed, he pictured the scene from "It's a Wonderful Life," where the bell on the Christmas tree rang because Clarence got his wings. *Better not tell her that nonsense,* he reconsidered.

So he wisely avoided any mention of bells and angels during the conversation, saying instead, "You said you had a bad week coming up. Is it your work? What do you do there?"

Stephanie explained her decision to resign; then she backtracked further to tell him about her parents' car crash and learning of her adoption.

He couldn't imagine how it must feel to lose one's parents and be all alone in the world. He came from a large noisy family, where everyone often talked at once without missing a beat in the conversations around them. He felt fortunate to have a big family to lean on in any emergency. Stephanie had been through grief and shock on her own without the benefit of any family support.

They learned they had a few things in common. They both liked the movie "Romancing the Stone" but hated the sequel. She found searching family history fascinating—all kinds of history fascinated him. Her favorite color was fire engine red—he drove red fire engines. Okay, that last idea's a bit lame, he admitted. But—he was determined to find a positive connection with her in any way possible!

He could have talked with her all night long, but when she suppressed a yawn, he realized they'd already talked for well over an hour.

"Oh, man, I'm so sorry. You must be exhausted and I'm keeping you awake—or boring you." He smacked his forehead and closed his eyes with a slight shake of the head. *Now why did I have to say that?*

"No, don't be sorry. I enjoyed the conversation. It seemed to be more one-sided on my part, though. Maybe I'm the boring one." Stephanie stifled another yawn.

"Lady, you are hell and gone from boring," he said in his best imitation of Michael Douglas' character in "Romancing the Stone."

Stephanie laughed. "Good night, Gage."

"Night, Stephanie."

When he hung up the phone, he didn't move, uncertain

what was happening. He barely knew this woman, had in fact only met her the day before. But he knew he wanted her to be his wife.

On that note, Gage decided to head to the gym in the back of the station house for a workout. He wasn't going to get any sleep, so he might as well make the most of his time before the shrill sound of the training alarm signaled the start of the exercise.

***

When Stephanie woke, she still clutched the cell phone in her hand, tucked under her cheek. She stretched and enjoyed the sensation of waking truly happy. She fluffed her pillows behind her head and smiled as her thoughts raced.

How could a few short days in life make such as difference?

Was it Gage? They didn't even qualify as acquaintances, yet they'd had an in-depth conversation last night as if they were old friends.

She'd never felt this way before, even with Ethan. Could love at first sight really be more than a cliché? She didn't know, but intended to find out. She wished the days would hurry by so she could fulfill the commitment of her resignation notice. After that—well, she just might have to go back to Portsmouth and research old history while making new.

Hopping from the bed, she headed for her desk and turned the computer on. While it booted up, she brewed a pot of coffee. When she checked emails, there were two new messages. She opened the one from Gage first, a smile curving her lips at the subject line: "Still not married!"

"Good morning! I enjoyed our call and hope you were able to get some sleep. I will be heading out to my next training exercise in five

minutes. I'll call soon as I can.
Gage

Stephanie immediately typed a response.

Slept like a log and woke up more refreshed than I have in months. I feel as though I can tackle any project that comes my way today. Stay safe, look forward to hearing from you.

She hit send and opened the second message, which contained an alert advising her of a new posting on her ancestry forum. Such posts no longer generated anticipation; contact from several other researchers resulted in disappointment when they did not lead to the records she sought.

Hi, I hope you don't mind me contacting you. My name is Kyle Avery, and I notice you have a family tree which has some members with the same names I am searching.

Whenever I compare my tree with someone else's tree and find they have reached a dead end with an ancestor for whom I might have details, I always feel compelled to share my information if it applies. If it is the same family, I might be able to give you some additional facts.

I'm researching an Arthur Wyatt, born about 1844 and died in 1902. His second wife Annette was my third great-grandmother. Arthur had two brothers named Thomas and Frank. I am pretty sure your relative Thomas Wyatt was born in 1847 and died in 1922. His wife's name was Emily Long. He served with the Union Army in the Civil War and was wounded in Virginia, then went home to New Hampshire to recover, where he lived for many more years.

Now, I have a lot of documentation for the Long side, which is actually an Americanized version of the French surname Longchamps. Emily Long (née Longchamps) Wyatt traced her connection to a prominent Revolutionary War figure, Etienne de la Rocher, to establish her eligibility for membership in the Daughters of the American Revolution. For this reason, you can trace your family line back to the early 1700's.

There is more! Emily's cousin Celestine married Frank Wyatt (Thomas's brother). In those days, it was not unusual for siblings in one family to marry siblings from another. Celestine retained the family's original surname of Longchamps. Are you still with me here? lol

I have more details I'd be happy to share. Feel free to contact me by email if you feel this information would be useful to you.

Kyle Avery

Stephanie's fingers skimmed excitedly over the keyboard as she typed an answer. "Thank goodness for spell check," she muttered crossly as she corrected her errors.

Dear Kyle,

Thank you so much for this information. I linked a possible connection to Arthur and Rosalee and added them to my tree today. This generated a lot of leads, which I haven't been able to review yet. Your Wyatt descendants *do* seem to correlate with what my mother found.

The information you provided might just be the breakthrough I've been seeking. Thank you for reaching out. I will compare your tree with mine and get back with you. I'll probably have a lot of questions, as I am just starting this work and have a long way to go.

Sincerely,

Stephanie K.

PS: Would this make us some kind of cousins?

Stephanie could hardly wait to open Kyle's online tree. Her fingers shook as she extracted the lineage for Thomas Wyatt and searched for matching information. As Kyle had stated, she found a few key clues leading to Thomas's ancestors, but the noted descendants exactly matched the basic names Jessica had already uncovered. For the first time, Stephanie had identified the full name of Thomas's wife, Emily Longchamps, born in 1849 and died in 1935. As Kyle mentioned, her surname was changed to Long, but so far he had uncovered no explanation of who changed it, when it occurred, or why.

Details in Kyle's family tree identified some of Emily's ancestors, whose lineage could be traced back as far as 1743. Her heart raced and then seemed to skip a beat when she read the first name of her seventh great-grandmother. Clothiste!

Stephanie's heart continued to thump wildly as she realized this might be the real name of the Revolutionary War woman lauded in the tales the old cousin Sadie had relayed to Jessica. The timing was perfect.

She started scribbling on sticky notes to post the names to the proper generation on her wall tree. Her hands shook as she pressed the sticky-note bearing "Clothiste" onto the chart, an unquestionably warm tingle surging through her fingertips.

She stumbled over the pronunciation of the name, and practiced variations as she repeated the name aloud. "CLO-teest; Clo-TEEST." The second version with the accent on the second syllable rolled more easily off her tongue.

She stood back and studied her growing ancestry tree, rubbing her fingers until the tingle ebbed.

Maybe the room was too bright—or maybe it was because she wasn't looking directly at Jessica's journal.

She didn't see the tiny, tiny light dancing on her mother's journal in a perfect rhythm with her heartbeat, but a definite scent of Chanel No. 5 filled the air.

CHAPTER SEVEN

ABIGAIL
Portsmouth, Virginia, 7 July 1781

Abigail prepared a list and ordered Lizzie the maid, who could not read, to take along the three step-granddaughters with her to the market. She preferred the girls out of her sight. Having the French women in her house unsettled her. Their presence caused her to remember the time in her life that created the fury she had tried so hard to tamp down.

She stared hard into the mirror at the reflection revealing a face ravaged by years of bitterness. Exactly thirty-five years ago to the day, James jilted her for his little tart. Her face tightened in anger and she turned away. She did not like what she saw anymore.

After maneuvering Monique into running away, Abigail moved quietly to console Phillipe Rocher and take care of his child. Phillipe had been shocked to learn his timid governess had run off with an unidentified man in the dark of night—the story Abigail ensured was told. They slipped into a natural relationship and she convinced him there was no need to engage another governess. Eventually Phillipe proposed and they were married by the end of the month.

Soon, Abigail managed to persuade him to anglicize his surname, suggesting it would result in business opportunities for trade, especially with the new colonists settling in America. It was easy enough to adapt the family name from Rocher to Roker, so he became Phillip Roker. He didn't mind. It was good for business and he had closed his offices in France anyway.

She helped him improve his English so barely a trace of French accent remained in his speech. As soon as Etienne was old enough, she convinced Phillip to send him away to school in France so he would retain his French heritage. Although she knew Phillip kept in touch with his son, Etienne rarely returned to England during his school years. She had not seen him since his twelfth birthday.

When she and Phillip finally immigrated to Virginia in 1755, they maintained well-established connections to England, and his mercantile trade continued to flourish in the new world. They easily—and profitably—became entrenched in the bustling seaport of Portsmouth, avoiding the dissention consuming their countries during the war.

Since its early settlement by the British, Portsmouth had always maintained its strong ties to England and, until recently, had not been affected by the war between England and America. Most of the early conflict occurred in the northern states, but now French troops had arrived to assist the American Army in moving further south and into Virginia. At a recent dinner with her neighbors, she had heard the rumors French ships were coming to the bay as well.

And now her stepson had sent his wife and children to live under her very roof.

The sound of glass breaking forced Abigail out of her reverie. She had clenched her hand so tightly in anger, she had snapped a wineglass in half, the sharp stem cutting deep into her flesh. She gasped as blood trickled from the palm of her hand.

Her gaze trailed the red liquid stream as it pooled in slow drops on the floor. Then she turned her glare towards the upstairs room.

It won't be much longer now.

A malicious smile curved her lips.

STEPHANIE
Alexandria, Virginia, present day July

During their Girls' Night Out, Stephanie was shocked to hear her best friend Jackie had received a promotion and transfer to the Caracas FBI office.

"Jackie, I'm so happy for you! But if you go, I will have no one left. Mom and Dad are gone, the houses are sold. I've quit my job. All my ties here will be broken. You were the only remaining constant in my life and now you're leaving." She raised the back of her hand to her forehead in a mock swoon, and in her best exaggerated Scarlett O'Hara accent said, "Wherever shall I go, whatever shall I do?" She changed back to herself, adding "You see how I am making this all about me, don't you?"

"Frankly, my dear, you know I give a damn." Jackie reached over and patted Stephanie's hand. "And that was a pretty good impression of Scarlett. Did she say it like that in the movie?

"I don't know; maybe something similar. When do you leave?"

"Soon. In all honesty, Steph, I've known for weeks. With everything else you've had going on, I just couldn't bring myself to tell you."

"But I'm truly excited for you, Jackie. I know it will be a welcome change to be closer to Alex. Aren't you excited about this?"

"Yes, I am. I have been waiting my turn for so long. Now, with Alex in the Bogota field office, we'll be so much closer." Jackie's long-time boyfriend was a DEA agent assigned to Bogota. "This long distance romance sucks. Our careers are going well—so we need to decide on our personal future now. I do want kids someday, but it may be a few more years before that happens."

Stephanie raised her glass in salute. "Let's have a toast to your promotion and romance in South America—and the future kids!"

Jackie mirrored the pose. "And to the sales of your houses. Which reminds me, you can stay in my apartment until you find something. I'm keeping it as a base for a while, because Alex and I will both have to return for some cases."

"Thank you, Jackie. You've just solved one of my problems."

They touched glasses and sipped.

Then Stephanie leaned forward, eyes sparkling. "Now, let me tell you what fantastic things have happened to me in the last few days."

***

By the time they indulged in their second helping of desert—German chocolate cake for Stephanie and strawberry shortcake for Jackie—the restaurant had grown quiet. Stephanie ended her conversation describing the morning emails from Gage and Kyle.

"Steph, for someone whose life was incredibly calm and normal for years, you've had an unbelievable amount of change in a short time. This Gage sounds like quite the charmer. You need to take things slow and be very careful."

"Yes, ma'am," Stephanie said between bites. "But Jackie, if there is such a thing as love at first sight, I'm experiencing it. But I am scared to death of it as well. And I can't even begin to explain this—whatever it is—this tug in Olde Towne. I feel as if some important part of my life is there, but I'm not sure if it's the past or the present drawing me to it. I can't explain it."

"Well, I wish I could just meet this Gage and see for myself. But I trust your judgment. And his family sounds intriguing with all of their projects. I love their idea for a kid's cooking school."

Neither woman spoke for a while as they sipped coffee, each reflecting on the pending changes in their respective lives.

"Well, I will miss our GNO." Stephanie sighed.

"Me too. We have to squeeze in at least one more before I go."

"Most definitely."

They both sat still a moment longer and then Jackie signaled for the check.

***

When Stephanie arrived back home, she checked her emails before she went to bed. Once again, she had emails from Gage as well as Kyle. For different reasons, she wanted to read both right away.

Her heart demanded she open Gage's email first.

Hi, Stephanie,

How was your day? Mine was not so good.

I didn't finish the training class until about noon today. One of our role-players in the simulated exercise was injured. He's from my former squad and he was playing the role of a rescue victim, but a nervous trainee lost his hold during the 'fireman's carry' and dropped him like a sack of potatoes. He landed on his side—the role-player, not the student—and broke his leg. He underwent surgery and I stayed at the hospital with him.

As soon as I got home, I hit the rack. I may have forgotten I've been awake for the past thirty-six hours, but my body hasn't, and it sure let me know.

I just woke up and thought it was too late to call. You were on my mind all day—well, during the times I was awake, that is. So I am just sending an email to say hello—still trying to avoid that stalker image and all.

Hope you had a good day. Sleep well.

Gage

She sent an answer right away.

Dear Gage,

I am sorry to hear about your colleague and I hope he will have a speedy recovery. Firefighting is such a dangerous job. You be careful out there.

I had dinner with my best friend Jackie tonight. She is an FBI agent and I just learned she's been reassigned to Caracas, Venezuela, so it's kind of sad knowing we won't have those get-togethers any more. She helped me cope after my parents died. I will miss her so much!

On the other hand, I received an email leading me to a lot of new information in the family tree. It looks as if the Civil War relative I looked for in Portsmouth received wounds there, but he apparently died many years later, and might be buried somewhere else. His brother may have been in the city during the same time. I have to research more on the brother.

Well, it's midnight and I'm still awake, so if you are too, call me. I will be up a while longer.

It's too soon to tell if you are a stalker, but I am giving you the benefit of the doubt. Oh, by the way, Jackie wants your credentials so she can run a check on you. lol. Otherwise, it's goodnight for now.

Stephanie

She hit the send button. Well, if his intentions were less than honorable, mentioning Jackie *and* the FBI might scare him away.

She read the email from Kyle next.

Hi Stephanie,

We aren't actually related by blood. My grandmother and her first husband Samuel are my direct family line. She married Arthur after Samuel's death, so I guess that would make us step-cousins. Or to be more accurate, we're 5th step-cousins, and only if my math is correct. Back in school, I was much better in history than math.

I have a chart to keep track of first cousins, second cousins, first cousins once removed, blah blah blah. Have you gotten into the dreaded cousin links yet?

I'm fascinated by the history in your family though. Have you researched Etienne de la Rocher? You will find there are a few mentions of him in history books about the French soldiers who fought in the Revolutionary War. I have some copies of the historical accounts, as well as some old news articles mentioning him. He served in a French unit, part of the militia who came from New England to assist Rochambeau and Washington. Etienne even had a mission in Portsmouth at one time. Maybe that is why you feel drawn there.

I'll be glad to help you find out more if you would like.

Cheers,

Kyle

Excited over this news, Stephanie was wide-awake and bolted from the bed to search the name Etienne de la Rocher on the Internet. Somehow she remembered French word *rocher* meant rock or boulder. How amazing—her high school French was coming back! She liked the idea that the family name meant something solid. It would be the foundation of her family tree.

She composed an email to Kyle.

Dear Kyle,

Thank you so much for the leads you sent. I'm now convinced I am a descendant of Etienne and Clothiste de la Rocher, who I figure are my seventh great-grandparents. I read if you could locate all of your ancestors for ten generations, they would total 1024 relatives! If that is the case, I'm at about 1 percent.

Please send me those clippings you mentioned about Etienne de la Rocher. Thank you for the offer! How exciting to hear my family tree traces back to colonial times, and I want to pursue it. I am also interested in any specifics you might have on Thomas Wyatt and his service during the Civil War. Since it is so close, I'll probably go back down to Portsmouth soon to try to search for records of Thomas and Arthur Wyatt and their possible time there. I'll let you know if I find out anything.

I have just gotten involved with the "dreaded cousins" and my mother's notes refer to her distant cousin Sadie, who was Arthur's granddaughter. I think she would be my second cousin twice removed but then again, math was not my best subject either. I am more interested in getting the information on Thomas and especially Emily, which I hope is going to lead to find out more about the ancestress Clothiste.

Anyway, I am looking forward to hearing from you again,
Stephanie

She had just typed in the name Etienne de la Rocher to try an online search when her phone rang and Gage's cell phone number popped up. For a moment, she waged war with the past and the present. Her fingers itched to stay on the keyboard, but those records would still be there later. She didn't want to miss this phone call right now.

"Hi, Gage!" she said. "Hold on one minute." Heading to her bed, she propped pillows under her head and settled back against the headboard. "Okay, I'm ready now."

***

Gage stretched his long frame in his own bed as well. He'd woken from a dead sleep, still exhausted from his long work day but starving even more. He'd started his laptop and as he waited for it to boot up, he fixed a bowl of Cheerios and poured a glass of orange juice. When he opened his email, he noticed Stephanie had sent her response just nine minutes earlier. He debated for a half second, then took the chance and called.

"Since you had just answered my email from earlier I hoped I could catch you before you went to sleep," he told her when she answered.

"I'm glad you did. I'm still wide awake. I've spent quite a while working on my tree, and got a hit on one of my family members—actually on several people in the family tree. How is your colleague?"

"He will be in the hospital a couple of days. He fell in an awkward way, and we heard the snap of his bone. It sounded gross." He winced in recollection.

"You sound tired. Are you home or at your station house?"

"Home. Well, not home-home, I live in Suffolk, too far to drive tonight, so I crashed in the apartment above my sister Terry's office. She converted the upper floor to a really nice living space, thinking she could live in it and save herself time and money. She soon learned what an albatross it is to live and work in the same building, so she rents it out. The old occupants moved out a month ago and she is still looking for someone to take it over. So when it's empty, I claim it every now and then, as I did today."

"Do you always work twenty-four hour shifts?" Stephanie asked.

"No, I am assigned to the training academy so I normally work Monday through Friday, eight to five. When we have a training course, though, the hours vary according to the subject matter."

"I'm impressed with the projects your sister has going on. They have quite a lot planned for those properties, don't they? Besides opening her own law office, she and Mary Jo have those ambitious dreams for the B and B and the kid's cooking school—which, by the way, I think is such a novel idea."

"Yeah, it is. Everything's a little complicated right now until Mary Jo gets home and goes to court."

"Terry mentioned that. What an awful situation."

Gage sighed. Mary Jo was like a sister to him and he was concerned for her. "When Jay died unexpectedly, he didn't have a will. Who expects to die at thirty-two? They just assumed if one went first, the other would be taken care of, but the emphasis has always focused on Mary Jo because of the dangers of her military service."

Stephanie remained silent, listening as Gage shifted in his bed before he continued. "As soon as Mary Jo was deployed to the Middle East, Della filed some kind of claim in court. I guess since she considers herself in the right, she thought the judge would just hear her side and grant her the property in Mary Jo's absence. Besides the fact that cases don't proceed based on one person's story, Mary Jo is protected by something called the 'Soldier's Relief Act.' She can't be sued while she's on deployment. Della didn't realize they would postpone it until Mary Jo came back from her deployment. Terry says Della doesn't have a case, but she still wants to be prepared. The buildings are Terry's investment, though, and so they will have to show Jay didn't have any involvement in them other than maybe doing remodeling."

"I can't imagine such a situation. Boy, I sure hope it works out for her."

"They're still planning for the B and B, with maybe a little girly shop for scents and candles, those things you women like. It's been in limbo so long now I don't know the plans anymore."

"It's a perfect location for a B and B."

"They probably won't get any customers. This apartment as well as the B and B are said to be haunted."

"Haunted? Oh, come on."

"Yep. Legends say someone died in one of these houses way back when. Some stories say the Revolutionary War, some the Civil War. Some say both. I don't know. Over the years, occupants of the house often reported seeing a woman's spirit; others say it's a little girl; still others say they see young women. No one ever hears them talk, but supposedly one ghost always has a tear running down her cheeks."

Stephanie shifted to get more comfortable. "So be honest. Have you ever seen them?"

"Me? Naw, I don't have that kind of imagination. Although I have to admit, I am always feeling warm spots around the apartment and I keep checking for hidden fires."

"I had a similar situation myself, just today. I picked up my mother's journal and it felt warm to the touch. I guess maybe I had it too close to the computer tower. It was strange."

"Maybe we are connected by ghosts from the past and they are trying to tell us something." Gage whistled, imitating the mysterious music of a low-budget sci-fi film.

"Stop it," Stephanie demanded with a laugh. "That sounded more like space aliens instead of ghosts, but now I'll be seeing spooky things in my sleep. My imagination is vivid enough to imagine them, but I don't want to encounter them in person." Her laughter rang out rich and clear and made Gage wish he could hear more of it.

"Hey, do you know something?" Gage said suddenly. "We have spent more time talking on the phone then we did in person, yet I feel like we've known each other forever."

Stephanie remained silent for a moment, and Gage feared he had said the wrong thing.

Knowing it was late, he tried to figure out what to say next, when Stephanie said quietly, "Gage—I think somehow we have known each other even longer."

They were silent for a moment. Then he repeated his ghostly whistle, and they both laughed.

"Goodnight, Gage."

"Good night, Stephanie."

Once he hung up, he couldn't sleep. He flipped through TV channels and found nothing interesting; he tried reading next, without success. He was wide awake and it would be a long night.

Not even lonely ghosts came to visit him.

Just to be sure, though, he got up and checked along the walls where he had sometimes felt warm sensations. The walls and floor were cool and normal to the touch.

He grabbed his laptop and got back in bed. Spider Solitaire always helped him through a sleepless night.

***

After she ended the phone call, Stephanie shuffled the pillows around and leaned back to think, arms across her chest, fingers interlocked and wildly tapping. Too tired to research Etienne de la Rocher, she slid under the covers and turned out the light.

"Well, whatever number great-great grandparents you are, Etienne and Clothiste, you've been waiting for me for more than two hundred years. I hope you won't mind if a few more hours pass by."

As she lay in the dark, she brushed at her cheek and touched a single teardrop she didn't even know she had shed.

Neither Stephanie nor Gage had any idea that in a corner of the attic of the apartment where he slept, two tiny little lights danced along one wall, and a little girl's delighted laugh echoed across the room.

CHAPTER EIGHT

CLOTHISTE'S DAUGHTERS
Portsmouth, Virginia, 7 July 1781

When she was sure her step-grandmother could not see her, Nicole slipped through the back door.

She missed being outside. Overhead the sun burst into a glaring silver ball and warm air swept across her skin. She was going to the market with her sisters and Lizzie. She skipped merrily toward the summer kitchen behind the house, dangling a small basket from the crook of her arm. She had lovingly tucked her baby doll under a checkered towel. All the way across the small yard, she could smell the smoky aroma of the hams roasting in the little building a few feet away.

She traipsed to the odd kitchen door, a kind she had never seen before she came to her grandfather's house. Cut in two halves, the top half could be open while the bottom half stayed secured, the way it was today. Her sisters told her they remembered seeing them at their uncle's house in New Hampshire. The doors allowed light to enter while keeping small children inside and animals out.

At the half-door, she stood on her very tippy-toes so she could see inside and watch. In the back of the room, a narrow ladder led to the tiny loft where Lizzie slept during the hot summer. During their stay, the older girls, Marie Josephé and Theresé, shared the space as well, as the wicked one had deemed the main house too small for all of them. Sometimes when their mother had been very sick, Nicole had slept with them, but usually she slept on a small pallet across the room from her mother.

At one table, Marie Josephé sliced potatoes with short, irritated movements. Theresé banged two pots together as she set them on a wooden counter, the metallic clang reverberating, while nearby Lizzie chopped something green on a butcher's table.

Penny, the lady with the wild red hair who sometimes came to help cook, stirred a wooden spoon inside a big pot on the woodstove. She looked toward the door and called out in a rich sing-song voice, "Don't look now, ladies, but there is a pair o' eyes dancing at our door." As the girls turned their heads, Nicole opened the bottom half and danced inside. The air was filled with the scent of cinnamon and cloves dancing a tango with the smoky aroma of the ham.

"It is just me, Miss Penny," she said with a laugh." I'm going to market with my sisters and Lizzie too." She took a deep breath and smacked her lips in anticipation. "It smells nice in here. I smell the ham—and apples."

"That you do. How do you like this?" The portly Irish woman held the spoon and waited as Nicole blew on it. The little girl tentatively tasted the apple slice on the spoon. Without waiting for a response, Penny called, "Well, you best hurry, girls. This is an important day for your grandmamma. She's having an important dinner party."

"She *is* not our real grandmother," the middle sister Marie Josephé said with a snarl as she irritably pushed utensils to the side. "She is just married to our real grandfather." She took off her apron and turned to the water bucket to scrub her hands with vigor. "I hate her and I am glad we don't have a drop of her English blood in us," she added as she angrily shook the towel she had just used to dry her hands.

"Sisters, we must leave now so we can get back here to finish." Theresé, always the voice of reason, removed her apron as well, and washed her hands. "We must be very precise in our time, Marie Josephé," she added in a warning tone as she retrieved an empty wicker basket from a hook. Her sister picked up a flat basket covered with a towel similar to the one Nicole had used to blanket her doll.

"What is in there?" Nicole lifted a corner of the towel and peeked inside.

"I baked something for some of the English soldiers," Marie Josephé answered.

"Why?"

"Sometimes it is nice to do something for the soldiers who are far

106

away from their families." Theresé gently pushed Nicole out the door, thinking perhaps taking the little one with them was not such a good idea.

But they had no choice. It was very important for everyone involved that Nicole and her doll made an innocent appearance at the market—and very soon.

STEPHANIE
Alexandria, Virginia, present day August

For the next two weeks, time rushed by as if Stephanie rode an express train on an endless loop with no stopping point. The good news was that her life continued to move forward.

First, the sales of the two houses continued to progress smoothly. In fact, her real estate agent Andrea advised that she had never seen a mortgage application proceed so quickly, let alone two at the same time. If things stayed on this course, both sales would close by August 31st. When she asked Stephanie what guardian angels were looking out for her, Marla and Jessica both came to mind.

She finished her last two weeks at work without a hitch, preparing her replacement, if there was one, to start fresh. Although her colleagues were genuinely sorry to see her go, it was no secret her departure would likely save another person's job. Her co-workers gave her a farewell luncheon at her favorite restaurant, and as always, conversation turned to work matters. Conversation buzzed as her colleagues lamented rumors of a six-month delay in awarding contracts. If true, temporary layoffs would be decided the next day. Collectively, nerves were on edge to learn who or how many would be affected when the dreaded announcements came. Stephanie departed the luncheon with a feeling of vast relief that she no longer had to worry about her job.

The most fascinating result of Stephanie's endless circle

was the daily progression of her long-distance relationship with Gage. They spoke on the phone every evening, and during the day exchanged dozens of emails or text messages. They each realized their attraction came at a busy time in both of their lives, with Stephanie juggling so many personal events in her life and Gage obligated to his duties at the fire school nearly twelve hours every day. After the graduation ceremony for the trainees, he would prepare his wrap-up report immediately and arrange to take some time off. As the ceremony coincided with Stephanie's last day at work, they agreed Gage would visit Saturday, the day after the fire academy graduation.

He would drive up to spend the day with her. They left unspoken the topic of whether Saturday would stretch into a full weekend together.

As it drew closer to the Saturday of Gage's visit, Stephanie panicked, fearing she would not have enough time to get ready. There just weren't enough hours in the day! Although she had already cleaned out her parent's home in preparation for the estate sale, the unexpectedly quick closing of her own little house threw her into upheaval as she sorted through things to store, sell, or donate.

Then she had to consider how much to prepare for seeing Gage. Although they had spent a few short hours together in person, they had spent dozens of hours on the phone, and exchanged literally hundreds of emails. Some were a quick hello no more than a sentence long; others detailed events in their daily lives.

The rush of the passing minutes brought a heightened sense of anticipation to Stephanie. What might happen when they spent more time together? Would the first strong spark still be there— or would it be a fire grown cold before the ember even had a chance to ignite?

She wasn't one to jump in bed with a man she hardly knew. Still, she thoroughly spruced her bedroom into tip-top shape, right down to a few strategically placed candles—just in case.

She checked the nightstand drawer, where a couple of square aluminum packets discreetly nestled in a small box assured her she was prepared—just in case.

***

During the same two weeks Stephanie rode her fast-moving express train, Gage's own life dragged by, as if carried on the back of a tortoise. *Did my watch quit working or something?* He tapped it. *Has every day become forty-eight hours long?* He loved his job, but nothing had ever caused such a distraction that he had to literally force himself to concentrate on teaching his classes.

Gage discovered long phone calls and frequent messages were almost as effective as face-to-face conversations. He had always considered electronic communications a necessary evil of modern society. Even text messages or emails replaced phone calls in today's world, severely reducing the need for human contact.

But hearing her voice over the phone brought her laughing face to mind, with that mesmerizing dimple. *It was funny about that little dimple. It doesn't always show when she smiles or moves her mouth, but when it does—wow!*

His stirring body reminded him of more than Stephanie's captivating dimple. His mind circled on a one-way track. He wanted Stephanie but wanted more than a casual sexual encounter. He wasn't going to scare her off by moving too fast, so he would take his time until he knew they were on the same track.

And damn it, it was time for class so he better stop thinking about her before he stood in front of the trainees. His lecture covered tools for the job but he was going to be a bit late until he settled down—no need for his own apparatus to become the next firefighter's hose joke around the station.

***

Stephanie woke at three-thirty Saturday morning. Gage planned to arrive at ten o'clock. She could not go back to sleep and got up to finish packing the things to take to her parents' house. She planned to have an estate sale there soon, and would include things from her own home to sell as well.

After an hour, she stopped her methodical cataloging and packing and flexed her back. Whenever she grew tired of sorting and storing, she rewarded herself with a little time to work on her wall chart for the family tree. The effort occupied her mind while giving her body a rest.

Stephanie looked at the wall chart filled with new sticky notes and hoped her mother would be proud of her progress. It occurred to her that she frequently referred to Jessica as her mother, but usually in the context of the family tree. At first, she felt disloyal to her adoptive mother Marla, but she recognized both women had given her the life she had now. She had room in her heart for both.

Convinced Kyle Avery had correctly identified the line of ancestry reaching back to the mysterious Clothiste and her husband Etienne, she could start filling in the family history generated by this discovery.

She counted the confirmed relatives in her tree. There were over two hundred on her father's Sullivan side. Eighteen listed on her mother's side. However, she had over four hundred clues to follow based on those few names alone.

Although she had minimal experience with genealogy research, she understood every lead would not necessarily apply to her family. Some would be duplicate references; many others would not be relevant at all. Still, any clue could identify other grandparents in her ancestry line.

For now, however, her "French Connection" remained

her priority. The documents Kyle Avery had sent were so extensive she had not yet had the time to examine them all. She planned to concentrate on the direct descendants of Etienne and Clothiste, adding relevant information to her online tree. She had yet to develop the discipline to concentrate on one person at a time, as she often diverted to clues to other ancestors and she lost track of the one she originally worked on.

She summarized the direct line of descendants of Clothiste and Etienne. Their daughter Nicole had married a man named Henri Lebegue. Stephanie already sensed a connection, because although she rarely used it, Nicole was her own middle name. Without knowing exactly why, she circled the name "Nicole" in red.

Nicole and Henri lived in New England, and he was killed in the War of 1812. Their son Edward earned a living as a shoemaker in New Hampshire; she placed a red circle around his name, as the direct descendant of Nicole. His daughter Genevieve married a man named François Longchamps and had a daughter Emily. She circled the two women's names. Thomas Wyatt married a woman named Emily Long.

At some point, the family name changed to simply "Long" and Stephanie put a sticky note by Emily's name to try to identify when that happened.

Thomas and Emily had a daughter Madeline Nicole. *There's my middle name again.* She circled the name, but it produced no particular vibe as she had felt with Nicole de la Rocher. Madeline Nicole married Richard Finch, and they had one son, Mason.

The final entry documented Mason's daughter Marsha who had a child out of wedlock with Mark Franklin and eventually placed their daughter Jessica for adoption. Neither Jessica nor Stephanie had uncovered much information on Mark Franklin or Marsha, except that she'd died at the young age of thirty-two.

Stephanie scribbled a reminder to send away for

Marsha's birth and death certificates. With no information for Mark Franklin, not even where he was born or how he died, she would have to search later.

Studying her chart, she noticed most ancestors lived well into their eighties and nineties. Her mother died at twenty-one and her grandmother at thirty-two, but longevity seemed abundant for most of the family line—she wondered if she would inherit this trait.

At six-thirty, the annoying buzzer on the alarm clock sounded from her bedroom and sliced through the quiet. She shut down her computer and closed the door to her study. An early riser by nature, she rarely needed to set an alarm, but wanted to be sure she was ready when Gage arrived.

She showered and took more time than usual with her appearance. Not one to use a lot of make-up, this time she applied more than a swish of mascara and a dab of blush.

She placed her hand to her heart once, as if to contain her excitement. *How can I feel this way, as if I've known Gage my whole life?* She peered at herself in the vanity mirror, fingers tapping noisily on the vanity until she forced them to stop. She leaned forward to study her reflection. Her skin glowed and her eyes sparkled.

Can I really be falling in love? She didn't know yet, but her heart flipped at the thought.

When the clock ticked eight, Stephanie couldn't contain her excitement. By now, Gage would be well on the road, but she called him anyway.

"Good morning, Steph," he answered. Her heart squeezed at the way he used her nickname. "How are you?"

"I'm fine. I figured you were on the road and just wanted to wish you a safe and quick journey."

He laughed. "It was quick all right. I'm already here. I couldn't wait and left at four. I've been sitting outside your house for more than an hour, waiting for the right time to call and tell you I was here."

"You're here already?" Stephanie looked out her bedroom window and her heart flipped again when Gage got out of the driver's side. Thank goodness she was ready! "Look in the upstairs window." She waved as he tilted his head back and caught her eye. He waved with a sheepish shrug.

"I'll bet my neighbors have been wondering if you were a pervert sitting out there." They laughed and she added, "I'm coming down right now," clicking off her phone as she headed downstairs at double time.

She paused at the door to take a deep breath to collect herself. She opened it to find Gage leaning against the doorframe, his right arm bracing the frame, his head tilted. He wore the same sheepish look on his face as he held his left hand behind his back.

"Sorry," he said. "I didn't want to waste a minute of this day."

"I'm glad you're here. Come on in." She gestured with her hand and he stepped across the threshold. They both leaned forward to brush cheeks with a chaste kiss, bumping foreheads twice as they each changed sides trying to line lips to cheeks. Finally, Gage simply touched his lips lightly to hers.

"Welcome to my home." Stephanie smiled shyly while she resisted the urge to plant one on him. How could she feel so timid and reckless at the same time?

"Thank you. These are for you." From behind his back, he brought forth his left hand tightly clutching a bouquet, this time all red roses.

"I love them." She inhaled the lovely scent. "Thank you. Please, sit down while I find something to put them in." She gestured to her cozy little living room couch, and went over to a box where she removed a vase.

"I'll put these in water. Excuse the mess. I have to be out at the end of the month so I am in the middle of packing. Would you like some coffee or something? I didn't fix anything yet. I'm not much of a cook, but I can

113

make a good cup of coffee."

"No, I'm fine for now. I drank a gallon of coffee on the drive up. I made good time. There wasn't any traffic."

"Weekends are easier. It's horrible during the work week. It takes—used to take—me over an hour sometimes to go seven miles to the office. Some days I just gave in and took the bus." Stephanie worried she was babbling, and clenched her teeth to stop talking.

"Phew!" Gage whistled through his teeth. "Insane. I guess I won't complain about a ten-minute gridlock when the downtown tunnel traffic blocks the route to the station again. Whenever the tunnel is backed-up, I can sit through six traffic lights waiting to cross blocked roads."

Stephanie filled the vase and arranged the flowers, bringing them into the living room to place on a carton serving as a coffee table. She then sat on the end of the couch opposite Gage, willing her fingers not to tap.

"What time do you have to head back tonight? I figured we could grill steaks later this evening, but there's a great little diner near here for breakfast. If we go now, we might avoid the weekend crowds."

"The diner sounds fine. So does grilled steak. I am off for a few days, so I have nothing to rush back for." He winced, glancing furtively toward Stephanie. She gave no indication he had spoken out of line.

Careful, Dunbar, his inner voice warned. Don't make it sound as if you want to jump her bones first thing—even if you do.

He paid attention to the inner voice, ignoring the little tug of lust trying to climb over it.

"Good. We won't have to hurry through breakfast. Afterwards, I'll take you on a tour of Old Town Alexandria." Stephanie said as she stood and reached for her purse. "Come on, I'll drive."

And maybe I will have all weekend for a chance to get my hands all over you, Mr. Gage Dunbar.

She smiled inwardly. She really liked this man.

CHAPTER NINE

CLOTHISTE AND NICOLE
Portsmouth, Virginia, 7 July 1781

The war between America and Britain raged on. Hessian soldiers from Germany moved further south with the British Army. Less than a year earlier, West Point had almost been lost because of the turncoat Benedict Arnold.

In fact, right now that very traitor was downstairs in this house, having dinner with the wicked one and several other British officers while on a return mission to Portsmouth. Clothiste wondered what would happen to them all if the wicked one knew that while she entertained—as if she were a queen, no less—her own step-son, Etienne, fought alongside the French and American armies.

Maybe it is time to stop writing in my journal. You write in French, silly woman, *she reminded herself with a small laugh,* you write in French and your secrets are safe.

In her opinion, the wicked one was as stupid as she was evil. Married to a Frenchman, yet could not even speak his language. English would only be spoken in her house, and Clothiste's family could make no reference to their French heritage, especially in front of visitors.

However, no one could prevent Clothiste from speaking French in private. All of her daughters were fluent in both languages and their English was far better than her own, but behind their own doors, they spoke only French. Her youngest, Nicole, God bless her, could speak either language without giving it any consideration. Her oldest daughter Theresé sometimes forgot her French, and could, if she tried hard enough, converse in English with either British or American accents when the occasion warranted it, as it sometimes did in this household. Only eleven months separated Therese' from her middle sister Marie Josephé, for whom languages seemed to come so naturally she could adapt her speech as she needed. Once she had easily mimicked a British accent, to convince the British soldiers she had unexpectedly encountered that she was a loyalist.

"Mama?" Nicole cautiously whispered, peeking in. "Are you sleeping?"

"No, ma petite fille, I am awake. Come in and snuggle with me." Clothiste patted the bed.

"Are you better?" Nicole scooted in beside her mother, pressing her hand to Clothiste's forehead as she had seen her older sisters do.

"I am much better, little one. How are you?"

Nicole laid her head on her mother's shoulder, then bounced up, and continued to chatter. "We went to market today. Marie Josephé had a basket of things she baked, and Theresé talked to a soldier man."

Nicole clutched the doll to her chest as if to protect it. "I showed my baby to the soldiers today. One kissed her nose—and mine." She rubbed her own nose without thinking. "They told me her new dress was very pretty. They were nice, even if they were British."

"And where are your sisters now?"

Nicole wrinkled her nose in disdain. "They are down there doing cooking and cleaning," she said, pointing to the floor. "Why does the step-grandmamma act so mean to us? Grandpapa is so kind and gentle."

Clothiste sighed and hugged her little girl closer. Although her stepmother-in-law detested Phillip's family, the wicked one was careful not to display this attitude around him. It was unfortunate his frequent absences for business allowed Abigail to run the house as she chose. In his absence, she was particularly hard on the girls.

Phillip knew her real story. In truth, Clothiste had been born of French parents who had settled in the French Canadian colony known as Acadia. When the British gained control of Canada, many Acadians, including her father, refused to swear unconditional oaths of allegiance to the British crown. Eventually many resistant Acadians were expelled, but her family remained. Clothiste was born there, and met Etienne de la Rocher, a young soldier of fortune nine years her senior. When she was just sixteen, they married.

In late 1775, the American Congress asked the French Canadians to assist the Americans in the war with the British. The American occupation in Canada was not successful, and the forces retreated. By 1776, many French families were displaced from their own homes and forced to follow their soldiers to America.

She and Etienne lost everything they owned when they fled Acadia—their land, their house, their property. Her uncle had earlier settled in New Hampshire, so they were able to take refuge with his family for a short while because she was pregnant with Nicole.

As soon as she could, she took her children and joined the other women following their husbands in camp. As the wife and daughters of a captain, they fared better than most. She acted as a nurse to the wounded men. Her two older daughters performed chores as needed, packing and following their father as necessary. She had not seen her only son, Louis, in years, as he too fought in the war and their paths seldom crossed.

Life had been difficult for the last five years and for that reason alone she despised the British.

Clothiste stirred restlessly, blocking old memories from her thoughts as she forced her body into a sitting position. On her mind now was the dinner downstairs. Two of the callers being entertained were the loathsome British General Cornwallis and that traitor Benedict Arnold, who would be returning to New York soon. The wicked one had infuriated her by demanding that Marie Josephé serve the guests. Poor Theresé was tasked with scullery duties alongside the unfortunate Lizzie, who often bore the brunt of Abigail's wrath.

One notion repeatedly crossed the ill woman's mind: could this event prove useful to her beloved Etienne? Perhaps her daughters would glean important information to eventually pass to Washington's army to end the war. Then her family could reunite.

With that idea giving her some comfort, she circled her arms around her youngest daughter and rocked her to sleep.

STEPHANIE
Alexandria, Virginia, present day August

Clatter from the kitchen and murmurs of chattering

guests permeated the small diner, but neither Stephanie nor Gage noticed. Tucked away in a small booth, leaning forward on their elbows as they talked, he sometimes stroked her fingers in a light but flirty touch, as she companionably rested her ankle against his.

Gage talked about how pleased his superiors were with the last class of fire recruits.

"All thirty students, including two females, passed every part of the rigorous training course. Thirteen graduated with grades of ninety-five percent or better. None of the remainder scored less than ninety percent." He leaned back to allow the waitress to refill his coffee before he continued.

"It's not unusual for one or two students to drop out at some point during the program. Some are unable or unwilling to meet the physical or academic requirements to graduate. Some realize this is not the job they want to do. We didn't lose a single recruit this session." He drank a few sips of coffee before he continued. "While I wish my training team could take full credit, this just happened to be an exceptional group. We may not be as lucky next time. We never know."

"I don't remember ever being inclined toward a career requiring such determination." Stephanie sighed. She tried to catch the eye of the waitress, who had turned to the next table after filling Gage's cup. "I had a year of community college but just couldn't seem to find a niche, so I dropped out when I got my job with the contracting company. My tasks were interesting but not particularly rewarding. They're a contracting firm which hires people for duties in countries experiencing internal conflict, such as Afghanistan or Liberia. I often envied the people who had the fortitude needed to assist in a foreign mission, such as the police, military or emergency personnel." Stephanie couldn't recall if he told how he became interested in firefighting, so she asked, "When did you decide to become a firefighter?"

"Oh, man, I guess about seven or eight. We had a school field trip to one of the fire stations, where we got to tour the buildings and sound the sirens, the kind of hands-on stuff most kids love. This particular station still had the old-fashioned poles but we couldn't slide down them. I tried to sneak back to it and slide down anyway but got caught by one of the firemen. He sent me on my way to my group but slipped a junior firefighter badge in my shirt pocket. I still have it." Gage's face softened at the memory as he absently tapped his shirt pocket, and she smiled.

"Of course, afterwards, every kid in class wanted to be a fireman. But the desire stuck with me. You had to be eighteen when you took the entrance exam, but you could apply earlier as long as you were eighteen by the date of the exam. I applied early and took it on my eighteenth birthday. I considered that a sign this was meant to be. And the first chance I had, I slid down that damn pole. About broke my ankles too."

Stephanie laughed, nudging hers against his, Gage bumping back.

The waitress brought more coffee to the table, casting admiring eyes toward Gage, who shook his head and moved the empty cup toward center of the table.

A slight tinge of annoyance rolled over Stephanie when the waitress ignored her empty cup, so with a deliberate move of her hand, she caressed her fingers along Gage's. The server understood the not-so-subtle hint and moved on, leaving Stephanie's cup still empty.

Stephanie narrowed her eyes and then drew her gaze to the firefighter watching her with an amused look. He started to raise his hand for the waitress and she pressed it to the table.

"I don't want the coffee that bad. Maybe she's just harried at the moment." *Ha!* She leaned on her elbows and propped her chin in her entwined fingers. "So you love your work."

"I do. My brother is a firefighter too, in Suffolk. He's

three years younger. Sibling rivalry being what it is, he chose a different city and has made his own mark. He's just been promoted to captain." Despite Gage's remark about rivalry, his eyes reflected pride for his younger brother, and smiled slyly. "But I still outrank him because I'm a battalion chief."

"I never minded being an only child, but there were times when I wished I had brothers or sisters." Suddenly, she slapped her hand playfully on the table and startled him with the abrupt movement.

"Okay. Now let me ask some questions." Her eyes twinkled mischievously and she asked in rapid-fire succession. "Are you married? Do you have any children? Do you kick your dog?"

Gage laughed and held his hands up. "Well, I'm positive to no on the first, pretty sure to no on the second question. And I don't have a dog." He teased her with a little tweak of her nose. Then he grew more serious. "Although when I was twenty I proposed to my high school sweetheart. But she didn't want me to be a firefighter and I didn't want to give it up. The break-up wasn't so nice back then, but we are on decent civil terms now." He grimaced. "Two months after our break-up, she married a guy who became a successful broker, and they now live in suburbia with their two kids, a dog and a cat."

"Ouch."

"Naw, it obviously wasn't meant to be. And you?"

"Never married either; never even engaged, for that matter. And I definitely have no kids. I spent two years with Ethan. We never lived together, but we each allotted the other closet and bathroom space in our homes, and came and went freely. We loved each other, but we reached a point where we agreed to move on. We probably had the friendliest break-up on record." She laughed. "He stayed in contact with me when my parents were killed in the wreck. He came by several times to check on me as I dealt with the funeral. We'll always be friends, but I guess we weren't meant to last either."

Gage leaned back in his chair, trailing his index finger along Stephanie's. It surprised him to feel a little twinge of envy when Stephanie mentioned Ethan. It was a totally new and different reaction for him. But the past was the past; he had to remember this was the now.

"So maybe I should ask the next question." He narrowed his eyes and leaned forward again, imitating Stephanie's earlier pose. "Are you opposed to firefighters as husbands?"

"Hmmm." Stephanie pretended to concentrate deeply, stroking her chin as a wise old sage might. "Hmmm. No, I can't say that I am."

"Okay, that's good news. You know—just in case."

"Just in case, indeed," she said with a laugh. "Let's walk off some of this huge breakfast on George Washington's old stomping grounds."

They window-shopped or slipped inside antique stores along the historic streets. Stephanie pointed out that Old Town Alexandria, like Olde Towne Portsmouth, played a significant role in America's colonial history. "I guess Portsmouth's use of the extra 'e' in the words is a throwback to the old English style, though," she added. As they strolled down King Street, she tucked her hand under Gage's arm, thrilled at feeling the firm shape of his bicep. His arms were strong but not bulky, and she basked in the warmth of his closeness as she discreetly steered him toward a surprise she had in store at their final destination.

Gage loved history, and noticed Stephanie enjoyed looking at practical antiques like lamps and furniture, not jewelry or old clothes. He didn't know why, but for some reason he found it appealing.

At one intersection, Stephanie drew Gage down a side-street and stopped in front of a small two-story building with an interesting cupola. Gage's eyes flickered to the sign and then widened in delight at a sign revealing they stood in front of the "Friendship Firehouse Museum."

"How cool," he exclaimed as he opened the double green doors of the old firefighting museum.

Watching him, Stephanie decided he looked like a kid waking on Christmas morning to find the presents under the tree. In her best guide's voice, she said, "The Friendship Firehouse was established in seventeen seventy-four as the first volunteer fire company in Alexandria." Having done her research in advance, she continued in the role of guide and added, "Most buildings were made of wood and heated with open flames in those days. This building was built in eighteen fifty-five and now holds early firefighting memorabilia and equipment."

Gage wandered over to the suction pump engine on one side, known as the "Rodgers Pumper" and built for the old Friendship Firehouse in 1851.

On the opposite side, a nineteenth-century hose reel carriage was on display. Once an elaborately decorated apparatus, as typical of the time, it now stood somewhat rusty, but still proudly bore the original fire company's logo stamped on the reel.

Gage bent low to peer at the machine, then turned to Stephanie. Mimicking her guide voice, he said, "Humans pulled both the pumper and hose reel carriage in their day. Horse-drawn carriages did not become prominent until the mid-nineteenth century." As he moved from display to display, he studied the axes, then the fire helmet, and water bucket, each made from leather and other materials.

Watching him, Stephanie decided not only was it Christmas morning for the handsome firefighter, he was a kid turned loose in a candy shop as well.

"I love this stuff." Gage grinned sheepishly as he caught Stephanie's amused expression. "Hey, what's upstairs?" He asked, his eyes skimming over the leather buckets and hoses from long-ago fire service, then to the ceiling. "And where's the pole?"

A museum historian standing nearby began to laugh. She wore a name tag identifying her as Catherine.

"That is our most frequently asked question here in the museum," she declared. "Fire poles didn't come into use until the eighteen-eighties. When this fire station came into existence, the firemen were citizens who did not sleep in the building like our modern firefighters do, but they responded from their own homes to fires when the bell tolled. Upstairs in the meeting room you will find more information about this fire company's history in the Alexandria community."

"Okay, let's go up." Gage tugged Stephanie toward the stairs. At the top of the steps, as they turned toward the room, Gage spied a ladder on the wall going into a narrow opening, presumably leading to the roof.

"I wonder what's up there," he mused out loud as he reached for a rung.

"Whoa, cowboy, I don't think that's part of the tour." Stephanie laughed, grabbing his shirt sleeve and steering him into the meeting room. "Now I just had a picture pop in my mind of you in the fire station when you were a kid, itching to slide down that infamous pole."

"Sorry, it's a firefighter's basic instinct to climb a ladder," he said, laughing. "I have to tell Connor about this place when I get back. He would love it too. It's small, but it would be a fun trip for him and Tanner." He entered and walked around the tiny room, peering at the bust of George Washington, prominently displayed between two white columns, then at the old ceremonial helmets and other regalia.

When he finished, Stephanie motioned for him to follow. "There's one more surprise for you downstairs," she said. Back in the engine room, she glanced at Catherine, who gave a nod of approval and pointed to two gold ropes hanging from the ceiling.

"As a real firefighter, you get to ring the bell," Catherine told Gage, who grinned broadly.

"I do? Way cool." He pulled Stephanie with him as he stood underneath the small opening where the ropes dangled, attached to the bell in the cupola. He stood still, his fingers twirling the end of the rope. The he looked at Stephanie.

"But I have to do something else first." Eyes turning smoky, he slid his left hand along the back of her neck and drew Stephanie close. Cupping her chin in his hand, he leaned in, stopping a whisper away from her lips until her half-opened eyes met his.

The unexpected move sent her heart pounding in her ears as he stroked her jaw line and brought his lips to hers. When their lips touched, the warmth was unlike anything she had experienced. Electric jolts sparked throughout her body. She was pretty sure her toes curled. Bells chimed in her head and she wondered how he pulled the rope with both arms still around her. She opened her eyes and stared into his, then realized the carillon echoes were all in her head.

"I have wanted to do that since I met you," he whispered, winking.

Her thumping heart did a flip-flop in her chest.

One arm around her, Gage grabbed the rope with his free hand and tugged on the bell as several other visitors in the room broke into applause.

"Let's go home," Stephanie whispered, and they scrambled hand-in-hand out the door.

She drove as fast as she could, pushing the pedal a bit above posted speed limits, then pulling into the driveway and hitting the brakes so hard both she and Gage lurched forward against their seatbelts.

"Oops. Sorry," she said as they got out. She fumbled with the key at the front door lock. Nervous fingers sifted through the ring for the right one. Gage placed his hand over her shaking one, and she stilled. She could feel his warm breath brushing past her ear, the scent of his cologne, and the key finally turning the cylinder. They stepped inside and she locked it behind her.

For a moment they paused in the foyer, staring face-to-face. As if on signal, they grabbed for each other. Gage backed her to the door and devoured her with his mouth while she ran her hands through his hair, returning kiss for kiss. Then she pushed him further into the foyer, her fingers working at his buttons. Without breaking the kiss, he took his hands off her long enough to let her tear the shirt down his arms and drop it on the floor. They did a half-circle as he spun her around and leaned her against the banister to the stairway.

"Bedroom? Which way to your bedroom?" he gasped through another kiss as he fought to find buttons on her shirt. Through muddled senses he was dimly aware that she wore a button-less pullover. She took her arms from the sleeves and left it around her neck like a Hawaiian lei as their lips locked again. He slid his hands across her breasts, causing her breath to hitch in her throat.

"Upstairs, left door," she mumbled, her smoky voice surprising her. She broke the kiss long enough to pull her shirt over her head and toss it aside. Like magnet to metal she returned her lips to his. Her fingers worked the buckle on his belt.

Scooping her in his arms, he climbed the stairs to her room, crossing over to and then falling with her on top of the prettily-made bed. His hands touched everywhere at once.

He unclasped her bra and tossed it over his shoulder, skimming his hands across her breasts and hearing her sharp intake of breath. He struggled to slow down. *Don't scare her, Dunbar; she's so tiny and delicate—so shy.*

Within moments, he realized he was only right about the first two descriptors. This woman was anything but shy. As he slowed his moves, she increased the intensity of hers, her hands roaming all over him. The button of his jeans resisted her nimble fingers, so he used the time to unzip hers and remove one of the barriers between them.

She stretched toward the drawer of the nightstand, allowing him the chance to gaze at her small firm breasts as she palmed the silver foil package. With one hand, he unzipped his jeans and yanked them past his hips. The other hand cupped her neck as he drew her in for kisses. He couldn't budge the jeans without breaking their embrace, but somehow—he didn't know how she did it, but somehow, bless her heart—she managed to hook her foot in them and push them past his knees where he could kick them the rest of the way off.

When Stephanie's trembling fingers could not open the foil package, he took it in one hand and clenched the edge in his teeth, deftly opening the corner so she could remove the protective content. Her hands stopped trembling as she unrolled it down the length of his shaft, the sudden confidence in her touch nearly bringing him to the brink.

Stephanie could not get her fill of touching him. She stroked his arms at the bulge of his biceps, over his chest and down across the taut surface of his perfect six-pack stomach. She inched her hands along his torso and then trailed her fingertips across his collar-bones.

Finally, he buried himself inside her. They matched touch for touch, kiss for kiss and thrust for thrust until hot release tore through them both, and they crested the wave together.

***

Gage didn't think he would ever move again—ever. He lay in an exhausted heap, still on top of Stephanie, not moving and barely able to mumble, "Wow! What just happened?"

With great effort, he rolled onto his back, drawing her over him.

She almost purred as she nestled to him, stroking one hand along his chest, smug with delight when shivers ran through him. "Did we just spontaneously combust or something?" she asked.

The keen of sirens drifted to their ears, followed by the air horn of a fire engine as it moved closer.

"They might be coming here. I think we just set the house on fire," she mumbled as she nuzzled his neck.

"Yeah. Probably we did." His lips found hers again, and of a sudden found he could move very well after all. "Do you think we could generate enough heat to start the grill from here if we repeated ourselves?" he asked with a mischievous twinkle in his blue eyes as he rolled on top of her.

"We should certainly try," Stephanie proclaimed, her eyes matching the twinkle in his.

CHAPTER TEN

CLOTHISTE AND NICOLE
Portsmouth, Virginia, 18 July 1781

Clothiste felt so much better. Her father-in-law had just returned home, which usually meant the wicked one would be on good behavior in his presence.

But the very best news—her stepmother-in-law would be gone for a whole week to visit some sick relative in Richmond. Clothiste nestled on the pillow with eyes closed as she enjoyed the first time peace filled her in this house.

The bedroom door squeaked on its hinges as it opened, and Clothiste recognized Nicole's childish shuffle crossing the room. She leaned on the bed and remained silent. Clothiste could feel tiny brown eyes staring into her, and she opened one eye to look at her daughter peering at her eyelids as if willing her mother to wake.

"Are you awake, Mama?" Nicole whispered, so near her warm breath brushed Clothiste's cheek.

"I am, ma petite, *but why are you awake? You should be sleeping."*

"I can't sleep. I am so happy. Grandpapa is here," she whispered excitedly. "And the step-grandmamma will go away today. She will be gone for a whole week."

"Yes, I know, darling. It makes me feel better already."

Nicole rested her head near her mother's, reaching up to pat her cheek. "I wish you would be better forever, Mama."

"I do too, darling. I want to be well again so we can leave here and be with your papa."

"Mama, I think I miss Papa, but I cannot remember his face anymore."

"Then I will tell you about him so you can never forget him, and

then you must sleep for a while, ma petite, *so you can see him in your dreams." Clothiste nestled Nicole beside her and spoke softly.*

"Your papa is so tall, and so handsome. His eyes are the same color as the eyes of your sister Theresé; blue like the cornflowers, so bright blue it is like the sky shines in them. His hair is dark, dark brown like yours. He has the little dimple in his face like you have sometimes, right there," she said, touching Nicole's cheek. "Then there are times he is too busy and forgets to shave, and his chin gets scratchy right here," Clothiste rubbed her thumb on Nicole's little chin. "And when he kisses us, he laughs when we tell him it tickles and he kisses us some more, like this." Clothiste nuzzled the back of Nicole's neck, causing the little one to giggle.

"You are not scratchy, Mama, you feel like silk," Nicole said with a yawn, her eyes heavy as she nestled alongside her mother.

Clothiste sighed and hugged her baby to her. The sounds of soft sighs signaled her little girl had drifted into sleep. She prayed her youngest would have pleasant dreams of her papa.

She closed her eyes and let the tears fall silently.

She would give anything to feel the rough scrape of her beloved Etienne's wonderful face against her cheek once more.

STEPHANIE
Alexandria, Virginia, present day August

The last remnants of the evening sun sent gold streaks through the slats of the bedroom blinds, fading rapidly into the dusk. Contentedly stretched beside Stephanie as the shadows lengthened to darkness, Gage twirled one of her curls around his finger. Without warning, his stomach growled and they remembered they'd skipped lunch.

"What do you say I just whip up an omelet for now and we grill those steaks another time?" Stephanie propped her arms across his chest, not wanting to move from the comfortable embrace.

"I like both of those ideas." Gage kissed her nose. "But how about I do the eggs? You've already told me you don't cook much, and I happen to be the firehouse omelet king."

"Well, your option is much better than mine," Stephanie agreed. Suddenly her expression turned serious.

"Gage?"

"Yes?" he answered as he looked around for his jeans.

"I don't—I don't do this kind of…" she waved her hand around, pulling the sheet across her chest.

He placed one knee on the bed and leaned over to kiss her nose again.

"I know, so just stop. Please. This…" he gestured his hand as she had done. "This has been the most incredible day of my life."

"Mine too. Gage, you brought out something in me I didn't know existed. You make me feel—amazing." She shook her head as her body tingled with memory of his touch, incredulous she could feel this way. Suddenly she burst into giggles. "However, if you don't mind, those are my skinny jeans you are trying to pull up."

"I am? Is that what's the matter here?" he asked, his ankles caught in the tight tapered leg. As he tried to pull one foot out, he lost his balance and fell over, disappearing from her view.

"I'm okay," his muffled voice called out. She was pretty sure he was trying to hide his own laughter.

She giggled helplessly and her heart flipped. Never had she known anyone like him. Could she be falling in love with this man? Was she ready to give her heart to this man?

She tamped down the nerves fighting with her feelings of happiness.

When Gage had kicked off his jeans earlier, they'd landed somewhere on the other side of the bed. He managed to wriggle out of the wrong ones, and crawled around until he found his own to pour into, barely zipping them as he trotted downstairs, shirtless and barefoot. Stephanie threw an oversized tee-shirt on over her panties and followed him—and their earlier trail of discarded clothing—down the stairs.

As she set the table, she watched him find his way

efficiently around her kitchen, as yet unaffected by her packing process. As if he were the star of an infomercial for some miracle kitchen knife, he expertly chopped peppers and onions, diced Smithfield ham, cheddar cheese, and in no time, had tantalizing smells filling the air.

Stephanie poured red wine in glasses and placed the salad she had originally prepared for their planned barbecue in the center of the table. As an afterthought, she moved two small votive candles to the table and lit them.

"Cute," he said with a wink as he slid two perfect omelets onto plates. "So are the candles."

"I'm quite impressed," she said. "Your kitchen skills rival your bedroom skills. And I cannot believe I just said that."

"Honey," he said as he leaned over to kiss her long and deep, "as the old song goes, 'ba-ba-ba-baby, you ain't seen nuthin' yet'."

As they ate, Gage tried to figure how to convince her to ignore packing for just two days and come back to Portsmouth with him. He began by explaining in a few days he would be temporarily reassigned at one of the station houses until the department selected a permanent battalion chief, which meant he would be working twenty-four hour shifts for at least a month.

If she stayed in Alexandria, his new shift work would make it difficult to see her as often as he would like. She wanted to conduct more research in Portsmouth. He wanted her close by, to be with her as much as possible. It had occurred to him it would be a good idea for her to see Terry's apartment before she rented it to someone else.

"I can show you around the historical area on Monday, and maybe we can find some information on your ancestor," he said, concluding his sales pitch. He even resorted to a bit of bribery, adding he would help her move on one of his off days to make up for her lost time.

"Oh, Gage, I would love it, but I have too much to do here."

"You can see the apartment tomorrow and get a feel for it, then maybe come back again after you sell your house." And, he was already counting on Terry's subtle support to convince Stephanie to stay and enjoy the fall and Christmas season events while she continued her research in the historical area.

Conflict tore through Stephanie. Her brain cautioned her that if she went tomorrow she would pay the price later, when she returned home and lacked enough time to complete the things she had to do before the closing. But her heart said not to miss the opportunity; she could always find the time to finish what she needed. Taking the cue from her heart, she told him she would come. After Gage rewarded her with a long kiss, she decided her heart was right.

As she carried dishes to the kitchen, she could see his reflection in the mirror of the china closet as he did a happy dance behind her, combined with a fist-pump identical to his sister Terry's favorite response.

"I saw that," she called out as she went to the dishwasher, not looking back.

"Weren't supposed to," he called back.

***

The next morning, Stephanie decided it was a fine thing to wake beside Gage Dunbar, wrapped in his arms, feeling his chest rise and fall with each steady breath.

A little twinge of concern pricked her. She had long moved past the breakup with Ethan, but she had only known Gage a short time. Was she really ready for another deep relationship? Gage stirred beside her and drew her close, his morning hardness against her hip revealing he was ready for—something.

So what if they had an unscheduled delay getting out of bed that morning? There would be plenty of time to hit the road before the weekend traffic turned Interstate 95 into a parking lot.

They had agreed to leave his truck at her house and take her new midnight blue Ford Escape to Portsmouth. He would drive her back to Alexandria on Wednesday morning and return home that evening.

During the drive south, they talked about childhood memories along the familiar I-95 corridor. Passing the signs advertising King's Dominion theme park, Gage recalled the first year he was tall enough to ride the roller coaster called the "Rebel Yell," determined to be brave but instead throwing up during one of the downward rolls. Stephanie told him about how she became separated from her parents at the park when she was about nine. She'd been missing for more than an hour, in the long line for her third spin on the "Rebel Yell" when her frantic parents finally located her.

"Ever since, they kept such a tight rein on me I wasn't allowed to cross the street alone until I turned twenty-one." When Gage turned his head to look at her with narrowed eyes, she laughed and said, "Just kidding—about the tight rein, not the ride."

A couple of hours later, they had a similar conversation when they passed Busch Gardens on Interstate 64.

"Okay. I might as well admit the 'Battering Ram' got me the year I turned nine," Gage divulged. "There I was, determined to avenge my 'Rebel Yell' debacle from the year before. Macho Boy here sat on the last row, because you feel more of the swing of the ride there, right? Well, on about the fourth swing, when the ride gains its greatest momentum, my row was on top looking down at the rest of the ride and...I barfed."

"Yuck." Stephanie wrinkled her nose, trying to make sympathetic noises. "Hey, I wonder if I was on the 'Battering Ram' the same day. I think I remember you. My mom waited patiently while I rode that thing at least four or five times in a row. She had sunburn on the tops of her feet, with white criss-cross marks left from her sandal straps. On my final ride, I wasn't in the last rows of the gondola, but about third from the top, when on one of the swoops, some kid on the other side heaved all over the people below him. Everyone screamed louder than usual. When I got off, I headed for a few rounds on 'Da Vinci's Cradle.'"

Gage turned and looked at her, shaking his head. "That is so wrong. Here you are, all little and dainty, you should have been scared to death. Or at least had the grace to lie and tell me you spit grits once or twice on those rides. I'm sure I wasn't the only kid in life to do so."

She threw back her head and laughed. Maybe she ought to tell him she made both stories up.

Naw. She chuckled inwardly. *Much more fun this way.*

***

After they arrived in Olde Towne, Gage pulled into a parking lot behind the buildings. Stephanie let out a squeal of delight. "Oh, gosh, what a gorgeous old magnolia. I've never seen one so huge. It must be very old." The graceful tree stood over forty feet, gnarly lower branches spreading nearly thirty feet over cool, dark and barren earth.

Gage glanced toward the tree. "Ah, the secrets that tree holds." He laughed as Stephanie grabbed his hand and tugged him toward it. "It's unusually old. Mom always wanted to have it dated but never did. When we were growing up and the parents dragged us here to visit ancient relatives, it became the perfect place for bored kids to plan adventures."

Stephanie reached for one of the saucer shaped flowers and sniffed appreciatively.

Gage continued, pointing downward. "See how those bottom branches spread out so close to the ground?" She nodded. "Nothing grows underneath, but it made for a natural tree house. It's been a pirate's cave, a clubhouse, a circus tent—you name it. Every year we invented some kind of secret lair. I think we all got our first kiss under that tree sooner or later." His eyes took on a faraway gleam. "Mine was with Maggie Underwood."

"Your first love?" She didn't like the pang of envy jabbing her like a needle stuck into a cushion.

Gage sighed dreamily. "Yeah, she was. An older woman too—ten to my nine." He let out an exaggerated sigh again and Stephanie finally caught on to his act.

"Oh, you stinker!" She lightly tapped his arm and laughed. "You had me going for a minute."

He crinkled his eyebrows mischievously. "Did I detect a touch of the green-eyed monster just then?" he asked.

"No," Stephanie denied as a creeping blush betrayed her words.

Gage threw back his head and roared with laughter. Then he gathered her close in for a long kiss. When they broke it off, he said, "If truth be told, Maggie said I kissed like a frog and she turned her attentions to Mack Reagan down the street."

"Well, she didn't wait long enough. You're a prince to me." She leaned in for another kiss. "And at this rate, we'll never make it to the front door." She gently pushed him an arm's length away.

He tilted his head back again, groaning this time as he guided her to the private stairway leading to the apartment.

"When the renovations started, Terry did not want any inside access from the office to the apartment," he explained as they entered. "She originally intended to live in it, but quickly learned all she did was work later than she wanted to, so she rents it now. It's been empty for about two months and there have been times when she's used it or I did instead of driving home."

"Where do you live?" she asked as they climbed the steps single file.

"I live out in Suffolk now. I'm restoring an old

farmhouse on a couple of acres. I used to get a lot accomplished when I did shift work, but now with the academy schedule I can only use weekends to get things done."

"Hmmm, it seems you've lost this weekend, haven't you?" she teased playfully.

He pulled her close and the long kiss sent fireworks off in her head. When she looked at him with dazzling eyes, he added, "Yeah, but, man, was it ever worth it."

"Oh, geez, knock it off already!" Terry yelled from the bottom of the steps. She started up and waved at Stephanie, who wore a culpable expression as if just caught in something unlawful. "And wipe that guilty look off your face," she commanded as she ambled to the top step and hugged Stephanie. "Welcome back to P-town, as we locals affectionately call this place."

"Thanks," Stephanie hugged back, surprised at how genuinely glad she was to see Terry, who was dressed in casual jeans and a tank top. She still managed to look classy and polished, right down to the elegant sandals on her feet.

"Did you guys eat yet?" Terry asked. "I'm starving. Beth has roast turkey on cottage rye at the bistro today. We could have lunch after we look at this place."

"Sounds good." Gage stepped through the doorway, followed by the two women.

"Oh, this is cute," Stephanie cried. A living area to the left covered the long-portion of an L-shaped room. A glass oval dining table dominated the entry space, and just beyond, an open counter separated the dining area from a small but well situated kitchen with sleek appliances.

"We always have to comply with historical area guidelines for the outside, but nothing says the insides can't be our own design," Terry said as her hand swept over the back of the powder blue suede sectional couch, accented with navy blue throw pillows. An afghan in vivid blue, navy and pale blue designs stretched artfully across the back of the couch. The geometric pattern of the drapes incorporated the same colors at two narrow windows. At each end of the sectional stood an oval glass end table; in front a matching coffee table, all complimenting the dining table in the eating area. A flat-screen television hung over an electric fireplace.

"Everything looks comfortable and so suited to the space," Stephanie remarked. *Sleek and contemporary, just like its owner.*

"Did I ever tell you I inherited this house from a great-aunt?" Before Stephanie could answer, Terry continued. "I turned the downstairs into an office, and designed the apartment, which is where I had planned to live. However, after spending two months pulling all-nighters on cases, I nixed that idea. Until a few months ago, a Navy couple rented it. They just transferred to San Diego. Gage says you may be interested in taking it for a few months?"

"Well, I don't know yet. I like it and I do have to move soon, but I haven't decided what I am going to do."

Terry grimaced. "Oh, dear, I have another young couple hankering for it now and I told them I'd let them know this evening if it was available. I wanted to give you first option after Gage mentioned you were coming down to see it."

"Oh. Oh, I see. I-I-I... Well, gee, I..." Lost for words, Stephanie stammered, biting her lip. Not ready to commit to anything yet, she looked awkwardly at Gage as if for an answer. She had no ties to Alexandria anymore, and could live anywhere she chose. A temporary move here would bring her closer to Gage, but she couldn't decide on such short notice.

Terry waited a moment and then burst into laughter. "Relax. I'm kidding you. Gage told me you might be here for a couple of days to check it out, but I haven't even advertised it yet. You have time."

Stephanie breathed a bit easier. "You looked so serious," she said.

"The look on your face was priceless, but I thoroughly

enjoyed watching the color drain out of Gage's."

"Yeah, well, not amused," he said, punching his sister lightly on the arm.

"Come on, see the rest. There are two bedrooms. The master has a full bath *en suite*." Stephanie entered the airy room, walls painted light pearl gray. A gray and lavender print comforter and shams topped the queen bed, dark gray and deep violet throw cushions scattered around the pillows. On either side of the bed, a glass-topped chrome stand held matching lamps, adding balance to the space. A long mirrored dresser lined one wall, and on the other, a small highboy held a flat screen television. The color scheme carried through into the bath, which boasted a shower stall in one corner, a garden tub in the other.

Next she surveyed the hall bath with two entrance doors. The first gave access to guests from the hallway, and the other gave occupants direct access from the second bedroom. The pleasant scent of gardenias drifted from a fusion bottle on the countertop.

Nearly as big as the master, the spare bedroom, decorated in a black and white color scheme, offered a modern but tranquil setting for guests. Pale gray walls with white trim framed a black futon couch loaded with throw pillows of red, white or black. On the opposite wall a small white chest of drawers stood diagonally in one corner, the other sported a three-cornered desk underneath a set of shelves.

Afternoon sunlight pored through the two windows, reflecting back from double-glass mirrored doors that encased the closet. The doors would be a perfect spot to showcase the ancestry chart for her "French Connection." She could work from the desk, although it did not offer much space to spread out her papers.

Ready to move into, low maintenance, and just big enough to serve as a temporary dwelling, the entire set-up could be a perfect solution to her upcoming housing dilemma—that is, if she chose to stay for a while.

At the end of the hall, a closed door separated the two bedrooms. Terry opened it to reveal a set of narrow steps leading upward.

"This leads to the attic. It's big enough for another room, but it's the one part I haven't had renovated yet. It was probably servants' quarters or something years ago. It has a window seat with a great view of downtown. There may be some old file boxes, and probably some of Mary Jo's things stashed there. I'm afraid we haven't been orderly about storage."

"Can I take a look?" Stephanie asked.

"Sure." Terry shrugged. She flipped on a light switch, illuminating the narrow stairs as she led the way. The roof arched high enough even Gage could stand upright. Two dormer windows with seats allowed light to shine in along the front wall. The rafters were still exposed, but light reflected off the white paint covering the wood paneled walls. One section of the attic was completely empty, but far to the left, items usually found in attics filled the floor space; storage trunks, plastic bins, even an artificial Christmas tree on a stand.

It had an old-world charm to it, though, and Stephanie closed her eyes, imagining an inspiring setting to work on the family tree.

"All of the utilities for this apartment are on a separate system from the office and included in the rent," Terry continued. She surveyed the room. "I should have insulation and a ceiling put in this attic before winter sets in, maybe it will save on the heating bills. Gage, I might need you and Chase's 'wrecking crew' in again." Before he could answer, she turned to Stephanie. "I assume Gage told you there was history in this house?"

"You mean, like there is a ghost here?" She asked, making a sound of "*woo-woo*" while Gage did his ghostly whistle.

"Okay, clowns, okay."

"Terry used to see the ghost when we were little and

visited our great-aunt Ida here," he added in a stage whisper.

With eyes wide, Stephanie turned to look at Terry.

"I did see one, several times" Terry replied haughtily. "From the time I was about seven through eleven, when I played up here, I sometimes saw a little girl about fifteen years old, dressed in colonial clothes. She never spoke, just looked at me with a sad expression. She always carried a book, but never did anything with it. You know, she just cradled in her arms like this." Terry crooked her arms in front of her chest as if holding schoolbooks.

"It doesn't feel spooky in here to me," Stephanie remarked as she gazed around. "I always expected a 'haunted house' to have creaking floors, slamming doors, or cold rooms where your breath whooshes out in vapors."

"Naw, but those kinds of things reportedly happened in the house next door. It's supposed to be haunted there, too. But I've never been afraid in this house. In fact, I feel kind of protected here."

"Yeah, I sense that too," Stephanie agreed. Terry's nonchalant manner discussing ghost sightings amazed her, yet her demeanor was totally credible.

Gage puckered his lips, the ghostly *woo-woo* sound resonating from his throat.

"He's just jealous because he never saw the ghosts," Terry said in a stage whisper.

"Yeah, well, let's get out of *the Twilight Zone* and go eat," Gage demanded, and began to hum the tune from the well-known old TV show.

They all laughed, and then headed back down the steps, Stephanie in the rear. A whisper of warm air brushed her cheek. With a last quick look around the attic, she followed, and shut the door at the end of the steps, her fingertips following the trail of the breeze on her face.

They walked single file, the hallway brightened by sunlight shining through the bedroom windows.

No one noticed the attic door behind them opening

slightly, and then swinging closed again with a subtle click.

CHAPTER ELEVEN

They stepped out onto the small landing and Terry secured the apartment's door behind her, then led the way down the outside stairs. She pointed and said, "This back path crosses over to the middle house and then to the bistro, but I want us to go around to the front door like customers. Business is slow on Sundays and we need lots of foot traffic to attract more patrons."

Stephanie asked, "Is there Internet access in the apartment, Terry? I need to check my email later."

"Yes, it has Internet and Wi-Fi. Don't you have it on your phone, though?"

"No, I hate learning all that new tech stuff. I have a tablet and a laptop, but don't have Internet on my phone."

"What? I'm in shock!" Terry pretended to clutch her chest. "How can you do it? I can't survive without my connections right at my fingertips"

Stephanie shrugged. "I just never needed it, I guess."

"You can't live without it, Stephanie, I'm telling you."

"Maybe I'll check it out when I get this entire house selling-and-moving business behind me. I better not take on anything new right now. I wouldn't even have time to learn how to work it."

"Once you start, you'll wonder how you ever got along without it. Let me know when you're ready, I'll help you out. I am the undisputed queen of electronic connectivity." She reached into a pocket and produced a sleek phone. "I personally never leave home without it."

"Yeah, she's so electronically connected, her brain is fried," Gage said, giving his sister a brotherly push into the bistro. The bell rang merrily overhead as they entered the shop. Terry leaned toward Stephanie and whispered loudly, "You really need to lose this pile of testosterone."

No other customers were in the dining area. Beth came into the dining area and looked disappointed.

"Oh, damn, I thought you were customers coming in."

"And we are...?" Gage asked.

"I meant *full-paying* customers, not discounted ones." She laughed as she walked over to the table.

"Mommy, you said a bad word." The little boy who Stephanie remembered as Tanner followed behind her, his face petulant.

"Thank you, little Mr. Profanity Police, Mommy made a mistake." She patted his head absently and turned to her in-laws, a little exasperated. "We've had zilch customers today. He's bored and I am so glad to see a-d-u-l-t-s."

"What's that spell, Mommy?"

"Lunch," Gage interjected lightly. "Come see me, Tanner Bear, and give your mama a break." He held out his arms and Tanner ran to him, clutching a multitude of tiny plastic figures as he wrapped his arms around his uncle's neck.

Beth dropped in a chair at one of the empty tables. "This is definitely my last open Sunday. Business is great during the week and good on Saturdays, but it's always dead on Sundays. It's nearly one o'clock and no one has been in."

"Well, you said you'd give it a try, and now you know it's not worth it," Terry said. "Beth, you remember Stephanie, don't you?"

"Yes, I do. How are you?"

"I'm fine, Beth, thanks."

"Stephanie came to look at the apartment. She may take it for a short while."

"I think there is a sibling conspiracy going on to get me here," Stephanie interjected.

"Well, watch out for the Dunbar technique. Before you know it, you'll be under their spell."

143

"Are you going to the 'partment, Uncle Gage? Can I go wif you? I want to see Nickel. She's there today."

"Nickel is his imaginary friend," Beth explained in an aside to Stephanie. "Sometimes I wish she were real. He needs a playmate."

"Well, he'll be in pre-school in a few weeks and then you will be crying buckets of tears for him." Terry laughed and turned to the others. "I am starving. I say we flip the 'Closed' sign around now and lock the door."

"Okay by me," Beth said, mustering enough energy to do exactly that.

"Tanner, do you want to know where my friend Stephanie took me yesterday?" Gage asked.

Tanner nodded as he arranged tiny yellow characters in a row. "Sure. Do you like my Minions, lady?" he asked, holding out one of the little cylinder-shaped characters from the *Despicable Me* movies. "Here's Dave—and Phil. Here's Stuart, he only gots one eye." Obligingly, Stephanie uttered appropriate sounds of approval as Tanner thrust a strange yellow character at her, its single eye encased in a goggle. He stuck it close to her face while Beth gently corrected his grammar. "*Has* one eye, sweetie."

"Tanner, this is my friend and her name is Stephanie," Gage said, "And I am sure she will let you tell her all about your Minions—all ten of them—in a minute. But she took me to a really old fire station near where she lives. It has neat old fire engines. They aren't the driving kind, like the ones in my station. Sometimes in real old days, the engines had to be pulled and pushed by people to get to the fire."

"Why?" Tanner split his Minions into two groups, lining them like miniature soldiers facing off in battle, obviously not the least interested in fire engines people pushed or pulled.

"Well, in later times they used horses, and now we have big shiny red engines to do the job. All right then, since I see the Minions are in control, maybe I will take you there one day and show you."

"Okay."

"Wait, we want to hear about it," Terry said.

"Yeah, do tell," Beth chimed in as she headed for the kitchen. "Speak loud; I'm getting sandwiches for everyone." Terry got up to help, waving Stephanie back when she stood as well.

So Gage described every minute detail of the fire station museum, down to the leather helmets—all of which was more than they cared to know.

"At the end, I got to ring the bell." He winked at Stephanie and left out the part about the kiss.

Terry made snoring sounds as she brought the plates to the table and shook her head as if waking abruptly. "Oh, are you done now?" she said sweetly, then called over her shoulder, "Beth, we need to rescue Stephanie from this primate. We'll have a GNO soon."

"What's G-N-O spell, Aunt Terry?" Tanner piped up, rolling the letters off his tongue.

"Trouble," Gage answered firmly, biting into a sandwich.

They lingered over the meal, talking companionably. Beth explained to Stephanie that her husband Connor, the youngest sibling of Terry and Gage, worked as a firefighter in another city and was on duty until eight pm. "Your parents are expecting us all as usual for Labor Day," she reminded her siblings-in-law. "Connor just got his day off approved. It's too bad Mary Jo can't make it."

"I hope she can. As for me, I start this temporary shift work in a few days and haven't seen the schedule, so I don't know," Gage said.

"Mom and Pops throw a killer celebration on Labor Day," Terry turned toward Stephanie and explained. "Then, once summer is officially over, they pack away all the water toys and barbecue equipment and start their travels."

"Reminds me of my parents," Stephanie said fondly. "They were always off on some trip or other."

Terry patted her hand. "I know you miss them. Are you making any progress on your ancestry?"

"I am, a little bit. Someone who, for lack of a better term, is a step-relative contacted me. It's complicated. A something-great grandmother of his became the second wife of one of my great-uncles. Through her, he gained information which matches my mother's—my birth mother's—research. This line of my mother's family is fascinating because it traces so far back to our early history. And it connects me to her as well. I've been able to trace one whole line of her family to French ancestors in the seventeen hundreds."

"Really? *Ooo-la-la!* And here we sit in our own little French bistro." Terry swept her hand around the room.

"What a coincidence. I just love it in here. It reminds me of an outdoor Parisian setting. You know, I might never have found this place if a downpour hadn't driven me here." Stephanie didn't add that the sudden rainfall eventually led her right into Gage's strong embrace. She bumped her knee against Gage's. Understanding, he returned the nudge. "While I am in town this time, I also want to see if I can find any Civil War records of this grandfather Thomas Wyatt. I didn't have the chance to look for detailed records the first time I came here."

"You should talk with our mom. Her maiden name is Wyatt."

"Oh, wow—another interesting coincidence."

"She has lots of old family stuff. I'm sure she would be glad to talk with you and let you see if anything is useful."

"Hey, don't dig too deep," Gage tapped Stephanie's arm. "I don't want to be related to you."

"What a shitty thing to say," Terry said.

"Aunt Terry!" Tanner admonished.

"Sorry, partner. But your uncle deserved that."

"It's not what I meant to say," Gage stammered. "I meant related by blood..."

"Oh, I see, as opposed to related by marriage," Beth

interjected with a twinkle in her eye.

Gage looked disgusted as well as flustered. He jumped to his feet and held his hand to Tanner, saying, "Come on, bear, we'll go talk man talk. Ladies, I'm taking my nephew with me," he said.

"He hasn't had a nap all day," Beth warned.

"He'll be fine. Thanks for lunch, Beth. Steph, I'll be in the 'partment with my little buddy here."

"Are we gonna burp or are we gonna fart, Uncle Gage?" Tanner happily wanted to know as they headed for the door.

"Shh, man," Gage said through his teeth. "You'll get us busted for sure." In a loud stage whisper he added, "Maybe both." He growled and Tanner imitated him.

Terry swiped her hands over her face and shook her head. "Oh, heaven help us," she said.

Beth shrugged. She'd married Gage's brother, after all.

"I'll help here and be right over," Stephanie called as they left through the back door.

"Like hell you will," Beth said, jumping up and going to the refrigerator, coming back with a bottle and popping a cork. "We pretend this champagne is for cooking deserts," she explained with a laugh as Terry retrieved glasses. "It's our emergency stash. We don't have a license to serve alcohol. But this is an excellent accompaniment to the dish you are about to serve us. So tell all."

"Not all," Terry interrupted. "I don't know what spell you cast, but my brother is absolutely smitten with you, Stephanie. I've never seen him like this." She set the glasses down with a thump. "If you did the deed with my brother, I don't want to hear about it." As Stephanie blushed, Terry laughed triumphantly, "So you did do the deed! Well, maybe you better just skim over those parts."

Over the next three rounds of champagne, Stephanie explained how she and Gage seemed to click the first night at the tavern. Terry interrupted her long enough to tell Beth how Stephanie had mistakenly thought she and Gage were married instead of siblings, which sent Beth into peals of laughter.

"May I continue now?" Stephanie assumed a haughty look, but her eyes twinkled as she told the two women how she and Gage bonded over phone and Internet conversation. She kept the private moments private, but did mention when Gage kissed her before he rang the fire bell.

Terry sat straighter and stared as she poured Stephanie another drink. "Oh my God, Beth, look at her. Look at the dopey look on her face. She's in love with my big brother."

"I am not!" Stephanie denied with a burp. "Stop pouring me drinks and *stop* asking me questions. Terry, you know how dree thrinks affect me. I mean, free drinks. I mean, three drinks, dammit!" She shook her head and shoved the glass away.

"Okay, calm down, tiger," Terry said, unable to avoid a grin. "We'll stop. I just wish you could see how you positively glow over my brother." She tamped down a touch of envy as she regarded the face of one happy sister-in-law and that of the woman she suspected would become the next one.

"I better go now before I reveal…" Stephanie shook her head again. "Never mind, I'm not that buzzed. But I do have to go."

"Oh, we *so* have to have a GNO," Beth said, "A full night of estrogen would be fantastic for me."

"My friend Jackie and I had a GNO whenever we could." Stephanie almost sniffled as she realized how much she would miss her old friend. "She's just been assigned to Caracas. I'll miss her."

"Well, we'll try to be good replacements," Terry said. "We can have a big bash when Mary Jo gets back."

Stephanie stood up, pleased when the room did not spin. "I'll go back to the apartment now—excuse me, the 'partment. Thank you ladies; this touch of estrogen was just what I needed."

"I'll come get Tanner in just a minute," Beth said. "Terry and I will finish here."

"All right," Stephanie paused. "Is it okay if I take my glass of champagne with me?"

"Technically, I'll say it's illegal to carry alcoholic beverages in an open container, seeing as we have a lawyer in the family and all." With exaggerated head movements, Beth inclined her head in Terry's direction.

Terry plopped a napkin over the top of the glass.

"Now it's covered. See you in a few."

"Bye. And thanks again." Stephanie shut the door behind her.

Terry waited a second before she turned to Beth. "What do you think?"

"I think they've fallen in love."

"I agree. Why is she resisting it?"

Oblivious to the topic of discussion in the café, Stephanie skipped her way to the apartment stairs, finding the door closed but unlocked. As she waited for her eyes to adjust to the change from sunlight to the interior room, a blue light shimmered in one corner and she figured Gage and Tanner were watching a sci-fi movie on television. Once her eyes became adjusted to the dark, she could make out Gage sprawled on the couch, asleep, and Tanner sitting cross-legged on the floor, his many yellow Minions spread around him. The television was off.

A little girl about the same age sat beside Tanner, holding a doll in her lap. Swathed in the blue light Stephanie first thought glowed from the TV, the translucent figure wore a colonial dress. She smiled at Stephanie and turned to Tanner, who laughed out loud. Stephanie could see the little girl laugh in return, but she could only hear Tanner's little-boy chuckle.

Stephanie took a step forward and the aura dulled. The figure turned her small face toward Stephanie, the sparkling

149

trail of a tear shining down her cheek as she faded further.

Tanner's hands shuffled Minions as he looked at Stephanie once and said reproachfully. "Nickel says it's about time you got here."

The shatter of glass pierced the quiet when the champagne flute slid from Stephanie's fingers and crashed to the floor.

CHAPTER TWELVE

CLOTHISTE
Portsmouth, Virginia, 19 July 1781

Clothiste no longer cried, but neither did she sleep. She glanced over at Nicole snoring softly beside her, doll clutched to her chest. She stroked her child's cheek lovingly.

The door hinges squeaked as Marie Josephé peeked around the heavy wood, rapping lightly.

"Mama?" she said, "I am so glad you are awake." She glided into the room and knelt beside her mother, taking her hand.

Clothiste struggled into a sitting position, and made room for her eldest daughter.

"I have a surprise for you, Mama," Marie Josephé whispered excitedly, her eyes shining. "It is from Grandpapa, actually. Let me fix your hair just a little, Mama, and he will bring it to you."

"What is it?" Clothiste found energy to push upright on the pillow. There were few moments of pleasure in her life these days.

"You will see." Marie Josephé fluffed her fingers through her mother's hair, and straightened her dressing gown. She took a small bottle from her sleeve and sprinkled a drop of perfume on her fingers, which she then tapped on either side of Clothiste's neck.

"Come in, Grandpapa," she called softly and the door opened.

But the man who stepped into the room was not Phillip, but his son Etienne.

"Etienne! My Etienne!" Clothiste threw back the covers, trying to get out of the bed. In three long strides, Etienne reached her side and she threw her arms around him, sobbing.

"Don't cry, ma belle," he said. "I have been so worried for you. I have prayed every day for your recovery."

"These are tears of joy," she whispered, wiping the tears away.

"Please, let us not talk of that right now, you have made me well just by being here. But tell me, how does it happen you are here? Are you safe?"

"I am safe enough for now, my love. My father's business remains a good cover, and I am here to find information for Washington and Rochambeau, to see how this city will affect us as we move south."

Tapping on the door, Theresé peered around it, Phillip close behind. Side by side they crossed the room to Clothiste.

"What did you think of your surprise, Mama?" Theresé asked, kissing her mother on the cheek and then her father.

"It was wonderful. Merci, mon beau-père," she turned to her father-in-law and gestured for him to come further into the room.

"With my darling wife Abby out of our way," he said, sarcastically utilizing the nickname she detested. He stepped closer. *"Etienne is able to stay here tonight. We will hide him and before dawn he will go back to camp, where they await his message."*

"But we may go with you then, may we not?" Clothiste clutched at her husband's arm. *"We need to be with you again. We must, Etienne."*

"I cannot take you tomorrow, ma belle, *it would not be safe. But my father shall make arrangements to get you back to our camp as soon as he can."*

Clothiste bit back another plea. She had been an army wife for too long, entrenched in the fields with her husband too many times to become a nag or burden to him at this point.

"Then we shall make the most of your time with us. Our girls will take care of you, and we will do whatever you need to make your mission a success."

Etienne kissed her and for a moment they clung together. Nicole stirred beside them, and he reached over and stroked her face.

"She seems to have grown quite tall."

Clothiste nodded. *"As have all of our girls. Marie Josephé, can you take Nicole to her bed?"*

"I will do it," Etienne said. *"I have not had the chance to settle my girls to sleep in a long, long time."*

"Would you care for tea, Mama? Papa?" Theresé asked.

Both parents shook their heads, Etienne lifting his wife's hands to *his lips and kissing them.*

"Then we will leave you until the morning." She leaned down and kissed her mother's cheek, followed by Marie Josephé. Etienne moved to gather Nicole in his arms, kissing her cheek as she nuzzled his shoulder.

Clothiste held her arms out to Phillip. "In my whole life, I have never had a surprise more grand or a gift more precious than what you have given me this night."

"It is a gift for me as well as for you, my dear." Phillip kissed her forehead as she hugged him. "I have missed my son and his family, and when this war is over, we shall be together again.

"And it is a pleasure to speak my native tongue with my family." He smiled as he reverted to French.

"It is not my place to speak this way, Phillipe," Clothiste said, trying to choose her words carefully. Her father-in-law winked at her use of the French pronunciation of his birth name. "But you are so different from your wife; I cannot but wonder how it is you are even together?"

He shrugged. "It is just a convenience now. In the beginning, we shared a good friendship. Money has been the basis for her interest ever since. I've always known this and it suited both of us. I am a far wealthier man than I might have been without her cunning sense of business. But now, it serves as the best cover to support the Americans in their fight against Britain. Few, if any, even realize I am a Frenchman, and I can count on my one hand how many know my exact role."

He raised a fisted hand and lifted a finger for each name he mentioned. "General Washington, General Rochambeau, my son, me—and now you. Oh dear, I must move to my other hand." He pretended to concentrate and then added with a twinkle, "I almost forgot my two most important spies—Marie Josephé and Theresé."

"You would be so proud of your daughters," Etienne said as he came back into the room and returned to his wife's side. "I do not know what Marie Josephé puts in the cakes she makes for the soldiers, but they forget she is there and they continue to talk around her. She has learned much." He reached over his wife and picked up Nicole's little doll.

"So this is our little carrier pigeon, n'est-ce pas, *aided by our innocent little Nicole?" He turned the innocuous doll over in his hands and lifted the little dress.*"Pardonnez-moi,mademoiselle," *he said to the doll as he carefully ran his fingers along the hemline of the dress Marie Josephé had created. When he found what he searched for, he pulled a piece of folded paper from beneath the loose stitches and held it between his fingers.*

"We may now know precisely how many ships are poised to block the harbors," he said, touching the paper to his forehead in a salute to his father.

"Business can be discussed later. This time is for you and Clothiste," Phillip said as he kissed his daughter-in-law again and squeezed his son's shoulder before he left the room. "Nothing will change between now and the morning."

STEPHANIE
Portsmouth, Virginia, present day August

The sound of breaking glass caused Gage to bolt to his feet. "What is it?" he shouted and leaped over the coffee table.

Stephanie's heart thumped wildly but she tried to remain calm so she would not frighten Tanner. She held out her hands to keep Gage away from the glass.

"I'm okay—we're okay. The glass slipped out of my hand, that's all." She raised her voice slightly. "Are you all right, Tanner honey?"

"I'm fine. You scared Nickel." He knelt upright on the couch, looked at the empty spot beside him and pushed his lips into a pout before face-planting across the throw pillows.

"I'm sorry. Can you tell her I'm sorry?"

Tanner lifted his head and shook it. "She's all gone." He petulantly flopped over and turned his back to them.

"Can you remember what else she said?"

"I don't want to." The child sulked.

"Tanner, if you could tell me what she wanted, I will be

sure to do it so she can come back."

The child rolled over, arms crossed as he glared at Stephanie. Then he seemed to relax. "She said you have to find her teardrop." He pouted. "Now she's gone again. She won't come back today." Without another sound, he rolled his face into the back of the couch.

Gage shook his head as if to clear it. "What is he talking about?"

Stephanie shook her head, her fingers to her lips. Her eyes never leaving Gage's, she drew him outside to the staircase landing, leaning against the door.

"Are you all right, Steph? You look as if you've seen a ghost."

She put her hands to his chest, shook her head again and rested it on his shoulder.

"Oh my God, Gage. I did see a ghost. I just saw Tanner's 'Nickel.'"

Gage grabbed her by the shoulders and drew her away from him, looking her in the eye. He sniffed. "Have you been drinking?"

"*No.* Well, yes, we had some champagne over at the bistro, but…"

Gravel crunched from the pathway as Terry and Beth walked into view. Beth started to wave but something in the looks on their faces immediately caused her mother's radar to kick in and she scrambled to the stairway.

"Is Tanner all right? What is it?"

"Everything's fine, Beth," Gage reassured her. "He's okay, no worries at all. He's inside."

Still, she pushed past Gage and entered the room, leaping over the shards of glass and spilled champagne to kneel beside her son, now fast asleep on the couch, Minions clutched in both hands. She checked him over, and satisfied he was all right, turned to the others.

Stephanie motioned them all to the dining table. "I dropped the glass and it shattered. Where is the mop and broom, Terry?"

"We'll get it in a minute. Tell us what happened. You look as if you've..."

"I have, Terry. I saw her, the little colonial girl playing with her doll. She sat right beside Tanner, in a kind of wavy blue fog. I could see them both laughing. But I could only hear Tanner, as if they could communicate telepathically or something."

She shook her head, her hand over her mouth. "I have never, ever seen anything like it. He called her 'Nickel.'"

Beth patted her hand. "It must be the champagne, Steph honey. We told you about his imaginary friend Nickel. It must have put some idea in your head."

"Beth, he said Nickel told him it was about time I got here," Stephanie whispered. "And that I have to find her 'teardrop,' whatever that means. But somehow I think her name might really be Nicole. I'm searching for an ancestor with that name."

They all talked at once until Terry's cool, calm voice broke through the chatter.

"Okay, everyone, wait a minute. Before Stephanie came upstairs, did anything unusual happen, Gage?"

"No. Tanner sat on the floor beside me and waged war on his Minions. I hate to admit it, but I dozed off. I could still hear him laughing every now and then, like he always does when he plays."

"Okay. And you didn't see any blue lights, ghostly forms?"

He shrugged. "I never have seen them, even when you used to say you did when we were kids."

"Okay," she repeated, "Can you tell me what happened next?"

"I heard the glass break and it startled me awake. Steph stood at the door, pale as a—sorry for this—ghost. No blue haze or anything, though."

"All right, then. Steph, tell us again exactly what you observed."

"I feel like I am on *Law and Order* or something."

Stephanie half-smiled and decided someday she wanted to observe Terry in action in a real courtroom. "I came up the steps and into the room. The sunlight kind of blinded me and it took a second to adjust to the dark room. I spotted the blue light and at first thought it emanated from the television, but then realized I could see the little girl, perfectly. Well, a ghost-like form, actually. I could see *through* her." She narrowed her eyes as she looked from one to another, daring any one of them to challenge her. She paced as she continued.

"*And* I know what I saw. She looks to be about four or five. She has on a little blue dress with a white apron, and one of those little ruffled caps from the colonial times; you know, similar to one of those dolls from the 'American Girl' series. She has dark brown curls under the cap." She touched her own hair absent-mindedly. "Exactly like my own color."

"All right, so after she appeared, what happened?" Attorney Terry asked.

"Well, I just stood there for a minute, not believing my eyes. As I already mentioned, she and Tanner seemed to be communicating silently with each other. They both laughed, but I could only hear sound from Tanner. Then he said she told him it was about time I got here, and I dropped the glass. She had a tear on her cheek and then she disappeared."

"And you say you have an ancestor named Nicole?" Now Terry paced around the table as Stephanie sat back down.

"Stop it, Terry, we're not in the courtroom," Gage reminded his sister as he patted Stephanie's hand.

"Sorry, sorry. I am just trying to analyze this." Terry stopped and rubbed her forehead as if to force her words out. "Stephanie's description isn't the same as my little childhood ghost exactly. The clothing sounds similar but my ghost was older—about fifteen. But she never spoke to me or laughed; she just looked sad and gripped her book."

"Okay," Gage interrupted. "For the sake of sanity, we are going to presume ghosts exist and come back to haunt houses centuries later. We will even—what's that legal word, Terry? 'Stipulate?' We will even stipulate this house has a ghost."

Terry smiled. "'Stipulate' is the correct word. And I concur."

"So what does it mean? Why show up now? When we remodeled this apartment for you, we stripped out walls to the studs and replaced everything on this floor. Nothing out of the ordinary ever happened to any of us. Of course, it was all guys on the crew."

As three pairs of eyes fixed a steely glare on him, he held his hands palm out. "Just saying."

"Let's go back to Gage's—'stipulation.'" Terry pulled out her cell phone and began to tap. "Let's just agree for the sake of this conversation ghosts exist. This is the first time Steph and Tanner were both together in this house, isn't it? Did it happen because of the presence of both of them at the same time, or because of Tanner, who has already had contact with Nickel? And is she the ghost of Stephanie's Nicole? So what are we dealing with: a ghost, a poltergeist, or a physic phenomenon?"

She studied her phone screen. "Listen to this—and I'm quoting exactly from this website called 'about.com.'" She held up a finger as she read, "It says 'Ghosts are spirits of people that have been caught between this plane of existence and the next. They are intelligent beings, often capable of interacting with the living.

"Skipping ahead, it then says 'They do not interact with the living. Poltergeists are neither ghosts nor hauntings, but are caused by the unconscious mind of a living person, usually under some kind of stress. It is worth noting that a combination of these phenomena can occur in one place. One can affect or even trigger another, which is why a variety of such phenomena can be found in a haunting.'"

"So—which is it?" Gage asked.

"I say we have a ghost," Stephanie interjected with a firm jut of her chin. "Poltergeists throw things, move things around, and create mayhem. Also, I am not under stress, so that leaves ghosts. And I don't get a bad feeling here at all."

She turned to Terry. "When do I sign the lease? And how do I get one of those damn phones?"

CHAPTER THIRTEEN

CLOTHISTE AND NICOLE
Portsmouth, Virginia, 20 July 1781

"Mama, Mama!" Nicole burst into her mother's bedroom. For the first time in weeks, Clothiste was fully dressed, combing her hair in front of the small mirror over the dressing table.

"You are up!" Nicole ran and wrapped her arms around her mother's waist. "Are you better?"

"I am wonderful, my little pumpkin. Is it not a remarkable day today?" She hugged her little daughter and whirled her in a half-circle.

"My baby," Nicole cried and ran to the small table where the doll sat. "I forgot her last night. But, Mama, guess what?" She ran back to her mother, clutching the doll to her chest. "I did not need her to sleep last night. Do you know why?"

"Tell me, ma belle."

"I dreamed of Papa!" Nicole danced around the room. "He came to me in my dream, and Mama, he is just as you said. Tall and handsome! He carried me, and tickled my neck with his kisses."

"Well, then, you had the most wonderful dream ever, did you not?" Clothiste hugged her daughter, relieved Nicole was still young enough to be convinced it was just a dream. They would all be in grave danger if the loyalists discovered their connections to the patriots before he accomplished his mission. Most frightening of all, the enemy would kill Etienne if they caught him.

"I too dreamed of Papa last night. But I have an idea, ma petite. *Let us keep our dreams a secret just between us. We shall not even tell your sisters. We will keep it all a big secret until we are together again with Papa. Can you do that?"*

"Yes, I can, Mama. I will. Now I can have a secret too." She pouted a little. "Sometimes Theresé and Marie Josephé talk to each

other in whispers, and they won't tell me what they are talking about. They say it is a secret and I am just a baby."

"Then we shall have our own secret. And maybe, if we wish very hard, Papa will visit you in your dreams tonight."

She turned back to the mirror. If Etienne could see how strong she was, she would be able to join him very soon. She pinched her cheeks to bring color to her face. Her husband was a man—he did not have to know where her healthy color came from.

STEPHANIE
Portsmouth, Virginia, present day August

True to his promise, over the next two days, Gage guided Stephanie around Olde Towne as they searched old records and visited several old cemeteries for clues about Thomas Wyatt or his brothers during the Civil War. To her disappointment, they revealed no known connections to her tree.

"I will have to tell Kyle Avery about this." She sighed.

"Who is he?"

"Remember, I told you before? I don't know him in person, we've just communicated through emails. He's the one who gave me the information which helped me find my mother's French roots."

"Oh, yeah, I do remember. He's a history professor at a college in Maryland, has taken a year sabbatical to study ancestry research, and may write a book about it, right?"

"Yep, that sums him up."

"Well. Tell him to stay in the state of Maryland," Gage growled as he pulled her in close for a long, slow kiss—right beside the historical marker on the waterfront at Crawford Parkway commemorating when General Benedict Arnold's British troops occupied Portsmouth in 1781.

"I'm only interested in the state you're in," she told him with a return kiss.

"Oh, yeah? Let's go back to the apartment and I can

show you what state I'm in right now."

"Lead the way," she replied.

Gage was very glad the apartment was just a few blocks away.

***

After she returned to Alexandria, she spent the rest of the week finishing the last of her tasks. Being able to move into a fully furnished apartment meant she needed to bring few necessities, other than her personal items, clothes and her genealogy materials. The single article of furniture she wanted to take with her was her mother's jewelry armoire.

Three suitcases of clothing ensured her she could transition from late summer to fall to winter; a fourth held all of her shoes and boots—of course. She filled a covered plastic bin with her personal mementos, including the family keepsakes once stored in the bank safe deposit box. She placed her laptop, printer and office supplies in another bin.

By the end of the week, Stephanie had finished packing and boxing. Although she could well afford to hire movers, Gage had insisted he, his brother Connor, and a couple of their friends would come to her house Saturday and move the items she had earmarked for storage, instead of paying movers. She readily agreed to his suggestion. It meant another chance to see him. She taped the last box, marked it with "donation" and shoved it to the side.

Gage's crew arrived bright and early. Throughout the day, she continually enjoyed the view of five strapping firemen in tight denims hefting boxes over their t-shirt clad shoulders as they emptied her little house from top to bottom. She flirted and laughed as she brought them iced tea or water, and they responded with easy laughs. However, she had the feeling Gage had established their relationship well in advance.

Still, there's something to be said for a man's finely tuned body, she reflected, as her gaze turned to the one that interested her most. *Especially* when it belonged to the man she continued to fall more in love with every minute. The realization struck her with a mix of fear and joy, two emotions she had to reconcile soon.

Nevertheless, she considered it her absolute civic duty to bring another pitcher of tea out to all of them.

***

By the afternoon, everything she owned went into her rented storage facility or to her parent's home for the estate sale. She piled discarded items at the curb for trash pick-up, and deposited useful items at a Goodwill drop-off.

And all it cost Stephanie was a half-dozen thick juicy steaks on the grill with all the trimmings, and a case of beer. The men refused anything else. She made a mental note to send a donation on their behalf to the little Friendship Firehouse Museum in Alexandria.

She stayed busy for the next few days, moving into Jackie's apartment so the cleaning crew could make the houses ready for their respective walk-through by each of the new owners. Jackie was out of town but still held the lease and still used her home as a base when she returned to Washington for her job.

The estate sales on Monday and Tuesday went off without a hitch. Although Stephanie had surveyed the items one last time with a hint of sadness just before the sale started, she realized her new direction in life made it easier to overcome the nostalgia and move on.

Finally, on Thursday, she closed on the sale of her two homes. Her attorney, Winston McGraw, conducted everything by fax from his office, closing on her parent's home in the morning, and then her own in the afternoon. She signed her name on the dotted lines more times than she could count, fiddling with the pen as Winston's efficient secretary juggled the files and faxes. The paperwork piled higher. After three working days, they would send checks by courier.

Thursday evening, Stephanie spent her last night in Jackie's apartment. As she wrote a thank-you note to leave behind along with the key for Jackie, she realized the door firmly closed on another chapter of her life. She pushed back the sense of sadness, knowing both she and Jackie faced bright new futures, albeit a continent apart.

With the long night ahead of her, she broke out her laptop and checked her emails. She had been too busy to work on the research during the week, and debated whether to do any ancestry research now—and decided her answer was no. She had already stowed her research in a small carry-on suitcase with wheels, her charts neatly folded and stacked.

She considered seeking Terry's approval to fasten the charts on a closet mirror but then considered the attic space of the apartment might be better. The height of the rafters allowed room to stand upright. If the lighting was sufficient, she might be able to create a small work area near one of the dormers. The one quick glance she'd made from the dormer window had revealed the view over rooftops would be much more interesting than gazing out a second-floor window into the bellybutton of the building next door.

She typed an email to Kyle Avery, describing her lack of success in Olde Towne. *He's far away in Maryland, so Gage won't mind.* She described the disappointment of spending two entire days searching old church records and scouring headstones in old cemeteries without finding a trace of her ancestor Thomas Wyatt or his brothers Frank and Arthur.

She continued the letter with the following:

Though I know it is typical in family research, it was disheartening not to find any records or facts here. I had so hoped to find something in this place.

However, I learned my friend Gage's mother is a Wyatt. I haven't met her yet, and I look forward to talking to her and seeing if it leads anywhere.

In the meantime, I am making a temporary move to Portsmouth. I don't know why, but I feel there is something I have not found yet. Perhaps the connection I will find is not to Thomas Wyatt, but to his wife Emily Longchamps.

If I have any luck, I will keep you posted.
Regards,
Stephanie

Almost immediately, she received a response.

Hi, Stephanie,

Too bad it was a bust re: Thomas Wyatt. I worked on something else that gave me an idea about my book. I'll focus on Frank Wyatt, not for his genealogical or familial value, but to use him as a foundation for my work. I have some family information through my step-great grandfather's side. I'm not a direct relation, but I can explain what leads I've followed, where I found records, and what information lead to what new clue. I don't know, too many ideas crammed inside my head at the moment.

Sorry—here I am babbling and boring you to death. Anyway, I have never been to Portsmouth, so I plan on heading down there for a few days at the end of the month, and then hit the beaches for Labor Day weekend.

If you are going to be around, let me know, we can meet for coffee or something.

The wandering researcher,
Kyle

She wrote back:

I hope to move down before the holiday weekend to avoid the traffic. Maybe we can meet and I can introduce you to Gage. I will let him know you are tracking a Wyatt, and maybe there will be a chance to meet his mother. Maybe you will find something I missed.

There are several cute little B and Bs downtown, and a couple of hotels in the Olde Towne area. Send me your phone number and we will call you to meet up.

Take care,
Stephanie

She added the last paragraph with "we" as an afterthought—just to be sure she didn't send mixed signals. She hit "send" and got his short answer a few minutes later.

He acknowledged the plan and he included his phone number.

As she copied it down, she had a feeling something very dramatic was in the wind.

***

It was September 1st and wind was certainly the topic under discussion on the radio Friday morning as Stephanie backed her car out of Jackie's parking lot. She headed straight for the interstate without looking back at her old hometown, listening to the weather report as she inched her way onto the entrance ramp.

It may be the last nice weekend for a while, she reflected, as the announcer reported a depression forming in the Caribbean with such strong winds it quickly could reach the level of a tropical storm. However, the newscasters expected the immediate weather to remain hot and clear through the middle of the next week. Even if the storm turned into a full hurricane in the next few days, it was still a long way from landfall.

She had calculated a six a.m. departure would be early enough to beat the traffic as travelers headed toward the beaches for the last weekend of the summer season, but quickly realized everyone else on the highway apparently had the same idea. By the time she reached the area approaching the exit for Occoquan, traffic already stretched bumper-to-bumper and she continued to hit massive backups in the usual pockets along the I-95 corridor.

Gage called her several times to check her progress, amazed when she reported during one conversation she had only moved three meager miles in the last hour.

"At that rate, I hope you make it here by Monday," he said and laughed.

"At least the weather is currently good. The news says a storm may be coming."

"Yeah, possibly. We'll worry about it when the time comes. I'll call you again soon."

Snail-paced progress put her at the exit to Busch Gardens when he called again.

"I moved a little further," she said, then laughed. "I'm fondly remembering your escapade on the 'Battering Ram' as I inch along past the park."

"I can see telling you that was a mistake." He grimaced. "Keep an ear on the traffic channel, you may be better off to go the James River Bridge when you get this way."

"Okay, I'll check. Thanks, Gage. See you soon."

"Be safe. Hurry, but be safe."

Feeling as if traffic moved on a slow conveyor belt, Stephanie glared as impatient drivers swerved in and out of marked lanes, trying to get one car length further on the road. She resisted the urge to follow the same reckless path and fiddled with the radio buttons on her steering column until she found a pop channel. The Beach Boys' hit song "I Get Around" blasted from the airwaves and she chuckled at the irony. Inexplicably the opening credits of the movie *Look Who's Talking* popped into her head. She envisioned the cars in front of her turning into sperm shapes, all competing for the same target. Bursting into laughter, she barely braked in time to avoid ramming a car that had stopped short in front of her.

She shook her head and deliberately straightened her posture to concentrate on driving. By the time she finally drove into the parking space behind the apartment, she was frustrated and exhausted. A quick glance at her watch confirmed it had taken nearly twice as long as usual. Gage's phone signaled busy when she called so she tried Terry's and got voice mail. She left a message she had arrived safely and would head to the bistro for a quick lunch.

She hefted the boxes with the computer equipment upstairs first, saving the other cartons until the temperature cooled down. It was just too hot. Absent-mindedly, she left her cell phone on the table as she went back downstairs.

She followed the narrow walkway behind the unfinished middle house and arrived at the back door of the bistro. *How convenient to have a café two doors away.* A pleasant tingle settled over her as she turned the knob: she belonged here now.

Until she pushed the door open and came face to face with the glaring Hannah.

"Oh, it's you," the old woman croaked as she brushed past Stephanie and stepped out onto the porch to light a cigarette. Today she wore baggy khakis and a bright green tee shirt emblazoned with the words "The coffee is bitter—and so am I." Lemon-yellow sandals covered her feet.

"Um-uh, hello, Miss Hannah."

"Just Hannah will do." She studied Stephanie with narrowed eyes and nodded once. "So you're the one that caged the Gage."

"I'm sorry?"

"You just take care you don't break that boy's heart, missy, and we will get along just fine." Hannah turned her back to Stephanie and puffed on her cigarette.

Crotchety old lady. Half amused at Hannah's attempt to accept her—welcoming was certainly too strong of a word, Stephanie's next thought forced her to suppress a smile. *Can the word "curmudgeon" apply to females? If so, Hannah is a shoe-in.*

The back entrance led through the kitchen and Stephanie strolled around the glass display case, where Beth carried empty plates to the sink.

"Welcome back, Steph," she called as they passed. "Seen any ghosts lately?"

"Not today."

"That's good."

Stephanie sat at a table by the window, her back to a tourist who was wrestling with the folds of a map. His back to her, he was so engrossed he didn't notice when she bumped his chair and offered an apology.

Beth brought out a pitcher of tea in one hand and a glass of ice in the other, stopping at the tourist's table to fill his glass before she placed the one with ice in front of Stephanie and poured. "You look hot, Steph. When did you get in?"

"Just now. Traffic was a bitch all the way down ninety-five. And the heat just got to me as I took some things to the apartment, so I'm taking a break."

"It's going to be a scorcher all weekend. How about our cold salad plate today?"

"Sounds perfect. What do you think about the predictions for the storm?"

"It's too soon to tell, but we'll prepare when the time comes. We always do."

Beth returned shortly with tuna salad mounded on crisp lettuce, sliced tomatoes, boiled eggs, and pickles decorating the sides.

"Did you forget your phone, Stephanie? Gage just called to see if you were here, said he's been trying to reach you."

"I guess I did." Stephanie patted her empty pockets.

"He said he'll drop by in a little while, but he wasn't sure when. He'll check here first before he goes to the apartment."

"Thanks for the message. Where is Tanner today?

169

"He's home. Connor has a firefighter's 'Kelly Day' so they are off doing father-son things."

Beth stopped at the tourists' tables to check with the other patrons before she returned to the kitchen.

A chair grated on the floor as the tourist rose from the seat behind Stephanie. She had a fork halfway to her mouth when he surprised her by stopping at her table.

"Are you Stephanie Kincaid?" he asked politely.

"I am," she replied, frowning for recognition and finding none. She stared into a pair of dark brown eyes with laugh lines at the corners. He was lanky, towering well over six feet. A shock of unruly brown hair tumbled across his forehead, as if he might have forgotten to comb it.

"I'm Kyle, Kyle Avery. We've been exchanging emails."

Her eyes widened and she stood up, shaking his hand enthusiastically. "Hello there. I was going to call you later. I just got here after a horrible drive on the interstate."

"I overheard just now and when the waitress called you by name and then mentioned Gage, I figured it had to be you. I don't mean to intrude."

"No, not at all. How nice to finally meet you in person. How did you happen to find this place?"

He laughed. "I don't know exactly. I was just following along the historical markers and realized the heat was becoming overwhelming. Next thing I knew, I was standing in front of this place."

"What a coincidence. The first time I visited Olde Towne, a sudden rain hit and forced me inside. I may never have found it otherwise. Will you join me?"

"Sure, but I don't want to take too much of your time. I've spent two days trying to find something about Thomas or Arthur Wyatt here in Portsmouth with no luck, but I think I have solved the mystery of why we can't find Thomas Wyatt here during the Civil War."

"Really?"

"Well, I haven't had time to check for sure, but I think the Portsmouth Army unit he served in was in New

Hampshire, not Virginia."

"We're looking in the wrong Portsmouth?"

"So it seems. That's why we can't find anything online. It didn't occur to me before now. As soon as I get back to my hotel, I will check to see if there are any New Hampshire records for him."

Stephanie's shoulders drooped. "Then I'm wasting my time here."

"No, you aren't. There may be a clue if I can find some property records for Celestine Wyatt, who was a cousin to your great-something Grandmother Emily. It seems she did own some property here at one time." He reached over to his table for a photocopy of a map.

"This is an old map depicting Portsmouth in the eighteen-eighties. Here's the area where this café is now, and it seems to be in the general vicinity of the old house—or houses—which Celestine Longchamps owned around the Civil War time," he circled the grids with his finger, exuding a boyish charm as he enthusiastically gestured with his other hand.

"Oh, my, this is exciting. If Celestine and Emily were Longchamps cousins, Celestine may lead to more information on that side of the family tree, which might add clues to mine."

"I am pretty sure there are a few old papers in the things I have," he continued, "on the laptop and at home, unfortunately. You see, I've been concentrating on the Wyatt side, not on their wives. It can get awfully confusing to try to research too many branches at one time."

"How well I know." Stephanie laughed, craning her neck to try to read the tiny print on the map. Kyle pulled a small magnifier about the size of a credit card from his pocket.

"Does this help?" he asked, his head bent near hers as she peered through it.

"It does. So you are thinking maybe this café is part of the old family site?" she asked, pointing to a spot on the map.

"At least one of these buildings could be—at least I'm pretty sure."

Gage and Terry came in through the front door; Stephanie too absorbed in the map to hear the bell announce their entry.

Gage saw though, and a blow punched his gut at seeing Stephanie sitting so close to a man he did not know. The guy was dressed like a professor or something, but in a young and handsome Harrison Ford/Indiana Jones way.

And he didn't care for it—or the feeling in his gut—one damn bit.

CHAPTER FOURTEEN

When Stephanie finally looked up, she inwardly drooled as she gazed at Gage in his uniform, entering with his sister close behind. She jumped to her feet and reached for him, delight dancing across her face. Gage was immediately ashamed of his temporary envy as she threw her arms around him and planted a kiss on him.

"Gage! I'm so happy to see you—and you, Terry." She hugged Terry, who glanced at the Indie look-alike with mild curiosity as Stephanie pushed the siblings to the table.

"Guys, this is Kyle Avery, who gave me so much information for my family tree. Kyle, this is Gage Dunbar and his sister Terry. Their mom was a Wyatt before marriage, by the way," she finished, breathlessly. She did not let go of Gage's hand as she gave him another kiss and sat back down.

Gage was relieved to find the green-eyed monster retreated rapidly, but glared through narrowed eyes. *I'll just keep my eyes on this Dr. Jones look-alike for a while.*

Kyle stood and shook hands with the two Dunbar siblings, explaining that this was his first visit to Portsmouth.

"Terry is part-owner of this bistro, Kyle. We're studying old maps of this property." Stephanie explained, repeating what she had just learned as Kyle pushed the map over to Gage and pointed.

Terry stood, her lips pursed, then sat down. She was used to men falling at her feet, not one who just shook her hand and sat back down to talk to another woman. She didn't care for this at all, studying her brother and this stranger as they inclined their heads on either side of

Stephanie's and babbled on about some old property once owned by some old dead relative. On and on and on...

She was annoyed—really annoyed.

But why? Was it because this scholarly looking guy—so definitely not her type, by the way—didn't cast a second look in her direction? Or could she be jealous, something she rarely experienced? She adored Stephanie, so obviously in love with Gage no other man even came into her radar.

Terry debated whether she was simply miffed that this stranger was not fawning over her in the style to which she had become accustomed, or had—God forbid—the green-eyed monster just bit her right in the ass?

Stephanie abruptly interrupted the discussion of old houses and long-dead relatives.

"Geez, Gage, Terry, I'm so sorry. You guys are here for lunch and here we are going on and on." She started folding the map and kissed Gage again.

"I apologize, too." Kyle stood to gather his papers. "I can get carried away."

"No need to leave, I am sure there's a lot of this tree stuff you can discuss." Gage motioned to the chair Kyle had vacated. "I can't stay anyway. I'm taking an order back to the station house with me. We have a planning meeting to discuss this upcoming storm. Steph, I can take your suitcases to the apartment for you before I go."

"No, thanks, I'll get them later. It's too hot. Kyle, you are welcome to stay. Maybe we can look over more records," Stephanie said. "Terry is an attorney, and she may know how to find legal records if you need them."

Kyle turned and acknowledged Terry with a nod. "I'd appreciate that."

"Terry, Kyle is studying genealogy practices and may write a book to help people find their roots. He is a—what did we determine—distant step-cousin?"

She turned to him and he nodded. "A grandmother of his was the second wife of a great-great uncle of mine. Kyle discovered a lot of family information through his grandmother's records, and when he noticed gaps in my online tree, he provided records I wouldn't have found otherwise."

"Our mother's maiden name was Wyatt," Terry said, nodding toward Gage. "I don't recall an Arthur Wyatt, though. Do you, Gage?"

"Not offhand, but Mom would. She had some stuff in an old trunk at one time. I remember she had some old Confederate money I took to school once for 'Show-and-Tell.' It's not worth much, more historical value than anything."

"I know Mom's great-grandmother lived into her nineties, and *her* great-grandmother was close to one hundred. Our family history passed down from those two ladies, so a lot of things are more anecdotal than factual," Terry, ever the lawyer, spoke.

"Family stories are often handed down from generation to generation by word of mouth, but they frequently provide anecdotal information that leads the researcher to factual records or information," Kyle said.

"My birth mother once talked to an elderly cousin of hers many years ago," Stephanie interjected. "She remembered stories told by her own grandmother, dating back to the revolution. It was enough to lead me here. I didn't find my past, but I did find my present." She turned to Gage and reached for his hand.

Gage gave her hand a gentle squeeze as he smiled at her. *And your future, Miss Stephanie. You just don't realize it yet.*

"I can call our mom and ask her." Terry offered and smiled inwardly as Kyle finally looked her way.

"I don't mean to impose. It may be there is no connection to the Wyatts we're seeking," Kyle said.

"She won't mind looking. She used to love that stuff, but her three children had no interest. Bitterly disappointed with us, she put it all away."

Kyle smiled. "I didn't pay attention to my family history when I was a kid either."

As Terry punched the keys of her phone, she asked Stephanie, "Did you get a Smartphone yet?"

"Working on it," Stephanie fibbed. She hadn't done a thing yet.

"Mmmm hmmm," Terry murmured skeptically. She brightened as her mother answered.

"Hey, Mom. How are you...have you got a minute? I'm here with Gage and Stephanie, and Kyle, who's another ancestry researcher. He's researching Wyatts from the Civil War era. Do we have any Wyatt relatives named Thomas or Arthur?" Terry shook her head and continued talking into the phone. "Just Grandpa Peter?...His dad?...hold on," Terry turned the phone from her mouth and said, "She is aware of four generations of male Wyatts before she was born; her father Peter Junior, her grandfather Peter Senior, and a Frank or two further up the line."

"Frank?" both Stephanie and Kyle said at the same time. Terry nodded, and made a quick decision. "Mom, are you free tomorrow? Could I bring these two ancestry geeks out to talk to you?" She glanced around the table. "About ten?" Kyle held his hands palm up in uncertainty, but Stephanie nodded affirmatively. "Thanks, mom," Terry said into the phone. "See you at ten. Love you...yes, I know you love me, the best of all your children."

She tapped the disconnect key and smirked at Gage. The she turned to Stephanie and Kyle. "Okay, you two sleuths, let's meet here at nine-thirty and we'll see if you find any information."

"I'll drive," Gage offered.

"That's gracious of you, but I don't want to impose," Kyle repeated.

"No problem at all. My mom will love it. The worst that will come out of it is you don't find anything you are looking for, but at least you looked."

"But I feel as if I'm imposing," Kyle started to say.

Stephanie patted his shoulder. "There's no saying 'no' to this woman, believe me," she laughed. "Just say 'yes.'

Besides, I want to go too."

"This heat has kicked my butt," Kyle admitted as he stood up. "I think I'll go back to the hotel and chill out—literally."

They shook hands, confirmed the nine o'clock meeting and each went their way.

Stephanie had observed Terry's interested study of the professor as he hunched over his maps. Ideas for matchmaking started taking root as she entered her apartment.

***

As she lugged her second suitcase upstairs, Stephanie regretted turning down Gage's earlier offer.

On her third trip, as she maneuvered a wide plastic box through the door, a ping signaled a text message arriving on her phone. She placed the carton on the counter, and searched for her cell around the boxes she had earlier placed on the kitchen table.

"I know I left it here on the table." Frowning, she grabbed her purse and felt inside, to no avail. She stood with her hands on her hips, fingers tapping.

"Hmmph."

After five minutes of searching, she still had not located her phone. She retraced her steps and poked around the boxes on the table again. Tapping her fingers on her chin, she stood back and tried to picture where she may have left it.

Reluctantly she left the apartment, running into an invisible wall of summer heat as she trotted down the steps. A quick rummage through her car confirmed the phone had not fallen to the floor. She dashed to the back of the café and called to Beth, who was scrubbing a pot in the sink.

"Beth, I can't find my phone. Can you give me time to

177

get back up to the apartment and call me so I can track it down?"

"Sure. I don't have you number." She reached into her back pocket and tossed the phone to Stephanie. "Punch your number in for me, and I will hit redial."

"Thanks. I thought it was on the table but it wasn't anywhere. Thanks a bunch. Give me a few minutes, though. It's so hot out there, I'm not moving very fast."

Beth laughed and waved a dish towel.

Stephanie trudged up the stairs and into the apartment to wait for the call.

One minute later, her phone rang and hummed with vibration.

She turned toward the sound and straightened her shoulders in confusion.

The cellular rattled against the side of a box—on the table where she had checked and rechecked.

"Okay," she said aloud. "This was not here five minutes ago. What's going on here?"

She was met with silence. After waiting a few seconds she flipped to the message on her phone.

Gage's message: Alarm just went off so we're going out. Will call later.

"Be safe," she said out loud as she typed the words and hit send. Since he would be on duty until eight in the morning, she could use the evening to settle into the apartment. She made one more trip to her car.

Dripping with perspiration as she carried her ancestry container upstairs, she dropped it at the door and headed for the refrigerator. The jewelry box was still on its side in the Ford, but she had locked the doors. She needed a break and poured a glass of ice water, turned the vents of the air conditioner directly toward her and sprawled on the couch for a moment—which turned into an hour-long nap.

Sudden laughter woke Stephanie, soft and distant. Disoriented at first, she wondered if she had left the television on, but the screen was dark. She bolted upright and looked around, straining her ears. The low hum of the air conditioner broke the silence now.

"I know I am not hearing things," she said indignantly. She stood and looked out the windows facing front, then out the back. Both street and parking lot sides were empty. She opened the door, and looked on the landing and down the steps. Nothing.

She searched room by room, finding each one empty. Then she stood in front of the doorway with the narrow stairs leading to the attic.

She rubbed her hand nervously on her jeans, gingerly flexed her fingers then touched the doorknob, not sure what she anticipated would happen. The handle turned and the door opened easily; her gazed swept along every tread to the top. Sunlight streamed through the dormer windows, casting late-afternoon shadows along the rafters. Her fingers tapped the toggle of the light switch and she flipped it on, illuminating her path as she climbed upward.

The room remained eerily silent. She looked around cautiously, her thumping heartbeat resounding in her ears. Nothing was out of place in the well-lit room.

She sat on the top step for a moment.

"Are you here, Nicole?" she said softly. Air brushed past her cheek.

"Are you trying to tell me something?" The air moved again. But she heard no other sound, saw no otherworldly being. She waited ten minutes longer, but nothing else happened.

The phone ringing in her pocket startled her so much she jumped six inches off the step.

"Geez." she blew out her breath, her hand over her heart as she glanced at the screen where Gage's number appeared. With one last look around at the normal attic space, she hit the answer button and said, "Hey, Gage," as she went downstairs.

As she reached the bottom step, she decided this was not the time to tell him what had just happened—at least not yet. She turned off the light and shut the door behind her.

She glanced over her shoulder as she walked down the narrow hall toward the kitchen. Her eye caught a sparkle of light blinking through the keyhole.

"Hold on, Gage," she said, tiptoeing toward the attic door. She glanced at the keyhole, bent and peered, seeing nothing but darkness through it. When she snatched the door open, the stairwell was dark. Only a slim shaft of dim light shined from the small dormer windows at the top.

"Is everything okay?" Gage asked.

"Yeah, all's well. I thought I left the attic lights on."

She turned back toward the kitchen.

This time, she did not see the tiny light shine before it faded away.

***

After breakfast Saturday morning, Stephanie and Gage stood at the kitchen counter. In between nuzzles and kisses, they watched the weather forecast on the small overhead television. Weathermen still predicted Labor Day would be hot and humid and a perfect way to end the last weekend of the summer season.

Gage reduced the volume and said, "We'll hear about this for days. Usually by now a few storms have already reached hurricane status somewhere. This is probably going to become the first named storm of the season, and everyone is abuzz."

On the screen, with the dramatic flair hurricanes often inspired in broadcasters, two weathercasters gestured on a wall map as they discussed how the tropical storm would continue to gain strength in the warm waters of the Caribbean. In sharp contrast to the indoor activity, cameras panned to show beaches already filling with early beachgoers determined to enjoy their last weekend, seemingly oblivious to the impending weather.

The newscast switched to a reporter standing in front of a huge map of satellite images. As she moved her arms to show a mass where winds were strengthening out in the ocean, cameras zoomed out to a map showing the ominous swirl located well away from land.

Stephanie turned from the television screen and pressed her hand to her stomach, feeling as if a Category 5 hurricane already churned within her. In a few short hours she would formally meet Gage's parents' for the first time. She had only seen them once, from the sidelines, that rainy day when they had come into *Pâtisseries a la Carte*.

As if reading her mind, Gage slipped his arm around her and drew her close.

"Stop worrying. They'll love you."

"I'm not worrying, but I am so nervous," she declared.

"Um—I think that's the same thing, babe," he replied, kissing her nose.

She laughed and shook her head.

"I remember seeing them in the bistro with Tanner, the day they left for Disney World. Terry moved like a constant whirlwind and your mom was absolutely unfazed at the commotion. So much bustle and activity overwhelmed me. The two of them were dressed so elegantly, and I felt like Little Miss Muffet sitting there all frumpy."

"Hey, for all you know, Miss Muffet might have been very elegant eating her curds and whey." He kissed her nose again and said, "How can they not love you? I already do."

They stood still for a moment, looking at each other.

"No, that wasn't what I wanted to say. I didn't mean to say it that way." When her face took on a glint of hurt, he panicked. *Why does it always come out wrong?* "I mean, I do mean it. I wanted to tell you. It's just that I wanted to say it for the first time in the right way." He ran one hand through his hair in frustration and then reached for her, his hand sliding to the back of her neck as he leaned in for one of her kisses that were guaranteed to curl his toes. When he was through, he looked her in the eyes and said, "I love you, Stephanie. I have from the moment I first saw your face. That's how I wanted to say it to you."

She drew her hands to his face, her eyes never leaving his as her fingers lightly skimmed down his neck to his shoulders.

"This is all happening so fast, Gage. I'm—I'm…"

He touched his finger to her lips. "Don't say it if you're not ready."

She touched her forehead to his, and he wrapped his arms around her.

"We have some time before we have to leave." He nuzzled her neck hopefully.

"No way," she said emphatically, pushing away with a laugh. "I'm about to meet your parents."

"Like they didn't have sex? They probably still do."

"Stop." She covered her ears and shut her eyes, laughing. "I don't want to have that image in my head when I meet them."

"Yeah, me either."

"Are you sure you don't need to sleep after working twenty-four hours?" she asked.

"Naw, we just had the one call yesterday, so we had a normal night's sleep—as normal as it can be with a dozen guys in a dorm room. Come on. Let's find out if Doctor Jones is waiting." He winced.

"Who?"

"Um, it's my nickname for Kyle. He kinda looks like Harrison Ford in 'Indiana Jones,' doesn't he?"

She laughed. "Oh? That was my impression of him, too. Scholarly without looking nerdy. Disheveled but cute. All that's missing is a bow tie. Does anyone even wear them anymore?"

"I hope not." He made a face as he laughed.

They walked toward the back door of the bistro. Hannah had just stepped onto the stoop for a cigarette. She had a hug for Gage and a narrowed-eye look for Stephanie.

"Morning, Hannah." He paused. "Have you by any chance baked any of those little éclairs you and Mary Jo used to make sometimes?"

"Not today, but I might be inclined to bring some to the cookout Monday," she rasped out as she stuck a cigarette between her lips.

"That would be great. And those things are gonna kill you," he said, taking the cigarette from her gnarled fingers and squashing it in an ashtray filled with sand as he kissed the top of her head.

"Yeah?" was all she said. As they went into the kitchen, they could hear the click of her lighter as she lit another one.

"Well, she does have one less in her pack now," Stephanie whispered.

"I heard that," Hannah snarled.

Kyle had just finished breakfast at one of the tables when Gage and Stephanie entered. He waved at them to join him. A harried Beth was in the process of clearing two other tables, Tanner on her heels as he whined about how bored he was.

"Honey, you are stuck here until I close, so you might as well go play at your table."

"Uncle Gage!" Tanner ran over and flung himself at Gage. "Hi, Step-anie."

"Hi, Tanner," the adults answered in unison as they sat with Kyle.

"Can I come to the 'partment wif you guys?"

"No, you can't, mister," his mother answered first, her tone firm. "Now go to your table and sit quietly please."

"Aw, gee," he whimpered as he stomped to a table in the corner, filled with coloring books, crayons, yellow Minions and other assorted toy figures.

"My baby-sitter pooped out and Connor is working his second job," Beth explained in exasperated greeting.

Gage draped an arm over Stephanie's shoulder and explained, "Most firefighters moonlight at second jobs on their off days, and Connor and I both do home improvement projects on the side for our friend, Chase Hallmark. In one way or another, we've all had some hand in the renovations of these buildings."

"Have you seen Terry yet?" Beth asked over her shoulder as she disappeared into the kitchen.

The door opened, the bell signaling Terry's arrival. Stephanie, already wilted from walking a couple of hundred feet in the heat, had to admire the cool elegance Terry exuded. She wore a sleeveless black blouse, crisp white shorts cinched by a thin gold belt which matched the trim on her white sandals at the end of long tanned legs, and tying the whole ensemble together were gold hoops at her ears.

Ignoring his mother's warning to sit still, Tanner ran to Terry and wrapped his arms around her.

"Aunt Terry, I'm bored. Where you going? Can I go wif you?"

"Hey, Tanner Bear, we're going to see Nana and Grampie, so I guess you can come if your mama says it is okay." Tanner's feet pounded the floor as he ran back to ask his harried mother, and Terry turned to the three sitting at the table.

"Good morning, all." She smiled brightly and sat down as each greeted her in return.

"I looked further at the information I have on Frank Wyatt, Stephanie," Kyle said. "There are records for both Portsmouth, Virginia and Portsmouth, New Hampshire. Let's see what information we get from the Wyatts here."

He looked toward Gage and Terry. "How would your mom feel if I were to ask her if I could use your family's research as a basis for my genealogy how-to book?"

"Ask her. She'll let you know," Gage said with a casual

shrug. "So, how are we doing this travel? Stephanie and I are coming back here, so we need to take my car. Kyle, you can ride with us and talk ancestry junk with Stephanie."

Kyle gathered a laptop and a backpack from the floor, following behind Gage and Stephanie.

Terry started to speak when Tanner ran to her. "Mom says I can, I can! Can I ride in your 'vertible wif you? Wif the top down?"

"Sure." She ruffled his hair, a slight frown forming between her eyes. "Let's go get your car seat." She sighed. Terry studied Kyle's departing back behind her sunglasses. *What a nerd. For sure, so not my type.*

She grabbed her purse and her nephew's hand. The little boy was not exactly whom she had planned to maneuver into riding in the convertible with her.

CHAPTER FIFTEEN

During the drive, Gage explained that his parents sold their Portsmouth home a few years earlier and bought a dilapidated old farmhouse on the Nansemond River.

"My best friend Chase Hallmark, the one I mentioned earlier? He had a fledgling construction company. They entrusted him with the restoration, and his once struggling business now flourishes. My parents lived in their camper during the construction of a huge garage-slash-workshop with an upstairs apartment." Gage laughed. "It's the closest I ever saw them come to arguing on a daily basis, whether it was about which materials to use on a project or who left the empty coffee pot plugged in. Moving into the apartment gave them some semblance of normalcy while they continued the restoration." He laughed as he remembered.

"Terry stays in the garage apartment for now. My own house, which I am restoring, is about five miles from them."

"It's nice of your mom to talk to us." Kyle leaned forward from the back seat. "I brought along my recorder in case she will agree to a recorded interview. Even if it turns out this doesn't lead to anything in the Wyatt trees we are looking at, it gives me material for my book."

Stephanie lifted a small three-ring binder. "I have a small version of my Thomas Wyatt-Emily Long family tree in here, as well as information I've gathered, including the notes from my mother Jessica's diary." She realized it was the first time she did not use the term "birth mother" when she talked of her to Gage.

"I brought along a scanner, too, a small portable one."

He laughed a bit sheepishly. "Not to mention laptop and cameras. If she allows us to copy any pertinent documents, I can scan them right then and there, and then put them on a memory stick for you later, Stephanie."

"Thanks, Kyle, I'd appreciate it. I'm excited about this part, but…" she bit her lip.

Gage laughed. "Stephanie is meeting my parents for the first time today, so she's nervous." He squeezed her hand reassuringly. "And there's nothing to worry about."

"I wish you'd tell my stomach that," Stephanie said as she placed her hand under her ribcage.

They came to a stop light and Terry's little red Maserati convertible pulled beside them. Tanner sat in his car seat in the back, sporting yellow Spongebob sunglasses over his eyes and a blue baseball cap turned backwards. He was waving and shouting, "Wanna race, Uncle Gage?" as Terry looked them over, eyes slanting to Kyle as if to say, "You could have been in these wheels, dude."

"Naw, we'll obey the law," Gage called back. The light changed and Terry zipped ahead of them as the road merged into one lane. Every now and then, she would raise her right hand high and wave back at them. They laughed when Tanner imitated her every move, his tiny hand the only visible part proving he was even in the vehicle.

Kyle whistled through his teeth. "That is some car."

"She bought it used and it still cost three times what my truck cost. She inherited the bulk of our great-aunt's estate, which made her a wealthy young woman. Plus, she handled a very successful litigation case a while back," Gage said simply, no trace of envy in his voice. "It enabled her to start her own small firm and make a down payment on that baby."

"*Wow!* Interesting." Kyle looked back at the car one more time, then turned to Stephanie. "So, Stephanie, tell me what information you have about Emily Long."

***

Gage followed the spiffy little convertible after it turned off the city street to a narrow side road.

Along the roadside, fields of cotton stretched to a forest. A cornfield with yellowed stalks followed, then several rows of symmetrically-planted evergreens.

The road curved. Stephanie's jaw dropped when the house came into view and she realized they were on a private road leading to the property. Among scattered trees nestled a large two-story brick house, with several dormer windows crowning the roof. Tall chimneys stood at either end. A covered wrap-around porch lined with rockers invited visitors; hanging ferns between large white columns graced the entrance.

Beads of sweat gathered on Stephanie's forehead. She turned to Gage as she rubbed her churning tummy. He reached for her hand and winked. "Relax. My parents will love you."

When she found her voice, she said, "Gage, when you said 'farmhouse' it conjured up images of Dorothy's white wooden house in the *Wizard of Oz*. This looks like the house in *Sommersby* or something."

Gage laughed. "Several farmers do lease the fields from my parents for corn, peanuts and cotton. One of them plans on harvesting those firs for Christmas trees in about six more years."

"*Wow*. Can't you just imagine the history of this place?" Kyle stuck his head out of the window and took a picture.

"It was built in the eighteen-fifties, I think. The brick is new but they wanted it designed to look old. They kept it as authentic to its origins as possible." Gage spoke with pride, repeating how his parents had entrusted his friend Chase with the awesome task; his meticulous workmanship and no-nonsense ethics had ensured the quality of the work.

What he didn't mention was Chase's rough teenage years, on the verge of a life of petty crime when Charles Dunbar put him to work in his woodshop and Chase discovered a talent for carpentry. The Dunbars had often been his beacon of light in an otherwise dim adolescence, and he had an undying loyalty for the entire family.

Two Irish setters raced each other to the cars. As soon as Terry released Tanner from his car seat, he scrambled out and fell on the ground, rolling around with the dogs as they barked and licked his face.

"Shit, now he's filthy," Terry complained. "Hope mom has clean clothes for him here."

"She probably has a change of clothes in that place to fit any one of us," Gage said, causing everyone to laugh. He took Stephanie's hand, and feeling her clammy palm, squeezed lightly. Terry and Kyle walked silently beside them. The dogs sniffed the group and nudged for head scratches before returning to Tanner, following him as he ran in circles.

"He's a bundle of energy," commented Kyle.

"Nana, Nana!"

Mrs. Dunbar came to the front door, mirroring Tanner's outstretched arms as she scooped him into a hug. After the hug, he raced along the wrap-around porch chasing after the dogs.

"Your canine alarm system works great." Gage laughed as he stepped on the porch and hugged his mother. He drew Stephanie to his side.

"Mom, this is Stephanie."

"Hello, Mrs. Dunbar, it's nice to meet you," Stephanie said. *Geez, how lame can you be?* She extended her hand, but Mrs. Dunbar shook her head and opened her arms.

"No handshakes for me, only hugs. I've heard so much about you already. And please, call me Joan."

"Yes, ma'am—Joan." Stephanie moved into the outstretched arms of the older woman and they both jumped as a jolt of static electricity passed through them.

"Oh, my, that was quite a little shock." Joan laughed as she shook her hands.

Terry stepped in to kiss her mom's cheek, and introduced Kyle.

"Kyle is thinking of writing a book on ancestry research, and might talk to you about using today's interview in it."

"Oh, this could be quite interesting." She shook Kyle's hand warmly.

"Due to lack of interest from my offspring…" She playfully narrowed eyes at her two children. "I put all my stuff away. Most of the older folks have all died. Now that I have a grandchild, I've been thinking it should be preserved before I'm gone."

"You're not going anywhere for years, Mom," Gage said.

"Yeah, well, there's a lot in here that's never made it to paper." She tapped her temple. "But it's waited this long, a few more minutes won't matter. Let's go inside. I baked fresh bread. Tanner, come inside with us."

She opened the door, and the smells of baking filled the air. Gage and Terry grimaced at each other behind their mother's back. In their opinion, she was a good cook, but a lousy baker.

"She doesn't know it," Gage whispered to Stephanie, "But some of her loaves of bread became the foundation bricks when this house was renovated."

"What?" Stephanie answered, eyes widening.

"Just kidding." He laughed.

"My son seems to think my hearing has gone," Joan said over her shoulder as she led them into the hallway.

"It just happened one time. I forgot to put yeast in the dough and the bread came out rather hard."

Her children held up three fingers. She flicked her wrist at them as if swatting annoying flies, but she laughed along with them.

Stephanie loved the house. Ten-foot high ceilings

embellished with intricate swirls and elaborate dentil trim graced the upper view. Gleaming hardwood floors extended from the living room to the left side, and to a huge dining room on the right.

"If you are interested, we can take a tour later and I'll show you the work Gage, Connor, and their friend Chase accomplished." Joan directed them down the hallway toward the rear of the house, where one huge open space combined the kitchen and family room. While the entrance rooms clearly conveyed the charm of the old home, this area obviously bore the mark of a modern family.

The kitchen was a cook's dream, decorated in shades of deep brown and tan accented with sage green, the same color scheme flowing into the family room area. Granite counters of brown and tan with gold specks filled one L-shape section to the right, anchored by the refrigerator on the short part and a double oven range in the middle of the long part. An island in the middle of the kitchen contained a copper farm sink and provided more workspace.

Large windows over the huge double sink graced the back wall, giving any dishwashing human a gorgeous view of the river at the end of the yard. On the left, a half wall of bottom cabinets, covered with the same granite countertop, created a dining bar. While separating the kitchen from the family room, the bar allowed occupants of both rooms to interact. While much bigger, this kitchen was the obvious inspiration for Terry's own apartment, Stephanie thought. As if reading her mind, Terry said, "Chase, the same friend who did Mom's kitchen, also renovated mine. I loved this feel of openness, and carried it to my place."

"Except Terry is ultra-modern and I'm more—traditional," Joan added with a smile. "These two rooms and the bathrooms are our concessions to modernized living. We had everything else restored to the style of this house as it was originally built in the early-eighteen hundreds."

"How long did it take?" Kyle asked.

"Two years. We lived in our camper for a few months, until the garage apartment was finished and we could settle there. Our marriage somehow remained intact, but my husband and I have not camped since then."

"Where is Pops now?" Gage asked.

"He went out for something for the Jet Ski, don't ask me what. He should be back soon."

"Well, I sure am glad Tropical Storm Abby decided to wait until after Labor Day," Terry commented as she took a pitcher of tea from the refrigerator while Gage got glasses from the cupboard. "The early weather report said it may be upgraded to a Category One this morning." She called for Tanner, who came charging into the kitchen and headed for the cookie jar.

Joan set a wooden plate on the table and a serrated knife, and then took a basket from the island. She removed a plaid cloth and placed a loaf of bread on the plate.

Gage tapped the loaf with the knife. He exclaimed as the knife bounced on the crust, "Hey, no resounding thud, I think she used the yeast this time."

"Very funny, wise guy." She added a tray with butter and small jars of jelly.

"We honestly just ate at the café before we came, Mom," Terry said. "Let's let Kyle start with his interview and we will have some afterwards."

"Don't think I won't hold you to that. Let's go to the dining room. I have things on the table there."

"I'll leave you all to that family tree stuff," Terry said. "I've got a couple of phone calls to make."

"Yeah, I am sure Pops will need me when he gets back." Gage grinned mischievously.

"Fine. I'm taking you two out of my will and putting these two in." She pretended to be perturbed as she hooked arms with Stephanie and Kyle and led the ancestry sleuths to the formal dining room, where various files, boxes, albums and newspaper clippings were stacked and spread around.

"Oh, boy," Kyle exclaimed. His eyes widened in boyish delight.

"Ditto," Stephanie added.

"Kyle, I looked through an old family Bible, which has some of my family tree four generations before me." She reached for an old leather-bound Bible and opened it to the front. "My great-grandmother Priscilla Garwood Wyatt started this in the late eighteen hundreds. There is a Frank Wyatt, her father-in-law, born eighteen thirty-four, but I don't see information for his wife. Most of the information describes later additions to the family."

She sighed. "I've always wanted to work on the family genealogy, especially the Wyatt line, but I just never knew where to begin. In all of these boxes and files you'll find every record or document that ever crossed my hands, all well-marked with names and dates. It's not perfect, but I think you will be able to locate things pretty well."

Suddenly she brightened. "Kyle—can I hire you to trace my tree?"

"Pardon?" Kyle blinked, immersed in the Bible.

"Oh, I'm sorry. I was just thinking out loud."

"I'm not a professional, although I hope to be. I've been working on ancestry for the past three or four years, and I think I am pretty good. But...'

'I tell you what," Joan interrupted. "Let's see if you find anything about the Frank Wyatt you are looking for first. Then we can discuss it again later."

"I'd like that. While I am researching your family, it could be a good foundation for my book, if you agree."

"Okay, we can discuss it later. In the meantime, let's start in the yellow file boxes. They hold my Wyatt files."

"Thank you so much for allowing me to be a part of this too," Stephanie said, impulsively hugging Joan as tears sprang to her eyes.

"I hope you find what you are looking for, honey," Joan said, returning the hug. "How do we begin, Kyle?"

"Well, can we agree to concentrate on this Wyatt branch for now, see where it leads us?"

As Joan pushed the yellow box toward the two amateur researchers, she said, "I remember there used to be a kind of numbering system you could assign to your ancestors, to identify who they were, and by the number you could always recognize the relationship to the main person. I don't know the name."

"*Ahnenetfel,*" Stephanie and Kyle said simultaneously, although she stumbled over the difficult pronunciation of the German word. Kyle smiled approvingly at her efforts as Joan nodded enthusiastically.

"Yes, that's it!"

Kyle continued explaining. "*Ahnenetfel* is a German word which translates literally to 'ancestor table.' It's a numbering system which uses a designated descendant as the first entry or the base. You determine a base person and assign the number one. Each ancestor receives a number in a special format—even numbers for males, odd for females. The number of each person's father is double their own number, and the mother is double plus one. So if Mrs. Dun—Joan is the base person, her number is 'One.'" He grabbed a napkin and sketched rapidly. "Her father is 'Two' her number doubled, and *his* father is 'Four', doubling his number. Her mother is 'Three'—doubling the base plus adding one. With this system, Joan's paternal grandfather is number four, and her paternal grandmother five, maternal six and seven, and so on. It sounds complicated but it's quite easy to understand once you see it on paper."

"I tried this with an online system and at first I was hopelessly confused, but after I studied it for a while, it makes sense," Stephanie added.

"Yes," Joan repeated. She pulled out a file and smiled. "Here's mine, with me as number one and Frank Wyatt as number sixteen." She set her neatly printed chart beside Kyle's rough sketch.

"Cool. I don't use this format myself anymore. Would you be amenable to me creating your tree in an online program?"

"Certainly. To be truthful, though, I would rather have the entire tree displayed on a wall chart eventually."

"We can do that, too," Kyle assured her.

Joan nodded as she reached in the box again. "This next file has various property records, including the buildings in downtown Portsmouth. My Aunt Ida left one of them to Terry in two-thousand and nine. I think there are other land deeds going back to the mid-eighteen hundreds, maybe further."

"Oh, man, this is such a gold mine," Kyle said.

"Even if this is not connected to my Wyatt line, I find it amazing," Stephanie added in agreement.

"Okay, the next files are either originals or copies of birth certificates, death records, marriage licenses, those kinds of things."

"If you agree, we should scan or photograph these papers so we don't have to handle the originals too much," Kyle said. "And I would also suggest preserving them in archival pouches."

"Good idea. Stephanie, can you push that third yellow box forward?" Joan asked.

Stephanie reached for the indicated box. Her fingertips tingled with warmth when she touched the box as she pushed it toward Joan. A crackle of static electricity passed between them when Joan touched it.

"Ouch, did you feel that static again?" Joan asked as she removed the lid. A flurry of activity in the kitchen distracted her as wild shouts emanated from the kitchen. The box top lid remained askew as the three of them scooted from their chairs and headed for the door separating the dining room from the kitchen. Tanner ran around in circles and the dogs barked furiously. Gage, Terry and Hannah stood shoulder to shoulder.

"Surprise!" They shouted as they parted and a woman

in blue military camouflage stepped from behind them.

"Oh, my God!" Joan shouted as she ran forward with open arms. "Mary Jo! When did you get here?" The soldier grabbed Joan and hung on.

"Let me look at you," Joan pulled back and looked at Mary Jo. "Are you okay? When did you get home? We weren't expecting you for another week."

"I'm fine," Mary Jo said with a chuckle. "Terry and I have planned this for weeks. We just weren't sure until a few days ago exactly when I would get here. Originally I planned to surprise you Monday, but I just couldn't wait until the cookout to come home."

"This is wonderful. Let's go sit outside and celebrate." She turned to Kyle and Stephanie. "Come on, you two, those ancestors can wait another hour. Come meet Mary Jo. I'll let Gage do the introductions so Hannah and I can get refreshments for everyone."

Gage extended his hand and Stephanie glanced longingly back to the dining room table before she went toward him to follow the family outside. Another day wouldn't hurt.

She was the only one who observed the tiny beam of light sparkle under the lid of the partially-opened box. *I will find you, Nicole, I promise.*

Stephanie joined the others as the light faded.

* * *

Following a moment of silence, everyone gathered around the picnic table. Mary Jo dropped into a chair, and Tanner immediately climbed into her lap and hugged her neck, playing with the dog tags dangling there. Hannah brought out a tray laden with glasses of tea and a plate heaped with cookies, and set it down. She stood behind Mary Jo, brushing her hand protectively on the soldier's arm. Mary Jo leaned toward Hannah, resting her head against the older woman.

"It's so good to be home," she sighed, and hugged Tanner to her chest.

"You look well." Joan sat beside her and patted her on the knee.

"Thanks. We all started to look better as soon as we were on the plane and actually heading home. We still had a twelve-hour delay at Bagram Air Base before we finally got out of there." She smiled, but it did not quite reach her eyes.

"I could hardly keep this a secret myself," Terry admitted as she munched a cookie. "Then when they were delayed, I was glad I hadn't told anyone."

"That can be especially hard for the families," Mary Jo agreed. When she didn't say more, Stephanie got the impression Mary Jo did not want to discuss her deployment at the moment.

"Can you stay home now, Aunt Mary Jo?" Tanner asked.

"Yes, I think I can, buddy."

"Good. Can I have your dog tags?"

Everyone laughed. Mary Jo reached into her shirt pocket. "Even better, Tanner Bear, here is a set of your very own." She put a chain of miniature dog tags around his neck and his eyes lit up.

"It's the bestest gift ever." He bit his lip and glanced at his uncle. "Except for the fireman's hat my daddy gave me. And the fireman's badge Uncle Gage gave me."

"They are all three bestest," Gage said as he ruffled Tanner's hair.

"So Terry tells me you are looking into the Wyatt family tree?" As Tanner fidgeted in her lap, Mary Jo directed her statement toward Stephanie.

Appreciating Mary Jo's thoughtfulness to include her in the conversation, Stephanie smiled. "Actually, I think Kyle might be the one who will be doing that. The Wyatts in my tree and Kyle's may be connected to Mrs.—Joan's. The first records indicated we may have some history here in Portsmouth but now it may actually be Portsmouth, New Hampshire."

"Whew, it's too confusing for me." Mary Jo shook her head. "Personally, I have no desire to find my real family anymore," she said grimly. "The Dunbars are all the family I need."

Joan reached over to pat her hand. The dogs started their raucous barking and headed around the side of the house. Tires crunched on the gravel, followed by car doors slamming. Tanner scrambled from Mary Jo's lap and thundered across the porch to follow the dogs, shouting.

"It's Grampie!"

Charles Dunbar arrived at the same time as Tanner's parents. Beth and Connor stood with outstretched arms Tanner ignored as he headed straight for his grandfather.

"Well, that's the loyalty I get for suffering through eight hours of labor," muttered Beth good-naturedly. Then her eyes widened and she headed for Mary Jo.

It amazed Stephanie to watch the welcoming ritual repeated. She had never experienced a big family environment before and found it somewhat overwhelming. Gage seemed to sense her concern and took her by the hand.

"Come on, babe," he said, pulling her toward the waterfront.

"The Dunbar clan can be quite a circus. Let's go for a walk."

"They're all amazing, but I am a little awe-struck by it all. I don't mean to pull you away from your family."

"Babe, we are one hundred feet away. To be honest, I don't think you pulled me far enough." He laughed and kissed her on the nose affectionately.

"I'm not used to all the commotion, although my life seems to have become a bit chaotic lately. It's as if I've been caught in a whirlwind and haven't stopped for months." She sighed as she tapped a finger each time she listed an event. "Losing my parents, quitting my job, selling the houses, and temporarily moving here. And still I have no idea what my future holds. Added to that, I now have ghosts in the picture. And there I go rambling again."

"Where do I fit into your chaos?" he asked gently, tucking her hair behind her ear.

She slipped her arms around his waist and leaned into his shoulder.

"You are the calm in my storm, Gage."

He circled his arms around her, and kissed her warm lips.

Watching from the deck, Joan Dunbar arched an eyebrow and caught her husband's eye. With a saucy wink, he nodded in approval.

CHAPTER SIXTEEN

Chaos ensued as Stephanie met the rest of Gage's immediate family. Charles Dunbar wrapped her in a bear hug after their introduction, and told her she was too good for his son. By the time Gage introduced her to Connor, Tanner was perched on his shoulders telling him how he and "Step-anie" had seen "Nickel."

Then Chase Hallmark arrived, and the excitement began anew as one and all shouted hearty welcomes. Stephanie observed the interaction between Chase and the Dunbars. The parents greeted him as parents would a son; their children as they would another sibling. His reception was as warm as Mary Jo's; to an outsider it would appear as if both were blood members of the family.

Hannah hugged him, moving into the same protective stance beside him as she did around Mary Jo, an observation Stephanie found especially interesting. She became even more intrigued by the interactions between Mary Jo and Chase. They embraced each other with a stiff reservation in their movements.

When they stood side by side, Stephanie noticed they were the same height, both nearly six feet tall and athletically fit. But they were as different as night and day.

Mary Jo had the delicate look of an Irish woman combined with the discipline of a soldier, Stephanie observed admiringly. *She's truly an all-American, "red, white, and blue" woman. Red-brown hair pulled into a tidy bun. Porcelain white skin with light freckles scattered across her nose. Blue eyes the color of sapphires.* Whether standing or seated, her posture was arrow-straight.

In contrast, Chase had a slightly-rough look, needing a

shave and a haircut, with his jet black hair curling over the collar of his shirt. A crisp white tee-shirt covered a rippling chest, neatly tucked into faded jeans with a slight tear on one knee. *Testosterone on two legs*, Stephanie reflected, as she enjoyed a moment of looking before she slid her hand into Gage's.

But Mary Jo and Chase did not exchange dialogue and to Stephanie they seemed more formal with each other than towards everyone else.

Even when they sat side-by-side for the impromptu barbecue Charles and Joan set out as "practice for Monday," they seemed to avoid engaging each other in direct conversation.

***

After they dropped Kyle off at the hotel, Stephanie casually mentioned her observation of Chase and Mary' Jo's polite but distant demeanor. She listened intently as Gage explained the complicated relationships.

"Chase and I have been friends since grade school. Terry and Mary Jo have been friends since kindergarten. Mary Jo grew up in a neglectful environment, Chase in an abusive one, yet it was Mary Jo who walked the straight and narrow, while Chase appeared headed for a criminal future."

As Gage pulled into the parking lot behind the apartment, he described Mary Jo's mother as an often indifferent parent raising her child alone. He turned the car off but did not open the door. Stephanie remained seated beside him, placing her hand on his knee.

"Child Services was about to take custody of Mary Jo when Terry urged our folks to step in as foster parents. She stayed with our family until the legal age of eighteen and maybe heard from her mother a handful of times in those five years." He drew the keys out of the ignition and they got out of the car. He circled the trunk and reached for Stephanie's hand, leaning in for a kiss as he took the care package his mother had sent with them after the cookout. He talked as they walked up the steps.

"Chase, on the other hand, came from a well-established home, the son of a Navy pilot and a trauma nurse. He was just six when his dad died, ironically killed as a passenger in a civilian plane crash. We were always at each other's houses. Along with Connor, we ganged up on Terry and Mary Jo and teased them ruthlessly. Although I have to admit, those girls outsmarted us on more than one occasion.

"Chase and his mother lived together well enough until she met and married a doctor when Chase was fifteen. But behind closed doors, this pillar of society turned out to be a wife-beater who then turned on the young son when he tried to protect his mother."

Gage's eyes narrowed and his jaw stiffened at the memory. She rubbed his arm and he relaxed, patting her hand. "His mother suffered the abuse in silence and shame, as did Chase, but it quickly took its toll on him. My mom first noticed the change in him, from a happy boy to one sullen and withdrawn. He once explained a bruise on his cheek as the result of walking into a door; another time marks on his legs supposedly occurred when he fell off his bike. Mom tried to inquire casually, but his mother insisted everything was fine. She did say she was grateful for his visits to our house, as Chase and her new husband were not getting along."

"And now I'll tell you about how we almost turned into juvenile delinquents." Gage broke off the story to open a bottle of wine while Stephanie put the containers of food inside the refrigerator. She wanted to nudge Gage to the story of Chase and Mary Jo but his comment about delinquency intrigued her more. She waited until he poured wine into glasses and they settled on the couch.

"Chase was savvy enough to remain polite and proper

around my family but his behavior elsewhere deteriorated. He twice received in-school detention for acting up in class and was suspended once for a fight on school property. A security guard caught him shoplifting at the mall and turned him over to his stepfather, resulting in his most severe beating yet; bruises he claimed were the outcome of crashing his skateboard into a tree. Following that, he was involved in a few other petty mishaps, but nothing serious.

"The turning point came when he and I were on a sleepover at the home of a third boy, Jeffrey Clarkson, the son of our high school assistant principal. At one in the morning, Jeffrey persuaded us to sneak out of the house and roam his neighborhood. We engaged in a walking vandalism spree. We used aluminum bats to knock down mail boxes and birdhouses and slashed tires on two sports vehicles." At Stephanie's gasp, he nodded.

"I know, I know. While he was the instigator and main culprit, Chase and I did our fair share. After that, we broke into a small corner restaurant under renovation, totally trashing the place by spray-painting obscenities on the walls, bashing holes in sheetrock, breaking windows.

"Someone in the neighborhood must have seen us. Police showed up at Jeffrey's house at eight in the morning, and confronted us. Chase and I admitted our involvement, but when they questioned Jeffrey, he denied being with us. Despite a witness reporting three boys returning to the home, the principal refused to believe his son was involved. Chase was already a known troublemaker, a very unfair accusation."

Stephanie stared at Gage in amazement. "Why, you little hooligan. I just can't picture you doing anything like that."

"I wasn't a perfect kid, but it was out of character for me and I'll never understand why Chase and I went along with it." He stretched his legs and propped his feet on the coffee table.

Stephanie curled her legs underneath her and nestled

close. She was so enthralled she forgot her original question as he explained how they refused to rat Jeffrey out. The police took Gage and Chase to the station and called their parents. Chase's stepfather was out of town, but his mother and Gage's parents picked them up.

They went back to the Dunbar home, where the truth came out, not just about the vandalism but about the stepfather's abuse. Chase's mother cried in fear of what he might do if they went to court.

Charles Dunbar kept it out of court. After speaking with the victims and making it clear what he had planned for the two boys, they agreed not to file charges. What Charles Dunbar had in mind was far more severe than anything the courts would have administered to first-time offenders.

"Even though I'd expected my parents to let me have it, Dad remained stoic. He gave one shake of his head and looked me in the eye, telling me he never expected to feel such disappointment in a child of his. It devastated me. I'd have preferred he yelled, or taken a swipe at me. Then he said 'You and Chase will repair the damages, cover the costs of the tires, and repay your debt to society as I see fit.'

"For the next two days, Dad only spoke to me when necessary. He'd say 'Pick this up, pass the salt, there's a phone call for you,' but none of the banter and fun we always had. I couldn't stand it and approached him in his woodshop. Even a backhand would have been preferable to the formal tone Dad used. I broke down and gave him my sincere promise nothing like that would ever happen again. Dad accepted that apology with a handshake." Gage finished the story. "And I will never forget what he said next." He paused for effect, sipping his wine until Stephanie prodded him to continue, causing him to inhale as his muscles quivered where her fingers dug into his side.

"Well, what did he say?"

Gage toyed with her hair until she again tickled his rib

in the sensitive spot she'd just discovered. He jumped and she formed her hand into a claw-like gesture.

"All right, tiger." He laughed and pulled her close for a long kiss until her wiggling fingers convinced him to continue.

"Okay. Here's the rest of the story. After Dad accepted the apology, his eyes hardened for a minute. He looked me square in my eyes with this steel glint I've never seen or caused since, and said 'And, boy, if you ever make your mother cry that way again, I will kick your ass between your shoulders and dribble you from here to kingdom come. You got that?' I nodded, and never got into any more trouble—well, of that magnitude, anyhow. I never wanted my dad to talk to me like that again."

Gage flipped the pillow under his shoulder and settled more comfortably, nestling Stephanie close. He continued, "He made us personally apologize to each family, promising full restitution. The main reason the victimized neighbors agreed not to press charges was because no one could prove Jeffrey had been involved, although they considered him to be the neighborhood troublemaker whose parents were in denial."

Stephanie settled her head on Gage's chest, listening to the rhythm of his heartbeat increase slightly at intense parts of the story. The Dunbars and Chase's mother paid for the immediate replacement of the tires and mailboxes. All of the parents agreed that every Monday that summer, both boys would have to mow the lawns at the four houses where they damaged property, for free. On Fridays, they would have to mow the grass at their own homes to repay the expenses their parents had shelled out on their behalf. The other three days they had to scrub away their obscene spray paint and assist the renovation crew until they restored the building to the point it was before the damage. They spent Saturdays in Charles's workshop building new birdhouses and mailboxes.

It took the entire summer to pay back their debts. They

were finally free the last week before school started, and they planned to bike and swim every chance they could. It rained the entire week.

"Whew." Stephanie whistled through her teeth when Gage finally finished. "How did you feel when it was all over?"

"Relieved. We paid everything we owed, Chase discovered he was a natural carpenter, and we stayed out of trouble. Jeffrey, on the other hand, has had occasional troubles ever since; petty crimes, DUI, and marijuana charges."

She still wanted to know more about the relationship between Mary Jo and Chase, adding, "Let's go back to Mary Jo and Chase. They seemed a bit formal with each other today."

"Well, we've all known each other for years, growing up together. They started dating the summer after they graduated. We expected at one time they might even get married, but something happened between them. They were together one day, then a week later she just up and enlisted in the Army and headed for boot camp. That was, oh, about eight or nine years ago. They haven't really seen each other much since then, although he did the remodel job for the bakery while she was on deployment. It will be interesting to watch them clash over the additional changes he wants to suggest once she is settled back home.

"And now you know the story of the extended Dunbar family," he concluded, drawing her in to kiss her nose.

"Gage, it's the most amazing thing I've heard. Your family is incredible—and so generous. Look how kind your parents have been to me and Kyle for our research, and they don't even know us."

"Well," Gage mused, "If they see people who need something, they find a way to help. It's what they do. Just don't get in trouble with them. They'll take it out of your hide without laying a hand on you."

Stephanie didn't hear the humor in Gage's voice; her

mind was on the close family she wanted to be a part of. A tear slid down her face before she could stop it. As he gently brushed it away, she framed his face in her hands and whispered, "I need you, Gage Dunbar. Take me to bed and let me love you."

Gage kissed her and slid his hand along her arm, brushing her breast gently with his palm.

They never made it to the bedroom.

***

On Labor Day, Stephanie remembered those stories as she watched the Dunbar men celebrate the holiday, and decided she was falling a little in love with each of them.

She had experienced her first ride on a jet ski, snug behind Gage's rugged brother Connor as they shot over the calm waters of the river, laughing as she lost her balance twice and fell from the back of the watercraft. Not quite ready for taking the controls herself when he offered, they returned to the dock, so he could take Tanner for a promised ride.

Later, she elected to observe as an enthusiastic volleyball game got underway between Gage's Portsmouth firehouse friends and Connor's Suffolk counterparts. Team members included non-firefighters Charles, Chase, and Kyle, the latter maneuvered by Terry into attending the cookout. Non-players lounged in lawn chairs scattered in strategic locations nearby. Hannah cheered raucously for both sides, pounding on the shoulder of a firefighter in a cast up to his thigh. Frank, the unfortunate colleague who had suffered a broken leg earlier during the rookie training class, sat in a lounge chair waving a crutch each time his Portsmouth team scored.

Stephanie joined the women of the family at the railing on the deck, where they companionably leaned together to watch the game. In honor of Mary Jo's safe return, Joan had draped red-white-and-blue bunting from nearly every banister and window on the back of the house. Miniature flags waved from potted plants or hanging baskets. Tableware carried out the rest of the color scheme.

"This looks like something from *Better Homes and Gardens*," Stephanie sighed in contentment.

"This is such a pleasant scene, isn't it?" remarked Joan as she sipped a beer and nodded toward the playing area. "The view from here is quite nice."

Stephanie turned her gaze to the volleyball court. Joan's husband Charles, patriarch of the family and once the summer bane of two miscreant boys, steadily held his own with men half his age at the volleyball net. He was as slim as his sons, not as tall but still a force to be reckoned with.

"They forget he was a volleyball champ in college." Joan laughed as Charles spiked the ball in front of Connor.

"You know, this nearly brings tears to my eyes, all those fine masculine bodies out there." Beth pretended to wipe a tear away as she fanned her face. "Shirts off, chests slicked with suntan oil, manly sweat glistening…"

"I've been around enough testosterone for the past year to last me a month or so," Mary Jo interrupted with a laugh as she removed the top off a watermelon wine cooler. "But I have to say this isn't bad—not bad at all. I like the looks of our newest guest out there, Kyle." She jutted her chin in his direction.

"Sorry, pal." Terry leaned on the railing and bumped Mary Jo with her hip. "Mr. Kyle doesn't know it yet, but he's on my radar."

"Okay, okay, calm down."

"Now, ladies, claws back," Joan admonished, but she laughed too. "Follow me. Let's guide all of that testosterone from volleyball toward the grill and get this picnic hopping." The other women followed like a trail of ducklings behind their mama.

When the final point—as declared by Joan— was achieved, the game broke up. The winners slapped high-fives while Charles called for his cooking crew to meet him at the barbecue pit.

Proving he was as much a master of the grill as the volleyball court, he good-naturedly donned a camouflage print apron on which the words "Grill Sergeant" were printed, and barked orders to his "minions." This prompted Tanner to show him the yellow plastic *Despicable Me* characters that always filled his pockets, pointing out none of his grandfather's helpers looked like "the real ones." Charles knew the characters well, having watched the video six times with Tanner, and had to agree.

"My minions have to follow my orders, though, just as Gru's have to follow him." As he ruffled his grandson's hair and took a deep chug of ice-cold beer, his eyes were on Gage, whose own gaze fixed on Stephanie while he stood behind the grill.

"She's a cutie," Charles commented.

"What?" Spatula in mid-air, Gage turned toward his father, who nodded toward Stephanie. "Stephanie? Yeah, yeah she is," Gage agreed, flushing slightly as he averted his gaze from Stephanie's cute little butt.

"She seems nice. Your mom likes her a lot. I do too."

Father and son watched in companionable silence as Stephanie and Joan reached for potato chips from a platter on the picnic table nearby. The women snapped their hands back and shook them, as if static electricity passed between them, and they burst into laughter.

"Am I thinking what you're thinking?" Charles asked.

"Aw geez, Dad, I hope not." Gage turned to his dad with a sheepish look, his flush deepening. *Is my lust that obvious to everyone?* He brooded inwardly, swigging a sip of beer to push the guilty thought out of his head.

Charles took his baseball cap off and lightly rapped his son on the side of the head. "You doofus. I was thinking she fit into this family quite well the moment we met her."

"Oh, oh that. Yeah, Pops, I was thinking that— almost." He turned to his dad, his look changing to serious.

209

"I know we just met, Pops, but she's the one for me. She's not ready yet, though. I just hope I can convince her soon."

His father nodded in silence. They watched the women a moment longer. Then Charles swatted his son again. "Minion, you're burning that burger."

Other Minions flipped dozens of burgers and dogs, and poked barbecued chicken as beer flowed along with manly laughs and guffaws. Those not designated as cooks at the grills passed salads and covered dishes in a bucket brigade from kitchen to table.

Heads bowed in respect as Charles stood, then offered a prayer of thanks for the gathering and Mary Jo's safe return. He added, "Hurricane Abby is still well off the coast but we ask God to continue to watch over those who serve and protect their fellow man in the military and public safety, especially with this uncertain weather."

Murmurs of amen sprang from the crowd, especially from those who did exactly that.

"And make the her'cane go away," Tanner piped up, prompting an even heartier "Amen!" from the guests, and signaling time to start the food line.

As Stephanie looked around her at the table, a happy sensation settled in her chest. She felt at home. She did not know this celebration of Labor Day would be the last respite she would have for days to come.

CHAPTER SEVENTEEN

Clothiste, her daughters
Portsmouth, Virginia, 25 July 1781

Thunder boomed over and over, with occasional lightning shooting across the sky. Clothiste had collected her meager belongings in a battered satchel and checked her daughters. They were ready to leave as well.

"How much longer, Mama?" asked Therese.

"Just about dark, I should think," Clothiste responded. "Are you sure you leave nothing behind?"

"We are sure, Mama," Marie Josephé confirmed. "We had so little when we came, we have it all in our satchels." She clenched her jaw and frowned in anger. "But we did not take the dresses the step-grandmother made us wear as her servants."

"I still have my baby," Nicole piped up, unaware of the anxiety permeating the room.

"And it is important for you to take very good care of her." Clothiste smiled through her tension.

Another crack of thunder seemed to shake the house, yet not one of the occupants of the room flinched. It sounded too much like the cannon fire which had been a near-daily part of their lives in the last years. Although Clothiste paced nervously, sudden noises did not frighten her or her daughters.

Her thoughts drifted back to earlier that morning and she clutched her shawl at her chest. Her marked improvement after the wicked one left for Richmond had amazed everyone.

But it was Phillip who'd discovered the odd bottle tucked far away in the cabinet. He put two and two together. Upon questioning Lizzie, he learned Abigail placed several tiny drops from the dark brown bottle into drinks before the maid took them to Clothiste.

"She said it was to help the missus sleep," Lizzie explained when Phillip had shown it to her. *"Sometimes when the missus did not eat her meal Madam Roker became angry, and she forced me to throw it away. She would not even allow me to give it to the hungry soldiers."*

"I knew she was ruthless," Phillip hissed through clenched teeth when he told Clothiste of his suspicions that Abigail may have been putting laudanum in her food. *"But I never suspected she could be capable of this kind of wickedness."*

Clothiste was shocked to learn her stepmother-in-law might have been slowly poisoning her. *"I should have realized it was not natural what I was experiencing,"* she said. *"I should have recognized it resembled symptoms many of the soldiers displayed when they were given too much laudanum."*

"This may have more implications than we realize," he said with deep concern. *"Was this something she was doing to you accidentally, or does she have some idea you were allied to the Americans?"*

"I do not see how she could even imagine that, we were always so careful. And the girls talk about how handsome British soldiers are and silly things like to pretend support of the Tories," Clothiste said. *"As much as it pains my girls to say it, they have allowed her to overhear them talking about how they want to find a soldier to take them to England when the British win the war. They display no interest in anything French or American at all."*

"Well, they are clever girls. Mayhap this is just a coincidence and she thought she was helping you recover. But, it is better to get you all out of here before she returns. We need to do this tonight."

Clothiste nodded, raising a hand to her throat.

Phillip took her hands in his. *"There is a shipment of arms they will retrieve from a Dutch vessel. It is destined for troops heading to Yorktown. The enemy thinks the supplies will go directly up the bay and they plan to capture it on the water. No one expects it to come inland here and when we get it, we will take it back over the river toward Yorktown. It is part of the arrangement Etienne devised when he was here. We have to get you on one of those wagons which we will separate from the rest. If you are stopped with the girls inside, the British may be less suspicious."* He glanced toward the window. *"The weather will not be good, but I will prepare everything so you can leave at dark."*

"I am grateful for all you have done and I hope we have not brought harm to you by being here."

"Do not have such concerns, Clothiste my dear. The harm is that I am not able to see more of you and my exquisite granddaughters. I shall continue to support the revolution. I am proud of you all, but as ridiculous as it may sound, you will be safer to return to the army camp than to stay here with my wife."

"What will you tell Abigail?" Clothiste asked.

"Why worry about her?" Phillip said with a wink. "I shall deal with her when she returns. I must go now to make arrangements."

"Merci, mon beau-père. Nous t'aimons," Clothiste told her father-in-law they loved him.

"Je t'aime aussi," he said as he left.

Thunder boomed again, and Clothiste's thoughts returned to the present situation. Now the hour neared when they would leave. She checked on her girls again. Nicole was curled on the window seat, playing contentedly with her doll; Theresé sat in a chair near a table with a single candle, using the stingy light to sew a rip in her skirt. Mary Josephé, as Clothiste had done earlier, paced.

"I want you girls to come close to me," Clothiste said. She reached through the secret slit on the side of her gown and into the hidden pocket over her petticoat and removed a brocade pouch. As her curious daughters gathered around her, she emptied the contents. Three smaller velvet pouches in the colors of red, white and blue fell into her lap.

"Mama, what are these?" Nicole pressed forward. "Are they for the Continental Colors?"

"Not intentionally, ma jeune fille." *Clothiste smiled but her eyes dimmed in sadness. "You know how my family lost almost everything we had during the war?" The older girls nodded. "However, thanks to your grandpapa we have some small treasures for your future. In each of these pouches is a special gift. I was waiting to give them to you when your father could be the one to put them around your neck, but somehow, I must tell you about them today. I want to see you wear them one time myself."*

She shivered unexpectedly and made the sign of the cross over her heart, hoping her girls did not notice. She shook the white bag and out slid a small chain with a tiny diamond in the shape of a teardrop. She looked at Nicole, who knelt beside her, eyes wide.

"For you, my innocent baby, this little jewel shining like my tears of happiness when you were born," she said as she slid it over Nicole's head.

"Then something special for my crusader Theresé," she smiled as she opened the blue bag, "You are the one who seeks justice for those who have no one to speak for them." Around Theresé's neck, she clasped a gold cross with a blue sapphire at each of the points.

"Finally, my warrior Marie Josephé." she smiled as she emptied the red bag. A ruby in the shape of a heart rested in the palm of her hand, and her middle daughter knelt beside her to let her mother place it around her neck. Then she beckoned her three daughters to come closer.

"I wanted you to see these for the moment, my daughters," she said, "To know they exist, and they will be yours when this war is over."

"May we wear them forever, Mama?" Nicole turned her diamond to watch the sparkles in the candlelight.

Clothiste smiled sadly. "Not for the trip we must take tonight. They are valuable, and we will have to put them away in my pockets for safekeeping. But for a moment, just this moment, I wanted to see each of my girls wearing her true color."

"But, Mama, may I put mine on my baby just once? Please, Mama?" Nicole begged, holding the necklace in one hand and the white cloth in the other. Clothiste nodded and her two elder daughters sat on either side to talk to her excitedly about their gifts before they took them off and placed them back in the colored pouches.

Nicole ran to the window seat and picked up her doll. Humming, she mimed putting the necklace over the doll's neck, then glanced over her shoulder. When she was sure her mother was still engaged in conversation with her sisters, she tucked the necklace into the secret place she knew Marie Josephé had sewn in the doll's dress, the place where sometimes she found the paper with funny markings on it. A few seconds later, she returned to her mother's side, placing the empty white bag inside the larger one.

"*Thank you, Mama, and of course, thank you to Papa, and to Grandpapa also.*" *She nestled her head on her mother's shoulder and looked toward her doll. She wanted to retrieve it but was afraid now. For one second, she imagined a light shining near her baby doll. She clenched her eyes shut, afraid her misdeed had been discovered. A tear slid down her cheek.*

She opened her eyes. There was no light.

Maybe it was the lightning outside.

The storm frightened her now and she turned her face away from it, back into the shelter of her mother's arms. The wind and rain increased, sounding as if stones were striking the glass window panes. Branches of the swaying trees scratched along the sides of the house and windows. Nicole buried her head further into her mother's arms as another clap of thunder shook the walls.

Her doll was on the window seat but she was afraid to reach for it, for surely the storm would punish her for keeping that necklace.

Stephanie
Portsmouth, Virginia, present day September

The bustle in historic Olde Towne on Tuesday morning after Labor Day was markedly different from what Stephanie had observed during her visit in the summer. The tourist traffic had all but disappeared, replaced in the early morning by yellow school buses making frequent stops on the streets of Olde Towne, and slowing commuters on their way to work.

The first day of school affects the whole community and the best news is that I don't have to deal with it.

She had a full day planned. She would meet Kyle at the Dunbar home at eleven o'clock and continue looking through the records they had started when Mary Jo's arrival interrupted the family. Afterwards, she would shop for supplies Gage told her she should have on hand before the hurricane arrived. She had never been through a hurricane before, and the constant bombardment of newscasts increased her anxiety.

Heading to *Pâtisseries a la Carte* for coffee, she found it packed when she entered. Instead of the usual tourists preparing for a day in the sun, however, working people crammed in for their caffeine kick before heading to their offices or jobsites. By the tantalizing smells of fresh bread, Hannah had started baking early. Stephanie noticed the usually dark television mounted on the corner wall was muted but tuned to the Weather Channel.

To save Beth from having to wait on her, Stephanie poured her own coffee. As she bent in front of the glass case to study the pastries, she waved to Hannah, who gave a sharp nod in response and turned back to her work.

"See anything you want, Steph?" Beth asked as she rounded the display counter.

"Just about everything," Stephanie sighed, and selected a fruit plate, then decided to "go for it" and added an éclair. She claimed a chair at a two-seater ice cream parlor table just vacated by a businessman who left with a briefcase and a newspaper. She cleared the table herself as Beth brought her food and thanked her.

"You know, we could use you part-time, if you're interested," Beth told her.

"Hmm, I'll think about that," Stephanie promised. She sipped the coffee. "Beth, I'm not much for coffee, but this is *good*."

Beth agreed. "It is good, isn't it? We get it from a little kitchen shop on High Street. We sell a lot of it."

"It might make me a coffee drinker." Stephanie laughed. As she nibbled, she perused the shopping list Gage had given her to prepare for the hurricane. They had discussed where she should go if the storm turned bad. She insisted she wanted to stay in the apartment. While he would have preferred she was elsewhere during the storm, he finally agreed. Downtown Portsmouth was notorious for flooding during severe storms, especially at high tide, but the waters rarely reached the area where the apartment stood.

He had even used magnets to post a map of the area on the refrigerator door, marking the locations of shelters and travel routes in case an evacuation was ordered, and stuck a list with critical contact numbers beside it. Once the city emergency operations center went into action, he would not be there to help her.

"Trees may blow down and damage buildings, block roads, or tear down power lines," he had explained. "At the height of the storm, emergency services may not be available until it's over, as there will come a point when even the police will be called back to stations to ride it out.

"Such storms are very unpredictable," he continued as he thought of another phone number to add to the list. "They create media hype for days. Many times the anticipated storm strikes another part of the country, or heads harmlessly out to sea, with little impact on the local area. This can lead to complacency among the citizens, who could be in trouble if they didn't heed the warnings and were caught unprepared."

Gage's ominous words returned as Stephanie glanced at the television screen displaying a map showing the storm's current location, still out in the sea off the southeast coast of Bermuda. It headed in a northerly pattern, gaining strength as it slowly moved along. At the moment, Florida and Georgia were getting heavy rain and winds but expected to be spared the brunt of the storm.

The new reports warned residents of the Carolinas and Virginia to start preparing immediately. During interviews with local authorities, emergency services coordinators advised if Abby continued on its present course, it might bypass much of the eastern US and make landfall in coastal New England and Canada. It could still bring those areas the same conditions as Florida and Georgia were currently experiencing and the viewing community still needed to be prepared.

Another weather bulletin described how the storm could turn west at any time and strike anywhere along the middle-eastern seaboard.

"I've never been through a hurricane before," Stephanie said as Beth topped off her coffee.

"I have been through a couple, nothing like Sandy or Katrina, but lesser ones. I think probably Isabelle was the worst one I remember, maybe back in two thousand three. This area lost a lot of trees, and a lot of houses were damaged."

"Well, I'm nervous, but a little excited by all of the hype."

"You won't be if one hits, believe me. Let's pray it ends as it often does in this area—much ado about nothing."

"You must worry terribly for Connor," Stephanie said.

"I do, but no more than usual because of his job. He's more worried about us, so we see to it everything is secured and we are well-prepared so he will know we are safe and he can concentrate on his job without his family being in the front of his mind. We live near his stationhouse, which gives us both comfort, but I have to be self-sufficient. He may not get home for days when a disaster strikes, so he needs to know I can handle anything in his absence."

Stephanie glanced again at Gage's carefully printed list. Later, As she drove out to his parents' home to meet Kyle she made up her mind to get into storm mode herself and be completely prepared so Gage could focus on his duty and not have to worry about her.

Charles and Joan Dunbar were already in storm mode when Stephanie arrived and located them in the backyard. With the help of Gage and Connor's firefighter friends the day before, all of the patio furniture and lawn ornaments had already been carried to the storage sheds. The lawn was devoid of any signs of the celebration occurring the day before. Today Joan was in the process of taking down hanging baskets while Charles backed the Jet Ski into a detached garage.

"It looks like a barren landscape compared with

yesterday, doesn't it?" Joan called as Stephanie strode up.

"It doesn't seem like the same place," Stephanie agreed. "I want to tell you again what a wonderful time I had."

Joan set down the two plants she was holding and gave Stephanie a hug, both bracing for the small shock which always occurred. It did.

"Thank you for coming. I'm just glad the weather held out."

"It's hard to believe there is the threat of a hurricane with such a gorgeous day as this. Can I help you with anything here?"

"I'm almost done, but thanks for the offer. We take the warnings seriously and always prepare in advance. If it hits, it hits, but we'll be ready." She nodded toward the house. "Kyle is already inside. Go on in and see if you can find any useful information for your search."

After greeting Charles, Stephanie met Kyle and found he had been quite busy. Three folding posters loaded with sticky notes stood propped on chair seats, leaning against the backs. A closer look revealed the posters had faint graphs about one inch square and the outline of a tree with bare branches.

"Hi, Stephanie."

"Hi, Kyle. You're making progress," she returned as she gestured to the posters.

"Well, Mrs. Dun—Joan—has good records. I can't wait to start plugging information into the computer and see what else I can find."

"Any Wyatt news?"

"Nothing more than what was in the family Bible, but we're just beginning. So far it's all I've copied, and look how much it generated for the tree." He pointed to the colored notes.

"I utilized sticky notes to start my chart, too, but as it grew I used the back of gift wrap instead of poster board so I could spread it out and see all the generations at once," she said with a laugh.

"Hey, what a handy idea. Listen, don't get your hopes up, but the Frank Wyatt in this family had a birth date close to the one I found on your side."

"Really?"

"Yes. Notations in the family Bible say this particular Frank was born the twelfth of November eighteen thirty-four, but my notes showed the twenty-first of November. Birth dates are often incorrect or transposed, and there isn't any reference in the Bible to Frank's siblings or parents so far. I haven't found a connection yet whether this Frank is brother to your grandfather Thomas."

"I always expect to find there may not be a link in the end anyway. Can I help you with anything here?"

"No, right now I have my own method for recording people."

"All right, then. I'll start with the box we were about to open when Mary Jo arrived and caused all the excitement." She reached over and pulled it toward her, expecting to feel the warm tingle again, but nothing happened, and her shoulders drooped in disappointment.

"Are you okay?" Kyle looked at her over his glasses.

"What? Oh, I'm fine. Why?"

"You just looked disappointed, as if nothing was in it and you were let down."

"Oh, no, not at all. In fact…," she peered inside. *What would he think if I told him I was looking for signals from a ghost?* She drew out a stack of envelopes. "It's full of old letters and correspondence. This might be fun."

"I brought a box of archival sleeves. I told Joan it would be a good idea to start preserving these keepsake items."

"I'll be extremely careful," Stephanie promised. Cautiously, she withdrew another bundle of letters tied with a faded ribbon and set it aside. There were four different packets of letters, tied with strips of the same faded ribbon.

"This stack seems to be letters between a Mrs. Frank

Wyatt and her husband Sergeant Frank Wyatt," she called out as she drew one of the bundles from the box.

"They would be Joan's paternal great-great grandparents," Kyle confirmed as he pointed to lines on the chart. "No first name or maiden name for the grandmother yet."

"These letters are old. I can see a postmark date. I can't make out the location, but it looks like the year eighteen sixty-two, maybe? Some still have stamps on them. And here is another stack of mail, simply addressed to 'Mrs. Frank Wyatt'."

Kyle came to look over her shoulder. "Yeah, I'm afraid we will see a lot of that. Women used their husband's names back then far more than they do today."

"Yes, the dutiful but unidentifiable little woman."

"Not answering to that." Kyle laughed as he looked at the postmarks.

"There are some letters of other people in here, from the eighteen hundreds, as well as old receipts, and sales slips. Here's one dated the third of August eighteen fifty-five, for the sale for something called an adz. I've never heard of one before. There's also a container with old buttons, maybe from a uniform? And look, here's a tissue, wrapped around a cameo. This is like finding a little treasure chest."

"I always felt the same every time I looked in there." Joan entered, squinting as her eyes adjusted to the room.

"Do you know what an adz, spelled a-d-z, is?" Stephanie repeated, fingering the receipt. "I just came across a bill of sale for one."

Joan concentrated for a moment, and then brightened. "I remember now. We looked it up in the encyclopedia when I was a girl—you know, back in the olden days." She laughed. "It seems to me some male in the family was a cooper or something, and an adz was some old woodworking tool sort of resembling an ax. If Terry were here she would just punch it in on her phone and get a picture as well."

"She's after me to get one of those new phones," Stephanie admitted. She hesitated a moment before she added, "Joan, I have an idea about this box of letters."

"Go on, tell me."

"Well, I was thinking maybe I could take them with me tonight and read them—well, actually, I'll scan them first and read from copies so the originals aren't handled too much. Maybe I could make a catalog of each letter to record the information, such as who wrote them, who the recipient is, date, maybe a summary. And if you agree, I could put them in protective sleeves, and do the same with the receipts and other contents."

"Hmmm…I like the idea of cataloging them and their contents. I am not sure I am ready to take them out of those envelopes for good, though. Let me think about it. I know they should be preserved, but there is something about seeing them in their bundle tied with the ribbon, probably in the same way they were kept by the recipient."

"I know what you mean," Stephanie agreed. "When I first found things around the house after my parents died, I wanted to just leave them in place, as if to hold on to them and the last things they touched."

"But you know what?" Joan nodded decisively. "Go ahead and do it. It's time. Catalog and preserve them. You're taking them back to the place where an ancestral house once stood—or in the general vicinity anyway. I know they'll be safe and in good hands with you."

She glanced over at the poster boards. "Kyle, that looks like a real family tree taking shape."

"Well, right now it's more so I can track your side of the family. I have one for your father and one for your mother." He slid the two chairs together to create one chart. "Side by side, they represent how your tree might look in a formal family tree chart."

"Clever. I can envision it already. It could become huge if we find a lot of ancestors, couldn't it?"

"This one would, absolutely, because you can already trace your family back quite a few generations." Kyle grinned. "Then I'll just cut the sticky notes in half to squash everything closer as we add names. But once this information is placed into a computer, you can have a nice commercial chart designed when you are ready."

"I like it already." Joan stroked her chin as she nodded thoughtfully. "You and I have to talk business soon, young man," she added.

"Joan, I found this tissue with a locket in it." Stephanie held out the small heirloom necklace in her palm. "It looks like a cameo."

"Aw, yes, I remember this. My great-grandmother Priscilla Wyatt wore this. In fact, she loved lockets and pendants. She had dozens that she passed down to all the females, including her daughters-in-law. Eventually I received a few. I passed one down to Terry when she hung out her shingle.

"I'm surprised it's in there instead of in my safe."

Joan took the cameo from Stephanie and continued to speak. "Now that was a lady who was well into preserving things, including herself. She always smelled like mothballs to me." She sniffed the locket and laughed.

"I swear I can still smell them now. She was the one who kept her mother's letters, and many of the old documents you see here." She glanced at her watch.

"Oops. I have some more storm prep to do, so I'll check back later."

Stephanie located another box that had small brown envelopes with clasps. She peeked inside one with the name "Priscilla Wyatt" containing a small leather diary.

At that moment her cell phone pinged a text message. She glanced down, and read a cryptic passage from Gage:

Quick hi. On break. City emerg serv prep busy. Meet for dinner @ 6 2night?

She sent her answer:

Miss you. Busy @ ur mom's finding good stuff. 6:00 fine. Where?

There was a slight delay before the next ping:

Dunno, pick place & txt me bck l8r

She smiled at the abbreviations in the text, which reminded her she still had her own storm prep shopping to do. "Kyle, I better stop so I can take care of some errands. I'll look through this at home. Would you like to join me and Gage for dinner tonight, maybe at six? I don't know where yet, but I can text you."

He looked up in surprise, caught in his own little world with one blue and one pink sticky note stuck on the tip of each index finger and looking very Doctor Indiana Jones.

"I'm sorry? I was thinking."

"I could see," she said with a laugh, repeating her invitation.

"Can I have a rain check? I'm probably going to stay here as long as I can today. I want to scan the birth and other vital statistics records in these boxes. I need to pack tonight and check out of the hotel tomorrow. I have to do some things at home over the next week or so, but hope to be back soon, maybe stay for a while."

"Okay, let me know if you find out anything else. It's been interesting working with you on this." They started to shake hands, but *à la* Dunbar, they hugged instead, promising to keep in touch.

Stephanie spent a few minutes talking with Gage's parents, telling them she had to shop for storm prep items.

"He knows what he's talking about when it comes to storms, so take it to heart," Charles said.

"I will. I plan to be prepared and then hunker down with these letters to see if they have any clues about my own Wyatt connection. I'm learning so much about how to research, and your documentation is so exciting."

"If nothing else, you will be accomplishing a task I've wanted to do for a long time," Joan said. "I appreciate it."

She stood on the porch until Stephanie had driven away. A satisfied feeling washed over her as she entered her house.

And all your work might just become part of your own family tree, young lady.

***

At the store, Stephanie noticed a few other people stocking the same essentials she had in her basket, but mostly, things appeared normal. Gage explained that people tended to wait until the storm was closer before they prepared, creating a buying frenzy in which panicked shoppers depleted store shelves.

Once she got back to her apartment, she realized how much she had to carry up the flight of stairs. The first things she removed were the two boxes containing the valuable keepsakes from the Dunbar home.

Next, she lugged bags loaded with toilet tissue, paper towels and plates, plastic eating utensils, trash bags, batteries, flashlights, and candles. She set the packages on the landing and went back down for the case of bottled water.

After that, she tried to carry the gallon jugs. With effort, she squeezed her fingers around jug handles and grabbed two jugs in each hand, managing to carry four at a time in one haul. Her fingers were pinched together from the weight as she clutched the handles. *Well that was stupid, I won't try that again.* The rest of the stuff would have to wait a little longer.

After shoving everything into the foyer of the apartment, she plopped on the couch for a minute, when she got a text from Gage and began a short exchange.

Gage: Finishing here early, on my way.

Stephanie: Just got here. Found everything u listed.
Gage: Wait for me and I'll help carry it in.

She rolled her eyes at the timing, but Beth's words came back to her. She drained a bottle of water and started back down the steps. It was important for Gage to see her as a capable woman so he could concentrate on the things he had to do.

Okay, so maybe I can't build a campfire rubbing two sticks together, but I can light a can of Sterno and heat soup!

She opened the car door and stopped mid-reach to stare at the magnolia tree. Some of the leaves turned inward, a light wind rustling branches at the bottom. In her imagination, the limbs waved helplessly, yet the top portion remained motionless. The foliage crackled as another gust wafted through.

A translucent figure stood amongst the lower branches. Stephanie straightened her shoulders and blinked, hand still poised above the bag. When she looked again, the form had disappeared.

Gage drove into the lot, parked, and walked to where she stood, staring.

He turned toward the direction of her gaze. "What are you looking at?"

"It's so muggy, yet I just noticed the leaves flutter in the breeze. And they're turning inward." She held her breath, wondering if Gage would see the image she had just seen.

He carried on in a normal tone. "Yeah, but it's probably because of the sudden increase in humidity before the storm. Small limbs become limp and the leaves turn over in the wind." He peered into the back of Stephanie's SUV and frowned. "Is this everything?"

"No, I'd already finished taking almost everything

upstairs when I got your text." Stephanie shook her head to clear the image, chalking it up to imagination, and smiled at Gage. "So is the storm about to hit?"

"It's hovering at a low Category Two and still pretty far off the coast, moving slowly but slightly northeast. If it stays on the present track we may just get the results of a heavy storm here."

"I hope it just goes away." Stephanie locked her car and they carried the last of the packages up the narrow staircase and set them on the table. She turned to Gage. "You look tired. How about we just stay in and order pizza tonight?"

"Sounds like a good plan." He pulled her close for a long kiss, then another, arching his body into hers. "But I'm kinda thinking you may have to help me put a fire out first."

"Then I should definitely hear you out." Stephanie brushed her lips along his neck and nipped his earlobe. Gage's slight intake of breath confirmed she had hit the mark and she led him toward her bedroom. "Let's go discuss firefighting techniques in our own command center down the hall."

CHAPTER EIGHTTEEN

The next morning, Gage showed Stephanie how to close the wooden shutters in preparation for the storm. He explained that most shutters used in modern homes were for decorative purposes and remained stationary, leaving occupants vulnerable to flying glass during a powerful storm. "During renovations, Terry insisted on using real wooden shutters that would be functional, yet preserve the historical integrity of the exterior. With working shutters, there's no need to place masking tape or plywood over the windows to prevent breakage." He demonstrated and the closed shutter darkened the room intensely.

"Just be aware it can become dark and stifling if they have to be closed," he cautioned as he returned the shutter back to its original position and the light returned. "I'm going to see if Chase can send someone to prune back one tree on the side so its branches won't be scraping the siding. Someone from Terry's office will take care of everything on the first floor, so there is nothing to worry about downstairs."

"I have bottled water and supplies, the building is taken care of, and fresh batteries are in the flashlights and portable radio." Stephanie ticked the items off on her fingers. "I'll keep my cell phone charged every night. I'll listen for periodic weather updates on the news. Are you going back to your station today?"

"We have a planning meeting first at Fire HQ this morning, then this afternoon I'll be part of the fire team at the EOC summit."

"EOC?" Stephanie was still getting used to hearing Gage talk in acronyms when he described something related to his work.

"Sorry. It means 'Emergency Operations Center.' The Fire Department already has a basic response plan in place, so we don't have to reinvent the wheel. We'll just go over the plans this morning, see what needs to be updated, and adjust according to circumstances predicted for this storm. Then we look at contingencies to cover the possible situations that may arise. We'll finalize operational plans outlining what personnel, equipment readiness, and supplies will be determined, but it probably won't vary much from the past."

"Okay, I see."

"I'm heading out to check on my house, since a certain lady has kept me occupied at her place for the last few days."

"Do you need me to help you? I haven't even seen it yet."

"No, I need to clean up before you see it." Gage laughed heartily. "Connor and I will check in with our families to be sure they're secure, get our gear ready for duty. If it gets too late, I may just stay out there tonight and see you in the morning. I'll let you know."

"Your folks were securing things at their place when I was there yesterday."

"They're prepared. We just check on them for peace of mind. What are you going to do today?"

"Oh, I might find a way to hang my homemade chart on the attic wall, and arrange a work area there. Terry said it was fine with her, and it will keep the clutter out of the apartment area. I can leave it all in one spot and not have to move it."

"Okay, then I'm outta here, babe. Catch you as soon as I can."

Stephanie wrapped her arms around Gage's neck and leaned in for a kiss so sweet and warm his heart turned a flip. When he reached the bottom of the stairs, he glanced back at her. She stood at the top, arms crossed as she fluttered her fingers in a wave. He returned her gesture with a smile. This time her heart flipped.

***

That kiss lingered on his mind an hour later in the briefing room. For the first time in his career, his attention strayed from the conversation at hand back to Stephanie. He was amazed at how swiftly and deeply he had fallen for her and contemplated how and when he would ask her to marry him.

When the sounds of chairs scraped across the floor as his colleagues rose to their feet, he realized he had missed most of the last few minutes of the assembly. Now he needed to discreetly find out what he had missed.

***

In a similar way, Stephanie's thoughts frequently drifted to Gage as she spent the morning unpacking her genealogy materials. Her chart would fit perfectly in the solid wall space between the two dormer windows. The graphs printed on the back which served as guides for cutting the wrapping paper were perfect to help her keep the generations in order on the same level. She longed to see her family information printed in a professionally designed family tree, but she was a long way from accomplishing that goal. Her lips tingled from his parting kiss as she imagined his picture beside hers, in position to start a new generation together.

After she tacked the last corner at the bottom, she sat back on her heels and stared at the chart. It resembled a drawing of a partially destroyed tree, with one long limb stretching far above spindly smaller ones. The tallest appendage identified the ten generations on her mother's maternal side, all the way back to the mysterious Etienne de la Rocher and his wife Clothiste. She still needed to research her mother's paternal side more thoroughly to fill in every set of those other sparse branches.

Her phone rang but she didn't recognize the number on the caller ID. She clicked the answer button and said hello.

"Hi, Stephanie, it's Beth. Are you busy?"

"No, just finished unpacking and arranging my research. What can I do for you?"

"I hate to bother you, but I was wondering if I could drop Tanner off with you for a few hours while I meet Mary Jo? Connor will be able to pick him up at four. We need to search for some files for her court case right away. There are some documents Terry needs urgently, but she has no idea where they are. "

"Sure, I can help. When will you bring him by?"

"In ten minutes, if it's okay. I'm closing the café now."

"What about—'Nickel?'"

"Oh, yeah, I forgot about her. I don't know. What do you think?"

"Well, I've been all around this place this morning, unpacking, checking windows to be ready for the storm. No ghosts—nothing unusual at all."

"Well, except for that one incident you experienced, I would still believe she was just his imaginary friend. Now I don't know anymore…"

"Bring him and let's sit with him for a while. If nothing happens, you can go on."

"All right, let's see. It's weird to even have this conversation."

"Tell me about it. I'm coming down from the attic now. See you in a few."

A few minutes later, the doorbell buzzed repeatedly, and she opened the door to find Tanner on the small landing, tiptoeing to lean his finger on the button. Beth followed a few steps behind him with a Spiderman backpack slung over one arm and a fat stuffed Minion under the other.

"Hi, Aunt Step-anie, I'm coming to see you. Mama says you're gonna watch me!" Tanner told her as she stooped to give him a hug. "Can we watch *Despicable Me*? I got my own DVD in my backpack."

"Well, of course. I've never seen it. We'll have fun." Stephanie glanced past Tanner to the black *Pâtisseries a la Carte* logo on a pale gray take-out bag Beth held in her right hand and squealed with delight. "Are those éclairs by any chance?"

"Oh, yes, tokens of appreciation and bribery." Beth laughed and handed over the bag. They stepped into the apartment and waited in silence for a moment. Tanner dumped the contents of the backpack onto the floor, sorting through action figures, cars and Minions to draw out the cartoon video.

"Did you say 'hi' to Nickel yet?" Beth asked cautiously as she took the DVD from her son and placed it in the machine.

"She's not here, Mama." By Tanner's scornful tone, it was obvious no one else was present.

In the meantime, Stephanie futilely jabbed buttons on the remote to try to get the video to play. "I can never seem to get this right on the first try," she said in frustration. Tanner bounced beside her, took the remote and in two expert clicks had the cartoon playing.

"Out of the hands of babes," she admitted ruefully.

"Don't feel bad. He starts ours at home faster than I can." Beth lowered her voice. "I swear there is something in the air today. It's bad enough I'm standing here waiting for apparitions to appear, which thankfully have not. Everyone's on edge waiting to see what this storm will do. And poor Mary Jo didn't even have time to catch her breath from her deployment and Jay's crazy mother is already hounding her, leaving voicemails when she doesn't answer, hanging up when she does."

"Why? I mean, I know a little about their history with the property and all, but …"

"She's a nut, that's why. Now we can't put our hands on the files with banking and receipts while Mary Jo and Jay were together, so Terry is in a tizzy until we find them."

"Did the mother take them?"

"What? Oh, no, no, it's nothing like that. Some things were stored at Terry's and some at Mary Jo's during the renovations. Terry still hasn't moved all of her files into her office yet. We just have to find the ones she wants. Those two women have four or five properties between them, and almost all are full to the brim with old things. Those files could be anywhere."

She paused and studied Tanner. He played contentedly, and nothing seemed out of the ordinary.

"All appears calm and quiet here—no sign of *woo-woo*. I guess I am going to run now. Connor should be here soon."

"Well, good luck, Beth. Let me know if I can help."

"Thanks again. Bye, baby boy," she called and left.

"Come sit here, Aunt Step-anie." He patted the cushion beside him "I will tell you who all the people are." For the next ten minutes, Tanner proceeded to introduce Stephanie to Agnes, her sisters Edith and Maggie, and the lovably despicable character Gru, as well as little yellow Minions with either one-eyed or two-eyed goggles and wearing denim overalls. The little boy's eyelids started to droop. He shook his head several times, but yawned and couldn't fight the battle much longer. He fell asleep with the stuffed Minion under his head.

After covering him with a throw, Stephanie turned to her dining table to catalog the correspondence. She first sorted the letters from Emily to her cousin Celestine, who apparently corresponded regularly from 1857 to 1863.

She carefully opened one dated December 1860 which contained general chit-chat about the anticipated birth of the first baby for Celestine. Stephanie entered information into the catalog, which she'd devised to record the full names of the sender and recipient, any addresses written on envelopes, and dates of letters or their postmarks. In a final column, she summarized the contents, and listed the names of other people mentioned.

Against the backdrop of cartoon characters on the television, she painstakingly handled each page, smoothing out the delicate paper. In a few of the letters, ink bled through the folds, but she was able to decipher most of the contents. She scanned the document to the computer, after which she placed each envelope and page of the letter in individual clear plastic sleeves. She filed these in a three-ring binder in chronological order. When she finished, she would prepare a table of contents. She counted one hundred letters in the box.

She was working on the sixth letter when Tanner's laughter drifted through her subconscious. Glancing over her shoulder, her smile froze on her face as a blue haze shimmered beside him. Tanner sat on the couch, holding up his stuffed Minion. The shimmer cleared and Stephanie could make out the translucent girl in colonial garb sitting beside him, a doll in her lap. Her image appeared stronger than the last time. She was laughing, but no sound came from her.

Stephanie stood slowly and moved toward the couch. The child turned toward her, a tear glistening on her cheek as the glow around her started to dim.

"Tanner, is Nicole—is Nickel here again?"

"Yes. She came to play wif me."

"Can you tell her to stay? I won't hurt her or scare her."

"She knows that."

"How do you know?"

"She talks to me in my head. I can hear her. She wants you to find her teardrop."

"Her teardrop? Yes you told me that the last time. I can see one on her face. Is she crying now?"

"Yes, she has to find her teardrop. She says to tell you Marla loves you very much."

Stephanie sank to her knees. The light around Nicole

dimmed again, but as long as Stephanie remained still, it brightened.

"Mom?" she whispered. "Mom?"

Tanner looked at Stephanie, speaking in a matter-of-fact tone, as if he was not at all startled by anything he was seeing.

"Nickel says Marla says hello."

"Is anyone else with her now?"

Tanner looked at Nicole and back to Stephanie. "She says it's Jessica. Jessica loves you too."

Tears rolled down her face as she pressed one hand to her lips. Her cell phone jangled in her pocket, startling her. She ignored the ringing and kept her eyes on Nicole, still surrounded by the filmy light. The tiny specter frowned and looked toward her with frightened eyes, sending a chill of foreboding along her spine.

"Nickel says you have to be real careful," Tanner warned, as the image dissipated into a thousand sparkling pieces and faded. As he nonchalantly turned back to his toys, another chill coursed through Stephanie. She remained where she was, and her cell phone stopped ringing.

A minute later, it rang again and she stood with shaking knees to reach for it and answer. It was Beth, telling her Connor was on his way.

"Are you all right, Steph? You sound funny."

"I'm fine, Beth. Um—Nickel paid another visit but we're ok. We're fine. It barely lasted a minute." She told her briefly, and could hear Beth turning away from the phone, repeating what she just said. She could hear Terry's voice.

"Are you sure you are all right? Tanner?" Beth was back on the line.

"Yes, we are, honestly. He said there was contact with other ghosts this time—all good ones. I couldn't see anything but the little girl. I will tell you later."

"I knew I was feeling something in the air today. We

want to hear more about this tonight, but one of the reasons I called is that we need you to look for a box of files for Mary Jo, if you feel up to it. Do you think you could do it after Connor comes by for Tanner?"

"Sure, sure. I think I hear Connor now. Let me call you right back after I get them on their way." She hung up and opened the door just as Connor was raising his hand to knock.

"Hi, Stephanie," he smiled, looking sharp in his firefighter's uniform.

"Daddy!" Tanner ran passed Stephanie to his dad and hugged his knee.

Oh my word, he's nearly as handsome in uniform as his big brother. She stepped aside as he reached for his son with strong sinewy arms and hefted him on his shoulder. A maternal tug pulled at her as she imagined Gage in a nearly identical scene, lifting his own child someday.

"Hey, little man, you ready to go?"

"Yes. Can we go to McDonald's, Daddy?"

"I don't know, Bud, we better check with Mom first. She may have fixed dinner already. Let's get your stuff together." He set Tanner down and helped him gather the scattered toys and put them in the backpack as Stephanie tried without success to turn off the DVD and remove the movie. Tanner skipped over to save the day.

"I need to have him spend a day with me to teach me how to work these gadgets," she said with a shake of her head.

"He's got me beat on some of them." Connor laughed. "He can get our PlayStation set up faster than I can."

"Any news about the storm?"

"It's still stalled off the coast, gaining a little more strength. It's just a 'wait and see' mode right now."

"Well, I think I'm prepared, thanks to Gage."

"Yeah, we are too. Thanks for watching our little man for us. Tell Aunt Stephanie thanks, Tanner."

"Thanks, Aunt Step-anie. I'll bring *Despicable Me Two* the

next time, okay?"

"That's a date," she promised as she hugged the adorable little boy.

As she closed the door behind them, she leaned on it for support, Nicole's message racing through her thoughts.

The phone rang again a few minutes later. After Beth had relayed the original conversation, Terry then called Stephanie to repeat the entire story step by step.

"Both of your mothers spoke to Tanner through Nicole? Both birth and adoptive mothers?" Terry repeated. "Hold on, I'm repeating the details for Mary Jo and Beth as you tell me." She murmured something and then came back to the phone. "Okay, what next?"

"Nothing. She told Tanner to tell me they loved me, and said for me to find her teardrop, and to be careful."

"Teardrop? I wonder what she meant by that?"

"I don't know. It literally gave me the shivers when she said to be careful."

"This is so weird, Stephanie. I would swear you were crazy except I've seen a few ghosts myself, something I don't tell very often. And an apparition appeared to Mary Jo many years ago, but she denies it now and doesn't believe in them anymore."

"Well, I still can't get over it, Terry, I really can't."

"Let's get together this evening and hash it out. Right now, I need to get my hands on several storage boxes, but one in particular. We've looked everywhere we imagined it could be, but it's not with her stuff. I know it's not in the law office because I organized those files myself. I haven't moved hers to the office yet. She has some things in the attic over the café, and some stored in the empty house where the B and B will be. Hannah checked the attic in the café and it's not there, so we hope it's in the B and B. Mary Jo just stored things kind of willy-nilly in her hurry to rent her house out during her deployment."

"Okay, what do you need me to do?"

"There's a set of three keys in the top right drawer in

the kitchen. One goes to my office, one to the café, and one to the B and B. Take a flashlight because there's only one light and it's not very bright. Look for white file boxes with blue stripes. About the size printer paper comes in. It was the last stuff we put up there. They should be right up front."

"All right, white boxes with blue lines."

"If you find them, we can stop looking here and come right over. I want to go through them before this storm hits."

"Sure. I'll go look now. I'll call you if I find it."

"Thanks so much."

Stephanie texted Gage to let him know she would be hunting for Mary Jo's missing files, adding about Tanner's seeing "Nickel" again, reassuring Gage all was well, and she would tell him about it later. She received a template response, "In meeting, will call back," so she went to search the attic of the B and B, armed with her new heavy-duty emergency flashlight.

At the back door to the house, the first two keys did not work.

"Of course, it's going to be the last one," Stephanie muttered in exasperation as the lock finally turned. She stepped into the kitchen area, which was partially renovated. Underneath plastic sheets, the shells of uncompleted cabinets lined the walls, giving a skeletal look to the room. Five-gallon buckets of paint were stacked in one corner, and a step-ladder stood open in an opposite corner.

Despite the warm day, the house seemed cold and she shivered as she walked from the kitchen to the dining room, then past the entrance hall to the living area. Each room seemed frozen in time, as if waiting for the work to begin again.

The foyer opened to the second floor ceiling. There was no railing on the stairs, but the steps were sturdy under her weight. They had been sanded down to the bare wood, not yet stained or varnished. Stephanie went to the second floor and reached the small landing at the top, where she found three bedrooms without doors. New drywall covered the walls and ceiling, taped and spackled but not yet painted. The bathroom was completely gutted to the studs, lined with insulation, but no tiles or fixtures were in place.

An incredibly sad feeling overtook her as she studied the small bedrooms. "Something heartbreaking must have occurred here." Her voice echoed in the eerie quiet. "Maybe it reminds me of Mary Jo's story and the difficult court battle she has ahead."

Remembering her own recent grief, Stephanie sympathized with both women; one who lost a fiancé, the other a son. But she could not understand the bitter route the mother had taken and hoped it would be resolved without a difficult court battle. She lingered for a moment, not quite satisfied it was the contention between Mary Jo and Della that created the feeling of despair.

Shaking off another chill coursing down her spine, she quickened her pace and reached the attic stairs. She turned the knob, but the door stuck fast. Underneath the ornate brass knob, she could see the old-fashioned keyhole was empty. She ran her hands along the door ledge to see if a key was hidden along the rim but came back with a film of dust across her fingertips. She rattled the door several times, finally heard something click and the knob turned in her hand. She glanced in at a narrow staircase, similar to the one in her apartment, leading to the attic, and flicked on the flashlight.

As she took the first step, she noticed the chilly air. The temperature outside was nearly ninety degrees; the attic should be even hotter. She frowned. Was it her imagination, or did the stairwell get colder as she took another step? Was the attic air-conditioned—or was she about to face another ghost?

Although the air stayed cold, no mysterious shape

formed or lights twinkled, as she had come to expect in these buildings. She flipped the toggle for the switch to no avail, and then carefully climbed to the top step, shining the light over the cluttered space. Boxes, containers, trunks and furniture filled every available nook. Pushed to one side stood the classic dressmaker's dummy that seemed to be present in every movie about a haunted house. The roof was not as high as in her apartment, and she had to stoop under the low beams to look around, dodging spider webs.

Despite her best effort, her hair caught in one, causing her to straighten in horror. She bumped her head as she straightened, vigorously shuffling her fingers across her scalp. "Ugh!" Grimacing, she raked her fingers through her hair one more time before she continued. Her gaze dropped to several boxes matching Terry's description, so she called to confirm which one to take.

"I am not sure now." Terry answered. "I'm afraid we weren't very organized when we placed stuff up there. The good news is you found the boxes we're looking for. We'll head over to sort through them. Can you bring them down to the second floor and we'll pick them up later?"

"Sure, will do. Terry, you are not going to believe this, but this attic feels like a refrigerator! Do you have an air conditioner running up here? It's freezing and it's spooky, so I am getting out as soon as I can."

"Please don't encounter any more ghosts, I can't take it."

"*You?* I'm the one that keeps seeing things. Okay, see you later, my battery is going dead."

"I thought you were getting a new phone."

"Well, I looked at them but it was too confusing. I need some advice."

"Yeah, yeah. We are so going tomorrow and getting you one."

"Yes, ma'am," Stephanie said. A fluttery beep warned her the battery was dying so she stuck the phone in her back pocket. She shoved two boxes to the edge of the opening, carted one down the stairs and placed it on the floor. She went back for the second box, and as she picked it up, cold air swooshed by and then the door slammed shut below her. She scurried down to the bottom and tried to open the door. It would not budge.

"Okay, don't panic," she said out loud, as she panicked and shoved her shoulder against the door to no avail. She reached for her cell phone but just as she tried to call Terry the battery died completely.

Then the flashlight beam failed and she was in total darkness.

CHAPTER NINETEEN

Stephanie sat on the base of the stairs, rubbing her arms for warmth as cold air continued to swirl around her. Her eyes adjusted to the darkness surrounding her, but she remained rooted to the doorknob. The other women would come to the building soon, so they would find her.

The thought offered mild comfort. It could be a while before they came.

She traced her fingers along the wall as she searched for the light switch. Finding it, she flipped again to no avail. As she had done on the other side earlier, she dragged her fingers along the interior doorframe for a hidden key, again without success.

Nervously, she drummed her fingers on her knees for a minute and then reached for the door handle. Icy cold in her palm, it still would not budge.

She clicked the switch on the flashlight again; it flickered and died.

She checked her cell phone; still no reception.

A new chill ran down her spine, and her teeth chattered uncontrollably. If malevolent forces were at work around her, they were doing a good job of spooking her. She looked behind her and found nothing amiss—although she was sure her imagination could conjure up something if she allowed it. Refusing to give in to the unseen influence, she took a deep breath and started to go back up the stairs, determined to find a blanket or something to cover her bare arms.

She froze in horror as a dull gray mist slithered toward her from the top step.

The slam of a door echoed below, followed by voices shouting. The vapor dissipated, and as suddenly as the cold air had enveloped her, warmth swept over her. Footfalls thumped on the floor outside.

She pounded on the door. "Hey, you guys, I'm locked in the attic," she shouted as loud as she could, looking up the stairs. The air was clear. "The door is stuck."

"Stephanie?" Mary Jo called back through the door, rattling the knob. "What happened?"

"I don't know. It was a little difficult to open at first, like the doorknob was stuck, then it popped open. After I got inside, it shut behind me and I haven't been able to open it." She braced her shoulder against the door to push at the same moment a click sounded. The door sprung open and she tumbled into Mary Jo's arms.

"Why, you're shivering cold," Mary Jo exclaimed as she steadied Stephanie and took her hands.

"Are you okay? Did you see another ghost?" Terry inquired.

"No, no, not here. I don't know what happened." Stephanie shook her head vehemently. "First, I had a sad feeling come over me when I passed the bedrooms. Then the air turned so cold in the attic staircase, I'd wondered if you were running the air conditioner up here. After I called you, I carried one of the boxes down stairs and went back for another. The door slammed shut behind me and wouldn't open. I had a sense of evil for a moment. Then the battery went dead on the phone and the flashlight went out, so I didn't have any illumination. The electric switch didn't work either." She clicked the flashlight to demonstrate, and the light beamed brightly. At the same moment, her cell phone buzzed in her pocket, indicating a voice message.

"Okay, I am *not* going crazy. Am I?" Stephanie reached inside the closet door and flipped the switch. Light flooded the attic. She put her hand to her mouth and looked at her friends in dismay. Now she was beginning to doubt herself.

"Well, I did try to call you twice and it went straight to voicemail," Terry reassured her.

"And the door was definitely stuck when I first tried it," Mary Jo added. "Not to mention, you were a chunk of ice in what should have been a sweatbox. If I hadn't witnessed it myself, I would think you'd imagined it."

"Well, as I said, I've never experienced such an eerie sensation and it lasted a few moments. It felt as if wickedness surrounded me. Have you—either of you— ever experienced that here?"

Neither woman said anything for a moment. Finally Terry spoke. "This house has always been rumored to be haunted. My Great-Aunt Ida, who left these properties to me, used to tell us ghost stories when we were little. Supposedly some triple-great grandfather died here during colonial times. But these houses received heavy damage during the civil war and family owners renovated extensively in the ensuing years, so very little, if anything remains from that time.

"However, it sounds similar to the young girl I used to see when we were kids. She never spoke to me, and as I grew older, she stopped appearing. The workers who were doing the rehab here recently said they often found their equipment and supplies moved around." Terry shrugged her shoulders. "So who knows?" She and Stephanie turned expectantly toward Mary Jo.

"What?" Mary Jo said, pursing her lips.

"Well?" Terry glared at her long-time friend.

Mary Jo rolled her eyes skyward as she blew out a breath that fluttered her bangs. Then she sighed heavily.

"Shit. Okay, okay. I'll tell you, but over a bottle of beer. I'm not saying anything else without a drink. Let's find those boxes first and get the heck out of here."

"I have Captain Morgan at the apartment," Stephanie chimed in. "And mojito mix with the alcohol already in it. And ice. We're prepared."

"This girl is my hero," Terry said as she pulled

Stephanie to her and gave her a loud smack on the cheek. "I'm designated driver, but after this scene, I'm having one drink anyway. Let's look for the right box and get out of here. But first..." She pushed the attic door open and wedged one of the boxes against it, looking at the other women with a sheepish grin. "No sense in taking chances."

"The temperature is normal in here now," Stephanie said as the three women went upstairs and crouched under the rafters. Terry began opening boxes and shoving them aside until she found the specific one she wanted. With a sigh of relief, she slid it over toward Mary Jo. "Here it is."

Next, she jutted her chin toward another file. "Take that one, Steph, if you will. I might as well move a few more over to the office in one trip. While I'm here, I'll take a quick peek around. There's an old satchel full of letters and papers somewhere. There might be connections to Mom's relatives. If I can find it, you might want to look through it for your research."

Terry rummaged among the clutter until she located the old burgundy leather case shoved under a high-backed chair. Her fingers tingled as she reached for the satchel to pull it out.

She stopped her movement midstream, the battered leather bag halfway out of its ancient hiding space, tapping her fingers in contemplation. A notion occurred to her; if she "found" the bag at another time, she had a good excuse to contact Kyle. The idea offered great possibilities. For the time being, she would leave the satchel securely wedged under the rungs of the chair, surrounded by old shoes and loose clutter.

"On second thought, Steph," she called back, using the toe of her shoe to slide it further under the chair. "I'll look for it later. I better get Mary Jo's things sorted first."

She went down the steps, flipped the light off and shut the door. The three women each picked up a box and headed toward the ground floor.

Behind them, a tiny light beamed out of the corner of

the bag and faded away as if in disappointment.

***

While Terry and Mary Jo took the boxes to the law office, Stephanie went to her apartment. She fixed a platter of cheese, crackers and fruit, mixed a pitcher of mojitos and turned the television to the local news channel to get the latest on the storm.

Hurricane Abby continued to travel on the same path. Veering east would keep the storm away from the coast; a westward turn could slam anywhere along the coast from South Carolina to New York. Reporters in raincoats and windbreakers broadcast from locations in South Carolina where the waves were churning and minor flooding was occurring, advising residents to be prepared.

"Well, I might have to go out for more rum after this get-together." Stephanie raised a glass and toasted the TV screen. "Screw you, Abby."

The clink of breaking glass startled Stephanie, and she whirled to stare into the kitchen. One of the tall glasses she had set out on the counter had crashed to the floor. A second one rolled on its side, wobbling precariously close to the edge. Stephanie stretched her arm and caught it in her hand before it fell to the floor.

Terry and Mary Jo rumbled into the apartment just as Stephanie was sweeping glass into a dustpan.

"What happened?" Mary Jo asked.

I don't know. The glasses just fell over and one broke. I caught the other."

Terry said, "Well, put the dustpan down, Cinderella, and come here." She carried a florist's box tied with a fire-engine red bow and handed it to Stephanie. "These came for you to the office today."

Stephanie's eyes widened. "Flowers? For me?" Stephanie reached eagerly for the box. "They must be from

246

Gage." She read the card and frowned in puzzlement.

"The card says, 'I always keep my promises' but it's not signed and that doesn't sound like Gage," she said. "Who else would send me flowers?"

"Well, open it and find out," Mary Jo urged, bursting with curiosity nearly as strong as Stephanie's.

Somewhat tentatively, Stephanie slid the ribbon and lifted the lid, rummaging through layers of pink tissue—and burst into laughter.

Instead of flowers, tucked away in the cloud of tissues rested a brand new pair of Manolo Blahniks with the geometrical pattern Stephanie had admired when she first met Terry in the café.

"Terry, they are gorgeous. But you shouldn't have done this."

"Well, give them back, then." Terry feigned grabbing for the box, and Stephanie snatched it out of her reach.

"Like hell I will." She cradled the shoes in her arms. "I love them! And I was completely fooled by the florist box."

"Well, as the card says, I always keep my promises and I did promise them to you. And you have to learn you'll never know what kind of package a Dunbar gift will come in."

"I'll remember that." Stephanie kicked off her sandals and slid her feet into the shoes, wobbling slightly.

"Oh, my, I'm not used to this altitude." She laughed as she swiveled on the toes. "I'll have to practice." She walked around in them as she pushed the flipchart closer to the table.

"What's that for?" Mary Jo asked, pointing to three columns drawn down a page on the flipchart.

"Oh, I'm creating a list to start documenting these recent incidents. I don't know what to call them. Sightings?" Stephanie looked at the other women. Mary Jo shrugged while Terry nodded.

"That sounds about right."

"Okay, they seem to be occurring more and more; twice to me today, once with Nicole and then in the attic. Ever since I found the letter revealing my adoption, I've had a series of these little occurrences. So whatever these events are, maybe we can find a pattern in them. "

"Like what?" Mary Jo sounded polite but skeptical.

"Don't think you are going to get out of talking about your experiences, either." Terry poked her friend in the shoulder with one hand while she reached for cheese on a cracker with the other. "Go on, Steph."

"Well, the first thing I remember seeing was a small light sparkling near my mom's jewelry box when I was in her room sorting things after she died," Stephanie said. "I was sure I imagined it, and moved around trying to see if there was a crack in the shades or something. I even remember resting my cheek on top of the jewelry box to look around the room, and the wood was warm to my cheek." She bent to lay her head on the table to demonstrate, and raised her head back up. "The wood tingled with a warm sensation on my face *and* to the touch. I opened the box and found the letter." She pressed her hand to her cheek as she remembered that day. Terry reached over and patted her free hand.

"I don't know when I would have gotten around to looking in that jewelry box," Stephanie continued as she scribbled "beam of light" and "armoire warm to touch" under her name. "It was one of those tall standing types." Stephanie held her hand about three feet above the ground. "And Mom didn't keep anything but costume jewelry there. Her valuables were in the safe. It was as if something directed me to the chest at that specific moment. It would have been weeks before I sorted through it." She sipped her drink and tapped her fingers.

With a smile, Terry reached over to stop the tattoo.

Stephanie stilled her fingers and continued. "And I had a very similar feeling when I first touched a box of letters from your mom's things, Terry, like a warm tingle to the touch. And Gage—he told me he has even felt along the walls for a fire in this apartment because they were warm to his touch but he never found anything amiss.

"Then there was another moment, when I was reading my real mother's journal, and it was warm to the touch. Now that I think about it, there have been other small things." She explained while she wrote on the chart. "The first time I visited Portsmouth, fate seemed to push me into the café just before the rain started. Of all the places I could have been, it was right in front of the café. I doubt I would have found it otherwise. And I met Terry."

She paused. "Then in my hotel room, I stretched on the bed after a crying jag. As I was dozing off, I had the sensation of someone brushing my tears away. Oh-oh, yeah, and then when I was looking at the apartment and we went into the attic. I felt a sudden swoosh of warm air just before I left, as if something brushed by me." She tapped her chin and turned in time to see Terry and Mary Jo exchange skeptical glances.

"Oh, humor me here," she said in exasperation. "I'm just thinking out loud. There's a trail of clues leading to something, but I just can't figure out what. Next, there was the time I heard laughing in the attic. I went up and looked around but didn't see anything." She scribbled furiously. "The first time I saw Nickel—Nicole—was with Tanner in the living room. And the second time occurred today, when Tanner said she warned me to be careful. She said my mother loved me. Then he mentioned both Marla and Jessica—the names of my adopted mother and my birth mother."

She nibbled on a cracker. "I had an incredibly sad feeling in the bedrooms of the B and B, followed by a disturbing sensation, like a premonition, when I was locked in." Stephanie finished talking and closed her eyes. "It felt as if something bad must have happened there. There's some connection between these three buildings here."

"Well, these properties have been in and out of family

hands since as far back as the seventeen seventies," Terry said. "The houses were practically destroyed during the civil war and have been rebuilt or repaired several times over the years. There are even legends about someone dying there, but those were old stories when I was little. I remember them as ghost stories, but nothing of historical significance." She touched her fingers to a cross encased in a ring of gold circles around her neck and suddenly fanned the chain. "Whew! I had a sudden warm sensation, like when you lean over a hot oven to take something out."

Stephanie leaned closer to peer at the pendant. "It's old, isn't it? I have noticed it before. Are those sapphires?"

Terry nodded. "Now this is going to sound weird," she continued, rubbing her neck where the cross lay. "This necklace has been in my mother's family for generations. Somewhere along the line, one of our relatives added these little circles around the cross, but we're told it was originally just the cross. It eventually passed on to Mom. She gave it to me when I hung my shingle on the law office. I've had sensations of warmth from it unexpectedly, you know, like when heat rushes from an oven as you open it. Like I had just now."

"And don't forget, every time I touch your mother's hand, we get shocked by static electricity."

"Oh, please, will you two knock it off?" Mary Jo snapped. "You're just getting carried away with your ghostly ideas. It's stupid, and you know it." She reached for her glass and swallowed the contents in one gulp.

Unperturbed by the outburst, Stephanie wrote "warm sensation from necklace" under a second column. She put Terry's name at the top.

Terry glared at Mary Jo through slit eyes. "Oh, we are going to get to your stories in a moment, madam." She turned to Stephanie. "I haven't seen my 'colonial' ghost for a long time, Stephanie. When I was a kid and we visited my great-aunt here, I used to see her sometimes. My brothers never did, although they had little strange things happen, such as their toys disappearing and showing up somewhere else." She shook her head. "Since we started working on these buildings, I've often heard doors closing, or furniture scraping the floor but I've never seen anyone—or anything."

Stephanie jotted "door closings" and "furniture moving" under the second column, and turned to look at Terry. "Anything you can remember from when you saw the ghost?"

"It was always a little hazy. I always felt as if she was trying to tell me something, but she never spoke. I heard her cry sometimes. Now that I think about it, sometimes I heard the crying first, and then she appeared." Terry strained to think. "It was nearly fifteen or twenty years ago. I just chalked it up to the 'haunted house' theory and forgot about it as I grew up."

"Well, sanity at last," Mary Jo said sarcastically.

"Oh, shut up, Mary Jo," Terry snapped back. "I remember you about peed your pants when your ghost materialized. And, you were always miffed because my ghost appeared more often."

"Girls." Stephanie raised her hands as peacemaker, but she couldn't help laughing. "Fight later. Terry, you described your girl to me before, but now I want to write it down. What was she like?"

"Probably eighteen, dressed in typical colonial garb; dress, apron, and little white cap. Vaguely brownish curls peeked out under it. She usually had a book or paper and pen, I think."

"Did anything specific occur when she appeared?

"No, not really. Seems mostly it was when I played in the attic of this house. Great-Aunt Ida would let me play dress-up in the old clothes and things. You could stand tall instead of stooping like we had to in the B and B. I just don't remember much more right now."

"Mary Jo?" Stephanie looked at her, pen poised to write.

Mary Jo sighed. She hated this. To her, it seemed silly and a waste of time, but Stephanie looked so earnest standing by the chart that she didn't have the heart to be rude. And after all—she *had* seen the ghost before.

"All right, I saw something once or twice. I remember one particular Easter gathering at your aunt's. I was in the back yard, sneaking a cigarette with Chase out by the magnolia tree. It was perfect to step inside the low branches and feel like we were in some secret room. We thought no one could see us. It never occurred to us smoke wafted in the air. Hannah caught us and read us the riot act, before she bummed a cigarette from Chase and left us there. Then I peered through the branches and caught a movement in an upstairs window. A young woman, maybe sixteen years old, peered down at me from a window. It was a house then, but it's where the B and B is now. It looked as if she was beckoning me. Chase said I was crazy and teased me so hard I didn't mention it to anyone until we were home and I told Terry. I was relieved when she said she'd seen ghosts there before."

"And…" Terry prompted.

Mary Jo rolled her eyes and huffed. "And she appeared when I first looked at the building to see if it would work if I converted it to a bakery and cafe. I heard noises and went to look. She was just standing there, where the glass case is now, looking at me. And like your ghosts—I can't believe I'm even saying that word—she was dressed in colonial garb, but holding a basket as if shopping."

"Hmmm." Stephanie tried to make sense of it all as she jotted notes. "Do you think we're all seeing the same girl? Maybe at different ages of her life, holding a doll, a book, or a basket? Terry, did a child or young girl ever die in this house?"

"No, I don't think so. I remember the old people talking about some grandfather who was shot during the revolution and died." Terry shrugged. "You don't pay attention to stuff about old dead relatives when you're a kid."

"Well, there's something going on," Stephanie said emphatically. "For me, it seems to have started when I found out about my adoption. I think I missed early clues, but the spirit's presence seems to be getting stronger. Whether it's all in my imagination or not remains to be seen."

"I don't think it is just imagination," Terry said slowly, breaking the mood as all three women straightened up. "I don't know exactly what it is, but all of this is connected somehow. I'll try to recall details about my encounters and jot them down for you. What about you, Mary Jo?"

"Well, I can't get my head around any supernatural mumbo-jumbo, but I do agree we each seem to have encountered unexplained events with some similarities. That's all I can say about it. Just do me a favor and keep this between us for now. I really don't care to hear any bullshit from the guys."

"Agreed," Stephanie said as she pulled the cover over the flipchart. "I hope by writing it down we may see what the link is. I'll want to talk about it with your mom at some point, I think, Terry. And, Mary Jo, if you think of anything else, will you let me know?"

"Yeah, sure." Mary Jo poured another mojito. There were certain advantages to not being the designated driver. "I do agree something is in the wind besides the storm, which, by the way, is picking up out there. Listen to that rain."

"Let's finish up and get out of here after we get the weather update," Terry suggested. As the three women listened intently to the weather update, Terry bit her bottom lip and leaned forward. She held the necklace, rubbing the cross between her thumb and forefinger as she zipped it along the chain. Mary Jo and Stephanie subconsciously mirrored Terry's pose, each touching a finger to the base of her bare neck where a pendant might nestle.

None of the three noticed their striking similarities at that moment.

CHAPTER TWENTY

CLOTHISTE AND HER DAUGHTERS
Portsmouth, Virginia, 25 July 1781

Though the rain had stopped, distant thunder still rumbled and lightning continued to flash in the darkened evening sky. Heavy hoof beats mixed with the boom of thunder, followed by a door slamming and footsteps pounding on the stairs. Nicole screamed in fright.

Marie Josephé did not have time to give the pendant back to her mother, so she shoved the small pouch inside the sleeve of her dress for the time being and would return it to her mother later.

The door to the bedroom burst open and Phillip stepped inside, his hair and dark cloak plastered with rain. "You have to get out now! Hurry, hurry," he shouted. "The soldiers are checking houses. I have been told they will come here. I don't know what they will do this time. I want you to get to Etienne's camp right away."

"Come, girls, we must hurry." Clothiste shoved her bag into the pouch under her gown, unaware it no longer contained all three jewels. She picked up the crying Nicole, following Phillip down the stairs and to the back door, where a carriage and driver were waiting. As a flash of lightning lit up the area, the driver's face took on eerie shadows, causing Nicole to scream louder. A second bolt of lightning immediately followed, striking a nearby tree. A huge branch broke away and crashed into a corner of the house. Nicole screamed again.

"Quiet, little one." Phillip tried to calm her as he took her from Clothiste and settled her in the wagon before he took the small satchels from the older girls.

"My baby, my baby!" Nicole suddenly remembered she'd left her doll on the window seat upstairs and she tried to climb out. Marie Josephé gently pushed her sister back into the wagon, not noticing the small red velvet pouch slip from her sleeve and fall to the ground. She

stepped on it as she climbed into the wagon, pushing it deep into the mud. As Theresé clambered in behind her, she too stepped on it and pushed it even further.

Many more footsteps and wagon wheels would cross over that small bag, burying it deeper into the muck long before the sun would shine again.

"No, child, you must stay in the cart." Phillip grabbed Nicole as she clambered over the side again, shouting "My baby, my baby!"

"We will find it later. You must go now."

Before Clothiste could climb into the wagon, three British soldiers came running into view, pointing weapons while shouting, "Halt!"

Without provocation, two soldiers fired, striking both Phillip and Clothiste. As they fell to the ground, the girls screamed from the wagon. The third soldier fired, his shots directed at his two comrades, stopping them dead in their tracks. Still holding his rifle, he stepped over them and ran to the wagon.

"Mama!" Marie Josephé scrambled to get out of the wagon to help her mother.

"Go, go!" the soldier urged. "There is no time. I will take care of them, but you must go. Father will be waiting for you at the camp. Tell him I will get word to him about Mama and Grandfather. GO!"

"Oh, Louis." Marie Josephé hugged her brother and scrambled into the carriage with her sisters, who were huddling together under a canvas cover. The driver whipped the horses into a gallop. Both Marie Josephé and Theresé knew they had to leave or they would compromise the identity of their brother Louis, a spy integrated within the British Army. They feared for their mother, but Louis would do whatever he could to protect her.

Amid the chaos at the house, Louis remained in control. As three more soldiers ran to the area, he shouted for them to look for two men in black cloaks, sending two in the opposite direction of the wagon's path and asking the one he trusted to remain with him.

"James!" Louis whispered hoarsely. "Help me get them inside." Terror ripped into him. His mother and his grandfather bled profusely. He cradled his mother in his arms while James tended to the unconscious Phillip. Three other soldiers ran into the yard, guns *drawn, asking what happened.*

"There was an ambush. Two soldiers as well as these people were wounded. Some of my men are chasing after them now. Can you find the doctor?"

"Yes, he lives not far from here. I will get him." One of the men holstered his gun and ran back the way he came.

"We need to get these people inside!" Louis shouted. He gathered his mother into his arms and carried her inside, while the men helped James carry Phillip. Stumbling in the narrow stairwell and again on the landing, Louis recovered and gently laid his mother on the bed in the room upstairs. He could see blood seeping in the area of her upper left shoulder area, and ripped a linen cover from a pillow, wadded it and pressed it gently but firmly to the wound.

"Mother," he whispered.

"Phillip? Is he…?" Clothiste clutched the lapel on Louis's jacket with her good hand.

"They have him in the next room. The doctor is coming."

"The girls—are they safe?"

"They got away, Mother. They will be safe in the camp in a few hours."

"I'm dying, Louis, "she whispered. She struggled to reach into her pocket for her brocade purse.

"Don't say that. You must not talk, mother."

"I love you, my son, and I am so proud of you." She used her good arm to reach into the slits in her dress for the brocade pouch and pressed it to his hands. "Take this and keep it safe. It has some small treasures for your sisters. I don't know when I shall see them again."

"Please, Mother…" Louis could say no more, as the door burst open and a man with a medicine bag came in, followed by a woman with a pan of water. The doctor knelt beside Clothiste and began checking the wounded area. He glanced toward Louis. "You can leave now, soldier," he said curtly and turned back to his patient.

Louis nodded and eased from the room, taking one last glance at his mother's pale face as he reached to shut the door. A sudden flash of lightning outside drew his gaze to the window and his heart froze. Nicole's doll sat propped up in a corner of the window seat, partially hidden under a knitted shawl bunched up to one side. He took a step back into the room, and the doctor turned to him, eyes slanted in question. Louis inclined his head and backed out, closing the door behind him.

In the next room, he found his grandfather lying on his stomach in the bed. James's hands dripped with blood as he pressed linens to the wound in Phillip's back while another man withdrew items from a medicine bag.

"What happened here? We heard the shots," the man said as he bent over Phillip.

Louis stepped into the room and answered. "My soldiers and I were returning to our camp when two men attacked this gentleman and the lady," Louis lied without flinching, catching James's eye with almost an imperceptible nod. "I believe it was a robbery attempt. The robbers fired several shots, hitting the man and lady, and my mates before we could act. I fired and am sure I hit one, but they escaped. The corporal's team came by and I sent them to look for the robbers as I tended the woman, and James took care of the gentleman."

"You likely saved his life, Corporal," the doctor said. "He has grave injuries."

"The two soldiers..."

"I checked them before I came upstairs. They are both dead," the doctor said brusquely.

Louis feigned regret. It was not the first time he had to kill someone in this war—it would not be the last. But now Phillip—if he could even hear—as well as James would know the story Louis would report.

"I will go see to my mates now," Louis told the others. He glanced for a moment at the closed door of the bedroom in which his mother fought for her life, knowing any inquiries he made would raise suspicions. He headed down the stairs just as the woman called the "Wicked One" stormed up them, followed by a wide-eyed serving girl.

"Who are you? Look at all this muck and mud." Abigail cried. "I demand to know what is going on in my home!"

"British soldier, madam," Louis answered. "We brought the gentleman and lady inside. They were accosted by robbers and have been shot."

"Who was shot? Is my husband here? Lizzie, see this soldier out

and then come upstairs immediately!"

"Yes, missus." As Abigail thundered up the stairs, the tiny maid turned abruptly and led Louis back down the staircase to the rear door. Without exchanging a word, the two embraced quickly, then Louis whispered, "Hide the doll," before stepping out into the rain. A hand to her mouth, Lizzie closed the door and scurried to the upstairs rooms.

Prepared to repeat his story as often as necessary, Louis walked over to the wagon that had just arrived to retrieve the two dead soldiers.

STEPHANIE
Portsmouth, Virginia, present day September

By the time Terry and Mary Jo left the apartment, the rainfall had increased and forced them into a mad dash down the steps to the parking lot.

Stephanie called Gage at his house while she tidied the kitchen. He had to report for the eight am to eight pm shift in the Emergency Operating Center, so he was preparing his gear. He promised to stop by on his way.

"I'll be fine. I wish you wouldn't worry."

"I don't like your being there alone," he said.

"Gage, you have me prepared for the zombie apocalypse. I am going to be fine. I'll keep my ear tuned to the weather channel, settle down with this box of letters, and read about the Wyatts in the Civil War."

"Yeah, well, that's the past. This is the present and I'm talking about you. And I don't like what happened to you in the B and B today." Although she had told him about the two episodes she had experienced during the day, she did not mention how the batteries on the phone and flashlight had not worked during the time she was shut in the attic of the B and B.

"Okay, while I'm reading the letters I'll have the cell phone in one hand. Would that keep you from worrying?"

She heard the smile in his voice as he answered, "All

right, I'm guess I'm being a bit overprotective."

"And I love it. See you when you stop by."

By the time Gage dropped by her apartment, the wind gusted in increasing waves. He checked around one last time, satisfied Stephanie was as safe as she could be. Reluctant to leave her, he held her close.

"Now I understand how Connor—or any of the married guys—must feel when they have to be away from their families during critical events."

"And I understand their loved ones as they worry about their firefighters," Stephanie responded, thinking of Beth. "But we'll get through this."

"We will, babe. We will." With a last firm kiss, Gage ran through the pelting rain to his truck as Stephanie stood watching from the window.

For nearly four hours, Stephanie read through the old letters, making meticulous notes in her catalog. Emily's detailed messages provided insight into everyday events happening in the area during the Civil War.

Stephanie found it a bit frustrating to read only Emily's letters. It was like eavesdropping on a one-sided conversation. She wished she could find the return letters to fill in the gaps.

Outside, the rain and wind intensified. She muted the television to quell the excited voices of the reporters broadcasting from various beaches as they shouted over the waves crashing behind them. She pulled another letter from the box as she yawned, deciding it would be the last one for the night.

She yawned again, but halfway through the letter, the contents jolted her. She abruptly sat up and re-read it from the beginning.

March 1861

Dearest Cousin Celestine,

I am so delighted to hear you are with child and that young Henry will have a baby brother or sister. I wish I could have been there to see your face when you confirmed this wonderful news, but my own confinement keeps me homebound. This baby is due in a few weeks, and I am so excited. I wonder what we each will have. Maybe our children will be able to play together someday. If I have a girl, I shall name her Madeline Nicole. If it is a son, well, of course he will be Thomas!

It is hard to believe you have lived in Virginia five years now! I know the climate is so much warmer and you love your life there, but I miss you every day.

It is calm here in New Hampshire, maybe even in all of New England, as the conflict does not touch us quite as severely as it does you who live in the south, and I listen for news every day, as there are many units from New Hampshire fighting for the Union.

I was saddened to hear Union soldiers occupied your house for a time and caused severe damage. That must be horrible. I know that the union fights for good reason, but the stories of the plundering and looting are as worrisome as the reports of the precarious welfare of our loved ones.

But how clever of you to hide your valuables while the soldiers were there! Have you been able to retrieve them yet? I am most intrigued by this secret compartment you have discovered, and the items you found already hidden.

It is hard to believe that a small doll and some French papers could have been placed there almost one hundred years ago and no one had found them! I am anxious to hear more about them. Why were they in that space in the wall? Do you suppose a servant girl, one who may have had to sleep in that garret many years ago, hid them?

I pray your own precious property shall be recovered soon and placed back in your home.

How long ago that seems, yet it is not even two months. And still, this war goes on, pitting man against man, brother against brother. We are fortunate it did not cause our men to take opposing sides, and Frank has been neutral, even with Thomas and Arthur in the Union Army. Indeed, this terrible war has taken a terrible toll on both sides, and I fear for you and Frank and young Henry so close to it all. I hope the fact that you have family in the North never causes you grief.

I will try to send you news when the baby is born. Thomas and *his parents all send you their best regards, and say they will write when they can.*

Dearest cousin, please write soon and tell me how you are.

Much love,

Your cousin Emily

Stephanie immediately photocopied the letter so she could write notes directly on the copy and save the original. She highlighted the name Madeline Nicole, which was also the name of her own great-great grandmother. Could she have found an actual link to her Wyatt tree or was it just so much wishful thinking on her part that she imagined connections that did not exist?

Next, she drew her yellow highlighter through the paragraph mentioning the doll. Could it possibly be the doll she often saw Nicole carrying when she made her appearances?

She sat back on the couch, shaking her head in disbelief. This was all too incredible. How she wished she had those letters written by Celestine to Emily. Surely missing pieces of the puzzle were in them.

When she analyzed everything and scribbled notes on the photocopy as well as in the catalog file, she had no new answers; nevertheless, she was encouraged that she would soon find something significant.

She read through several more letters. Emily later wrote that indeed, her baby was a girl, and she named her Madeline Nicole. She found no further mention of the doll or the secret hiding place in the subsequent letters.

In an email to Kyle, she sent a copy of the letter, noting that this was the first information that validated her Wyatt connections. She briefly relayed her two sightings of Nicole during the day. Because of the storm, she immediately shut down her laptop without waiting for a response and unplugged the power source from the wall.

She expected to be too excited to sleep, but as she reviewed her notes, her eyelids drooped. She left the television on but still muted, not bothering to turn out the light on the end table as she curled up on the couch and slipped under the afghan. Within a few minutes, she fell into a deep sleep.

***

Confusion surrounded Stephanie as she followed a small beam of light up a set of stairs that led to nowhere. It seemed as if the stairway simply floated into the dark of night. There was no ceiling, floor or walls, just black emptiness surrounding the steps. The beam lit each stair as she followed, its light fading every time it rounded a corner, leaving her in darkness for a moment until she turned. Each time she came to a landing at the top of the steps, the light turned a corner and when she followed, there were more stairs. But it never ended. There were just stairs, turns, and more stairs, but she didn't seem to get any higher in whatever place it was she was in.

Noise filled her senses. Loud knocking became more and more frenzied. Then a bell tolled, echoes resounding as if far, far away. Finally, a booming clap of thunder freed her from the dream and she woke with a start. Shaking the image from her mind, she realized her cell phone was ringing, and at the same time, she heard erratic banging overhead.

"Hello?" she answered.

"Steph, it's Gage. Are you watching the weather?" Gage's voice crackled through static.

"No, I fell asleep. I was in the middle of a strange dream about ringing bells, but in reality, it was my phone. What is it? What time is it?"

"It's three o'clock. Steph, this may be my only chance to call you. Keep a check on the weather. This hurricane has changed its course, turning a complete three-sixty and heading for a direct hit between North Carolina and

Virginia. We're going to get hammered later this morning. It could be bad, with flooding and falling trees. Close the shutters as soon as you can."

"All right, Gage. I have the television on now. I'll get the shutters closed."

"Just hunker down and stay inside. You should be okay there, but sometimes nearby streets have flooded in the past."

"I will be fine, Gage. I'll stay alert. Don't worry…" The line went dead as a second clap of thunder exploded overhead.

The incessant banging continued from a loose shutter in the attic. Before she went upstairs, she struggled to close the shutters on the downstairs windows. She scrambled to the attic doorway, flipping on the light switch, relieved when light illuminated the room. After her earlier experience in the B and B, she fully expected it would not work.

Outside, one of the shutters had broken loose and slammed constantly against the window. As she knelt on the window seat to push the sash up, silhouetted tree branches clawed wildly in the wind, sending a shiver down her spine. The heavy frame of the window stuck and it took all of her might to force it upwards.

After she finally opened the window, she tried to reach the loose shutter as it moved, but the wind snatched it from her hands and smashed it back against the house. She managed to draw the left shutter inward with her left hand and slide the tiny latch in place. She ignored the pelting rain as she leaned forward and stretched her right hand to try once again to pull the swinging shutter towards her.

A streak of lightening followed by a single clap of thunder startled her and her grip slipped on the knob. As she steadied herself and reached again, lightening crackled once more and a claw-like grip encased her arm. She looked into the unearthly face of a woman who glared at her, eyes wild with madness. The specter hovered in the air, seeming to fly in reverse as she tugged. Stephanie's fingers inched away from her grip on the sill as she screamed inwardly and engaged in a tug-of-war with the banshee. The skeletal fingers dug into her wrist.

As Stephanie struggled, the room behind her lit up in a shimmering rainbow haze, and reflected in the glass. The outline of a woman formed a shadow behind her, as another shape appeared, then a third.

The violent struggle continued with the ghostly form on the outside as unseen hands tugged her back into the room. Finally, the apparition outside let go of her arm and swirled into a gray cloud before it dissolved into night.

Stephanie fell backward and off the window seat as she broke free. She tumbled into the wall, the wood panel cracking under her weight as her shoulder struck it.

She looked around her. For one brief moment, she could clearly see the three forms in the iridescent blue mist. One appeared to be a woman of about forty wearing a colonial dress. Beside her were two women in modern clothes; one was older, one was younger. Stephanie immediately recognized her adoptive mother, and from photos she had seen, her birth mother. All three specters extended their arms toward Stephanie, but as she reached for them, they smiled and faded away as if in a vapor, and the room returned to normal.

Stephanie sat where she was for fully five minutes, oblivious to the powerful winds howling outside as she waited, hoping to see her rescuers' images again. To her disappointment, nothing else happened.

Although she managed to close the two shutters against the window, she had not fastened them and they rattled noisily, bringing her back to the task at hand. She tentatively reached for the clasps and secured them without further incident. She still needed to close the shutters on the other window, and with reluctance moved to do so.

She knelt on the window seat in front of the other window for several seconds and stared out. The thunder and lightning seemed to have stopped abruptly. Finally, she raised the sash and waited, hoping whatever was out there would not reach in and grab again. When nothing did, she leaned out and pulled the shutters across the glass, noticing for the first time the long scratches on her right arm illuminated in the blue flash of lightning.

Staring around the room, she eased into a sitting position, and drew her knees to her chest. She clenched her eyes tight and willed the benevolent figures to materialize again.

Stephanie opened her eyes and looked around, disappointed no spirits appeared before her. Then she tilted her head toward the paneled wall she had fallen against, walked over and knelt before the crack where her shoulder had struck the wall, peering closely. A small shaft of light slivered behind the gap in the wood panel.

Before she could reach for the thin board to look, an explosion seemed to rock the house, followed by a loud crash. Then the overhead lights went out and she could not see anything beyond the beam of the flashlight.

Then that too disappeared, and the room plunged into total darkness.

CHAPTER TWENTY-ONE

Stephanie gingerly groped her way out of the attic to her kitchen, fumbling at the table until her hands touched the backup flashlight. Flicking it on, she swept the arch of light around the room and observed nothing amiss. With the shutters closed, she could not see outside, so she opened the wooden apartment door to look out, driven back by the rain falling sideways from the force of the wind. The raindrops pelted her face like sharp needles.

She shined the flashlight from side to side; limbs of the tree that had crashed behind the apartment had broken the outside landing and steps. It was too dark to see the extent of any other damage. Another tree crashed nearby, wood splintering. Loudly. The house shook again, jarring the tree limbs outside her door, breaking away more of the landing. She hastily slammed the door shut.

The storm was arriving, just as Gage had warned. Wind had swept into the room, scattering her papers. She gathered the loose pages by flashlight, placed them in the file box alongside Emily's letters, and moved it to the hallway. Next, she gathered pillows and the afghan from the couch and placed them near the box. Even though the wooden shutters secured the windows, she felt vulnerable in the open room and decided it might be safer to wait between the solid walls along the hall. She located the portable radio and fiddled with the dial to find a clear broadcast through the static. As she settled with her back to the wall, she glanced at her phone. The "No Service" indicator illuminated the screen.

Gage mentioning during their preparations that if the hurricane were to hit, she should fill the bathtub with water in case there was a water shortage came back to mind. She got up to check, relieved to find the water worked. First, she filled the tub and then placed a small trash container nearby to bail water if needed. The master bathroom had a separate shower stall so they could still take showers. She returned to her spot by the wall and waited.

Although she had never smoked a day in her life, she had the urge for a cigarette, just to give her hands something to do. She tapped her fingers nervously along her thighs until the actions began to get on her own nerves.

For the next five hours, the hurricane raged non-stop. The entire building creaked as the wind battered at the shutters and the siding. Outside, the house vibrated as large thuds—probably tree limbs—hit the house. At the sounds of howling wind, Stephanie winced and hunkered a little further down the wall. She had never heard wind blow in such a manner. It didn't fluctuate or gust in spurts, but droned steadily, as if in a never-ending exhaled breath.

Between scratchy static sounds from the portable radio and her own weariness, she did not notice when the wind died down. The sudden quiet caught her attention, as if someone had muted a television screen and thrust her into abrupt silence.

She stood and listened cautiously to the eerie hush. Even though this was her first experience with a hurricane, she knew of the misleading calm when the eye of the storm passed over, the time when those who were in the storm often thought it was safe to go outside and inspect the damage. The second wave of the storm could often be far stronger than the first, and therefore even more deadly.

Stephanie tentatively opened the shutters covering the window in her kitchen. The sky was a fuzzy blue-gray but clear.

Branches and debris littered the rear parking lot. A tree had crashed across the back fence and into a building behind her apartment. Another tree had fallen parallel to the back of the house, narrowly missing her car. Leaning out of the window, she could see where the branches from this tree had torn siding from the building.

She went to the door and opened it. Less than a foot of the landing was still intact at the doorstep. The treads and railing were completely destroyed by branches from the fallen tree, effectively trapping her inside her apartment.

One corner of the B and B next door had considerable damage from heavier branches of the same tree scraping and puncturing the siding. Amazingly, the trunk of the tree itself had not hit anything.

It appeared *Pâtisseries a la Carte* might not have fared so well. The magnolia from the back of the lot had crashed directly onto the back of the building, but the B and B between them blocked her view and she could not see the extent of the damage. The uprooted tree left a gaping hole and also tore up the old-fashioned brick pavement covering the parking lot.

Sirens sounded in the distance as Stephanie moved to one of the front windows to look out that side and she prayed for Gage's safety. Leaning out of the open window, she could see the damage further down the street. A tree had fallen there as well, destroying two cars and completely blocking the road. In some places, heavy tree limbs had crashed down on power lines, snapping them in half. A live wire arced ominously at the intersection.

Residents began to step outside their doors to assess the damage. Even with her limited experience, she knew this was a dangerous thing to do. She shook her head in amazement as one couple walked within fifty feet of the arcing wire, gawking and pointing before they backed away.

The neighbors directly across the street from the B and B, an older man and woman, came out on their second floor balcony over their porch. Seeing her at the window, they waved and called out to ask if she was okay.

"I'm fine, but my staircase has been wiped out by the storm. I'll be stuck here for a while."

Small splatters of new rain began to fall. "We'll check

on you again later," the man shouted back.

She waved and ducked back inside, shuttering the window once more.

Stephanie fixed a bowl of cereal but found she had no appetite as she listened to the harsh rain, which sounded like pebbles hitting the building. She thought of her chart upstairs, and remembered the crack in the wall and the tiny beam of light she had seen just before the tree crashed outside. She approached the door leading to the attic and stopped, with her hand on the knob.

She wasn't sure what she expected, but the knob felt normal, and opened easily. The door did not slam shut or lock her in. No blue haze swirled mysteriously as she climbed the steps and the temperature in the attic was muggy and warm; no freezing cold suggested a ghostly presence.

With a cry of dismay, she realized her chart had been torn from the wall and her loose papers scattered by winds sweeping into the attic. She gathered the sheets and stuffed them in a file to take back downstairs.

Warily, Stephanie eyed the window where the apparition had earlier appeared, but it looked normal. She then turned her attention toward the crack in the wall where the tiny beam had shone through earlier. Now a wide swath of daylight streamed through the split in the panel. Short walls had been built to accommodate the window seats in the dormers under the roof, so there were no eaves on this side of the attic. On the opposite side, as is typical in most attics, the roof slanted right down to the floor.

Stephanie poked and prodded the paneled wall until she could get her fingers under the wood and pulled, breaking a small section to peer inside. She could see light coming through where the storm had torn away siding during the storm, exposing the triangular-shaped nook hidden by the short wall.

Her heart thumped with excitement as she recalled

Emily's mention of a secret place where Celestine had hidden family treasures. She shined the flashlight around the small space, just big enough for a person to crawl around in. Perhaps two people could have crouched inside it at one time, but it would have been cramped.

Cobwebs draped in front of her, and she marveled at how the delicate threading remained intact despite the ravages to the sturdy wood frame of the house inches away.

The tiny area appeared empty at first, but as she moved the flashlight around, the beam revealed an old leather shoe, an empty brown glass bottle and a small pile of cloth. She gingerly dragged the material toward her, hoping it was not the dwelling pad of rabid critters, but it was a remnant of a heavy brocade drapery.

Considering the walls were damaged anyway, Stephanie broke more of the paneling until she could get both shoulders through the opening. She tore down the spider web with a piece of the panel. Then, using her elbows to scoot on her stomach further into the opening, she pushed the brocaded drape into the hole of the outside wall to plug it up. Most likely, the wind would just blow it back inside, but it made her feel as if she was protecting the area until it could be repaired.

She gingerly inched out of the space, sweeping the flashlight beam side to side, drawing her eyes to the right and a reflection of metal. A small tin box leaned on its short side, protruding from a crack where it had fallen between loose floor boards just out of her reach. She struggled to extend her right arm until she got hold of the box and dragged it toward her. The now-familiar warm tingle surged through her fingertips as she held it while wiggling her way out of the hole in the wall. She prayed no unseen hands waited inside or outside the compartment to grab her.

Outside the secret compartment, she lay on her stomach on the floor for a full minute, not moving, head resting on one arm while the other gripped the box protectively to her side.

She propped the panels back in place against the opening, securing them upright with a box full of Christmas decorations. Rain pummeled the roof steadily now and she could hear the wind pick up, the strange droning sound increasing.

She scurried down the steps to the hallway and slammed the attic door behind her. Whatever was in the box would wait until she was safely downstairs.

***

Gage and his colleagues intently tracked Hurricane Abby's every movement. The storm that had danced for so long offshore abruptly started an unusual about-face, turning a 360° loop as it crossed its own path and aimed west. A direct hit was expected somewhere between the Outer Banks area of North Carolina and the Hampton Roads area of Virginia.

When Hurricane Abby finally hit land as a strong Category Two, close to the Outer Banks, its residual effects tore through the southeastern Virginia area.

Essentially striking in the middle of the night, many people slept through the turn of events. The biggest danger would come from a storm surge, which could be deadly if it combined with high tide.

At the height of the storm, police officers were ordered to fire stations located within their beats to ride out the storm in safety. Some sprawled out in chairs, others stretched in sleeping bags, trying to take advantage of the chance to rest before they had to head out to the waiting calls.

Others reported to the Emergency Operating Center, listening to their radios while they tapped away on tablets or cell phones to pass the time.

Gage monitored the radio calls while he worried about Stephanie, real fear slicing into his gut. He'd had the chance to call her before her phone went out so she was alerted. She had a good head on her shoulders, and they had prepared well for the hurricane.

He should have already finished his shift at eight a.m. but it was the height of the storm. The raging storm delayed the arrival of the oncoming shift and he would not leave until they were there to take over. There was no telling what other turmoil the tempest caused.

By now, most citizens would be awake and were probably aware of the severe change in the storm's direction, but with power and phone outages, Gage wondered how many might get into trouble, thinking it was all over. As the eye passed, it brought the temporary calm which citizens could mistake for the end of the storm. When Hurricane Abby passed over the area for the second time, however, it could be more powerful because it was the stronger right side of the storm that would pass, possibly spawning water spouts or causing storm surges.

Several police officers dressed in their foul weather gear to head into the brief lull to answer a report of a nearby domestic dispute turning violent. Gage shook his head disgustedly. Even during emergencies, some people managed to find a way to cause trouble. He hoped they could resolve it before the storm resumed.

With great restraint, he did not ask them if on their way back they could drive by a certain apartment to check on the situation there.

***

Stephanie could hear the sounds of the returning storm outside as she steadied herself against the downstairs wall and prepared to open the rusty tin box. Originally lacquered black and covered with pink roses, rust now showed through chipped paint.

For a split second, her memory pulled her back to the moment when she held the safe deposit box in the bank before she opened it. It already seemed so far in the past. She shook her head to clear the image. Ignoring the increasing tattoo of a thousand drums beating on the roof, she lifted the lid and drew in a sharp breath at the sight of an old doll that resembled the one Nicole always held in her appearances. It nestled on top of other contents, and with the beam of the flashlight centered on the doll, the box reminded Stephanie of a coffin. A chill ran through her and she hurriedly but gingerly withdrew the doll.

Under the ragged toy, she discovered brittle papers tied with ribbon nestled on top of a stack of confederate currency. The rest of the contents consisted of old coins, buttons, a pair of yellowed lace gloves, a dried corsage, and a little enamel case that may have once been a compact or a pill box. Unraveling a piece of wadded tissue, she found a pair of pearl earrings and a matching necklace tucked inside.

There were at least half a dozen loose pages with writing smudged in several places. The first pages she glanced at were written in French. Her high school French was adequate, but it had been many years since she practiced it. She could make out words as she glanced through the missive, but the small and stilted handwriting was difficult to decipher.

Stacked neatly behind the French version, the next papers were in a different hand and in English. After reading a few, she realized someone had already attempted to translate the original papers. Two of the names that jumped out were Etienne and Nicole Suzette; however, when her gaze drew to the name at the bottom, her heart nearly stopped. Clothiste!

Grateful for the distraction from the weather outside, Stephanie painstakingly copied the translated page onto a notepad, moving the flashlight back and forth, as she first read a passage in French, compared it with the translation, and then copied it in longhand.

Nearly two hours later, between her moderate French skills and the translation already attempted by an unidentified person, she surmised the gist of the note from Clothiste.

I did not want to come to this place where my husband's father lives, this place called Virginia. Here there are too many who are loyal to the crown, but Etienne says we will be safe, for although his father is married now to an English woman, they are family and they will protect us. We will be closer to him while he fights in some place called Yorktown. When this war is over—and Etienne is confident the British will be defeated—he wants to settle in the warmer climates. Too many hard winters have taken a toll, and he wants to feel the warmth of the sun on his face and the absence of a weapon in his hand. I myself wonder if we will ever have the peace we once knew.

He says his father has lived here for many years without incident and his business success can help us. Indeed, Etienne has even visited his father while carrying out special tasks for the army, right under the very noses of the despicable British. What great satisfaction that gives me. If he was able to do this undetected, than perhaps this place will be safe for us as well.

My darling Etienne says it is for a short time, but he does not see the trouble I feel will come. When the British were victorious in Canada, everything but our lives was taken from us there. Our homes were destroyed or stolen, our treasures confiscated, and we were forced to flee. I will never forgive them for what they did to us. And I fear it will happen again if we lose this war.

But I know it has become too difficult to follow the army right now with three little girls. Poor children. In my sickness, much of the burden of my tasks has fallen to the older ones. Marie Josephé, I suspect, would rather be fighting the battles than washing the clothes or cooking, but I believe if she could have her way on the battlefront, the war would be won the next day. Theresé is barely eighteen, and already works as hard as a grown woman, scrubbing and serving. She fights against the wrongful things, not with the force of her hands such as Marie Josephé might, but with her words and mind. She does not hesitate to speak up for children who are bullied by the older ones in camp, or even bullied by soldiers who drink too much and tease the children who are doing their small chores. Marie Josephé is more inclined to take a poke at the offender rather than talk to them, but Theresé does not back down when she speaks, and while the guilty ones may laugh at her tenacity, they cease their unkind actions.

Both of them are reaching the age where the eyes of too many soldiers look their way, and with their father so far off, we may not have the protection we had before. Perhaps there is a blessing in this unwanted move after all.

And my baby Nicole Suzette is now four, and camp life is all she has known. She does not cry as much as she used to, and is kind and charming to everyone. She would even share her water with the redcoat prisoners, which Theresé tells her is right and Marie Josephé says is not.

Still, her young life has been hard, but her little doll baby makes her happy and her sisters repair the worn-out clothes when they can. They have promised to repair the yarn hair when we are back at camp. Soon, I hope.

We have to do this, and we must stay here until I am well. Etienne thought it best, but strangely, I feel worse now than before. Sometimes I feel as if I might die here.

I do not understand why Etienne's stepmother hates us so, but I hope we can leave here soon. Something wicked is present here and I want to get away. But I hope we can be of use to the Americans and that gives me some small comfort. All we have to do is keep our eyes and ears open in this house as there is always some activity.

I hear footsteps on the stairs, so I must hide this now. I do not know when I will have the chance to continue…

Stephanie wished that she had a pocket translator or French dictionary to ensure her interpretation was correct, but overall, it paralleled the original translation attempt. She was confident her former French instructor, Madame Dumas, would have been pleased.

Next, she studied the doll. The face was made of wood

and covered with a thin layer of painted plaster, chipped and cracked. Little paint pieces flaked away as she turned the doll over. The yarn hair withered to a wisp, the muslin body yellowed and brittle. The handmade dress was nearly as fragile as the doll. She lifted the skirt, noting the neat, even stitches along the seams and hemline, imagining the love someone had conveyed in sewing that dress.

Her fingers brushed over something nestled in the dress. She rubbed the material. The hem gapped open in this section. She slipped her finger along the hemline, which split the delicate material.

Something fell through the ripped material and onto her lap. She jumped and shined the flashlight, hoping desperately it was not a bug.

The arc of light illuminated a tear-shaped necklace on a chain and she picked it up.

She leaned back on her heels and pondered the small piece of jewelry.

Could this be Nicole's "teardrop"?

A child's laughter tinkled like wind chimes far, far away.

CHAPTER TWENTY-TWO

While Hurricane Abby steadily lost strength outside, Stephanie all but forgot about the storm as she continued to look through the contents of the box. She found a few more loose pages with the same French handwriting, but without translation. The final paper item in the old tin box was an envelope addressed to "Mrs. Thomas Wyatt." Stephanie's shaky hand withdrew folded papers. As she opened one page, her heart thumped a little harder when she realized Emily's cousin Celestine had started a letter.

April 1861
My dear, dear Cousin Emily,
Your recent letter did so much to cheer me up. It is good to know all is calm there at home. How funny I still call New Hampshire "home," even after living in Virginia for five years. I do like it here, very much. But my fondest memories are of the fun we had growing up together. I so look forward to your visit when this bloody war is over. (Forgive my coarse language, dear cousin!)

Today I am not feeling well at all. The shipyard is burning and although a distance away, we can smell the horrible smoke even here on our street. We have already suffered much damage to our house and I pray desperately that the fires do not burn their way to us.

But I must tell you of the excitement we have had, in spite of this awful war. I have had someone help to translate one of those French papers I found. I will tell you about it later in this letter, but it is from our great-great grandmother Clothiste. I am so ashamed I did not pay much attention when my great-grandmother Nicole and yours talked of their beautiful and courageous mother and the mysteries surrounding her. I remember they smelled of rosewater, and I hated that smell as a child. However, I have come to enjoy it as I have grown older.

I think back to when we were children and we sat near them, making faces and mimicking them. What horrible little monsters we were! I wonder if we will live to be two old biddies ourselves. I shall watch my grandchildren like a hawk to see if they are making fun of me.

But if I had paid attention, perhaps I would recall more about Clothiste and her daughters. Could it be true they were once spies for the American army? How intriguing!

I will finish this later. There is some commotion outside…

Smudged ink obscured the words following "outside." Stephanie set the letter aside, disappointed with the unfinished sentence. She surmised Celestine started the letter and simply tucked the unfinished letter into the envelope during the commotion. Through a path of unknown ownership, the old letters eventually ended up in the small tin box, containing information that finally cemented her family lineage to Clothiste and Nicole.

"I've got to email Kyle," she cried, scrambling to her feet. The flashlight fell with a thud, a reminder that power had been knocked out. She checked her cell phone and the "No service" message flashed.

She tilted her head and listened to the gentle patter of rain dancing on the roof. The storm was over.

Stephanie cautiously opened the wooden shutters covering the living room window, and removed the screen to the window so she could lean out to survey the damage. She was dismayed at the number of tree limbs cluttering the street and sidewalks.

She opened the apartment door. There was nothing left of the landing and the steps. All she could see were the branches that had swept them away and speared through the house next door. She could hear sirens in the distance and worried about Gage. His shift ended nearly four hours ago, and she prayed his delay was due to duties and not some unknown harm.

The sirens grew louder and stopped nearby. She went back to the front window and leaned out. A fire truck stopped somewhere in the middle of the road, blocked by a downed tree. The truck was not in her line of vision but she could see the red emergency lights reflected in windows of nearby buildings and could hear the radio squawking from the apparatus's loudspeakers.

Two firefighters walked cautiously toward the downed wire, now dormant and stretched placidly across the sidewalk, no longer arcing.

Then she heard Gage shouting her name. She looked down as he ran toward the building and she called out to him.

"Up here, Gage." She waved.

Gage, in full turnout gear, turned his face upwards, cupping his hands to his mouth and shouting, "Stephanie, are you all right?"

She gazed down, the sight of Gage's upturned face reminding her of the day he first visited her in Alexandria, when he stood under her window in much the same way. Even with the helmet shielding much of his face this time, she could see the relief and her heart squeezed in appreciation.

"Yes, I'm fine, Gage. Is the storm over now? Are you okay?"

"Yeah, it's pretty much moved inland and dissolved. I'm fine, babe." Something about the way Gage said "babe" caused Stephanie's already dancing heart to race harder. *I admit it. I am truly and madly head over heels in love with this man.*

She leaned further out the window. "A huge tree broke through the staircase and I can't get down, but everything's okay in here."

"We can't get the equipment through until we get some of these trees out of the street. Public Works has to get these roads opened first."

"There are two huge trees down in the back here, Gage.

This building seems okay, but I think the B and B and the café took a hit from the old magnolia."

"Oh, man, I hope not. I'll check and be right back."

Her gaze stayed riveted on Gage as he headed toward the two colleagues who had been checking the area where the wires had arced earlier. Apparently, the wire was no longer an issue, and the three men walked out of Stephanie's sight toward the rear of the building. She ran to the other side of the room and threw open the sash to a window on the back wall. Moments later the firefighters picked their way through debris to scurry over the tree closest to her apartment, the trunk within inches of her new car.

One of the firemen gave a low whistle, which she surmised was due to the proximity of the tree to her vehicle. As far as she could tell, the sporty SUV escaped damage. Gage picked through branches to the area where the staircase once stood. He shook his head and called back, "Nope," toward his colleagues, followed by words she could not discern. The three then returned the way they came and walked back to the front of the building, where they once again disappeared from her line of vision.

She left the windows open, but sat on the couch. Trapped as she was, there was little she could do but wait. Periodically, she got up and tried to see where Gage or his colleagues were. Surely he wouldn't be much longer, after working well past his twelve-hour shift. In case he was hungry, she had prepared a sandwich platter, with chips and pickles, and occasionally she nibbled on a chip, crunching nervously.

Through the window, she saw the elderly couple across the street step out onto their balcony. She threw the sash up and waved. The husband cupped his hands to his mouth and called out, "How are you doing over there?"

"Okay, so far," she shouted back. "Some trees are down behind the building. We have some damage back there. How about you?"

"We have a huge leak in the roof, but otherwise we're lucky."

"Good. I'm glad you're safe. Can you see what the firemen are doing?"

"It looks like they are using the ladder at one of the buildings down there. Someone must be trapped."

Then his wife screamed and clamped her hand over her mouth, eyes wide.

"I can't see a thing from this angle," Stephanie cried. "What happened?" The firefighters were out of her range of view, blocked by the buildings on her side.

"A fireman fell from the ladder," the man shouted, his face displaying shock at what he had witnessed.

"No!" Stephanie screamed and leaned further out, but could not see the fire truck or the firefighters. She cupped her hands and called, "Can you see what they are doing now?"

"He's on the ground. They are surrounding him, trying to help." The old man shouted back. "We can't see him anymore."

A fear unlike anything Stephanie had ever known punched her in the gut, and she fisted one hand under her ribcage.

Gage! Could it have been Gage who fell? *Please, God, no.* Bile rose in her throat as she stumbled to the door. She threw it open with such force, it banged against the wall, leaving a hole where the doorknob struck.

At sight of the sheer drop below, she became woozy with vertigo. She clutched the doorframe, and closed her eyes. Then she opened them, and gathering her resolve, leaned out to peer down the side of the building.

There was no way to get down from the apartment. The staircase had been obliterated by the tree limbs, leaving only small chunks of broken wood attached to the house. She tested one and felt the strain under her shoe. Even if she tried to scale down using the sheared remnants still attached to the building, one could easily break under her weight and pitch her into the protruding branches spearing out in all directions below her. A vision of her impaled on a branch sent another wave of vertigo and she stepped back inside, still clutching the door frame.

The wail of a siren echoed through the air, increasing as it neared, then stopped abruptly. She slammed the door shut and scrambled back to the window, striking her shin on the coffee table. Ignoring the sharp pain, she leaned out of the window, calling to the couple still standing on their balcony.

"My boyfriend's down there. Can you see anything?"

"No. We can see several of the fireman bent over him, but not him. The ambulance is down there too."

Stephanie clutched her throat. She slid to her knees in front of the window, arms on the sill. Minutes ticked by as she prayed, "Please, God, please let him be okay." Tears streamed down her face, and her chest racked as she broke into harsh, gasping sobs. Guilt washed over her as she thought of the moment Gage had told her he loved her, but she wasn't able to tell him in return. She loved him from the very depths of her heart. What if he was hurt—or worse—and she could never tell him?

"You idiot!" She smacked her hand to her forehead in reproach. "Why couldn't you just say it?" She sat with her back against the wall, shaking her head every few minutes as she tried to clear images of a broken, injured Gage on the ground.

The waiting and lack of communication was driving her crazy. *Much longer and I'll be tying bed sheets together to get out of here.*

Five minutes later, a sharp rap on the window sill startled her. She turned and squealed with relief. As she scrambled to her feet. "Gage!"

Within the window, as if framed in a portrait, Gage grinned at her. He rode in a "cherry picker" on a telescopic ladder, stretched as far as possible to enable him to reach the window.

"I'll have a double cheeseburger and a large fries, ma'am," he said, laughing, until he saw Stephanie's terror-stricken face. Nimbly he scrambled over the edge and into the room, scooping her in his arms. He gave her a bear hug, and then stuck his head out the window. With a shrill whistle, and wave of his hand, he let his on-duty colleagues know he was inside and all was well. He closed the window and took off his helmet, letting it fall at his feet with a resounding thud.

"Oh, Gage." Stephanie clung to him, sobs jerking her body. "Are you okay?" She kissed his face, hands skimming down his arms until her fingers touched his. "The neighbors saw a fireman fall, but I couldn't see anything. I was trapped in here by the broken stairway. I was so frightened, not knowing whether you were hurt or not."

"I'm fine. One of the guys lost his balance and fell off the ladder. He was knocked out cold and gave us a scare, but he was awake by the time the ambulance got there. He's probably got a nasty concussion but he'll make it."

"I was so afraid I might never have the chance to tell you—to tell you I love you. The thought of losing you without ever having told you broke my heart. I promise you I will never go another day without telling you how much I love you."

Gage brushed his lips to hers and said, "I love you, Stephanie." Water droplets ran down his coat sleeves and a tiny puddle formed under his boots.

Stephanie helped him out of the heavy jacket.

"I'll call in the cleaners before Terry finds out I did that." He smiled but she noticed the worry and fatigue in his eyes. He unbuttoned his shirt and dropped it on top of his helmet. She leaned in and kissed his cheek.

"You look so tired. Are you sure you are all right?"

"Worn out but I'm okay." He touched his forehead to hers. "I worried about you the whole night. I was so relieved when I saw you at the window."

"How bad was it out there?"

Gage sighed, a grim expression crossing his face. "If the short distance from the station to here is any indication, we got hit pretty hard. Power is out across most of the Tidewater region. A communications tower got knocked out by a falling tree and a lot of phone service is disabled. Downed trees and power lines block most residential streets, but so far, no injuries or deaths have been reported. A couple of police officers got hurt responding to a bad domestic a little while ago, but they'll be all right. I'll tell you about it as soon as I catch up with myself."

"Are you hungry?" She wanted to know more about the extent of the storm and to tell him about the ghosts and her escapades in the attic, but could see he was too exhausted.

"Not too much. They fed us well at the EOC. I hitched a ride with the unit sent to check on downed wires so I could get home quicker. I'll get my car tomorrow."

"Those wires were arcing earlier."

"Yeah, it'll be a while before the power is restored around here. Unfortunately, the downed trees are going to hinder any recovery. It may be days before electric and phones are restored. This building looks pretty good, just has some missing siding and a few shingles from the roof. The middle house has some damage but Mary Jo's café is busted up pretty bad in the back. And the parking lot is destroyed."

"I could see the trunk of the magnolia and heard it hit her place, but the B and B blocked my view of the building. Is it bad?"

He nodded grimly. "We'll have to deal with it. Later."

Stephanie still held the heavy fire coat and glanced at Gage. She slipped her arms through the sleeves.

"I've seen you in your blue uniform, but this is the first time I've seen you in your full gear." She smiled and trailed a finger down his bare torso. "But I kind of like this sexy bare-chested look too."

"Cute picture." He pulled her close for a long kiss.

She returned the kiss, then gently pushed him away, and said, "Well, the water still works and I have the shower all ready for you. I lit candles so you could see. Go take it and then I'll bring you a sandwich you can eat in bed. Maybe it will make you feel better."

"That sounds like a winner." He smiled, but leaned his forehead to Stephanie's and held on for another minute. "I was so worried about you."

"It was a bit hairy after the electricity and the phone went out," she admitted. "Knowing what was going on outside and worried you were out in it made it worse. It sounded horrible out there. I heard those trees crashing down, and sometimes I was sure the wind was going to blow the roof away. But you prepared me well, Gage. I wasn't afraid—very much. I'm just glad you're here safe and sound."

"Well, I have to go back in tonight at eight. I better get that shower now." He headed wearily down the hall.

Still wearing the turnout coat, Stephanie picked up the dropped uniform items. The lingering scent of old smoke mixed with his cologne, and she buried her nose in the heavy material, grateful for his safe return home. She hung Gage's uniform shirt on a coat rack attached to the back of the door. She ran her hands lovingly over the helmet emblazoned with his name and shield, tears brimming in her eyes as her heart squeezed with love for this brave man. Placing the helmet on the same peg as the shirt, she kissed it.

Next, she swabbed the trail of small puddles with a towel and took it to the bathroom to drop in the hamper. She glanced inside. Steam coated the mirror and fogged the room. Dropping the towel, she stepped back into the hall and shed all of her clothes. She slipped back into the turnout coat and stepped into the steamy room, planning on adding a little more to the mist.

She leaned her left hip against the sink, and pulled the coat to the right side. Anchoring it back with her hand firmly fisted on her hip, she posed so that only her side and right leg were exposed. A coy smile curved her lips. This would be the first of many times she would tell Gage Dunbar how much she loved him.

"Gage, I just thought of something," she called, barely raising her voice over the sound of the water. "How are you going to get out of here to get to work tonight? The stairs are gone."

He thrust his head around the glass shower door and called, "What?" Water dripped as his jaw dropped. "Oh, *wow*!" His eyes trailed down the exposed portion of her body.

Casually, she repeated her words and he just shrugged. "Ah, I'll worry about it tonight. Can you hand me a towel?"

Slightly annoyed at his indifference, Stephanie reached for the oversized bath sheet and held it to him. He thrust his hand from the side of the shower curtain, but instead of the towel, he grabbed her arm and hauled her into the shower beside him.

"You madman! What are you doing?" she sputtered and laughed at the same time as he maneuvered her away from the water spray, leaning her shoulders against the wall as he wrenched the coat down her arms.

"You were so right," he said, trailing kisses down her neck. His tongue chased a bead of water trickling from her neck to her breast. "This shower is making me feel better already."

"Well, allow me to assist," she said as she ran her hands along his taut torso.

***

Almost as soon as he stepped out of the shower, Gage found his spontaneous burst of energy faded as fast as it had heated up. As Stephanie slipped on a robe and went to the kitchen to get the sandwich tray, he sat and flopped backward on the bed, still wrapped in the huge bath towel, and sighed with the exhaustion of being awake for almost thirty-six hours. He heaved his feet off the floor and rotated his body until his head hit the pillow.

Stephanie entered the room laden with the tray. Gage, still draped in the towel, stretched out on his back and snored lightly. She set the tray aside and drew the covers over him, then realized she hadn't slept much either and joined him, quietly snuggling under the covers. Gage turned on his side and drew her close. Within seconds, she too was fast asleep.

In her whole life, Stephanie Kincaid had never felt so safe.

***

Gage woke first, his internal clock tuned to his duty hours. He could see by the illuminated dial on his watch that it was six-thirty—two hours from the start of another night shift.

He eased slowly from the bed and used the watch to light his way out of the bedroom and down the hall to the kitchen.

For such a small beam, it sure illuminates the room.

Then his eyes focused and his heart pounded like a marathon runner's after a race, and he wondered if he would have a heart attack at the vision in front of him.

Sitting on the couch in a shimmering blue haze, a little girl played with a doll. Her eyes settled on his and she smiled before fading away.

In the sudden dark, Gage struck his shin on the coffee table and knocked over something that crashed to the floor. He tried to muffle his cry of "shit, damn it!" but the noise had already wakened Stephanie, who moved quickly in the dark living room, where she found the battery-powered lamp and turned it on.

"Geez, you must have eyes like a cat," Gage muttered grouchily, adding a few stronger swear words in his head as he continued to bump furniture.

"What happened?" Stephanie asked as she turned the beam toward him.

"I was planning to forage for that sandwich tray, but your ghost just appeared and I knocked the shit out of my shin on the coffee table."

"What did you say? You saw Nicole?"

"Is she the ghost with the doll? She sat right there on the couch, looked me square in the eye with a smile, and then 'poof.' She disappeared. Everything went dark and I banged my shin on the table."

Gage hobbled to the dining room table, turned on another lantern and plopped into a chair. "Geez, I can't believe she was sitting there. I can't believe I'm talking about it." He turned his gaze toward the empty couch and shook his head.

"Well, the sandwiches are still in the bedroom. Stay here and I'll get them." She squeezed his shoulder. "I want to tell you what happened to me during Hurricane Abby."

While she set the food on the table and got a pitcher of tea, she told Gage of the drama during the storm. When she got to the part about the specter trying to pull her from the window, he put a hand on her wrist and stopped her.

"Wait! Did you just say it tried to pull you out of the window?"

"Yes—I know it sounds crazy, but it's what happened."

"After seeing your Nicole myself, I believe you. But as soon as I can, I am taking you out of here. You won't spend another minute alone here."

"No, Gage. No. Now you stop." She said it firmly. "I am safe in this house. Just let me finish." She continued with the story, watching as emotions flickered across his face.

Then she got up and brought the metal box to the

table.

"I think I was guided here to find this, Gage," she said as she opened it. She took out the doll and the letters. "Some of these older letters are in French, and I am sure they were written by my ancestress Clothiste. Somehow, one of her descendants during the Civil War found these letters, translated them and hid them when the house was occupied by Union troops. The letters are one sided and don't give all of the information. It's too complicated to explain the relationship, but suffice it to say many connections have me convinced."

As Gage looked at her, she held the doll and showed him the pocket in the unhemmed section of the dress. "Do you see this place here? I think this doll was used to hold secrets when Nicole was a child. And look here." She held her clenched hand toward Gage and opened it slowly to show the necklace.

"I found Nicole's teardrop."

Before he could answer, there were thumps coming from the floor, and they realized someone was in the office below, banging on the ceiling to get their attention.

"Someone must be checking on us," Gage said. He stomped on the floor twice in answer, and then went to the window. They could see two figures standing in the parking lot, shining the light towards the window. It was his father and Chase.

"Terry, I've got them," Chase shouted, tilting his head upward and adding, "Are you guys okay?"

Terry came out of the doorway of the office and turned her head upwards.

"We're fine, just trapped with the stairs gone." Gage called down.

"Yeah, we see. The streets are blocked, but we drove over sidewalks to get back here. I've got a generator and an extension ladder. If we can get some of the tree branches cut and out of the way, we can put it up to the door so you can get out."

"Is everyone else okay? Dad, how's your place?"

"We're fine. We didn't even lose power, but we have lots of limbs and debris in the yard. Some of the streets are flooded. Connor and Beth are safe. Your mom is with Mary Jo now, looking at the damage to the bistro."

"All right," Terry said, narrowing her eyes in warning. She waited impatiently as the three men cut the tree with chainsaws, their silhouettes outlined in a silvery glow from the spotlight Chase had set up.

"I'm coming too," Stephanie said. "I'll get dressed."

Gage didn't argue. He wanted her out of this place anyway.

Stephanie ran to her closet and pulled on jeans and a sweatshirt. A sudden roar announced the start of a heavy generator. Lights illuminated the room, and the whirr of the refrigerator kicked in. She dug a pair of sturdy boots from the closet and returned to the open window. Gage had already climbed out and was down on the ground, removing the ladder from the window.

Stephanie was furious. "I'm telling you right now, Gage, you'd better put that ladder back or I'll jump down. If you think you are going to leave me up here..."

"Calm down, Steph, I'm just going to move it to the door so it will be easier for you."

"All right," she said, narrowing her eyes. She waited impatiently as the three men cut the tree with chainsaws, their silhouettes limned in silver light from the spotlight Chase had set up.

Finally, they cleared away enough of the tree limbs so they could prop the ladder at the door and she could climb out. She stepped out cautiously, ignoring the slight wobble as she took each rung gingerly. At last, her feet touched the ground. She hugged Gage, then his father and finally Chase.

Terry came out of her law office announcing that the interior seemed okay there. She rushed to Stephanie and grabbed her in a hug.

"We could see your flashlights moving around when we arrived, so we knew you were okay," Terry said, her voice tinged with relief. She turned to her father and added, "I was lucky, Dad. The offices are fine inside. And, Stephanie, it's amazing how that pine tree completely missed your car."

"Oh, I know, I couldn't believe it myself. And the apartment seems okay too." Stephanie told her.

"Let's go see what happened to the café," Terry called, directing a huge flashlight toward the building. Stephanie scrambled over the bulk of the tree trunk, then over the magnolia crashed into the back of *Pâtisseries a la Carte*. Joan held one arm around Mary Jo and tucked her hand in the crook of Hannah's arm. The three stood, bodies rigid together with horror, flashlights illuminating the destruction.

Stephanie's heart sank at the extent of the damage revealed by their many flashlights.

CHAPTER TWENTY-THREE

The next morning, a bright blue sky dotted with billowy clouds revealed no hint of the violent weather that had blown through overnight.

The luxury of the generator Chase provided enabled Stephanie to watch news coverage as local reporters spread out among the largest cities in the area to showcase the damage. She flipped the channel in time to catch a seasoned broadcaster in the middle of a city street as the cameraman panned the cluttered area.

"While Hurricane Abby was not the most destructive storm that ever passed through this area, it was full of uncommon features. Thunder and lightning rarely occur during a hurricane, but Abby was full of both. Even rarer—the three-hundred-sixty-degree loop this storm took. Hurricane Jeanne in two-thousand and four was the last hurricane that followed such a full-circle pattern."

The reporter moved and stood on the trunk of a fallen tree, sweeping his arms wide to indicate several trees behind him blocking the roadway. "There were no deaths or serious injuries reported, but extensive damage occurred in northeastern North Carolina and southeastern Virginia, mostly from falling trees. Local nine-one-one centers received at least nine hundred and twenty calls reporting downed trees in the region, reported by those lucky enough to still have telephone communication. Emergency operators list only the trees that crashed onto power lines or block public streets and require removal by city Public Works Departments."

Walking as he talked, the reporter and his news team moved from the street and zoomed in on a tree protruding into a roof. "But, of course, not all fallen trees landed onto public property, so unless they pose an immediate danger, trees on private property aren't included on the dispatcher's list. Many more crashed between houses, onto them, or alongside them. Property owners are responsible for clearing those downed trees on their property."

Another news team covered the hardest-hit areas across the region. A female correspondent used exaggerated hand and facial movements as she described the scene behind her.

The sharp edge of the woman's voice grated on Stephanie's nerves and she flipped to another channel where local coverage continued.

Shaking her head at the images, she turned off the television and opened her door. Although Chase said his crews would put a temporary staircase in so she could come and go, she did not wait. She gingerly backed down the ladder still in place at the same time as a crewman dropped a stack of two-by-four studs on the ground. He nodded as she skirted over the fallen pine to reach the parking lot. He asked if she could move her vehicle and she obliged—after she traversed the ladder again and retrieved her keys.

She marveled again at how close the tree had come to her car and winced at the sound of pine limbs crunching under the tires. The debris made driving bumpy as she headed for an open space on the side street and parked.

The light of day revealed a number of trees had fallen in Olde Towne. One of the repeated crashes she'd heard during the storm resulted from a tree striking a main transformer where she had seen the wires arcing.

She stood by, keys in hand as she observed a crew from the power company traverse through the cluttered roads on foot to reach the damaged structure. They determined it would take at least another day to get the power back in service in this area of the city. To enable faster response, neighborhood men got busy with chainsaws and axes to cut through trees blocking access to the transformer. Chase sent two laborers to assist.

Olde Towne was lucky. Many other areas of the city could be without power for as long as a week while crews worked their way to them.

Chase had three men cutting the pine behind the law office, and another ready to build a temporary staircase to the apartment once the tree was cleared.

"You'll be able to get in and out in a little while, Stephanie," he called.

She thanked him and added with a smile. "I'll wait. I'm not going back up that ladder again until it's done."

"If you're looking for Terry, she was in her conference room, but may be at the café now."

The building housing Terry's law offices and Stephanie's apartment had comparatively minor damage. Fallen limbs struck the short fence along the left side of the lot. A few strips of siding had been torn loose and fluttered in the light breeze. Some water damage had occurred from one opening near the cubbyhole where she'd found the box. In spite of the destroyed staircase, damage was minimal.

Following the path to the café, she had not yet comprehended the full extent of the destruction. The magnolia tree had torn through the various layers of bricks and paving covering the parking lot over many generations. Orange plastic fencing cordoned the area around the gaping hole.

The trunk missed most of the B&B, but the upper limbs had demolished the small back porch. Branches wildly speared through parts of the back walls, breaking most of the windows on the back side and allowing rain to pour in. The damage could be repaired, but much of the interior repair work already in progress would have to be torn out and started all over again.

The beloved old magnolia tree had completely uprooted and fallen squarely onto the back of the structure.

The porch roof was crushed but it had also absorbed some of the impact. Two large holes gaped in one section of the main roof. Most of the shingles were gone.

She found Mary Jo and Terry kicking debris from the pathway and they greeted her with subdued expressions. Hannah and Joan huddled together as they surveyed the damage.

"That beautiful old tree caused all this damage," Joan said with a deep sigh as she swept a hand toward the café.

Hannah patted her shoulder. The two older women who had been surrogate mothers to Mary Jo each had tears on their faces as they looked into the destroyed kitchen.

The impact of the tree had crushed the roof of the porch, which had also absorbed some of the impact. A section of the roof had two large holes, and most of the shingles were gone. A large limb had smashed through the back wall of the kitchen, and they could see through the gaping cavity into the devastation beyond the wall.

The shiny countertops lay in twisted heaps of metal; the attractive stoves bent by the trunk; the huge refrigerator dented. Glass display dishes were shattered by debris blown in by the storm. The little room where she planned to have her *"Boutique de le Petit Chef"*, her kids' cooking section, was demolished.

Chase assured them the structure was sound in spite of the damage. The women entered through the front door to salvage what they could from the undamaged sections of the building.

Mary Jo led the way in stoic silence, shaking her head often but not speaking. The destruction to the back looked more devastating from this angle. The bright red and white striped awning she and Chase had argued about hung in tatters over the glass counter, as if in defiance of Abby's attempts to destroy it.

The wide-screen television dangled precariously to one side, but otherwise appeared intact. The delicate little paintings of French scenes were blown from the walls; the little sets of tables and chairs were scattered about.

The copper plaque of the bicycling Frenchman still hung in his spot on the wall, although he now appeared to be pedaling furiously uphill as a single hook on the front wheel held the bike in place.

"I never even had a chance to cook anything in this kitchen," Mary Jo spoke wistfully, causing Stephanie to jump at the unexpected sound. All eyes turned to the woman speaking slowly but strongly.

"But this can all be fixed. No one we love was hurt in this mess. After everything that happened in Afghanistan and Iraq, after seeing the death and destruction there, the loss of lives or limbs, I realize there is nothing here that can't be replaced." She touched the glass display case, which had miraculously survived intact. "I was so proud of this beauty when Jay found her, and at such a good price."

With purposeful strides, she marched over to the wiry little bicyclist on the wall and yanked him down.

"But Francois-Pierre here," she smiled at the figure, "You I want. You've been with me since my visit to beautiful *Paree,* haven't you, *mon ami?*" She blew a kiss to the mustachioed profile wearing the red cravat and black beret, and turned to her friends.

"There's also a three hundred and thirty-two dollar bottle of *Dom Perignon* in the wine rack, which I bought to celebrate my homecoming. When that damn tree is removed, I'm gonna be wanting that champagne first thing." With a last look around, she headed for the front door. "Come on, ladies, let's blow this joint."

Mary Jo locked the door and moved toward the law office. Flanked by Hannah and Joan, she turned her back on the café and walked away.

"Wow," Stephanie said admiringly as she walked behind the other women with Terry at her side.

"You don't know the half of it," Terry responded, pride in her eyes as her friend walked with her head held high.

As if on second thought, Mary Jo looked toward her

crushed dreams, and said "Screw you, Abby, you haven't beaten me, you bitch. You haven't beaten any of us."

Next door, in the attic of the future Bed and Breakfast, a dank cold vapor swirled angrily around the rafters and along the floor, slithering like a snake through the boxes and containers that held mementoes from generations past. With a hiss, the livid mist turned the color of tarnished silver before it dissipated into nothing, leaving no evidence behind—this time.

***

By mid-morning, the conference room in Terry's law office was re-established as the Dunbars' command center. With the generator providing electricity, they charged batteries and kept food cold in the refrigerator. Joan and Hannah worked in the small kitchen to keep food prepared for the crews outside.

Beth stopped by with a hamper of food and a cooler full of canned drinks but couldn't stay. She took a quick look at the damaged café, tears in her eyes as she hugged Mary Jo and said goodbye to the family.

Then the heavy work began.

While construction crews labored to cut the trees into manageable sections, another crew rapidly built a temporary staircase to the apartment. Stephanie worked steadily with Mary Jo and Terry, dragging debris to the side of the road.

As soon as the work crew took a lunch break, she asked the other two women to come to her apartment. They went one at a time, each tentatively testing the new stairs as they walked single file.

"I hope these hold up," Terry called on her turn behind Stephanie.

Chase knew the quality of his crews' work and sent a withering look that said, "As if."

Mary Jo unexpectedly shot him the bird as she went last. Stephanie, who had reached the landing first and looked behind her, gasped in surprise.

"I'm sorry," Mary Jo said through clenched teeth, stomping her feet as if daring the staircase to fall. "That man brings out the worst in me."

Stephanie made a mental note to find out what was going on with those two as she headed for the dining table and pulled out a chair.

She filled the women in on the events that occurred the night of the hurricane, adding even Gage had seen Nicole. As she described everything for them, she knew by their expressions they were seeing it all in their minds.

"Hold on, I have something to show you." She jumped up, dashed to her bedroom and returned with the tin box. Terry and Mary Jo leaned forward, eyes widening as Stephanie gently removed the worn-out doll and showed them the rip in the hemline where the necklace had slipped out.

Then she uncurled her hand and showed them the chain with the miniature pear-shaped diamond resembling a droplet of tears.

"I think this must be the 'teardrop' Nicole wanted me to find."

Neither of the other women said anything. Mary Jo said in ramrod perfect posture, taking the tiny necklace and staring at it, still warm from Stephanie's grasp.

Terry absently stroked the cross at her throat, fanning the chain which warmed on her skin. She closed her hand over Stephanie's extended one.

"Then it's yours."

Stephanie's protests were interrupted by the start of chainsaws. The three women broke from their inner reflections without saying anything and together headed to help where they could. The present was more critical than the past at this moment.

At dusk, Chase called it a day. His crews had cut the

bulk of the two trees into manageable sections, the heavy branches that had scraped and poked the houses shorn back. Stephanie, Terry and Mary Jo had dragged the limbs to the side of the street, building mounds five feet high. Tarps were placed over the holes in the roofs, broken windows were boarded up.

The weary work crews headed for home, prepared to come back and repeat the same tasks the next day. Gage and Connor came back in the late afternoon, still looking tired from their long shifts.

Terry asked her family to stay for a summit in the conference room of her law offices, including Chase, Mary Jo and Hannah. She sent her brothers to the pizza shop around the corner on High Street, which was doing a brisk business due to its large brick oven stoked by wood. She gave them an order for plenty of pizzas with various toppings.

When Stephanie turned to head for the makeshift stairway leading to her apartment, Terry asked, "Where do you think you're going?"

"I'm sorry?" Stephanie replied, her hand reaching for the railing as she looked back.

Terry rolled her eyes upward. "I said where do you think you are going? You are part of this family now. And you have a big story to tell the others."

With emotions fluctuating between elation and embarrassment, Stephanie followed the extended Dunbar clan into the office. She shyly hovered in the background as Charles and Joan took a seat on one side of the table, Hannah and Mary Jo on the other. In a moment of panic, she drew Terry to one side and whispered desperately, "Don't make me tell about the ghosts."

"Oh, come on, Steph, it's important to know everything that happened. It also answers some questions that have lingered about this house for a long time."

"But do I have to tell the part about the ghost trying to pull me out of the window? They'll think I'm crazy."

"Look, my mother still talks about the ghosts she saw as a kid and no one would dare call her crazy." Terry patted Stephanie's arm reassuringly. "I want you to tell everything, to everyone, here tonight under one roof. Get it all out and over in one fell swoop. You've found out some history that apparently goes back to the both the Revolutionary War and the Civil War. So apparently you are connected to this place in some way. We still don't know how or why."

Stephanie sighed. "All right, I will. But I'm not telling what Gage said he saw. That's for him to do if he chooses."

"Yeah, yeah, he saw, you saw. We all saw. Now go sit."

"Do you run over the opposition this way in court?"

"Every chance I get," Terry grinned as she steered Stephanie back into the conference room.

Over pizzas, the family discussed the damage to the buildings. Chase advised they could salvage everything; the structures were not beyond repair. Once his crews removed the big magnolia, and as long as the foundation was still intact on the building housing the bake shop, *Pâtisseries a la Carte* was included in his assessment of recoverable property.

"We're lucky your insurance agent started her rounds on this street first," Joan said. "Of course, it helps that her office is right around the corner."

"And since she insures all of our homes, she was relieved to hear these were the only ones damaged," Terry said. The stack of full pizza boxes quickly dwindled as the topics of conversation centered on the family-owned buildings damaged by the storm, the activities Connor and Gage had experienced in their respective fire departments during the storm, and the aftermath that would take days to settle.

Stephanie observed the dynamics of the extended family, awed but a little overwhelmed at the same time. There were agreements on the extent of the damage and disagreements on whether to continue with the plans for the B and B. Sometimes two or more people would talk at once, and Charles would calmly rap on the table and dryly remind them to speak "one at a time please." She remained quiet, nervous knowing she soon had to give an accounting of the events she had experienced—stories that would seem to the others implausible at best.

By the time the last pizza box circulated the table, Terry—and a reluctant Mary Jo—agreed Chase would determine the course of repairs and the priority they would receive for completion. When there seemed to be nothing left to discuss about Hurricane Abby, Terry announced, "Stephanie had some excitement of a different kind during the storm."

As all eyes turned expectantly to Stephanie, she sighed heavily and looked at Gage. He patted her hand reassuringly and said, "Go for it."

With a deep breath, she started to speak. Her voice shook as the first words came out, but then she steadied. She reminded them of the afternoon before the storm, when she was babysitting Tanner, how Nicole suddenly appeared, and through the little boy she received the message to find Nicole's teardrop. Then she relayed the melancholy atmosphere that overcame her at the B and B when she searched for the file boxes, the strange cold enveloping her and the door jamming behind her. When she reached that part, Mary Jo and Terry both confirmed the scene when they found her.

No one said a word as she continued in a stronger and steadier tone. She could see varying degrees of skepticism around the table and suspected the silence had more to do with respect for Charles and Joan Dunbar than acceptance of her story.

"I fell asleep before the storm hit, and had a weird dream about following endless stairs. I could hear loud knocking at the same time as bells rang. I finally realized the sounds coincided with a shutter upstairs knocking against the house and the ringing of the phone when Gage called to warn me. I went to the attic, and found the shutter swinging madly." Keeping her gaze directed at Gage, she described the banshee clawing at her and nearly dragging her from the window. How unseen hands tugged her back inside. She showed the scratches on her right arm, and finally looked around the table. Chase frowned and rubbed the back of his neck. Joan stroked her forearms. By various facial expressions, Stephanie wondered if others at the table had gotten goose bumps or the hair bristled on the backs of their necks.

Suppressing a new shiver of her own, she continued. "Next, I hunkered down with a blanket and supplies to wait the storm out. During the calm, I went back upstairs to check the wall where my shoulder struck. I found a small box with an old doll, letters and old buttons and things." She described the contents of the tin box, Clothiste's letter, and the unfinished missive from Celestine.

She ended her story with a description of the doll and dress where she found the necklace.

Everyone started talking at once, until Gage called out for them to wait.

"Let me add one more thing," he said, and told how Nicole appeared in the dark of the night, smiling at him before her shimmering blue form faded away.

For a split second, silence permeated the room. Then the babble started again.

Before the night was through, Stephanie had retrieved the box and its contents so everyone could look at them.

Terry brought up ownership of the jewel, stating in her opinion the pendant and doll belonged to Stephanie.

"Whether or not anyone believes ghosts or some supernatural entity brought them to light, or whether it was just pure luck, it's obvious they would not have been discovered without her. And if nothing else, I own the property so I'm giving them to her anyway. Maybe when she transcribes the rest of the papers from the box, we'll know more."

Stephanie thanked Terry and looked at the faces around the table. Maybe a little less cynicism was evident now. No one questioned her sanity or said it was just her imagination; they just agreed to accept it all for the moment and tried to offer suggestions to answer the mysteries.

No riddles were solved in the ensuing discussions; no one provided logical conclusions about what had happened. Finally, Charles Dunbar wrapped on the table with his big hands and suggested they call it a night.

"Whatever is going on has been in the making for years," he said logically. "I'm not saying there are or there are not ghosts. I'm saying we can continue this tomorrow. Let's all go home and get some rest. We have a lot of work ahead of us over the next few days."

***

Stephanie and Gage had a couple of hours before he had to report for duty, so they cuddled on the sofa, rehashing the earlier discussions.

"You know, with all of these events going on, I've been doing a lot of thinking, Gage," Stephanie began.

"Have you now?" he asked, propping on one elbow to look at her while he toyed with a lock of her hair.

"I've been comparing myself to my mother—my real mother. She revealed so much of herself in her journals." Nestled in the crook of his arm, she began to tick off on her fingers. He never quite understood her lists, her charts, and her habit of neatly linking things and events that were significant to her, but he found them all endearing. He tilted her chin and kissed her.

"We were both adopted and found out under shocking conditions." Stephanie continued. "She knew the night she met my father he was the one for her. I knew the moment we met you were the one for me. Their favorite song was 'The First Time Ever I Saw Your Face.' You whistled that tune when you left the café the day we met, and it stayed in my head for the rest of the day. Until Hannah came at me with the broom." They both laughed.

"Mom wanted to know where her roots were, and started her family research, which I am continuing. She quit college to be with my dad. I quit everything to come here—and be with you." She settled on her side and faced Gage, stroking his cheek tenderly.

"I think some predetermined course of events occurred to bring me here, whether you want to call it fate, destiny, chance—whatever. Many things over the last few months have guided me to this place, at this time. Every day I find something that connects me. Those letters from relatives convinced me I'm finally on the right trail. I found the doll and necklace that further connects me here and subsequently to you. And I love it every time something clicks—well, maybe except for ghosts. And even then, there is a connection." As she stretched along the length of Gage's body, she added, "And you finally saw my Nicole. I've come full circle."

Gage kissed her nose. "I don't know what brought you to me, Stephanie Kincaid, I am just glad it did." He paused and added, "And I have a present for you."

"You do?" Stephanie's eyes sparkled with interest. "Where is it? Where? Where?"

He rolled on his back and reached as if stretching lazily, and came back with a small package wrapped in flowered tissue in his hand.

"With all those relatives of yours leaving their legacies in writing, Steph, I think it's only right you tell your story so it can be found a hundred years from now," he said as he handed it to her. She opened it and found the small jade green leather diary.

"Oh, Gage, how sweet. Thank you so much. I love you," she said as she rained kisses across his cheek. He laughed as he reached on the side of the sofa again.

"This isn't exactly how I planned to do this, so nothing is wrapped right, but tonight seems very fitting," he said as he held a slender wooden box with the words *"Mont Blanc"* stamped across the lid. "I think this is a connection to add to your many lists."

Stephanie beamed as she opened the box, expecting to find a set of the elegant pens inside. But instead, she found a brilliant Marquise-cut diamond engagement ring nestled on the velvet band. Her hand flew to her mouth, and Gage watched her eyes grow wide. Tears slid down her cheeks. "Oh, Gage, it takes my breath away."

"Will you marry me, Stephanie?" he asked as he took the ring and reached for her hand.

"Oh yes, yes, I will!"

Gage slid the ring onto her finger. She straddled him and threw her arms around his neck, planting more kisses all over his face until they both burst out laughing.

"Look, Gage." Stephanie held her left hand to her throat, tapping her right finger back and forth between the ring and pendant. "This ring matches Nicole's teardrop." She strained to peer at the two pieces of jewelry side by side, then added, "You know, Terry warned me to never trust the packages you Dunbars put your gifts in." She wrapped her arms around Gage's neck, stretching out her hand to admire the glistening stone on her left ring finger. "I better keep it in mind from now on."

***

The next morning, the mind-numbing work started all over again. Stephanie could not bear to risk wearing her sparkling new ring as she worked outside, but at lunchtime she wore it long enough to take it downstairs to proudly show everyone. Charles and Joan Dunbar hugged her warmly and welcomed her to the family. Mary Jo and Terry checked it out happily, although Stephanie had an inkling the entire family had already known about the ring. After showing it all around, even to the crew members ready to start on the carcass of the tree, she turned to take it back upstairs and nearly bumped into Hannah coming from the law offices.

A little apprehensively, Stephanie extended her hand to show the ring. The wizened old woman took Stephanie's hand in her gnarled ones, peered intently and then gave a gentle squeeze.

"It's pretty," the old woman spoke, her voice catching. "You caged the Gage after all. You take care of him."

"I will, Hannah, I will."

"You better or I'll be after you with my damn mop. Now scat and quit holding me up. I've got people to feed."

"Yes, ma'am," Stephanie said, and then impulsively leaned forward and kissed the wrinkled cheek of the old lady.

"Scat, I said," Hannah said, her scratchy voice a little rougher as it rasped past the lump in her throat.

Stephanie skipped up the stairs to put the ring safely in the upright jewelry box that once belonged to her adopted mother.

"Mom Marla, Mom Jessica, I'm engaged," she said, touching the top before she placed the ring in the velvet ring slot. She stayed there a moment, disconcerted by ringing in her ears.

It took her a moment to realize the ringing came from her cell phone. Her service was back on! She grabbed it excitedly, Kyle Avery's name lighting the screen.

"Hi, Kyle," she answered. Static crackled but she could hear Kyle's relieved voice.

"Stephanie? Hello. I am so glad to finally reach someone. I have been trying for two days to get through. How is everyone there? Are you all okay?"

"Our connection's not great, Kyle, but we are all okay. Everyone made it through. There is a little damage to my apartment building, but both the B and B and the café both got hit hard. Trees fell and caused a lot of damage."

Kyle's scratchy response asked about Mr. and Mrs. Dunbar.

"Charles and Joan are fine. They had very little problems out in Suffolk compared to here."

Kyle said something else, but she couldn't make it out.

"I can't hear you, Kyle. What did you say?" She had to ask him to repeat it again, finally understanding that he would come down as soon as the way was clear, that he had big news for the Dunbars.

"Did you say you have big news to tell us? I have a lot to tell you too. I'll email as soon as I have Internet."

The phone crackled in her ear, causing her to flinch in discomfort. She could hear Kyle talking from far away until his voice faded into nothing.

"Damn it," she said. Silence greeted her as she tried to dial his number.

She headed outdoors once more, called to Terry, who was dragging a heavy pine branch toward the refuse pile.

"Holdup, Terry," she called as she clambered down the steps. Just as she reached the bottom, a high-pitched whistle pierced through the drone of machinery, followed by a hair-raising shout from one of the workers. He waved wildly and then pointed downward. As the buzz of machinery and tools silenced, she heard him as he called out again.

"My God! Come over here!"

Mary Jo and Chase were closest and reached the area first. Chase shouted for his workers to stay back.

Stephanie leapt forward, followed by Terry. They scrambled over debris and stopped dead in their tracks.

The root system of the fallen magnolia tree stood at least eight feet high, perpendicular to the ground. Right in the center, held upright by the myriad fingers of the old roots, a skeleton stared straight at them.

Stephanie stopped suddenly and tilted her head,

straining to hear. She heard the soft sound of crying mingled with the breeze. As the translucent figure of Nicole appeared near the trunk of the tree, she raised her hand to wave as she faded away.

Terry turned her head to follow Stephanie's gaze. "What is it, Steph?"

With a hint of sadness, Stephanie sighed…

"Nicole just said goodbye."

Epilogue

Portsmouth, Virginia 1781 to present day

When the red pouch containing the tiny heart-shaped pendant plopped unnoticed onto the mud, hurried footsteps trod over it, trampling it deeper and deeper into the wet muck. It was further buried by the wagon wheels passing over it as the desperate family made their getaway.

A few days after the hasty exit of her husband's family, Abigail Roker ordered the planting of a new tree at the far corner of the summer kitchen. The spindly magnolia would suit her purpose once it grew. Until then, the outbuilding blocked the corner of the yard and all it represented. For years, heavy boots or dainty slippers pounded steadily over the dirt. More horse hooves and carriage grooves packed the earth firmly, burying the necklace more than a half a foot down.

Nearly a century later, the thunder of heavy artillery roared through the South during the Civil War. In Portsmouth, the weaponry created ruts and mounds rendering the yards of the Wyatt homes useless. Frank Wyatt planned to remove the ancient magnolia tree to make way for the cobblestones that would soon cover the area, but his wife Celestine begged him to spare the huge old tree.

"It's been there so long, Frank. Let's leave it to be enjoyed by the generations to come after us."

A man who loved his wife dearly, Frank agreed.

So the Wyatts, never knowing how close they had come to unearthing old secrets, left the tree standing in one corner of the lot, and paved around the area with cobblestones.

Over the years, the war-ravaged homes underwent repairs. Macadam, then bricks, covered the cobblestones.

But it was the felling of the mighty magnolia in a 2st century tempest that finally revealed what lay beneath.

The End

Stephanie's "French Connection" Notes

PHILLIPE DE LA ROCHER aka Phillip Rocker m. 1st wife unk, m. Abigail Weston, 2nd wife

/

ETIENNE DE LA ROCHER (1741-1812, age 69) m. CLOTHISTE JANVIER (1750- d. unk)

/

NICOLE SUZETTE LA ROCHER (1776-1859, age 83)[1] m. Henri Lebegue (b. unk - 1812)

/

EDWARD ETIENNE LEBEQUE (1802-1900-age 98) [2] m. Monique

/

GENVIEVE LEBEQUE (1830-1917, age 87) m. Francois Longchamps[3] (1823-1908, age 85)

/

EMILY LONG (née Longchamps1849-1935, age 86)[4] m. Thomas Wyatt[5] (1847-?)

/

MADELINE NICOLE WYATT (1885-1970-age 85) m. Richard Finch

/

MASON FINCH (1926-1988-age 62) m. Lucinda Banks

E [1] Nicole marries Henri Lebeque and moves to New England, where her husband is killed in War of 1812

[2] Edward, Nicole's son, is a shoemaker in Massachusetts

[3] Francois' family name was "Longchamps" but after a while some records dropped the "champs" part to anglicize the name to "Long". Francois' daughter Emily was married under the name Long. Her cousin Celestine married Frank Wyatt, Thomas and Arthur Wyatt's brother, under the name Celeste Longchamps, the French version of the surname. Through Kyle Avery's information, Stephanie confirms that Celestine is actually a cousin to Emily Long.

[4] Emily established ties to DAR while being helped for her application for a Civil War widow's pension. She received civil war benefits after Thomas died.

[5] Thomas Wyatt served in the Civil War. He is one of 10 children. His brother Arthur is married to Rosalee, who worked on the family tree to establish ancestry for Civil War pensions. They have a son Jeremy and a granddaughter Sadie, who is Stephanie's distant cousin. Sadie never married. While researching for the pensions, Thomas's wife Emily Long establishes she is descended from Revolutionary War hero Etienne de la Rocher, and this helps her to also establish DAR eligibility. Celestine is at first thought to be Emily's sister but in reality are cousins whose fathers are brothers.

MARSHA FINCH (1950-1983-age 33) m. Mark Franklin
/
JESSICA FRANKLIN KINCAID (1966-1987, age 21) m. Stephen Sullivan(1964-1987, age 23)
/
STEPHANIE NICOLE SULLIVAN KINCAID (1987-) engaged to Gage Dunbar (1986-)

Turn the page for a sneak preview of
HEART OF COURAGE: The Red Ruby Story
Book Two of the True Colors Series

Coming winter 2016

MARIE JOSEPHÉ and the Red Ruby
On the way to Yorktown, Virginia, July 25, 1781

I huddled with my sisters under the heavy canvas covering the cumbersome wagon. We were already bruised from the bumps and jerks caused by the constant jolting. Every new crack of the driver's whip caused another painful lurch as the animals responded.

At the driver's shout of "Easy!" the horses' pace slowed. We scrambled into upright positions. Theresé and I sat protectively on either side of our baby sister, Nicole, who now slept fitfully, dried tears smudging her cheeks.

I rose to one knee to ease Nicole's curled form from my lap to Therese', and groped my way toward the back of the wagon. Another jolt when the wheel crashed over a rock sent me tumbling. My shoulder struck the side board with a loud crack. A crate overturned and raked the side of my arm. I bit back my cry of pain, but could hear my sister's gasp of concern.

In spite of the horses' slowed gait, I slid from side to side until I reached the back and pushed the oilcloth covering to the side. Rainfall from the earlier storm had gathered in the fold, fat drops plopping on my head as I peered into the night.

A bright moon and crystal stars lit the open field to my right, the thrashing of the storm long since passed. White rocks stood out like flat sentries forming a motionless barrier along a tree line that cast shadows on the wagon. The air was thick with humidity and pungent with the smell of wet grass and dirt. Small pools of mist swirled low to the ground. A stench, unique to tidal marshes, soon overpowered the other scents.

I crept back to Therese's side, and settled on the hard floor, bracing my back against the back of the wagon. At the slower pace, my sister and I could talk with ease. We leaned our heads closer together so only we could hear each other's whispers.

"The storm has passed," I broke the silence first. "The thunder only rolls far in the distance now."

"What did you see?"

"It is dark, but the moon lights the way. No one follows. We ride alongside a range of trees, perhaps to conceal the wagon. I can smell the river nearby."

Theresé arranged the scant coverlet across Nicole's shoulders and said, "The driver has slowed his pace. We must be far enough away from Portsmouth. How much longer do you think it will be before we reach Father's camp?"

The sigh escaped before I could prevent it. "I know not. Mayhap hours."

We fell quiet, swaying in unison with the horses' gait. Only hours earlier, we had fled our grandfather's house in advance of British soldiers. We'd had no time to ask questions as we raced through pouring rain to the waiting wagon.

Neither of us mentioned the crack of gunshots or the awful confusion that had ensued as our party was confronted by two soldiers. Rifles roared, blasting in time with the lightning, drowning our screams as both our mother and grandfather fell wounded to the ground.

Two more shots echoed, muzzle flashes searing the night as next the soldiers fell.

From the shadows, our brother Louis emerged, pistol in hand. Disguised as a British soldier, he'd pushed us into the wagon and shouted to the driver, "Go. Now!"

We older sisters obeyed without hesitation, fearing any delay could compromise his cover. Little Nicole screamed for her doll, left behind in the chaos. She is only four, it is understandable that her doll is a source of security amid the chaos.

Theresé's voice broke through the dark. "Sister, I fear for our mother. I worry so about what happened back there."

"Louis will do what he can to protect her and grandfather." I spoke in a voice strong with courage I did not feel. I wondered if my sister experienced the same clutch in her chest as I did, not knowing whether our loved ones had even survived.

I reached into my sleeve to retrieve the small pouch I had tucked away in the confusion of our departure.

It was gone.

"Theresé! I cannot find the pouch with the necklace Mama gave me!" I ran my fingers along the material covering each arm. "I did not have time to give it back to her, so I pushed it inside my sleeve. I thought the cuff would hold it in."

"Are you sure?" Theresé ran her fingers across my sleeves.

"We had to leave in such a hurry. Mayhap it fell out when you pushed Nicole inside. Let us hope Louis will find it."

"As I hope he also finds Nicole's doll. She left it in the room."

Therese dug fingers into my skin, her voice thick with tension as she whispered hoarsely, "Louis' message…"

I interrupted. "His message is safe. I did not leave it in the doll's dress this time. Some odd feeling overcame me and seemed to warn me to take it." I peeled a layer of cloth from my dress cuff and touched the small flat papers hidden in the false hem. Warm air brushed my cheek as my sister sighed in relief. A rumble from deep in my belly made us both giggle, as we had not eaten for hours.

Suppressing her laughter, Therese whispered, "We must soften your hunger growls or it will lead the British right to our wagon."

"I would be happy just to have a firecake right now. I long for this war to be over so we can be in our real home again. I will prepare such deserts and treats. No more firecake; that tasteless bread made with flour and water."

I have never liked to cook, but I loved to bake fancy pastries. "What shall I bake for us when we are in our own home again?"

"Crusty bread, just the way Mama baked it."

At mention of our mother, we fell into sad silence.

"We should rest now, sister," Therese suggested, and we settled in the uncomfortable space.

As I rested my head against the wooden crate on my left, I touched the sleeve of my dress. I again lamented the loss of my mother's gift, but quickly banished the selfish thought.

My family faced grave danger over the next few days. We knew the importance of the mission that Louis and our father were conducting, and willingly obeyed our brother's orders. How I wished I could have remained behind, to fight alongside my brother! He was a soldier, however, and I a mere girl.

I was doing my part. I fingered the cuff of my sleeve, once again satisfied the hidden flap protected the vital secrets I was trusted to *deliver.*

As slivers of moonlight sliced through rips in the canvas, my gaze drifted to the floor of the wagon. Hidden in a false bottom beneath us, firearms and ammunition were crammed in every space.

If the British army stopped the driver and discovered the smuggled weapons, we would all be taken prisoner—or more likely shot on the spot. If we could reach the edge of the James River where a boat would ferry us to the north side and our father's camp, we should live to see another sun rise.

Author Allie Marie grew up in Virginia. Retired from law enforcement, she recently embarked on a new career writing fiction. Besides family, her passions are travel with her husband Jack, and genealogy, which inspired her to write the <u>True Colors</u> series. The first book, *TEARDROPS OF THE INNOCENT: The White Diamond Story*, is her debut novel.